Downward Dog, Upward Fog

Downward Dog, Upward Fog

A Novel

MERYL DAVIDS LANDAU

Alignment
Publishing
company

BOCA RATON, FLORIDA

Library of Congress Control Number: 2010918456

ISBN 978-1-936586-35-6

Book design by Michele Anderson

Visit our website at www.AlignmentPublishing.com

Printed in the United States of America

For Gary,
with my deepest love

Downward Dog, Upward Fog

Chapter 1

I never even saw the bright red Mazda enter the highway, but suddenly it's right behind my car, like a leopard pressing in for the kill. My heart pounds wildly; my palms feel so slippery, I can barely grasp the wheel. I swerve into the center lane just in time to avoid a crash.

"Crazy driver, are you trying to kill me?" I scream, even though I'm certain the teenager can't hear me through my closed window. Not only is his bass thumping and rattling, he's already slalomed past a dozen cars up ahead. But my rage is roaring, and I can't tamp it down. "How did you ever get a license?" I fume. "When a kid comes into the Motor Vehicle Commission, they need to hand him a bus map and shove him out the door: 'Off the road, buster, till you're more like twenty-one!'—the minimum the driving age should be! They should—"

I spy my twisted red face in the rearview mirror, and come up short. My gaping mouth closes; my fist releases its midair punch. Sheepishly, I peek to the lanes on either side, relieved to see no one's watching me: a lone lunatic railing at the world.

Where does this anger boil up from? I wonder. It's the second time in the past few days I've found myself shrieking at a stranger, for reasons I can't fathom. I know I'm really a sweet person. On this same drive, after all, didn't I happily oblige a woman's request to duck in front of me on her way to the highway entrance ramp? But this guy doesn't ask permission, I remind myself. He just drives like he's king of the road. No wonder I lost it.

I check myself again, unhappy with the direction in which my thoughts are zooming. *Lorna, this is not a good way to begin your week.*

There aren't many distractions when you're alone in your car, so I flip on the radio, fumbling till I find the station my sister, Anna, keeps begging me to hear. Anna's five years older than me, but she's a hundred years more together. Not just because she has a loving husband and an amazing daughter while, at thirty-three, I'm still struggling to find the right guy. Anna became an interfaith minister a few years back. (She assumed the name Angelica when she took her vows, but I never seem to remember to call her that. Old habits certainly die hard.) Belief has helped her settle so comfortably into her skin; Anna radiates a contentment I can only dream of.

Still, I've been avoiding this WNOW station since she first suggested it three weeks ago. It just doesn't seem like something I'd be into. But after my highway tirade, I need something to calm myself down, and checking out Anna's recommendation seems as good a course as any.

My patience wanes as I wait through three commercials—for a natural energy booster (I once read about a woman who needed an emergency liver transplant after taking one of those!), a special gum that claims to improve the brain, and that ubiquitous radio ad to enlarge my penis. (*Don't you know half your listeners haven't got one of those?* I want to inform the dashboard, but I refrain.) Finally, the talk show begins.

"Goooood morning to you! So wonderful for you to be here, sharing this moment in our lives together. This is Serena Robbins, host of *Onward and Upward,* hoping to remind you we're all on a journey to create heaven right here and right now. The world is always filled with beauty and perfection, and if you wake yourself up, you'll be able to see it. Let's get right to my first caller, Liz from Cleveland."

Cleveland? Cleveland, Ohio? That's a long way from New Jersey, where I've lived nearly all my life. I'm surprised to learn the show is syndicated nationally. I assumed it was produced on hand-me-down equipment in a local basement right here in Hoboken, taking calls from area residents like Anna. After all, how many people can possibly be interested in this stuff?

"Hello. Am I on the air? I'm not hearing myself on my radio." Liz's nasally words shout through my speakers. "Oh, wait—there I am. Oh, cool. There's like an echo." After a major pause, I wonder if I've lost the signal. "Oh, sorry," Liz breaks in, just as I'm about to fiddle with the buttons. "I was listening to myself. I really am on the air, huh?"

"Yes, Liz, you're reaching out to all of our listeners. Let's share your wisdom with them, shall we? What can we in this inspirational community do for you today?" Serena Robbins's voice strikes me as a unique combination of loving girlfriend and efficient librarian.

"Well, um, it seems like no matter how hard I try, I can't get people at work to like me. Let me give you some examples. I keep inviting women I consider my friends to hang out after hours, but they're always too busy—or at least that's what they say. And every time I leave a meeting, I fear my coworkers are talking behind my back. . . ." A long silence follows. I wonder if Liz is talking on a cell phone while driving and avoiding her own near-collision. Finally, she speaks. "Oh, sorry. I was hearing my voice on the air again. I sound nice, don't I? Why do other people think I'm a loser?"

I can tell Liz is about to cry, and my heart goes out to her. Then again, maybe people avoid her for a reason. I certainly work with enough troublemakers to know they're as pervasive at the office as problem drivers are on the road.

"I don't think you're a loser, Liz. In fact, I don't think any person can be a loser, since we're all made from the loving energy of the universe itself. It sounds to me like you're caring too much about what other people think. Just go about your day noticing the well-being that surrounds you, and ignore everything that doesn't feel good. If you do that, every day will be magnificent— and as a bonus, I guarantee your coworkers and friends will start treating you better, too."

This message, while empathic, strikes me as a bit Pollyanna for so early in the morning—especially after such a lousy commute. So I'm grateful to pull into the parking lot of my company's headquarters. I click off the station as I slide my silver Jetta into an open spot.

"Liz," I say to the silent radio. "You should have to work with the piranhas in my department. You wouldn't have to wonder if people were talking behind your back. You'd *know* they are."

I gather up papers strewn around my backseat. As on most weekends, I thought I'd work at home a bit, but I never made the time for it. Before I leave my car, I take a minute to assess the status of my career, in what is becoming my Monday ritual.

I've been at Favored-Flavors, a national premium ice cream manufacturer, for nearly six years. Part of me adores my job, especially the fun marketing events I get to plan and attend. Plus, I have tremendous freedom—now that I run the whole Special Events department. (Okay, it's a department of two, but who's counting?) I make enough in this position that I was able to buy my own adorable house last year, rather than wait, as my none-too-optimistic mother constantly nagged, until I "maybe, someday, reel in a man."

But the other part of me wishes— well, let's just say there are probably nicer people in Sing Sing than around here. In truth,

I've started to dread having to deal with them. I'd love to find a job where I didn't have to constantly watch out for sharpened knives aimed at my back. And wouldn't it be great to do something meaningful? I mean, when you get down to basics, I spend my day shilling some of the world's most copiously caloried concoctions. I'm well aware that our product is part of the reason so many kids have type 2 diabetes that it's no longer called an adult-onset disease. But I have no idea what that better job might be.

Now I also let my mind roll into an area I've been avoiding: assessing the status of my life. With all this anger and road rage I've had lately, I don't even recognize myself. I mean, haven't I always taken pride in being nice? Well, at least there was the woman at the on-ramp. And last week, I did let a guy at Saks have the last pair of purple cashmere gloves for his girlfriend's birthday gift, even though my credit card was already out of my wallet when he sauntered up to the counter. Those gloves were adorable, but I felt joyful handing them over. Plus, my girlfriends would describe me as caring and considerate—or they would have, until recently. I'm not actually sure what my pals would say today. With all these short-tempered bursts of indignation. . . .

Resigned to the fact that I'm not going to figure everything out today, I button my coat to steel myself against the winter morning and step outside. The chill bites my nose, so I keep my chin tucked into my bright green wool coat. As I trek to the front of the building, lulling myself into a mental trance with the steady click of my boot heels, I wonder if there's anything to what that Robbins woman said. *Maybe if I emphasize the good things more. . . .*

ॐ

When I get to my company's sixth-floor lobby, I can't help staring at the walls. They're decorated with dozens of paintings of enticing ice cream, the sight of which makes me smile.

Our receptionist, Hallie Johnson, a petite brunette with the longest eyelashes I've ever seen, nods to me.

"Morning, Hallie. Hope you had a great weekend," I say, barely taking my eyes off the paintings.

"It was fine." After a pause, Hallie chuckles. "I would've thought you'd stop glowing by now."

"Never! I love these paintings. And all the artists who did them!"

"I have to admit, it was a genius promotion. Getting some of the most famous modern artists in America to paint our little ole product."

"And with barely a dent in my annual budget."

"I still can't believe you got them to do it so cheap—some token money and a year's worth of delivered ice cream. They'd have to eat an awful lot to make that worth their while."

"Ah, but you're forgetting I told each of them to choose three others to get a weekly delivery, too. I had them eating out of my hand—pun totally intended!—once I revealed that each package would come with a card reminding them of the artist's generosity."

I glance around and practically inhale my favorites: mint chip dripping over a chandelier; a cubist banana split; a girl sitting in a field bursting with colorful flavors. Last summer, these canvases graced the walls of several museums. The buzz in the press catapulted our ice cream to the top supermarket seller, where it has stayed since.

Hallie suddenly leans in close, her voice sinking to a whisper, eyelashes aflutter like hummingbird wings. "Did you hear the latest about Stella?" she asks.

"You mean that she had the baby?" Stella Crandon is our office manager. She's also a single thirty-seven-year-old who accidentally found herself pregnant a few months after she'd started dating a long-distance trucker. Stella tried to hide her growing girth under empire-waist dresses well into her second trimester, but when she began frequenting the bathroom so often that we could have held our weekly meetings there, the gossip mill went wild.

"No. That's so last week. I mean about her not coming back," Hallie whispers gleefully. "That she's moving to Vermont to be near her mother. Apparently her boyfriend doesn't want any part of little Jackson."

"What a shame. Stella has a good heart, even if she didn't always show it around here. And I know she dug that trucker."

"Will you stop being so compassionate?" *Hah! You should have seen me on the road this morning,* I think, as Hallie barrels on. "Stella made her own bed. That guy's probably got a woman off every highway exit. Anyway, it's not confirmed she's going, but I say, good riddance. It'd be great if we get a replacement who doesn't ask me to justify every pencil and sticky pad I use."

And isn't quite the gossip you are? But as always in this shark tank, I keep that opinion to myself. I have enough enemies here without tipping my hand to every person who annoys me.

And speaking of enemies, here comes my truest foe, Carletta Milborne. That woman has never made a secret of coveting every job I've had here.

"Carletta, my dear, how are you this beautiful morning?" I tilt my head in her direction as I wave bye to Hallie and start walking.

As I breeze past, I catch a glimpse of Carletta's startled expression. "Lorna Crawford, what are you up to?" she demands.

"Nothing at all," I say sweetly, unwilling to engage her this morning. I flash a smile and head down the hall without turning around.

As I enter my cubicle, I recall how my coworkers got so worked up last summer when they tore down the walls in our office and replaced them with these Dilbert-esque cubes—the better to keep an eye on us, everyone theorized. Getting unhinged about office space didn't seem worth my energy at the time, although the way I'm feeling this morning, I can appreciate their annoyance.

One thing that does drive me totally bananas is having to deal with marketing people at other companies. When I first moved up to run Special Events, I enjoyed chatting with the folks who were eager to have us donate our ice cream or sponsor their programs. Now I'm convinced they conjure up their ideas after way too many gin and tonics.

Take last Friday's call: a pet store wanting to host a reptile pageant, with kids bringing in their snakes and lizards, and our ice cream as awards. "We're desperate to get the attention of little boys," the woman explained. *Forget reptiles! Have a Nintendo DS contest, and they'll come flocking,* I wanted to tell her. I've seen so many boys with one in their hand, I'm starting to think God is welding them onto male fetuses right in the womb. But she probably knows that; it's all those virtual pets that are undoubtedly keeping kids from wanting the real McCoy anymore. I simply thanked the woman for contacting us and told her that our awards budget for the year is fully committed.

The day before, a guy kept me on the line for an hour as he begged us to sponsor his plan to drive cars on top of one another, monster-truck style—on the streets of Chicago! When I told him we put our name only on events where the ice cream is an integral aspect, he offered to smear it on the hoods. Ugh!

I don't know why these ideas irked me so much. In truth, their schemes aren't that much weirder than some of the creations I'm paid to come up with. Two weeks ago, in a meeting with Doug Stevens, my boss, I offhandedly tossed out a proposal to create a new world record for the biggest ice cream sundae. I was sort of kidding, but Doug pounced on it the second the words passed my lips. It's now on deck for this summer in New York's Central Park. I'm meeting with Doug and our president, Hunter Stanton, in a few days to create a timetable for the next five months, which I know from other large promotions I've done will fly by fast. The biggest challenge will be keeping all that ice cream (exactly how much do we need? I must check the old record this morning) from melting on the grass before the sundae gets started. My heart palpitates as I picture chocolate ice cream running all over the lawn, and tabloids and bloggers gloating about the park looking like army of escaped dogs had a romp through it. I calm my jangling nerves by reminding myself I've got plenty of time to work out these details.

My final work frustration: Brendan Bunker. I *am* better at keeping my issues with Brendan under wraps than I am with Carletta. Partly because he's our top-accounts liaison, so we work side by side a lot, and partly because I feel sorry for a guy who's so insecure, he needs to rattle off his 800 math SAT score a decade after graduating from college.

No sooner does Brendan enter my thoughts than here he is, walking into my cube. That's so weird! Anna keeps telling me there's no such thing as coincidence, that people don't wander into our lives—or our cubicles—as randomly as dice fall on a craps table. (Anna says dice rolls aren't coincidence either, but that's just ridiculous.) Last time something serendipitous happened to me, she quoted this fellow, Deepak something, who wrote in some book that coincidences are messages. "They are clues from spirit," Anna told me over the phone, "urging you to open yourself beyond your familiar patterns of thinking." I don't actually believe that. But how to explain this impeccably timed appearance?

"A very good morning to you," Brendan says in an affected British tone that obviously took this rural North Carolina boy years to cultivate.

"So nice to, um, see you," I stammer.

"Lovely to see you, too, Lorna."

"How was your weekend, Brendan? You had a date, right?"

"Yes. Quite lovely. Went to the Guggenheim with my new girlfriend, Desiree. You should see the Jasper Johns they recently acquired. Wonderful interplays of color and light. Took my breath away. I studied art in college, you know. Or maybe you didn't. I'm sure you all think of me as a math whiz, which I suppose I am. But I've always adored art. Minored in it, actually."

Despite my fragile mood, I force myself to stay positive. "I'm glad you had a good time. And I didn't know about your art skills. Thanks for telling me." I don't want to hear more about his education, though, so I spin toward my desk to signal an end to the conversation.

Fortunately, my phone rings, providing me with a natural out. I wave Brendan off as I lift the receiver, and he takes the hint.

Unfortunately, it's my mother.

"Lorna. I'll cut right to the chase. It's Uncle's birthday today, and I'm sure you didn't remember."

"Actually, I did, Mom. Mailed him a card the other day. I'm sure he got it by now," I say, exasperated by my mother's typical lack of faith in me.

"Just a card? With the nice way he's always treated you, I would think a gift—"

I cut her off. "Thanks for the reminder about his birthday. If I get a chance, I'll give him a call. You know I adore Uncle. But I gotta get to work now." I hang up the phone and try to ignore the criticism that flows so easily past her lips. As usual, it gets the better of me. I spend the next thirty minutes searching online for a company that will e-mail my mother's brother a gift certificate today, and once that's sent off, I leave messages on his house, office, and cell phone voice mail so he's sure to know I tried to reach him.

For the next few hours, I'm in such a dither worrying about pleasing my uncle—and, yes, I realize, by extension my mother—that I'm surlier than I've ever been. First, a woman from HR calls to inform me that I overused my personal days a few months ago. My boyfriend, Brad, and I—back when he wasn't so caught up in his work—had sneaked up to Woodstock for a glorious weekend looking at the foliage. We quickly realized that what we most wanted to watch was each other (in the hotel bed!), and a weekend somehow stretched to four luxurious days. The HR woman tells me, in the nastiest of tones, that they're docking this week's paycheck because I didn't have any personal days left at that time. The old me would have accepted the financial hit or graciously pleaded for a onetime exception. But no. Feeling the bile rise up my throat, I retort that *HR* stands for "horribly ruthless."

Later, I have to drop a rush package in the FedEx box outside our building to make the morning pickup because my assistant, Michelle Chen, whom I do adore, is out running an errand. When I turn to reenter the building, I'm jolted by a pointy elbow in my lower back.

"Get out of my way, lady! Some of us don't have all day!" A balding, heavyset man with a beaky nose nudges me aside, eager to get the door swinging.

"Assho—," I start to say as I ready myself to poke him back. And while I do catch my tongue before the "le" slings forth, and I stop myself from shoving him out of *my* way, I'm not proud of this uncharacteristic hostility.

To top off my unhappy morning, the leather digital clock on my desk—a present my best friend, Gretta, gave me two years ago when I got promoted to this position—suddenly flips to one o'clock. I can't fathom where the hours went. Until a few months ago, I would have thought, *How glorious!* If every workday could whiz by so quickly, I'd be the cheeriest employee on earth. I could put all my energy into the weekends, a kid joyfully splashing in her wading pool from Friday night to Monday morning. When I hit my thirty-third birthday, however, that living-for-the-weekend notion began leaking water. My life consists of seven days a week, I realized. If I zone out for five of them, by the time I'm seventy, an astonishing fifty years will have sneaked by me unawares.

Hoping to rouse myself out of my doldrums, I slip out for a lunchtime walk. Breathing in the crisp, cool air definitely clears my head. I circumnavigate a park a few blocks from the office. I'm happy to see the "nice me" make an appearance when I assist a woman who asks if I can hold the leash of her chocolate lab while she straps her flailing child into his stroller. I even coo to the little boy, my funny faces banishing his fury. I grab a hot dog from a street vendor before returning to my desk.

The next thing I know it's three o'clock. *Darn, how does a day slide away like that?* I reach into my overstuffed desk drawer and feel around for a rainbow-sundae-shaped sports watch, a giveaway from a promotion during last spring's switch to daylight saving time. (My clever tagline: "It's always the right time for an ice cream treat!") I strap the timepiece on my wrist and set it to ring every half hour. I hope the dings will jar me into paying attention to my day. I also want to remind myself to stop letting this weird, mean-girl side bore through.

I'm typing some ideas for the summer Central Park sugarfest. At 3:30, *beep beep*. Okay, Lorna, observe how you've just spent the last who-knows-how-many minutes panicking over how we might keep those fifty-five thousand pounds of ice cream and toppings (the old record sundae turns out to have weighed fifty-four point nine) in the deep freeze on a hot June day. To shift my thoughts, I gaze around my office, then sniff the air: mocha coffee. Somebody just went to Starbucks.

Beep beep, 4:00 P.M. I catch myself still fretting over the Central Park logistics; I didn't even realize until the beep that my mind had wandered there again. I need a change of scenery, so I leave my office and walk downstairs to get our favorite coffees for Michelle and me.

Beep beep, 4:30. I'm plodding through the thirty-ninth of forty-seven e-mails that have arrived this afternoon. Not one is from Brad, which sends me into a little tailspin. I want to feel like I'm the center of his world, but lately I'm not even a blip on his radar.

He's been working so much on that blasted software launch, we hardly speak, not to mention that we haven't had a date in weeks. The beep reminds me to shift my perspective. "I know Brad adores me. I bet he's thinking about me right this minute," I force myself to say, even though I only half believe it. I reach for my Venti-sized coffee, and am startled to see the cup's nearly empty. Did I drink the whole thing? I barely recall taking more than a sip.

Beep beep, 5:00 P.M. Thankfully, I'm doing something thoughtful when this one goes off. In the bathroom processing my coffee, I noticed the toilet paper running low. With Stella on leave, I took it upon myself to replace the rolls in all the stalls. When the timer rings, I'm hooking in the final one.

Before I know it, 5:30. *Beep beep.* I'm in Doug's office, describing a remarkable phone call I just got from a movie producer eager to feature our product in an upcoming film.

"But we don't want our ice cream associated with a terrorism thriller," Doug insists, adding to his list of concerns about allowing our brand in this movie. *How can you not see what an amazing opportunity this is? Don't you get where this could take us?*

The beep reminds me to rein in this thoroughbred. "I know it's risky to say yes," I say, giving credence to Doug's apprehension. "But it could be riskier to say no. Think how M&M's must still feel, knowing they turned down *E.T.*! And we can write into the contract that no terrorist scenes include our product."

"Look, Lorna," he says, giving me a meaningful look with his riveting, deep black eyes, which I've always found so gorgeous, matched up as they are with his chocolate-brown skin. "I agree that movie placements could be a good direction. Definitely explore it. But this film ain't it."

Caught up in my vision of Will Smith being chased at 120 miles per hour, navigating his steering wheel with one hand and scooping vanilla praline fudge with the other (with me on the set, making sure everything goes perfectly, of course), I lose my cool. "Don't be so afraid to take a risk, Doug!" I sputter. "It could pay to go out on a limb."

"I think I go out plenty," he replies evenly, but he's clearly pissed.

The conversation clearly over, I turn to hurl myself out the door. In the mirror by the exit, I see that same twisted red face I'd seen in my rearview earlier. *When did I become so unbearable?*

Back in my cube, after I've calmed down, I compose a heartfelt apology e-mail to Doug. The second I hit SEND, Carletta appears, her shaggy blond mane visible before I even look up from the computer. She plops into my visitor's chair.

"What do you want?" I ask curtly, raising my eyes to meet hers directly. Carletta's the only person in this office I truly don't mind offending. In fact, I'm happy to have an outlet for my angst.

Beep beep, 6:00.

Shit.

No, a part of me realizes. *This is perfect.*

"I need to borrow Michelle for a trade show Wednesday," Carletta says. "Turns out my new assistant Danny's gonna be having minor surgery. It's a big show, as you well know—all the top supermarkets. I need a body, and Michelle'd be perfect."

Of course I should lend her Michelle. I have no special events this week, so I can spare her. It would be the right thing to do from our company's perspective, and even more important, the right thing from my own. Lending Michelle would demonstrate that I can be openhearted even to a woman who has hated me for years, a woman who openly desires my job.

But to have Carletta over a barrel is a joy as satisfying as spending a day on the crystalline beaches of Aruba, or tasting a moist chocolate mousse cake topped with homemade whipped cream. The kind of moment whose exhilaration lingers long afterward.

"Sorry, Carletta. I need Michelle Wednesday. You'll have to make do."

"Oh, come on, Lorna. You know lending her is best for our department—something you should care about."

"Maybe you wouldn't have this problem if you didn't run through assistants the way Santa runs through toy paint."

"I told you: Danny's having surgery."

"Might his surgery involve sawing through steak during a job interview?"

"Fine. If you won't lend Michelle, I'll take it up with Doug."

"Please do. Doug's the one who wants me to work out the plans for the sundae gig. He knows I need Michelle's help."

Carletta stands and turns on her heel. I notice she heads for her own office, not Doug's. I'm not surprised she's backing down; she knows that Doug and I are pretty tight, despite our tiff earlier.

I'm clear that with all these confrontations my productivity is shot for the day, so I log out of my computer and head to the elevator. I walk quickly and purposefully across the ground floor lobby, eager to feel the cool air. Outside, my breath pools around my face. Rather than go directly to my car, I lean on the side of the building and take a moment.

I should be elated after putting Carletta in her place. But, like so many other things in my life right now, the victory feels hollow and disappointing.

Chapter 2

I'm in my Saturday-night party uniform, pushing through the crowd at my girlfriends' favorite hangout, Scoffo's. You can't go wrong with a short spaghetti strap top under an open denim crop jacket, A-line mini, and black leggings, not to mention funky faux fur–trimmed designer leather mules, which I scored at a yard sale for a mere twenty dollars. My shoulder-length brown hair is tied with a suede scrunchie in a high, off-center ponytail—what Gretta laughingly calls the Leaning Tower of Pebbles. I admit wearing it this way does make me look almost as young as the Flintstone toddler. But it puts me in a fun mood—something I'm desperate to recapture.

I toss my coat to the check girl and scan the wood-paneled room for the table filled with my giggling pals. I've known these women forever, and we've been meeting monthly at Scoffo's for years.

The air in the bar feels stuffier than normal, triggering a single deep cough, like the blast of a backfiring car. I pray this doesn't mean one of my rapid-fire attacks is on its way. Coughing long and deep is practically my trademark, a medical misery I've been stricken with since girlhood. It's always baffled the doctors, since my lungs are otherwise fine. Fortunately, the barking stops. I regain my bearings and search for my friends.

"Lorna. Lo-or-na. We're over heeeere." Mallory, of course. The singsong vocals perfectly match her personality: she's always searching for the dramatic action she laughingly calls "the delicious chili peppers of life."

I spin in the direction of the crooning and see all the girls have gathered. Darn, I know I'm late, but I thought at least Sarah would get here last: she who can't leave her house without changing her outfit thirteen times. I once asked what she was hoping that baker's dozen would do for her that the first ensemble—or even fourth—didn't. She held back tears as she replied, "I don't have the sense of style that you have, Lorna. You just grab pieces out of your closet and know they'll go perfectly. I can't see how an outfit'll come together until it's on!"

I find Sarah's underconfidence baffling, and constantly tell her so. Whenever I see her—usually arriving an hour after she's supposed to—she looks terrific. And she does again today, in a stunning lime green wool wrap shirt with plunging neckline, her skinny jeans tucked into high-heeled crocodile boots. (The boots are fake, of course. Like me, Sarah would never sanction the killing of those creatures.)

"So happy to see you all. Everyone looks so fabulous! Sorry I'm running late," I ramble, blowing kisses to each of my buddies. "Had to stop for gas on my way over, and this guy pulled his Jag next to my car and started this long conversation. Not that I minded: he *was* adorable."

"Lorna!" Tina says, feigning shock. Tina's our most cerebral member, and an accountant. Naturally, she's the one who divvies up the bill at the end of our evenings to the penny, based on what each of us ordered, even though we've suggested a hundred times that it's easier to split it evenly. "I thought you were committed to Brad these days."

"I am," I reply. "I adore Brad. But he's been so busy with work, it's been weeks since we got together. Anyway, till I'm dead, I'll never stop talking to hunky guys." I squeeze into the empty seat next to my best pal. "Hey, Gretta, how *are* you?" I say, giving her an affectionate pat on her shoulder.

Gretta and I met in seventh grade, when we were paired up in gym class to spot for each other on the balance beam. That first day, I tumbled into her during a failed somersault, knocking her to the mat. She could have been angry, but she took it in stride. "If you wanted to flip for me, there are better ways of showing it," she joked as she did a straddle leap off the floor. I knew right then we'd be great friends. We survived junior and senior high together—our best-pal status fused by our mutual love of Keanu Reeves, posters of his sexy torso plastering our respective bedrooms for years. We fell out a bit when we went to college, her to Syracuse and me to Swarthmore, but when we both moved back to New Jersey after graduation, our friendship reignited, and we've been buddies since. In the past few months, though, there has been a strain between us, for reasons I can't quite put my finger on.

Our regular waitress appears by my side right on cue. My throat is collapsing from the room's dry air. "Crystal, you're a doll! I'd love a seltzer with a lime twist," I say, holding back a gathering cough as I squeak out the words.

"No martini, or even wine?" Mallory sings. "What's gotten into you?"

"Nothing. I'm just thirsty. I might have a glass of wine or an apple martini later." Unlikely, but I'm not ready to admit this to my drinking buddies. I'm taking a cue from my sister, who practices the Eastern precepts of keeping one's mind clear. I'm not convinced laying off booze will pull me out of my doldrums, but I think anything is worth a try. When I compare my unyielding gloom with Anna's perpetual blissfulness, I feel a bit like that woman watching Meg Ryan fake an orgasm in *When Harry Met Sally*: I definitely want what she's having.

"Who's seen the new Brad Pitt movie?" Sarah asks. "I've been dying to, but can't get Tommy to go. Says it's a chick flick."

"I didn't realize you were still with Tommy. You talked about moving on ages ago," I say after Crystal mercifully appears with my club soda and I'm able to lubricate my Gobi-desert throat.

"I do want to dump him! But I figure a bird in the hand, you know . . . Keep him around till somebody better flies in."

"I saw that movie," Mallory trills. "Brad Pitt was sooo hot. Especially when he took off his shirt in that love scene. Perrrrfect!"

"Well, he might be perfect on-screen," Gretta says, immediately animated by any discussion involving a Hollywood star. "But I'll never forgive his leaving Jennifer Aniston, regardless of the beautiful arms that were waiting. I read practically every magazine article at the time describing how devastated she was—apparently couldn't drag herself out of their house for months. Of course, what a house it was! Tennis courts, art studio, enormous movie screening room . . . something like ten thousand square feet . . . ."

I tune out the rest of her virtual home tour. Thanks to the hours she spends digesting those supermarket tabloids and online gossip sites, Gretta's a walking celebrity encyclopedia. Everyone who's anyone in Hollywood is filed away in Gretta's brain. The stars' own agents can't possibly know as much about their clients as she does. For a long time I was smitten, too, although never to the same degree. But somewhere along the line, it just stopped mattering. I know this upsets Gretta. "I miss how we'd lie across the couch reading celebrity magazines, pointing out juicy tidbits to each other," she whined to me two weeks ago. *But why should we care how people live in plastic*

Hollywood? I wanted to reply. She was pained that I no longer share her passion, so I simply shrugged.

I glance over to the bar. I'm surprised to see a priest on one of the stools—and even more stunned to realize I know the guy. Really, though, it's just like Jimmy Preston to come to a joint like this. Jimmy—Father Jimmy now—was my neighbor in grade school, and has always enjoyed being around lively people and places. I reminisce about all the fun we used to have with the kids on the block. I notice that he's lost a lot of weight—and hair—since those preadolescent days. Still, he looks fabulous, something I didn't pay attention to when I saw him a few months back, when my mother dragged me to Mass at his church. I'm convinced she switched from her own longtime parish just so she could brag to people about how well she knows the Father. *She* swears it's because her old church is modernizing. Change is something Mom definitely abhors; that much is true.

"Earth to Lorna. Come in, Lorna."

I look up. The girls are staring.

"You haven't been paying attention," scolds Gretta. "We're going around the table, naming various celebrity jerk men who've cheated on their fabulous wives. We get to you . . . and nothing. You aren't much fun tonight." She eyes me with the nasty look of a teacher who's just discovered thumbtacks on her chair—the hard way.

"I'm just not much in the mood to discuss celebrities," I say, trying to sound nonchalant, even though I now find this kind of gossip futile.

"Watch out for Lorna," Gretta continues. "She's in a real funk these days."

"Really? What's kind of funk?" Mallory asks. It's clear from her consciously perky voice that she doesn't want too much depressing detail.

"Nothing. I'm fine," I protest, hating for my ongoing malaise to be the focus of our evening together. "All right, a cheating male celebrity jerk. How about—?"

"Actually, you don't seem fine," Tina says. "Haven't since you walked in. And I don't know what was up the other day. I sent you that long text about my problems with my brother—because you're usually so understanding—and you answer with a three-word reply."

"Lorna. If something's wrong, we deserve to hear it. I mean, we've been your good friends for, like, forever," Sarah adds.

I'm searching for the right words—although I'm not sure myself what's got me bothered—and finally I apologize to Tina for being so brusque. "I'm sorry about that text. I guess I have been in a mood. But I really can't say why."

"Well, if you had to guess, what would you think?" Sarah prompts.

I take another sip of club soda and swish it around my mouth, buying some time. I place the glass down carefully and look toward the ceiling. "I guess I've been asking myself that proverbial, 'What is the meaning of life?' question, and not coming up with a satisfying answer," I confess. "The things I spend my time on don't seem to be that important—to me or to the world. I'm wondering if there's supposed to be more." I pause, sensing blank faces all around. "Never mind. It's just a phase. I'm sure it'll pass."

"I sure hope so," Gretta jumps in. Her irritation hasn't lessened one bit.

Mallory drawls, "Whatever do you think about these things for, Lorna?"

"That's what I'm wondering," Gretta says. "Why run your brain in circles, trying to get answers to unanswerable questions? The meaning of life? Unless you're talking about the old Monty Python film, I'd rather focus on more important things—like Brad Pitt!"

I stand abruptly, eager to put an end to this discussion. "I see someone I know," I say, and stride toward Father Jimmy. The girls' faces brighten as I depart, each of them wearing that same look of relief we share whenever a nerd we're afraid will crash our table mercifully walks on by. I feel relieved, too. These are my drinking, hanging-out, having-fun buddies. What am I doing making such depressing conversation?

"Hi, Jimmy—er, Father Jimmy," I say, remembering when this tall, lithe man used to crawl around his mother's couch as a boy, pretending to hide from the attacking enemy (me), with gun (or rather, popsicle stick) at the ready. *You have grown into a man,* I think, noticing his blazing green eyes and that jutting jawline. *Stop it, Lorna—the guy is a priest, for God's sake.* I smile at my own irreverence. "Nice to run into you, although I admit it's an unusual place to find a priest."

"It's so good to see you," he says, giving me a peck on the cheek. "And I'm only having soda water," he says, tilting his glass in my direction and smiling. "You know I've always loved a warm atmosphere where people are having fun. I suspect some of my parishioners might not understand, but you—"

I interrupt, wanting to ease his discomfort. "No need to explain. I think it's great that you can continue being a real person, being a man of the cloth now and all."

He shifts his weight and straightens his back, embarrassed. "Haven't seen you at church since your mother brought you. Been attending Mass nearer your home?"

"No." I wonder how proper it is to talk about doubt to a believer. "I haven't been going much lately. Organized religion doesn't seem to do it for me right now."

"I see," he says. I watch him bite his lower lip. I guess it's hard to reprimand someone with whom you've played Monopoly marathons. After a few seconds of silence, he offers, "If you ever want to talk about your confusion, give me a call.

I'm happy to . . . help you sort out your thinking."

"That's very kind of you," I say in a voice I hope is more neutral than dismissive. "So . . . how are your parents doing?"

Our exchange meanders to pleasantries about his sister and mine. Eventually, I notice my gal pals are laughing so loudly, the other patrons must be desperate for earplugs. Mallory's cackles peal especially high. I'm pleased they're having a good time. I'm even tempted to rejoin them—they *are* my most treasured buddies—though I'm afraid I'll feel as out of place as a polar bear in the Sahara.

"My friends are waiting. Nice seeing you, Father Jimmy. You certainly do look terrific," I say before ambling back to our table.

". . . a recovering cocaine addict who recently relapsed. He went on a bender and shot his own dog. The woman he's with is his dealer, thrilled to have him back in her stable," Tina is saying when I get close enough to hear. They're all hysterical— even Sarah, despite her lifelong devotion to dogs. "That's why she's smiling so broadly; he buys her best stuff."

"Okay, my turn . . . Oooooh. I've got that man." Gretta giggles, pointing to a small olive-skinned guy sitting at the other end of the bar from Father Jimmy. "Let's see. . . . He's a fundamentalist terrorist who believes Islam's rightful place is at the center of the universe. He's having his farewell drink before he straps on his belt of explosives and goes to blow up the Fort Lee mall. Fortunately for us shoppers, the man over at *that* table—" She points to a bodybuilder type sitting in the other corner. "—is with the FBI. He's stalking the terrorist and will wrestle him to the ground before he sets the thing off, saving everyone. My hero!"

"That's so against the rules!" Mallory cries, her lilt straining. "You're not allowed to predict the future. You're just supposed to give us your fantasy about what brought the guy—or the two guys, in your case—to this bar right now: funny stuff about their recent past and present."

And maybe something not quite so racist, I think, locking eyes with Sarah, who's obviously thinking the same thing.

"Oh, it's all in good fun," Tina says, aiming to defuse the tension. "Besides, the guy's clearly Mediterranean, not Middle Eastern. Maybe he'll go out with you if you ask, Mallory. I hear Greek or Italian guys adore forward American girls. And maybe not *all* his parts are small!" More giggling.

"What do you think, Lorna? Should we approach the guy to ask him out? Or maybe the FBI man. Certainly none of *his* parts will turn out to be tiny," Mallory's laughing so hard, she snorts her sip of cosmopolitan out her nose. This brings another round of guffaws to everyone at the table but me, laughing that continues as Mallory makes a big show of dabbing it off her face with Gretta's napkin.

"Girls, I think I'm gonna call it a night." I throw down a twenty even though I had only the one club soda, and gather my purse to leave.

"That's not right," Tina says. At first I think she means my walking out before the rest of the group, but then I see she's eyeing my Andrew Jackson. She's not even sorry to see me go. Ouch.

"It's fine. You girls use the extra money to take cabs home rather than drive in your condition."

"Since when did you get so prissy?" Gretta asks. "You used to be fun."

I don't reply. But inside, I know she's right, even if I have no idea how or what needs changing.

ॐ

I drive home awhile in silence. I've never felt so alone. Could I have tried harder to laugh with my buddies? If I'd gotten as tipsy as I usually do, I'm sure I would have found their conversations merrier.

I click on the radio to WNOW, hoping it might lift my spirits the way I suspect it does Anna's. The same host as the other day, Serena Robbins, is on the air, filling in, she says, for a late-night colleague.

"Gooooood evening to you! I hope you're having a magnificent Saturday night."

"Not really," I say to the tuner.

Amazingly, she hears me. "To those not having a magnificent time, I say you need to shift your mindset. It's a glorious evening— the moon is full, the crisp air is sweet to breathe, life is waiting for your appreciation. Don't let situations, or other people, even if how they act seems awful, separate you from the inner glory that is you. . . . Steve from Lanville, you're on the air."

"My evening was the pits. I was supposed to have a date with this girl. I've had my eye on her for, like, forever. She stood me up! I don't think she ever planned to meet me. What a fool I was, sitting at this restaurant for nearly an hour. I've spent the evening since then walking all over. I've no place to go right now, so I'm still walking. I feel like such an ass."

"You can't be responsible for other people's actions," Serena Robbins coos. "No one can make you feel like an ass but you. Remember that you're here on this planet to have your own joyful time. Don't let someone else ruin that. And don't feel lonely because you were alone tonight. A lot of people spent this evening with other people, even lots of them, yet some of them felt alone, too."

"Amen," I say aloud. Maybe this woman is on to something.

"Keep walking, Steve. But instead of feeling sorry for yourself, use this time to notice how breathtaking the world is, and how you, too, are plugged right into that magnificence. I guarantee it will transform the rest of your night."

By the time I pull into my driveway and walk toward my house, I'm feeling more upbeat. Standing on my front porch, I look up to see that the full moon *is* striking and that the air is indeed sweet and crisp. There's a lone fly walking around my light fixture. I smile as I stand still for several moments, watching the insect contentedly strut its stuff.

But when I enter my empty house and notice the red light on my phone is not blinking—no *Are you okay?* voicemail from my girlfriends or *I miss you* kisses from Brad—the internal darkness descends again.

Chapter 3

Anna—Angelica—has already grabbed a booth for us at the diner near my house by the time I arrive. It's been more than a week since my evening with the girls, and I've been under a cloud ever since.

"Thanks for meeting me—especially on such short notice," I say to my sister, leaning over the Formica table to peck her cheek before sitting across from her on the red vinyl banquette. She beams as usual in her sequined white blouse, festive heart earrings, and, of course, the ever-present twinkle in her eyes.

"No problem. You sounded like you needed a pick-me-up. I consider that my specialty."

I look around the diner. It's one of those modern places that strives to look old-fashioned; meanwhile truly authentic places are closing down all over town, victims of rising rents and changing palates. I picked this spot because I've always adored the vintage 1950s Coke signs adorning the walls, though when I spy them now, they strike me as grimy.

Anna leans forward, eyeing me intently. "What's up?"

I swivel my attention back to her. "I wish I knew," I reply glumly. "It's nothing I can put my finger on. I mean, I'm bummed Brad hardly calls me, but I know he's busy. Work's fine. My friends are okay, even if we didn't have the greatest night out last time. There's Mom, of course, but nothing new there: just her desire to knock me down at every turn."

"You know she doesn't mean—," Anna softy defends her.

"You know she *does* mean it," I interrupt firmly. "Not with you. Only me. But Mom hasn't done anything worse than usual. Nobody has. *They* haven't changed; it's *me* who has. Stuff that used to be fun grates me like nails on a chalkboard. I can't seem to gin up a passion about anything."

Anna looks at me for a full minute without responding. This habit of hers, taking her sweet time to reply, always drove me crazy. But now I appreciate that she wants to clarify her thoughts rather than spout the first, maybe off-the-mark idea that springs to her mind.

"You're having a spiritual crisis," she replies at last. She says this with the certainty of a doctor who, reading the X-rays, has diagnosed a broken bone.

"Well, when you're a minister, I suppose everything looks like a spiritual crisis," I say lightly. "Like when you're a hammer . . . ."

The waitress comes by to pour me coffee and Anna, tea, and we pause our discussion while she fills our cups. Anna turns to fully face the woman. She looks about twenty-five, with rosy cheeks and dark hair pulled into a wispy ponytail with fringed bangs. Anna asks the woman how she likes her job, if she has any kids, whom she prefers in the upcoming special election. This desire to speak to everyone as if they were her BFF is another trait of Anna's that I never understood. I mean, Anna doesn't ever eat here, so it's not like she's going to see the woman again. But this Queenie, if the perky HI, I'M QUEENIE name tag pinned next to her very open neckline is to be believed, grows more animated with every exchange. After a few minutes of this, she pumps Anna's hand with unbridled joy, flashes a hundred-watt smile on both of us, and practically skips away. Anna watches her flit behind the counter for another minute before resuming our conversation.

"I know you think I'm single-minded, Lorn. But the reason I can recognize the symptoms of spiritual drifting is because I had it, too. In my early twenties. I just stopped feeling like my life had meaning. It's what set me on my ministerial path."

"I will not become a minister!" I jokingly protest, screwing up my nose like I've just eaten something awful for added effect.

"I'm not saying you should," Anna laughs. "But it sounds like you're disconnected. I think you'd benefit by developing . . ." She pauses, reaching for the right words, and for some reason I feel incredibly patient. "Well, I think it would help you to develop at least a passing acquaintance with the amazing energy of the universe that's inside you—that's inside everyone."

"Have you been listening to that Serena Robbins radio host?" I demand, smiling.

"Oh! You've finally heard her," she shrieks. "I love that woman! So what did you think?"

"Dunno. At first she seemed so airy-fairy. But I've listened a few times now, and I have to admit she does always make me feel better. Like she's tapping into something meaningful and deep."

ॐ

I guess my response was all the opening Anna needed. In any event, that's how I wind up in the foyer of her house, arms teetering under the dozen spiritual books she's insisting I read. The names on the spines are either new to me—Thich Nhat Hahn, Ernest Holmes, Gregg Braden—or people I had no idea concerned themselves with spirit, like Ralph Waldo Emerson, that essayist we were forced to read in high school.

"When you finish those, I've got plenty more," Anna says, giving me such a massive good-bye hug, I'm surprised the books don't tumble from my overwhelmed arms.

A few days later, I'm sprawled on my living room couch,

tearing through my ninth book. Until now, my spiritual repertoire has pretty much been limited to the Bible (from childhood religious classes; I haven't cracked it since). But these very different spiritual tracts—encouraging my personal union with my highest essence, and offering various road maps to get there—are opening me up to a different world. I'm starting to see that life isn't about what happens; it's about how I decide to react to those things. It's up to me whether I choose to react by feeling angry, sad, and aimless—or, as my higher self does, loving, appreciative, and joyful. It's my call whether to live from a place of connection or separation.

Although I can tell that putting these ideas into practice won't be easy, I feel a bit like the baby boom generation must have felt when it got its first taste of the Beatles. There's a whole world out there I never knew existed. I am awed by these teachings. And I am on my way.

Chapter 4

I'm sitting in my silk pajamas before bed, in the corner of my bedroom that I've set up for *sujaling*—my made-up word for "meditation." After voraciously ingesting Anna's dozen books, then the dozen more I picked up from her before raiding the public library for another huge stack this week, I felt compelled to give meditation a try. Pretty much all these teachings extol the value of sitting serene like the Buddha. When, in the most recent book, I saw an illustration of him under the Bodhi Tree, I realized I had to go there. Not to the tree (although jetting off to India would be fun). To where it took him. It struck me that behind those closed eyes, the Buddha is joyfully cantering on a graceful horse along the beach at sunset, or serenely staring into a newborn baby's eyes.

I hate the word *meditation,* though. The *med* part reminds me of that sticky red liquid my mother used to ply me with for my unyielding cough, while the *tion* sounds so hard and commanding. I want a word that is as gentle and sweet as the state I am hoping to experience. Yesterday, the first time I tried this "sitting cross-legged, focusing on my breath" thing, the word *sujal* popped into my head. The *sue* sounded like the wind, the *zhul* so dreamy and otherworldly. Although it has no meaning, I adopted it immediately.

Just as I'm crossing my legs on the floor, my cell phone rings. I know I'm supposed to ignore the sound and get down to business, but my curiosity wins out. Besides, I haven't really started yet.

I lean over my nightstand and grab it, pressing the green button right away. "Hello?"

"Babe. How are you?" Brad's chipper voice rings out.

How ironic that I've been praying all day for Brad to call, and when he does, I'd rather be sitting in silence. Since I haven't yet told Brad about my spiritual explorations (it's not something I want to discuss by phone, and I'm not sure how he'll take it), he won't understand. "Hey. So good to hear your voice," I reply.

"I've been staring at your picture on my computer for the last ten minutes, and I finally just had to connect live."

"Glad you did. I thought about calling you earlier, but I didn't want to bother you. I know how busy you are."

"Hearing from you's not a bother!" He sounds genuinely hurt. "So I should have called?"

He pauses a second before answering. "Uh, no. My cell was turned off, and my secretary was instructed to hold my calls. Tons of meetings. But we're talking now! I miss you so much."

I'm eager to get my sujal going, but I do also want to chat with Brad, so I plow on. "I miss you, too. If it wasn't for your picture on my cell phone—okay, and my key ring, my dresser, my desk—I might forget what your adorable kisser looks like."

"Don't forget too much! I know I've been a shitty boyfriend, but I'm gonna make this up to you big-time. I promise."

"Sounds good." I pause. "Listen, hon, I'm beat—so if you don't mind, I'm gonna head off to bed."

"You know I'd love to be heading there with you."

"Is that an offer?"

"It is if you'll take a rain check."

"You've got it! Tell me it will stop raining soon?"

"Soon enough. Just bear with me a little longer."

After some noisy air kisses, I hang up and return my focus to my altar.

Last night I vowed to sujal every day for ten minutes in the morning and ten more each night. I read in some books about dedicating an hour or more, but after last night's and this morning's racing-mind sessions, I'll be thrilled now if I can do those ten minutes without my mind constantly pulling me out of focus.

I light a stick of sandalwood incense resting in a teak wooden holder, items I picked up the other day at a New Age shop to adorn my bedroom altar. Well, it's not an official altar, just a small end table I dragged from the living room and covered in an old scarlet scarf. I've topped it with things Anna—*why can't I remember to call her Angelica!*—gave me from her own altar, along with that second set of books: five stones, each carved with a word like *faith, love,* and *contentment;* a Tibetan singing bowl; and a small golden statue of Kwan Yin, the Chinese goddess of compassion. Official or not, it feels elevating to look at it, which I'm clear from my reading is the whole point.

I close my eyes and rock my butt back and forth until I get comfortable. Then I flare my nostrils to concentrate on the smell. I suspect that to get into the present moment in any kind of real way, I have to engage all my senses. Otherwise I go right to my brain, the brain I learned to use long ago to shield me from my inner essence. But now the guard may be loosening its grip, and I'm desperate to feel the full range of desires I know are hiding underneath, too scared from years of having bricks thrown at me by my mother to come out to play. No, not desperate, I correct myself, because *desperate* implies that I'm running breathless with the enemy at my back, and all the books I've devoured emphasize that the key to meditation is accepting and allowing and waiting patiently for things to unfold in their own time.

I suddenly realize that I've lost my focus on the smell, what with all this mental yammering. *Let me try sound.* I listen into the silence until I hear the whoosh from the hall of the tabletop waterfall I bought at the discount store the other day. It's been running since I flipped the switch on my way into the bedroom. This is why I need to practice sujaling: so I can get to the place where I'm fully awake and aware. Otherwise, years from now, I'm going to be an old woman lying on some saggy mattress in an antiseptic-smelling nursing home, wondering why I never much listened to the sound of running water or sniffed the sweet scent of sandalwood.

There I go again! Well, at least this time I caught myself running off course midstream—unlike this morning, an unmitigated disaster from a meditation standpoint, when I didn't stop the ruckus at all.

My awareness moves to my body. I notice a tightness between my shoulder blades, thanks to my earlier coughing session. I really should do something about it, but I have no idea what. I'm certainly not taking any more of that medicine my mom used to insist on, but doctors have tested me for asthma and allergies and say I don't have them, and the over-the-counter cough remedies I've tried don't seem to do anything, and—

Lorna! Keep your focus on the here and now! Why do all those authors make it seem so easy?

Suddenly, my timer dings, indicating my ten minutes are over. Damn. An unstoppable mental train. My cantering Buddha will have to wait for another day.

ॐ

A few weeks later, I'm practically breathless as I head for my yoga studio. My afternoon meeting ran so long that now I won't make my hatha class on time. I'm in a lather.

I've taken up yoga in the hopes it might help with my horrible sujals. I've discovered that I can't sit for more than a few minutes before one body part or another cries out for attention. I always thought yoga was just another exercise, but recently I read that it was invented by ancient Indian meditators who couldn't sit on their rumps, either. Not having flat-screen TVs or tabloid magazines, they spent hours watching dogs and cats and lions and cobras in the natural world, and realized these animals never get stiff because they constantly stretch their bodies into contorted positions. The yogis emulated the animals and credited them with the names of the poses.

I discovered this Om Sweet Om yoga studio by searching the Web, and had to laugh when I realized it's only a few blocks from my office. I must have passed it on the way to my favorite pizzeria dozens of times, but I never noticed. Although I love the idea of stretching my body, plunging in proved harder than I expected. The first time, I just stood at the entrance, chilled to the bone but suddenly feeling too intimidated to go in. There was something about those foreign Sanskrit words in the window, not to mention the illustration of a woman doing a back-bend with one leg up in the air, that told me this was a club to which I'd never belong. My eyes kept darting around, looking for my mother—not that she lives anywhere near there. But I know she'd never approve of my doing these weird Eastern practices. (Even though she's okay knowing Anna does. Double standard is Mom's middle name.)

I stood there for a long time, frozen in every sense of the word, wearing the bicycle shorts and tank top I'd changed into at my office (the only exercise clothes I owned). Even though I wore a long coat, my teeth began chattering and my legs became numb. I did everything I could think of to coax myself inside— reassuring myself that surely not everyone here does that one- leg-up maneuver, and that if I really stink, I can bolt from class midpose—but it proved useless.

I was about to slink away, when an attractive blonde about

my height and age rounded the corner. The tight pants and fitted T-shirt under her open coat revealed a firm but not impossibly taut body. When she saw me, she stopped short in front of the entrance. "Is it closed?" she asked, confused.

"No, no. You can go on in," I replied, praying she'd enter swiftly and leave me in peace.

Alas, she didn't budge. "Are you waiting for someone? You can stand inside, you know. It's a lot warmer."

"I'm embarrassed to admit this," I confessed, amazed to feel comfortable being honest with this stranger, "but I'm too nervous to try a class."

"I know what you mean. I was the same way my first time. I'm Janelle," she said, extending a hand. The second she touched my frozen fingers, she dragged me inside, spouting warnings about frostbite and shock.

Janelle took it as something of a personal mission to reel me into the class. She prattled on about how yoga isn't a competition, so it doesn't matter how flexible I am, but anyway I have the perfect body to do it, and how she loves it so much, she'd come three times a week for the past six months. She was very persuasive. Not fifteen minutes later, I was lying next to her sticky mat (me on a rented linty towel), awkwardly trying to get my limp legs off the ground or to twist my rigid torso more than ten degrees.

The class was intoxicating. It didn't matter that I was no good. And much to my relief, the instructor spoke clear English—tinged with the most adorable Spanish accent—not the Sanskrit gobbledygook I'd feared. Any poses she named in the ancient Indian language she swiftly translated, her lyrical voice informing my untrained ear that *Bhujangasana* meant "Cobra" and *Dhanurasana*, "Bow."

Afterwards, Janelle took me to this cute little tea shop in a tiny alley around the corner. I'd never noticed the alley before, either; chalk it up to the constant mental chatter that distracts me from seeing what's around. She and I yapped for hours, our talk flowing as easily as the Mississippi River, and a deep friendship was born.

Now it's almost six thirty, the time our class is scheduled to start. I was supposed to meet Janelle twenty minutes ago, and I'm crazed by the thought that she's waiting, that I'm making her late, too. Why does nothing ever seem to go according to plan? Now she's going to be pissed, and instead of having a fabulous yoga experience, we're going to embarrass ourselves by having to tiptoe through the silent classroom, avoiding all the outstretched arms and legs strewn about the floor.

As I rush down the final block, I suddenly recall a passage I read yesterday in *The Peace Book,* by Louise Diamond: "To find our natural self, we must learn to calm the inner battles . . . to touch, at will, that deep pool of serenity and clarity that is the soul's birthright." It hits me how ridiculous it is to work myself up about getting to a place I've chosen to go to specifically to relax. As I near the front door, I begin an exercise from that book: I breathe in deeply, inhaling peace, then breathe out deeply, exhaling acceptance. Another breath of calm in, loving-kindness toward myself out. If I'm tardy, *c'est la vie*.

I twist the doorknob and spy Janelle in the lobby store, sitting on a pile of meditation cushions like a queen on her vast yogic throne.

"So sorry I'm late!" I pant in a frenzy that reveals some remaining angst beneath my patina of calm. "You'd think since I've been working on plans for this ice cream sundae event for weeks already, I wouldn't still be in crisis mode. But every time I think I've figured out how to pull this stunt off, something causes my brilliant idea to evaporate. Anyhow, you should've gone up without me."

"Girl, your tongue's gonna fall off if you keep wagging it at that speed." She smiles widely. "Stop worrying. The class is running late—I checked with Consuela. She's gonna start in a couple of minutes, so we won't miss anything."

"You're the best. Thanks for waiting for me." I love Janelle. No matter the situation, she always scouts out the positive, sure that everything will turn out okay. The way I see it, we're like a photographic image—but she's the lovely print and I, more often than I would like, especially these days, the corresponding negative. Janelle's become my idol, someone who, along with Angelica, can nudge me toward the vibrant version of myself I long to be. Relieved, I shoot the woman at the front desk a loving grin as I flash my monthly pass card and sign in.

"My day was so great," Janelle says as we hustle into the locker room to change for class. "I slipped out at lunch and did a half hour of deep, three-part breathing at the park. When I came back, nobody could touch me. Even when Raymond tried to do his blame game for why his project came in so far over budget, I didn't lose my peace. There's a lot to be said for staying connected to your calm inner being."

"Yeah, there is—or rather there would be, if I could remember to do it more often," I sigh. Occasionally, I'm able to put these teachings to work, to relax and revel in the beauty of the universe—even the gems I know are hiding somewhere within Brendan and Carletta. And when I do, it's magical. But most of the time I'm oblivious, slopping anxiously and haggardly through my day.

"Patience, my dear. Good things come to those who keep at it."

We pull on the yoga outfits we scored at a sale at Bloomingdale's last Saturday. After thousands of years of baggy white cotton as year-round attire, yoga clothes suddenly have a season! Bloomie's was trying to clear out its winter gear (even though it's still solidly winter) to make room for the incoming spring stuff. Janelle was practically choking from laughter, and while I admit to being something of a fashion plate, I, too, thought it was hilarious. The stuff on the sale rack looked exactly like the new outfits coming in at triple the price: stretchy pants with white piping down the sides, spaghetti-strap tops with drawings of teeny people in these impossible ankles-over-ears or fingers-behind-their-toes poses. The only difference was that the spring items came in brighter shades of the blue, brown, and lavender. As I kick off my pumps and hang my work clothes in the locker, I'm confident I look as terrific in my navy yoga outfit as I feel.

In the studio, I roll out my sticky mat and settle in just as the session begins. Consuela, the woman who taught my first class, is still my favorite instructor. She's a lithe dancer with petite shoulders and muscular thighs. She's also so bendable, I affectionately think of her as Miss Gumby, after that old rubber cartoon character, but with delicious brown skin rather than green. Although I now do some poses I thought were beyond my body for this lifetime, I'm still incredibly inflexible, especially when compared to the abilities of not only Miss Gumby, but all the other women in this classroom. They rise effortlessly into the bow pose, balancing on their abdomens while holding their ankles, while I struggle mightily to reach my shins. I lift my thighs and torso a meager three inches off the ground—more like the arrow than the bow!—feeling as stiff as that oversprayed piled-up hairdo my great-aunt Ethel has worn practically since the Civil War.

I glance around at the women in the room. *How do they do it?* They seem to lack some of the bones I have. These women pull their legs up as if no fibulae stand in the way, and arch their back as if their spines contain fewer vertebrae than mine, and more verve. Plus, my thighs, back, and shoulders seem to be guarded by a platoon of intractable joints and muscles, which don't desire to lay down their swords and let the limbs do their thing.

Even though I'm pretty thin, I was never good at sports, as my dear mother constantly informed me. As a kid I couldn't do the cartwheels on my lawn like my friends, and I was the last one picked for every game of kickball we played in the street. But now I realize I was taught to think badly about my body. If Mom had complimented my flexibility and speed, I could have been an athletic star. But my mother had the creaky body of the Tin Man, and she hated to think I might be more limber. Mom planted the notion that my physique wasn't cut out for anything more strenuous than cleaning up my room, until I not only believed it to be so, I made it happen.

Thought is "the first step in creation. . . . Your thought is the parent which gives birth to all things." The minute I read that in Neale Donald Walsch's *Conversations with God,* I knew the God in that book was talking to me. What you put out to the world with your thoughts gets returned in hand-delivered hard copy. You think it into being, and, like a boomerang, back it comes. Now that I'm trying to live these spiritual principles, I need to change my thinking, to use that universal creation machine to my advantage.

I have a flexible body, one getting more limber with each pose, I silently declare as I arch into the pigeon pose—or the highly modified version I do that makes it more of a turkey. I glance at the woman next to me, her back a perfect crescent, hands delicately grasping the foot behind her head. *Who am I kidding about getting limber?*

We move to the full forward bend, *Uttanasana*. Consuela has us hold the pose for probably two minutes, and to my rigid lower back, that's way too long. To make the time go faster, I decide to scoot forward a little more. I inch over, retreat back, then relax down, farther than I've ever gone. Practically sniffing my knees, I'm sure I can't move a millimeter more.

Miss Gumby, however, has other ideas. She walks over to me and leans her entire torso onto my back, urging me onward. It isn't much—maybe a quarter of an inch if someone were to come around with a ruler. But to my flaming back and legs, it feels like a mile.

"Breathe, breathe," she whispers gently into my ear.

"I'm breathing!" I retort.

"Slowly inhale a bit more air, to open your muscles. It will also return your face to its natural, lovely, pink complexion."

I breathe. Long and slow and through the nose, like Miss Gumby has taught me. My back opens wide up, and I sink down ever farther. It feels like I've discovered space inside my body and dived in to stake my claim. I'm feeling such bliss, I don't want to move, so I linger in that pose a few minutes after everyone else has progressed to another asana.

By the end of class, my thigh and back muscles are rebelling. But my face is tranquil. More important, my mind has expanded, like I'm connected to a world beyond my body. There's something about yoga that makes it a spiritual experience, I'm realizing. It's opening me beyond myself. A good class seems like a dose of LSD—without the worry you'll find yourself jumping off a roof into a swimming pool.

Miss Gumby is prancing around the room, handing out flyers about a weekend silent mountain retreat the studio is hosting next month. "Sorry for the short notice," she says. "We were originally planning this for late spring, but the retreat center made an error. So this is the only date we can reserve enough rooms." No annoyance as she mentions the screwup. No hint of *Can you believe those dolts?* I am in awe.

The second she dismisses the class with her loving, *"Namaste"* (Sanskrit for, "I salute the divine light within you," Consuela explained during my first class), Janelle is all over me.

"Let's do this!" she says, waving the flyer so close, it misses slicing my nose by inches. "You've been saying you want to deeply explore yoga. Well, this certainly would do it."

"A weekend silent retreat? No way can I keep my trap shut for two days!"

"Sure you can. This'll be such a perfect chance for both of us to ratchet our practice up a notch."

"You mean a mile! Look what the flyer says." I scan the paper. "Two daily yoga classes and two meditations . . . lectures on yogic philosophy . . . silence the entire weekend. And get this: a yoga cleansing practice. I haven't the foggiest idea what that is, but I'd rather not find out. Anyway, maybe that'll be a weekend I can see Brad."

"Since when do you plan your life around Brad? You told me yourself you don't expect to see him much till his software launches." She pauses, but I don't give her the satisfaction of a reply. "Anyway, didn't we agree we wanted to be more like Miss Gum-by?" she smiles as she elongates her pronunciation of our now shared nickname for Consuela. "I'm sure she does all these practices. And look at the results she gets."

I glance at our teacher as she rolls up her lime green sticky mat. She's fit and gorgeous, her short dark hair falling into a perfect bob even though she did a headstand during class. (I didn't even try; I just lay on my back with my legs at a ninety-degree angle.)

But I know that's not what Janelle's talking about. Consuela has a glow about her, like she's lit from some internal pilot light that's always on. You can tell she's entered a room without turning to the door because it's a shine you feel as well as see. She definitely doesn't get that radiance from any dermatologist-tested cream or elegantly scented lotion.

"Plus, this could be a great chance for you to stop worrying about whether your mother would approve," Janelle piles on relentlessly. "You know she'd think a silent retreat is bonkers. Treat it like a test: Can you go a whole weekend without mentally seeking her approval?"

"Okay, okay! I'll do it for you," I smile, worn down by arguments I know are dead-on, even if my mind's still resisting. "In any event," I laugh, "it'll be a great chance to show off our new kick-butt yoga clothes."

Chapter 5

I'm sitting in my cube on a Friday afternoon, staring at the light fixture and wondering yet again how I got snookered into signing up for that retreat. I haven't told anyone about it since Janelle and I registered two weeks ago—a sign, I'm certain, of my reluctance to attend. Whenever I think about a whole weekend of silence—not to mention cleansing practices, which I don't even want to ponder—my stomach flips over.

The phone rings. I pause before answering and shove my thoughts about the retreat to the back of my brain. I lift the receiver, and a voice starts talking right away.

"Hey, gorgeous! So glad I caught you in!"

His enthusiasm reminds me how much I adore my boyfriend, even if I haven't seen him since that one day before a yoga class when he dropped by on his way to a meeting for a quick hello.

"Hey, hon. How's your day going?"

He ignores my small talk and gets right to business. "I pray you're free tomorrow night. I've got a lull before the big storm and am eager to take you out for dinner—and maybe collect on that rain check you promised a while back."

I smile at the thought of finally getting him into bed again. But the man hasn't made time for a proper date in ages, so I'm hesitant to seem too available. A few months ago at a garage sale, I found a tattered copy of *The Rules*, a book that was all the rage back in the mid-'90s. Its recommendation for manipulating relationships was such a hoot, I'd brought it to our girls' night at Scoffo's; we had some great laughs over its very un-feminist advice. Still, the part about not being an easy catch seems relevant right now. Of course I'm free tomorrow night—and pretty much every night—but isn't it better if I leave Brad wondering? After all, haven't little white lies been part of man–woman encounters since, well, Eve equivocated about where she got the apple?

"I'll have to check. Figured you'd be working, so I kinda made tentative plans."

He pauses, taken aback by my hesitation. "Well, let me know as soon as you can, okay? My colleague Philippe here is the brother of one of the silent partners backing LeHot, and Philippe has pulled strings to get us a reservation. No easy feat for a Saturday night, I might add."

LeHot! The Trendiest—capital *T*—restaurant in Manhattan! I heard LeHot's been so popular from the day it opened that it's impossible to get reservations, even for a weeknight. *The Rules* be damned.

"Okay, I've checked my calendar: I'm free!" I exclaim, to his bemused chuckle. "What time will you pick me up?"

"Eight o'clock," he replies through more muted laughter. "Dress sexy. Can't wait to see you!"

As soon as we hang up, I dash an e-mail to Gretta. She and I used to gab several times a day, but that's been drastically reduced since our awful evening at the bar. From hints she dropped last week, I suspect the girls are going to Scoffo's this weekend without having invited me. At first I felt crushed, but when Gretta rambled on about having run into Conan O'Brien at a fund-raiser she'd been to—endless details about what he wore, how he looked her in the eye when she said hello, how he signed an autograph with her pen and now she wants to frame them both—I decided maybe a breather was a good idea. But it was Gretta who told me you couldn't get a reservation at LeHot until it was practically LeCold season next year, so it's only natural I want to reach out to her now.

To: Gretta
From: Lorna

My excitement builds with every keystroke.

Subject: Guess who's heading for LeHot!

Message: Brad just asked yours truly for a date to LeHot for tomorrow night! We all know it's impossible to get reservations, but he's got connections! I need your advice, girlfriend: What should I wear???

As I extend my finger to click SEND, I realize that this communiqué is far from loving. This is my oldest pal, after all. So what if we're in a little slump? If I'm trying to be more spiritual, shouldn't my words to such a good friend—and really, to everyone—be more uplifting and generous? I hit DELETE and start again.

To: Gretta
From: Lorna

Subject: Help!

Message: Hey girlfriend, hope you're rocking. Let me know what's up with you. My big news is that Brad's taking me to LeHot tomorrow night. I'm thrilled, but haven't a clue what to wear. I need your gifted fashion insight, pronto.

I feel much better sending this message, although I admit a small part of me does hope to get at least a little rise out of

Gretta. Isn't some of the joy of going to an "in" place derived from the fact that you're no longer one of the "outs"? I'm sure my ego will inflate tomorrow night when I join the elite few stepping over this restaurant's threshold. Not exactly in line with my spiritual aspirations, but I already knew I was a long way from enlightenment.

To: Lorna
From: Gretta

Subject: I'm green!

Message: I'm dying from jealousy picturing you at that restaurant!

I feel surprisingly ambivalent, although that's clearly the reaction I'd been after.

I've been trying to get a reservation there forever. I can't believe you're going on a Saturday, when everyone who's anyone will be there! I have some news of my own. Remember I joined that gym, Tonies? The name is a play on the owner, Tony Farraway, a gem of a guy. I crashed into Tony there on Tuesday and we hit it off great. He invited me to lunch next week with his "friend who will be in from out of town," who turns out to be none other than Scarlett Johansson! I'M GOING TO HAVE LUNCH WITH A MOVIE STAR! I know she'll be as breathtaking in person as she is in the movies. Anyway, about your big night. Wear that rose-colored number we bought in Saks last summer: sexy but chic. Do remember, red lips and nails are out. Pink is in—and add some sparkles to look delicious. Let me know how it goes—and who you see there! Love you, too!

A tinge of sadness washes over me as I finish reading Gretta's e-mail. She met a new guy earlier this week, and I didn't find out till now. In the past, this scoop would have been delivered to me not two seconds after their encounter. But Gretta's excitement about LeHot does stoke my enthusiasm. Maybe *I'll* see Scarlett Johansson, or someone even more thrilling, like my idol, actress Eva Longoria.

I picture myself in that plunging rose halter dress, accidentally bumping into Eva outside the ladies' room.

"Oh, I'm so sorry. I didn't see you," I would trill.

"No, I'm the one who's sorry. I hope I didn't wrinkle your dress. It's spectacular, as are you."

Okay, maybe this particular scenario is about as likely as Carletta walking in tomorrow and announcing that she's quit. But in such a place, on the arm of a man like Brad, isn't anything possible?

ॐ

I'm standing in my underwear in front of my bedroom mirror the following evening, the rose dress abandoned, along with four others, across my bed. None looked as fabulous as I'd remembered. I feel a bit like my friend Sarah, my self-confidence withering with each attempt. Finally, I slip on a jungle-print miniskirt, tight black sleeveless turtleneck, and faux cougar pumps. *It's not ideal*, I think, eyeing myself once more, but then I realize maybe I'm trying too hard to please the phantom Eva. After all, the skirt shows off my newly firmed thighs. All that yoga definitely has made them tighter.

I groan as I apply the pink lipstick, knowing (as does Gretta) that red is so much more flattering on my lips. Pink loses the battle waged by my yellowish skin tone. But in is in, and I will not be caught in New York's most chic restaurant in last year's colors.

I'm excited to be seeing Brad, and not only because it's been ages since we had a date. I've read so many spiritual books these past six weeks, I'm able to quote Neale Donald Walsch or Louise Hay the way English professors cite Shakespeare. In fact, when I browsed through a recent One Spirit book club catalog, I was thrilled to realize I'd read all their bestsellers. But knowing these principles is not the same as living them. I'm humbly discovering what a tall task I've set for myself: joining forces with my soul rather than my ego to be loving, appreciative and joyful—especially with people in my office. I suspect it will be far easier to reach this goal while hanging out with a sweetheart like Brad.

My doorbell rings as I'm giving myself a final glance in the mirror. I spy a gray strand I missed when I pulled out some others earlier. *It's fine*, I tell my rising agitation. *Nobody but you expects perfection.* For a second I debate whether to yank it (and hunt for other infiltrators), but I'm pleased I'm able to let it go.

I race for the front door and eagerly throw it open. "I'm so happy to see you! You look better than ever," I say, scanning his black shirt and blazer and trendy rectangular glasses, not to mention those piercing blue eyes.

"I was about to say that to you!" He plants a long, perfect kiss on my eager lips. I close my eyes to savor the musky smell of his skin, and feel him press something into my hands. When I open my eyes, I'm holding an enormous bouquet of bright red roses.

"They're magnificent!" I exclaim.

"Consider it an I've-missed-you gift."

"Well, don't miss me so much, then! Try seeing me more often," I snarl, surprising myself with the resentment pie I hadn't known I was baking.

"I'm sorry, Lorna. I hate us being apart, too. But you know this launch is a once-in-a-lifetime opportunity. I should be working even now."

"I do know it's a big deal for you," I say, softening.

"For us!" he counters. "When this software's a hit, I should make enough to jet you off to dinner in Paris, or even Fiji," he laughs. Then he turns serious. "But I admit I've been a lousy boyfriend. I brought you something to make amends."

"Yes, they *are* beautiful. And you remembered red's my

favorite color flower," I say, inhaling the luxurious fragrance of the bouquet in my arms.

"I'm glad you like the roses. But that was only the appetizer. I've got something else for the main course." He hands me a rectangular box wrapped in gold foil, the size of a pair of shoes.

"Brad, you shouldn't have! I didn't get you anything," I say.

"I didn't expect you to. Open it." He smiles with eager anticipation.

I dig my nails under the tape. When the lid pops open, I'm astonished. It's not new high heels, but rather a gleaming statue of a meditating Jesus. I can't speak, and not just because it's breathtakingly beautiful. This is a gift from Brad—someone who clearly doesn't share my spiritual yearnings. When I finally got up the courage to tell him on the phone last week about all the books I'd devoured and the practices I'd been doing, he joked that Eckhart Tolle—the author of my latest favorite, *A New Earth*—sounded like a Pacific island, and that in his mind, a meditation cushion resembled a giant toadstool.

"I was online finding a gift for the bride of one of my engineers, a guy who's working crazy hours like I am. The second I saw this, I knew it had your name on it."

I stare at the statue, transfixed. I've never seen an image of Jesus meditating. Even though I've read that scholars believe he was an avid practitioner, most artists prefer to depict him on the cross. The sight of Jesus in perfect contemplation fills me with admiration for his abilities, and inspires me anew to aim for this bliss in myself.

"Like it?" he asks, and only then do I realize I haven't said a word.

"Like it? I *love* it! You are a terrific boyfriend. Especially since I know you're not really into this stuff."

"Well, I know you are. Besides, how could you go wrong with Jesus looking so beatific?"

"You're incredible," I say, feeling my appreciation, love, and joy reach new heights.

ॐ

A few minutes later, after I've placed the flowers in water and the statue temporarily on the kitchen table, I settle into the sumptuous leather of Brad's BMW convertible. I can't help staring at him during the drive. His thick blond hair looks positively ravishing. But as usual, his most striking feature is his smile. I suspect one reason it's blazing is because all the female drivers we pass look admiringly in his direction. Instead of being jealous, I allow myself to feel proud and happy.

When we pull up to the restaurant, Brad hands his keys to the valet—another heartthrob, if I am allowed to observe this while on a date. The chill bites my bare legs, but Brad stands transfixed, watching the guy speed his car down the block to the parking lot. I understand Brad's concern for his Bimmer, but I'm cold enough to wish he'd stop worrying. I'm also coming to understand that instead of bringing you what you want, worry actually increases the odds the feared thing will happen. I'm not sure I completely believe this notion—it's definitely a little odd to think you energetically call the things you focus on into your experience, including things you don't want—but it's a constant thread in many spiritual teachings, and it does strike me as at least plausible. In any event, I'm clear that it feels better not to fret.

The valet (mercifully!) finally steps out of the car, and Brad guides me to the entrance. A twenty-foot-high, black-and-gold awning telegraphs that this will be one lavish place. In case a person might somehow miss that message, six well-dressed doormen stand at attention on either side of the churchlike bronze doors.

"Thank you so much," I say to the men as they swing open the doors. Several of them look surprised, like they don't hear such gratitude often.

The second we walk in, I'm completely dazzled. I've been to plenty of fancy restaurants in my day, but I've never seen anything near this elaborate. This is a Matisse painting come to life: a veritable kaleidoscope of colors and swirl—walls ablaze in orange and lemon yellow; tablecloths of pink, red, or lime green; the plates a whirl of purple, yellow, and orange circles and lines. I glance at a waiter carrying a tray of food and realize the decor isn't the only thing over the top. At other posh spots, fish and beef may be stacked on hills of mashed potatoes, but here they're veritable mountains. As the whimsically dressed hostess walks us past a table, I spy a waiter serving a medieval-banquet-sized platter of turkey. I'm astonished when he places it not in the middle of the table for sharing, but in front of one—hopefully very hungry— guest. LeHot nothing. This is LeHedonism.

We follow the hostess to our table, passing others brimming with celebrities and politicians I instantly recognize: Gwen Stefani, Dwyane Wade, New York's mayor Collin Jones, and a top fashion model whose name escapes me.

After we're seated, a waiter dressed in an Elton John–ish lilac-and-green-patterned silk shirt places menus before us.

"Welcome to our charming little restaurant," he says. "Have you dined with us before?"

"No, it's our first time," Brad answers. "I guess you could say we're virgins." He tosses a knowing wink in my direction.

The waiter doesn't take the bait. "Well, I trust you'll have a marvelous experience here. I'll be back in a few minutes to answer any questions about our menu," he says before walking away.

"Virgins, huh?" I smile at Brad. "Who knew?"

"Well, we're LeHot virgins. As for anything else, we can leave him guessing."

I lean over and give Brad a long, slow kiss, savoring the love and satisfaction I knew would come easily this evening.

"So much for leaving him guessing," Brad laughs when we break apart, and so do I.

After a few minutes of admiring both my boyfriend and the astonishing decor, I glance down at the menu. I expected the prices at a restaurant like this to be steep, but like the piles of food served, they're way over the top.

Ever since I insisted on our first date, Brad has been clear about my need for us to each pay our own way. I spent too many years under my mother's control to allow myself to feel beholden to anyone; letting someone pay for me feels like restraint, even though part of me knows Brad certainly doesn't intend it that way. I have a thriving career and my own paycheck. As long as I keep myself financially independent, I'm much more comfortable in a relationship.

As if he's reading my mind, Brad leans over and whispers, "It's my treat tonight, so don't even think about splitting the bill." I don't know why this gets my back up. Maybe it's the way he commands it. Or maybe it triggers those deep-seated issues about being owned.

"No. I'll pay my own way like I always do. I don't need your charity," I say sharply.

"It's not charity. It's my final gift of the evening. Another way to apologize for being so busy, I hardly see you."

"You've apologized plenty. And given me enough gifts. This would be charity, and I won't take it."

Brad's clearly bewildered by my quick turn of mood. And honestly, so am I. "Lorna, I *want* to treat you. It would be my pleasure."

I feel my ire relax a bit. "I love being with you, Brad. But you've already given me two spectacular gifts today. That's enough."

"Is there a limit on gift-giving? Weren't you the one who sent me that beautiful Italian wallet a few weeks ago, when I didn't have a present for you?"

"That was different. It was our six-months-since-we-met anniversary. Anyway, we have a deal about meals."

"And if I remember correctly," he continues, ignoring my protestations, "didn't you once say 'Taking a gift is as generous as giving one'?" *Yes, I did*, I think. But his bringing that up only irritates me further.

My voice rises in anger inexplicable to me. "Don't be throwing my words in my face!"

"Calm down, love. We're only talking about a dinner."

My rational brain knows that Brad is being kind and generous. These are traits that I love him for. But somehow, I feel my emotional dukes rising, and I can't put them down. It's like I'm playing the role of a nasty character in a Broadway show, and backing down isn't in the script.

"You're. Not. Paying," I say again, my words loud and emphatic enough to cause a lavishly painted middle-aged woman at the next booth to turn and cluck her disapproval. "If we can't settle this now, we might as well go home."

Brad bobs like he's taken a right hook to his jaw. "Lorna, we're finally together, in a fabulous restaurant, ready for a delicious meal. Why are you getting worked up over nonsense?"

"I don't appreciate that you're trying to change our agreement."

"I'm just trying to be nice. Is it such a big deal if I pay for your meatballs?"

"Oh, so now you're ordering for me? I never said I was having meatballs."

"It's just an example! Lorna, I've never seen you like this." Suddenly his face lightens. "Maybe you're not well. Are you feeling okay?"

"No, I guess I'm not. I'm sorry, Brad," I say, getting a modicum of control over the powerful emotions welling up in me. "Let me freshen up in the restroom. When I come back, hopefully I'll be the sane, sweet woman you thought you'd invited to dinner."

Chapter 6

I open the door to the bathroom, barely registering its marble ceiling or the soap counter that, with its dozens of lotions, soaps, and cosmetics, better belongs on the ground floor at Macy's. I ignore the bathroom's sole occupant, an elderly attendant commandeering a pile of colorful towels, and quickly shuffle into a stall—eager to avoid her cheery face that threatens to burst into song. Right now I'm not in a mood for merriment.

I plop onto the toilet seat lid and close my eyes, trying to regain my center. I'm furious at myself for this uncharacteristic and, worse, completely unspiritual behavior with Brad.

What's going on? Why did his offer to pay affect me so deeply? I rummage through my brain, but can't uncover a single clue.

After about five minutes of wandering around this mental wilderness, I whip out my cell phone and dial Janelle. If anyone can help, she can.

"Hey, what's wrong?" is how she answers her phone. "Aren't you supposed to be having the time of your life tonight?"

"Well, I'm at LeHot with Brad, if that's what you mean. But I'm calling from a bathroom stall." I explain what happened: how one minute I felt happy and contented and the next I was picking a ludicrous fight. "This craziness is ruining what should have been a fabulous evening," I conclude, my level of annoyance with myself rising higher.

"It isn't craziness," Janelle replies, her voice calm and soothing. "Remember what you read in *A New Earth*? All that discussion about the 'pain-body'? I think that's your problem: *It's* been trying to eat in that restaurant the same as you are."

I didn't understand about the "pain-body" when I read it in Tolle's book. But now it makes sense. The pain-body is his term for the residual, toxic energy carried by each person, derived from decades of negative thoughts. Thanks to my mom, I've certainly had plenty of those. Tolle warns that the pain-body periodically awakens from its dormant state, overtaking and transforming its host—and not for the better. A passage from his book pops into my head: the pain-body "periodically needs to feed . . . and the food it requires to replenish itself consists of energy that is compatible with its own."

"That's it!" I say, relief washing over me.

"Well, it's the only thing that makes sense. The pain-body is dense, so it thrives on drama and conflict. Which would explain why you've been creating that," Janelle says.

"But even if that's true, why couldn't I control it? Isn't it a sign that, even after all this reading and yoga and sujaling, I'm still in the spiritual toilet bowl?" I chuckle at the apt metaphor, given where I am sitting.

"Nah, you'd have to be a master like Tolle himself not to let the pain-body overtake you once it gets going. It happens occasionally to everyone. The main thing is to remember his advice for putting the genie back in its bottle."

"Something about witnessing the negative energy, rather than letting myself get caught in its claws, right?"

"Right. If you stop identifying with it, the pain-body will go back to sleep. And you'll return to being your fabulous self."

"Janelle, you're a lifesaver!"

"Well, I hope a date-saver. Now, go have the fun you intended. I love you, girlfriend!" The line goes dead.

How do I witness my pain-body? From yoga class, I'm learning that stepping back from my thoughts comes easiest during deep-breathing exercises. So for the next few minutes, I perform *nadi sudi*, a calming "alternate nostril" technique that Miss Gumby adores. Closing off my right nostril with my right thumb, I exhale long and slow through the left, an invisible feather floating down. An even longer, slower inhale through the left draws the feather back up. I switch my fingers, opening the right for the next exhale.

On my sixth go-round, the bathroom attendant does start singing, as I'd predicted—a tune from that classic musical *South Pacific*, about washing a man out of her tresses. Fortunately, the breathing practice has calmed me enough that this doesn't upset me. Her choice of lyrics is even intriguing. She obviously overheard my phone call with Janelle.

I ponder whether my outburst *was* unconsciously designed to wash Brad from my life, but that doesn't ring true. I adore the guy. He's kind, smart, generous, handsome, and soon to be incredibly rich. Not to mention he's great in bed. He's a fabulous guy, and I know it.

When the attendant starts in on the second chorus, I return my focus to my breath. I have no idea where I left off, so I arbitrarily exhale out my left. By the time I get to the right, her song becomes a mere background hum. A few minutes later, I'm calm enough to enjoy her accompaniment. I exhale through the right once more, then realize the exercise has indeed helped me separate from my negative thoughts. It's almost like I can sense a heavy energy surrounding me, but I'm no longer merged with it. I'm in the middle in a peaceful light.

After a few minutes observing the pain-body as a separate entity, I'm ready to exit the stall. Standing at the troughlike sink, I relish the feel of my soapy fingers under the warm, flowing water, washing the pain-body away. When the attendant passes me a towel, I feel such a deep joy flow through me that I offer her a hearty thank-you and a ten-dollar tip. Now I know how Angelica feels being super-generous with both time and money to those waitresses!

When I return to the table, Brad is smiling, as eager as I am to close this ugly chapter.

"Feel better?" he asks, leaning over to kiss my lips.

"Yes, much," I say as I sit down. I'm ready to change the subject and put the evening back on track.

Thankfully, Brad's on the same page. "I ordered us a bottle of German Riesling. And—" He hesitates. "—when the waiter came over, I also got us an appetizer to share. Don't hit me— but it's meatballs. The waiter was gushing about them nonstop. Wouldn't take no for an answer, really." He pauses, eyes lowered and lips pursed, waiting to see if I'm going to explode at the mention of meatballs.

My wine sits before me. I lift my glass and take a luscious sip, wanting to make sure I'm in complete control. "Sounds wonderful. You're such a sweetie!" I say finally.

We each smile, and I'm happy in the knowledge that my inner peace has held.

ॐ

I don't expect the meatballs at a place like this to look like Mom's holiday platter, but I'm still amazed when they arrive. On a plate between us, a pyramid of savory balls swims in a swirl of tomato sauce, but that's only the foundation; a dozen more mounds of meat climb single-file up the middle, each fastened by a colorful bit of wood. It looks incredibly phallic. Brad and I eye the pile warily. Finally, he bravely digs his fork into a ball in the foundation, an action that plops it and several others into the sauce.

"I guess you're not supposed to actually eat these babies," he laughs. "Maybe that's how we save our appetites for their enormous entrées."

Emboldened by the crazy look of the display and eager to keep things light between us, I stand up and lean over the plate, arms clasped behind my back. "Maybe you're supposed to eat 'em like this," I whisper. I lick my lips in a slow, sexy motion, then, using only my mouth, bite off the ball on top.

"Lorna!" Brad feigns horror, and then bursts out laughing.

I sit, giggling so hard I can barely swallow. Brad's grinning, too. "Hope you don't mind, but I'm not doing *that!*" he says. He lifts his fork and gently removes the balls one at a time from the tower, settling them safely on the plate. As we dig into the pile, I have to admit they are outrageously delicious.

A while later, the waiter clears a plate picked so clean, a raccoon wouldn't be able to scavenge a morsel. He refills the wine with a flourish. Just before walking away, he flashes us a wicked smile. I'm not sure whether he's thrilled that we have quelled our fighting, or whether he saw my little meatball demonstration—and remembers Brad's "virgin" joke. Brad and I sit in comfortable silence.

Again I survey the boisterous room. I'm amazed anew at the circus-colored decor, the rampant portion distortion, and the patrons' incredibly chic clothes. I'm sure there must be more celebrities I haven't yet spotted, so I start scanning.

Brad points across the room. My eyes follow his finger, eager to see what A-lister he's discovered, but it points to an unfamiliar man in a herringbone suit, sitting with a nondescript woman. "I had a business deal last year with that guy; the one in the purple tie. Alex Simpton, a total jerk. Tried to screw me at every turn. Fortunately, I got back at him good."

I feel my stomach flutter. I'm not sure whether it's because there's no celebrity, or because this is a side of Brad I've not seen before. "Sorry to hear he caused you problems," I finally reply.

"Well, I caused *him* problems after that! Bad-mouthed him to a client I knew was his client, too. I doubt they did business again."

"Did you say really awful things?" I ask, not sure I want an answer.

"Horrendous." He chuckles, apparently thinking I'm enjoying the sordid tale as much as he is. "The thing is, they were kinda true; barely had to exaggerate—like I said, he's a real jackass."

"Did it bother you to say those things?"

"Nah. It might be tough to talk bad about a saint, but it's easy when the person's a jerk. You know that yourself: Remember when you told me that stuff about your neighbor?"

"Ruth? Yeah, I did go through a stretch of disliking her," I say, squirming that I've been caught talking ill of others. Since reading a book on mystical Jewish teachings, I've been trying to stay away from negative gossip, known in Hebrew as *lashon hara* ("evil tongue"). "That was before I started my spiritual practice. Now I try to focus on Ruth's good points," I continue. Of course, as I say this, I recall Ruth's catching me the other morning on my way to my car and me brushing her off. With her single-minded prattle about her garden, Ruth can be a bore. I push the memory aside.

"Well, you had no trouble complaining when it came to your lawn watering," Brad continues.

"Yeah," I confess, "although I've since made peace with her actions. Really, what I changed was my reaction to her actions."

A few months back, Ruth kept resetting the time clock on my automatic sprinkler, telling me when I finally confronted her (after I continually put it back) that she doesn't like hearing the whirring motor in the morning. Annoyed, I pushed it to noon, even though I've heard this is the worst time to water the lawn because the sun evaporates the liquid before it fully sinks into the roots. I was able to put it out of my mind until a new suede blouse I'd ordered online got caught in the midday fountain when the delivery guy left it by my door. I fumed. A week later another package—a designer handbag!—got so soggy it was ruined. It was after this second episode that I bitched to Brad.

A few weeks ago, however, it dawned on me that those sodden items were a spiritual lesson of sorts, the universe's way of showing me that I can choose how I react to any situation. I'd been failing as badly as a Hollywood celeb in detox. I decided to stop focusing on how annoyed the whole thing made me, and right away I got the idea to buy a big plastic storage box to set near my front door and write a note for the delivery people to please put items inside. My sprinkler still goes on at noon, and I do feel bad about wasting some water, but I haven't had a problem with my packages since. (A huge batch of mail-ordered spiritual books stayed pristine in the box the other day.) The best part: I now feel good about accommodating my neighbor.

My thoughts return to the present just as the waiter arrives with Brad's rack of lamb and my fish and vegetable stew. Mine is served in a massive tureen, the kind you'd use to make soup for a party. It's a blend of melt-in-your-mouth shrimp and whitefish, new and sweet potatoes, the teeniest baby carrots, buttery turnips, crisp green beans, tasty black beans, even cabbage and brussels sprouts, two veggies I always thought I despised until I taste this culinary masterpiece. When the waiter later returns, I insist he send my utmost compliments to the chef.

The evening passes without another hitch. Brad spends most of the meal entertaining me with stories from his recent trip to Moscow, where he successfully sold Russian rights to his software. The ancient architecture and interesting characters that pepper his tales have me so envious, I'm drooling. (Of course, Brad's periodic nibbling of my ear may also play a role!)

Then he tells me about an adventure a Russian colleague told him about that he's eager to experience sometime: a flight in a MiG jet that comes as close to breaking through the atmosphere as one can outside of a rocket ship. This leads us to a long, earnest discussion about the huge expanse of the universe.

"It doesn't make sense that you believe we're the only living beings out there," I summarize after our fifteen-minute back-and-forth. "Consider the billions of stars in our teeny galaxy alone."

"But if others exist, where are they? Why haven't these extraterrestrials revealed themselves?"

"Maybe they've no reason to bother with us. Maybe they spend their time with more evolved beings elsewhere. Or maybe they *are* here, and they don't tell us."

"Like *Men in Black*! Perhaps our waiter is an alien," he laughs.

"I'm serious. How could there not be others in such an enormous universe?"

"What can I say? I was taught that we're the center of everything."

"I learned that, too. But we don't have to keep believing it."

"Maybe I like the idea of being the center of everything," he says.

"I think we *are* the center of everything—but I don't think that has to mean it's us and nobody else. I interpret it to mean we're all plugged into the universal energy that animates all of life, here and across the universe."

"You know, this conversation's getting a little spooky," Brad says. "I know you're hot on all this spiritual stuff, but how 'bout we get back to more practical matters—like what we're having for dessert."

I'm disappointed that Brad won't explore these concepts with me. But the grin on his face as he scans the lavish dessert menu reminds me how much I treasure his boyish appreciation for the here and now.

Soon we're digging into our triple-decker chocolate soufflé, which could satisfy the sweet tooth of all of China, when Brad calls out to a passerby. At first I fear it's his nemesis, Alex. Fortunately a different man heads our way, one Brad whispers that he knows from business school.

"Jim Stevenson! So great to see you!" Brad says when Jim is close enough to take his outstretched hand for a rugged shake. My mouth unhinges when I see that Jim is not alone. Behind him is a celebrity I'd recognize anywhere.

"Brad, Brad. How the hell are you, man? I assume you know this woman, Veronica Swanson," he says, grasping her around the waist and pulling her forward.

"Of course. So nice to meet you, Veronica," Brad says, extending his hand. "And this is my girlfriend, Lorna Crawford."

I want to say hi in the same nonchalant manner as Brad, and to tell Veronica how much I adore her work. She's still one of my all-time favorite actresses; I was heartbroken years ago when she left her long-running TV series. Each Monday after the show, I'd spent hours trying to get my hair into the gorgeous updo she always sported. (Despite applying reams of volumizer, fistfuls of mousse, and gobs of extra-hold hair spray, I never did get it right.) My mouth hangs as limply now as my hair did then. I can't manage more than a wan smile.

"I'm trying to interest Veronica in being a spokesperson for my company's new skin-care line. She's a tough sell, but I'll sweeten the deal enough that she'll have to sign on," Jim says to us, but I suspect, really, to Veronica.

"Jim's products are lovely," Veronica replies to us, but really to him. "But my schedule's so full. I'm about to shoot a TV movie about a woman who falls for the wrong guy. A story as old as time, no?" She nods in my direction.

I hope to say something witty, but what emerges is a snortlike giggle. I can't believe I'm so starstruck. This is exactly the behavior I chide Gretta for all the time.

After several minutes of polite chitchat among the three of them, Jim wraps up the discussion. "We should get together for lunch sometime, Brad. Of course, with you, too." He smiles at me. Before I'm able to get out a single word, the pair departs.

When the bill comes, Brad and I split it down the middle without comment, although I have to admit it gives me pause to hand him close to two-hundred dollars for one dinner.

After we leave the restaurant, Brad and I stroll arm in arm. A few blocks up, he stops and turns to me, taking my face between his strong fingers. "I don't know how I let so much time go by without seeing you. I promise it won't happen again," he says earnestly.

I soften under his gaze. "Want to see even more of me? How about coming back to my place to collect on that rain check." Brad doesn't need the invitation repeated. We rush back to the valet to retrieve his car—this time he's the one who's impatient as the man again takes his time in the car. Finally, we pull into my driveway.

Uninhibited because of the alcohol and eager to feel his body against mine, I steer Brad straight for the bedroom. After all, we've had a whole evening of foreplay. Surprisingly, he resists.

"Lie down in the living room. I'll light a fire and give you a back massage."

"Now?"

"There's never a time when a back massage isn't good, is there?"

"I meant the fire," I retort, as if he didn't know.

"There's never a time when fire isn't good either. Ask any caveman."

I strip down to my bra and lacy underwear. After tossing a

cashmere throw from the sofa onto the floor, I stretch out on my abdomen. I hear Brad fussing with the kindling, but I'm already too relaxed to get up and help. In a few minutes, the fire goes live.

"Wow, another of your astonishing skills," I marvel, purring as the warmth of the flames mingles with the heat rising inside me.

He opens a bottle of massage oil he must have pulled out of my bathroom cabinet, who knows when. "Now relax and let Brad's wandering fingers work their magic," he says.

Time melts away as Brad presses and pinches my shoulders, arms, back, and thighs. Meditation has even helped in this area of my life, I chuckle to myself. I'm completely at one with his moving hands. After a while—I haven't a clue how much time has passed—I simultaneously become his touch and the skin he's caressing. It's a wonderful (dare I say, spiritual) sensation. I moan several times, hums of pleasure involuntarily escaping my happy lips.

"Let me know when you want me to take you to the bedroom," Brad finally whispers as he strokes the melting muscles of my thighs.

"I don't want to move—ever," I reply, even as I flip over and raise my arms so he can carry me.

Afterwards, in my bed, I lie curled in the crook of Brad's tender arm. I feel entwined not only with Brad but, in a way I've never experienced after sex, also with what I can only imagine is the pulsating energy of the universe itself. The expression "best sex I've ever had" seems a massive understatement. This feeling of expansiveness, of being at one with the world, is the best *anything* I've ever had.

"That was amazing. Way better than any meditation I've done," I say, surprised to be speaking these private thoughts aloud, since I'm sure Brad wouldn't understand. But when I glance at him, it's obvious he hasn't heard. My sweet, beautiful, sexy boyfriend has his head tilted back and his mouth slightly ajar. He's fast asleep.

ॐ

I awake in the morning feeling my skin abuzz, like someone's fluttered tulips all over my naked body. Brad's sleeping torso is spooned against me, which could very well have something to do with this sensation.

I turn to face him, watching with pleasure as his chiseled chest floats up and down.

He must sense that I'm watching; he opens his eyes. "Morning," he says, smiling. "Been up for a while?"

"Long enough to have my eyes on you, if that's what you're asking."

"I had that feeling. I guess now you have to let me have my turn—it's only fair." He sits up on his elbows, ready to push down the blanket.

"Cut it out!" Embarrassed, I grasp the covers tightly. Then I have a different idea. "Unless, of course, you're wanting a replay of last night."

"I'd love that . . . but I can't. Gotta get back to work. I don't even wanna know what time it is. My boss probably called the missing persons bureau."

"On Sunday? You're kidding."

"Wish I were. I've been gone since, what, seven last night. And now it's what?" He reaches over and turns the clock to him. "Oh, geez—nine. This is the longest I've been gone in weeks." He sits up and throws his legs over the side of the bed, preparing to stand.

"Can't you at least stay for breakfast? I'll make your favorite: scrambled eggs."

"Sounds heavenly. I appreciate the offer. But I really gotta go," he says. Leaning over, he plants a kiss on my mouth, then swallows my bottom lip completely.

I retrieve my lip from between his. "That's not fair! You tell me you gotta go and then you make me want you to stay!"

"Maybe I'm just trying to keep you from giving up on me before my project launches," he replies, smiling. But in fewer than fifteen minutes, he's showered, dressed, and out the door.

For the rest of the day, I float on cloud nine. Actually, that isn't quite right. My mood certainly is soaring, but my body is exquisitely grounded, fully experiencing every sensation. The soles of my feet register every surface I walk on, from my bedroom's warm bamboo floor to the kitchen's cold tile. My fingertips, too, seem to have sprouted extra nerve endings, tingling under the backyard dirt I'm inspired to dig up later in the day. (I've had these packets of floral seeds for nearly a year— from a "Cones and Coneflower" ice cream promotion we held last Earth Day—but today I'm driven to plant them.)

As the sun drops from the sky, I carry my soup-and-salad supper out back and, wrapped in a blanket on my backyard lounge chair, eat al fresco. Nature provides a magnificent show with its chirping birds and crickets. During the grand finale, when the sky shifts from blue to orange and finally to purple as the fiery ball drops behind Ruth's roof, I actually applaud. I inhale deeply, and the crisp evening air fills my lungs not merely with oxygen, but with a love of life itself.

As I head inside, I start to croon a karaoke medley of ain't-life-grand tunes. Soon, I'm belting them out as I dance around the living room—everything from The Rascals' "It's a Beautiful Morning" to Mary J. Blige's "Beautiful Day." I top my evening off with a warm lavender-scented bath, an hour of yoga, and an amazingly focused fifteen-minute sujal.

I slip into bed, contented from my fingers to my toes. As I drift off, I wonder if maybe living the spiritual life really isn't so hard as it has sometimes seemed.

Chapter 7

At four o'clock on Friday, I find myself downing a last-minute cup of coffee. I've left work early so I can be ready when Janelle picks me up for our weekend retreat.

If I had any lingering doubts about going, this past week at work has convinced me that a silent retreat is a necessary shot in my spiritual arm. So much for thinking I'd mastered this stuff. On Monday morning, Brendan tripped in the corridor outside my cubicle and spilled coffee all over the rug. When he loudly accused me of leaving some invisible trash he swore he slipped on, I found myself secretly willing him to fall again, and was delighted when he later stumbled.

That same day, I was rude to my good pal, Jamal Thompson. He'd swung by my cube innocently asking, "When you get a chance, could you give me some details about your sundae event, especially any celebs who've already committed? I wanna run some teaser ads in *New York*."

A reasonable request from an advertising copywriter. But I found myself snapping, "You think I'd look this frazzled if I already had stars in the bag?" Of course, I apologized immediately, but from the hurt look on Jamal's face, I could see the damage was done.

This morning, when I heard Carletta whispering on the phone, something about her mother, it took all my effort to resist the urge to spy and tell. I succeeded only by forcing myself to consider all the negative things people would say about my own mother, should they ever meet her.

Plus, I'm still plowing through my days unmindfully. Nine o'clock morphs into six o'clock without much awareness of what's happened in between. Once in a rare while, I'll remember to feel the computer mouse under my fingers or notice the stunning almond shape of my assistant's eyes, but mostly I'm slogging through.

I'm hoping this yoga weekend will be the prescription that gets me back on track.

The phone rings. Thinking it'll be Brad saying good-bye, I grab the phone without looking at the number.

"Lorna, it's your mother." Drat.

"Hi, Mom. What's up?"

"As if you're interested. You haven't bothered to call in weeks."

"Sorry, Mom. I've been a bit busy. I'm kinda tied up now, too; I'm racing out in a few minutes."

"Yes, they told me you were going away when I tried you at your office. How come I'm the last to know?"

Maybe because you're as open-minded about a yoga retreat as Homer Simpson would be, I want to say. But I refrain.

"It's only a weekend trip, Mom."

"And where are you going for the weekend, may I ask?"

"To, um . . . to the mountains." I'm pleased that this isn't even a lie.

"The mountains! At this time of year? Wouldn't you be smarter waiting till summer?"

"The mountains are lovely any time of year, Mom. Listen, I gotta run. Did you call for anything special?"

"Nothing that can't wait until you're not too busy for your mother," she sneers.

"Okay. Well, I'll call when I get back." I hang up the phone and realize my chest has tightened. I take a few deep breaths while I remind myself of the happy thought that Mom won't be joining us for the weekend.

I take my final sip of coffee. An hour ago, I read the fine print on the brochure: There will be no meat, alcohol, or coffee. I have no problem temporarily eschewing flesh or booze, which I have been limiting anyway in my (so far futile) attempt to generate Miss Gumby's inner spark. She's talked a lot about the precept that yogis should keep a clean mind along with a healthy body. While she hasn't told any of her students not to drink alcohol or eat meat, I know that she refrains.

But coffee? How the hell am I gonna survive without my morning mainline? I'd considered calling Janelle, fake-vomiting into the phone, and pretending I'd gotten the flu, but that didn't feel right. Living spiritually has to include such old-fashioned virtues as honesty and responsibility. To weasel out of my commitment with a lie is going down the slope with the DANGER: KEEP AWAY signs plastered all over.

Perhaps this cup will tide me over. Maybe when I wake up tomorrow morning, I'll recall this moment: the scintillating smell of ground beans; the feel of thick stoneware on my lips; the warm liquid sliding down my throat; the taste of that bitter yet sweet bite—and it will be enough.

Who am I kidding? I'm screwed!

My cell phone beeps in a text message. SUGAR, I'LL MISS YOU! HAVE A FAB TIME, I read. Things have been great between Brad and me since our date; we text or talk dozens of times each day, even though with his work schedule, another evening together won't be happening for a while. I text back that I'll miss him, too.

I'm in my bedroom zipping up my suitcase when I hear the

honk outside; I recognize the horn of Janelle's Prius. I grab my hot pink overnight bag, purple yoga mat, and green Lilly Pulitzer purse—a veritable botanical garden—then pause by my altar. *Kwan Yin, am I doing right by going on this weekend—without coffee, no less?* I silently ask my statue. I'm hoping to sense a reply, but nothing comes. She may be the goddess of compassion, but she isn't showing me any.

When I step into Janelle's car, my anxiety skyrockets. I'm petrified about the weekend: Can I take two yoga classes a day without collapsing? Stay silent without going nuts? And not drink my morning coffee? Yet when I look at Janelle, she's beaming, and I trust her instincts better than I trust my own—mine having been so manhandled not just by my mother, but also by the echo of her voice, which I seem to have internalized so completely.

After hellos and how-are-yas, I snap on the radio. I fiddle to find WNOW, which I know Janelle won't mind me doing and which will definitely soothe me. Serena Robbins has a show on Friday afternoons, so I'm not surprised to hear her hosting. I'm amazed, however, to hear that her caller is Loser Liz.

". . . I know you said I shouldn't care if other people don't like me. But I do," Liz from Cleveland declares.

"Liz, and everyone else," Serena Robbins responds. "The only person you can control is you. And it sounds like you're falling down on the job by deciding to stay stuck in unhappiness when you could be choosing joy."

"Well, I *am* unhappy! You would be, too, if you thought everyone hated you."

"By wanting other people to change before you let yourself be happy, you're actually keeping that happiness from coming. I know this is hard to fathom, but what other people think of you can't be your concern."

"I don't have a clue what you're saying," Liz says, and I laugh because I sort of don't either. *How can other people's thoughts about me not be my concern?* I do agree, though, with the notion that happiness is a choice: some people select it even when they're in the most awful place in the world, while others make themselves miserable in a beautiful, lakeside home—my mother being the prime example.

Hopefully Liz sticks around long enough to understand what Serena Robbins is getting at, because Janelle doesn't let me hear more. "I feel like getting out of my head right now. You mind if I turn on some chanting music?" she asks, mostly as a formality since it is her car, and she's already whipped out a CD.

During the rest of the drive, we listen as a beautiful female voice repeats a single, monotonous Sanskrit phrase over and over . . . and over and over . . . and over and over. At first, this drives me crazy. I keep praying the singer will discover a new sentence, or at least slip in one teeny extra word. But after a while, my resistance lessens and I find myself chanting along: *"Shri ram jay ram jay jay ram."* The phrase, which the CD liner note describes as "a tribute to the Hindu incarnation of God as an idealized being," pushes everything else from my mind—especially my fear about what's ahead.

As soon as we pull into the retreat center parking lot, however, my panic returns.

"Is it too late to back out?" I ask, only half in jest, when Janelle stops the car. "I don't think I can do this."

"Sure you can. It'll be fun!"

"For you, maybe. When you do yoga, you look like those photos in *Yoga Journal*. My asanas are more like the 'before' shots—you know, the wrong way to do the poses. Plus, I don't think I wanna 'cleanse' my insides!"

"Relax, will you? You know you have a tendency to expect the worst—so remind yourself that the worst never comes to be."

"What if I hate it here?"

"Then we'll leave early. I won't hold you captive—I promise."

"What if they hate *me* here?" As the words tumble out, I realize this is what I most fear.

"How could they hate you? You're a doll!"

"I'm not always a doll—especially lately. Anyway, you're just saying that because you're my friend," I say.

"And I'm your friend because you're a doll. And no one is all the time," she replies. "So stop this useless self-doubt."

I zip my jacket and grab my things from the backseat of Janelle's car without saying another word. Otherwise, I'm afraid the word might be *See ya.* (Okay, that's two words.) I head for the entrance to the charming rustic resort, steeled to face whatever lies ahead.

ॐ

"*Om Shanti.* So nice to have you here!" We're greeted by a grinning, effervescent woman at the reception desk. I know that her bright orange clothes are the traditional garb of the Hindu monk, but I can't stop feeling like I'm in the presence of a smiling cantaloupe.

"Thanks. It's great to be here," Janelle replies.

"We're grateful you decided to spend your weekend with us. We're well aware you could be passing your valuable time in any number of places."

Part of me thinks that this woman is a phony—someone who's deferential while we're standing here but sneers at us stressed-out urbanites the minute we leave. But the other part, the more embracing side I'm trying to cultivate, senses her genuine love. I spend a moment trying to tip my balance in that direction.

The woman sweetly asks for our address, yoga experience, and payment information, waiting with an angel's patience while Janelle fumbles through four separate compartments in her backpack to locate her credit card. While Janelle's searching, I'm jolted by the realization that it would be *me* judging us if

I had this woman's job, that *I'm* the one who's too quick to ascribe unwholesome motives to people—even when they're monks who have taken vows of service and compassion.

"Your room is on the second floor; stairs are down the hall to the end," the woman says after we're checked in. "We hope you're okay with our accommodations; they're kind of primitive. We're mostly an ashram, you know; that's the Hindu term for the residence of practicing monks."

"Don't worry, we're not expecting the Wynn," I say, eager to relieve her concerns. "I'm sure it'll be wonderful."

"Glad to hear that. Dinner, also unlike anything you'll find at the Wynn—to my mind ours is tastier—starts in half an hour. The orientation and silence begin at eight."

The thought of being zippered for the next forty hours launches Janelle and me into immediate, simultaneous babbling.

"Isn't the weather lovely?"

"So unexpectedly warm."

"Adore your new top."

"Yours is even nicer."

We continue this pointless chatter all the way to our room, naming items we pass in the hall like toddlers delighted by their first spoken words: "Nataraj statue." "Delicious incense." "Beautiful tea set." "Elaborate tapestries." It's as if we fear that, unless we exercise them now, by Sunday our vocal cords might waste away.

We reach the end of the long hallway and trudge up the stairs. I push open the door to our room—and spot two other women inside.

"Sorry. She must've given us the wrong room number," Janelle mumbles behind me, looking down at the paper the swami gave her as we both back out the door.

"No, this is right. Room eight," one of the women replies.

"They told us two more were coming."

"You mean there are four to a room?" I ask incredulously. When Janelle made the arrangements, I assumed she would have clarified the sleeping arrangements. Her *I didn't know* expression makes it clear that she hadn't.

"All the guest rooms here are quads," the woman says. "I'm Lucinda, and this is my friend Carole."

Lucinda is a tall, fair-skinned woman, older than me, I judge from the strands of salt in her pepper bob. Her body is as lithe as Miss Gumby's, and she gives off a slightly muted version of the same radiance. Carole is shorter and heavier, but she, too, emanates a *life is good* glow from her smooth skin, which looks to be Native American. Maybe I won't mind getting an up-close view on how to transform my own listless complexion.

"You're both lovely," I say as I walk in and heave my bag onto one of the two empty beds, feeling good about myself for surrendering to the moment.

Janelle looks mortified that I might be mad at her. "It's only for two nights," I offer, to let her know I'm fine.

"I guess you haven't been to a retreat here before," Lucinda says.

"I guess that's pretty obvious," I laugh, warming to her further.

"Carole and I come every few months," she says, nodding to her friend. "We find it's a great way to inoculate ourselves against life's craziness. Every time we go home, we're so much calmer about our jobs, our husbands, the city. We live in Manhattan, which I don't have to tell you pretty much invented stress. Where're you two from?"

"Hoboken . . . in New Jersey," I say.

"I know Hoboken!" Lucinda brightens. "There's a great scrapbooking store there; after I shop, I always eat at a marvelous café. A different one each time—it seems they spring up daily."

"Yes, there's quite a bit of change going on there," I say.

Janelle abruptly shifts direction. "What about the silence? Is it hard to keep mum for an entire weekend? I mean, two whole days!" Funny, I thought I was the one who was anxious about that prospect.

"Of course it's hard," Lucinda replies. Not the answer I expect—or want. "It's shocking how much chatter goes on in your mind. At first, you think you'll burst if you can't spill it. I've come here many times, and I'm only now at the point where I can watch my thoughts leap—and believe me, they still do—without needing to share every last one of them. But if you can't stay silent, you can always go out to the gardens for a quiet talk. Plenty of people do."

"Really? People come to a silent retreat and don't keep silent?" I say, feeling relief wash over me.

"Silence is tough for everybody," Carole says. "We all think we have brilliant ideas we absolutely have to share! Plus, silence can feel like punishment. Remember when someone in your second-grade class was mean to the teacher and she made everyone pass recess sitting quietly at their desk?"

"Were you in my class?" jokes Janelle. "My teacher did that!"

"I think I had your teacher, too!" I snort. "She must've leapt from one school to another." We all laugh.

Carole gets back to business. "For some people—and this was true for me the first time I came—a few hours is huge. That's way longer than you're usually mum. But the monks are fine with the fact that not everyone can do it for two days."

"You mean they won't throw us out if we utter a word?" I realize I'd unconsciously clung to an image of Swami Cantaloupe scooping me up by my beaded belt and flinging me through the doorway if I so much as cleared my throat.

"Hardly," Lucinda laughs. "Believe me, if this is your first time, they'll be thrilled if you last till Saturday afternoon."

"That is so good to hear," Janelle and I say together.

ॐ

The buffet dinner consists of vegetarian chili, stir-fried vegetables, and steamed brown rice, which leaves me feeling light and energetic. Afterwards, we're ushered into the orientation room, where pillows and chairbacks line the floor. About forty people mill around. Somehow I'd expected only a handful of crazies like Janelle and me would choose to spend a weekend in a place where you can't have coffee or, for crying out loud, conversation.

I recognize about a half dozen women from my yoga center, although I don't know any of them well. I search the corners of the room, hoping to locate Miss Gumby. She promised she'd be one of the teachers here (we had discovered when we signed up that the retreat combines students and faculty from several yoga centers), but so far, her comforting face is absent.

Janelle and I select pillows next to each other and sit down. I scan the rest of the row, and notice two men sitting with sleek beauties who I'm guessing are their wives. The men's bulging, tattooed muscles peek out from sleeveless T-shirts. If I had to wager, I'd say the men were dragged here, off the construction site, perhaps, by their yoga-loving wives. I hope they know how much yoga and meditation they're in for!

One of the husbands looks at me and smiles, so I decide to break out of my comfort zone and say hello. As I walk over, I see that the women and the other man are chatting with people in the next row. The guy who acknowledged me extends his hand.

"Hi, I'm Lorna," I say, shaking back.

"Vinny," he replies. *Naturally.*

"Where you guys from?"

"Pennsylvania . . . near Philly."

"Wow, long drive. Did you get in today? You must be tired."

"We got in early, so we've had time to unwind by walking around the grounds; they're so beautiful."

I realize I hadn't so much as looked up when we arrived, not being in the best of moods. "I hope we have time to walk outside tomorrow," I say sincerely. "I'm a little concerned we might be too booked up with classes."

"Nah, there's plenty of time for everything. Anyway, time expands when you stay in the moment."

"Sounds very Zen," I say, surprised by his deep philosophy.

"My friend Carl and I study Zen. As well as yoga. We're disciples of Swami Davananda, the swami who founded this center—although to our great disappointment, he's not here now. Goes off to India once each year."

"Oh, I thought your wives would have been the yogis."

Vinny laughs heartily. "Tina and Cynthia have never done yoga. They've always left it to us. Carl and I are thrilled we finally got them to join us at a retreat."

Busted, Lorna! So much for not pigeonholing others.

The swami from the front desk enters the room to begin the program. I shake hands with Vinny, then head back to my pillow, happy that I've already learned a spiritual lesson about the importance of looking beyond appearances.

The swami introduces several staff members, including a male swami who, with his long, dark hair and serene expression, looks like Jesus. *Well, at least I'll be in good hands*, I think, smiling.

The Jesus swami explains that they're Hindu monks who view serving others as their path to God, so we should let any staffer know right away if we need anything. *How do we do that if we can't speak?* I wonder. As if he's reading my mind, he passes out pads and pencils, instructing us to use them to communicate our needs or ask questions.

He then explains the rationale for the silence: "Our culture's become so used to living in the mind, we forget that our true identity is not our thoughts. Our essence is spiritual, a state that is best experienced not in words, but in the space between them. Being silent, even for as little as one weekend, helps us go beyond our usual way of experiencing our world."

Did he say, "as little as one weekend"? A weekend without words will be an eternity! Who, other than a born mute, can handle more?

Again, he reads my thoughts. (*Do swamis have ESP?*) "For those who want to give a longer period a try, I highly recommend our ten-day silent retreat. The next one isn't till summer, but once you see how easy and powerful this is, we hope you'll sign on. Observing silence for an extended period is magical and transformative."

I look at Janelle and mouth, *Ten days!* as my eyes swell to the size of golf balls. She smirks, as if she finds the idea intriguing.

The swami then describes the morning schedule: Our wake-up time will be 6 A.M., with mandatory meditation promptly at 6:30. A thought washes over me, accompanied by an appropriate tsunami of panic. *We're four women. With one bathroom.*

I don't have to be a Brendan Bunker math whiz to know those numbers won't add up. How will we all manage in half an hour? Maybe I should shower tonight? But I hate going to bed with damp hair, and besides, I'm exhausted.

After a brief introduction about the history of the yoga center and its lineage traced to esteemed swamis in India, the staff declares that our silence is to begin. They dismiss us with a prayer for a good sleep and a reminder that they'll welcome us at daybreak. Janelle and I eagerly head to our room.

Now that I've adjusted to the idea of the four of us staying together, I'm able to appreciate the ambience when I open the door. Much of the space is taken up by the four single beds, each topped with a neatly tucked, organic brown cotton blanket. A small chest for clothing sits at each foot. The look is clean and uncluttered. Draped across the ceiling is a large peach silk fabric, a softening effect that I decide would look nice over my sujaling corner in my bedroom. Tomorrow I'll have to see how they fasten it up there. An altar holding candles, incense, and fresh flowers sits by the door. In our absence, someone must have lit the incense: the room smells like cinnamon. It's a smell I happen to love, but one I pray doesn't linger till morning. It reminds me too much of coffee—the coffee I will not be having.

I change into my pajamas and head to the bathroom to brush my teeth. I feel awkward standing next to Lucinda as we take turns spitting into the sink. For a moment, I worry I won't be able to sleep in a room full of strangers. And what if the mattress is too mushy? What if Lucinda snores? What if Carole talks in her sleep? Then I fret again about the morning: How will four women fare in the rush?

As soon as I settle under the comfy blanket, however, my trepidation melts away. I quickly fall into a deep and satisfying sleep.

Chapter 8

I am alone in a peaceful, dimly lit cave. Although it's deserted and chilly, I feel only joy. I walk in meditation through the long empty space, mindfully taking one step in front of the other. My eyes fix on each spot where my heel is about to land; my ears ring with the echo of the rhythmic footfalls. After I cross the cave, I look up in wonder at the stalactites. Dripping for thousands of years, one fraction of a millimeter at a time, their journey seems as long and as timeless as my soul's. Suddenly, bells ring out, and the cave transforms into a breathtaking cathedral. A warm, golden light hovers before me. As the bells angelically peal, I feel beckoned to merge with this light, which I know with all my being is pure love, pure bliss. I eagerly step forward. But before my body makes contact, a knock erupts from somewhere outside. I draw back. Is it a sign of danger? A signal that I'm not yet elevated enough for such a union?

"I want to make sure you're all up. I don't hear any movement in there," a man's voice gently calls. It takes a few seconds for me to realize the knock is not coming from the cathedral. It is not my higher spirit warning me that I'm not prepared or worthy enough for an experience of enlightenment. I open my eyes, spy the peach silk stretched across the wood-beam ceiling, and remember that

I'm at the ashram. The bells and the voice come from the swami. It's time for me to wake up, even if not yet to merge with the divine.

I'm about to shout, *Okay, we're up,* when my tongue comes up short at the roof of my mouth; I recall that I'm supposed to be silent.

Lucinda's experience from prior retreats becomes apparent as she rouses from her bed and knocks twice on our side of the door.

"Very good. I look forward to seeing you all in half an hour in the meditation room," the voice says before moving on.

Suddenly the bathroom door closes. Lucinda has gone in. I start to sweat. The unbalanced equation comes roaring back: thirty minutes, four women. That's seven-and-a-half minutes each, assuming that each takes only her allotted time, a hope that is immediately dashed when I hear Lucinda turn on the shower. My mind flips to my college freshman year, when an obnoxious roommate used to spend hours reading romance novels in our bathtub, ignoring my desperate pleas for her to move on. This memory only adds to my agitation.

What am I doing here, my blissful sleep interrupted at six-damn-o'clock, without even having enough time to shower and get ready? Anxiety mixes with annoyance. Soon my head joins the pounding, as a caffeine-withdrawal grenade explodes beneath my skull. Oh, joy!

After what seems like an eternity but when I look at my watch is fewer than ten minutes, Lucinda emerges, dressed in black and turquoise workout gear, her damp hair slicked back. Carole immediately closes the bathroom door. How did I miss my chance to go in? Although I have a feeling my category 4 mental storm has played a role, I nonetheless find myself unsettled again.

Eventually I look over at Janelle, eager to throw daggers her way. *Why did I let you talk me into attending this stupid weekend?*

I silently berate her. Yet she remains peacefully on her back, her eyes softly open, the corners of her mouth turned up in what I can only describe as a state of grace.

Maybe it's Janelle's ease in the face of this time crunch, or that I suddenly remember my spiritual goals. Or perhaps all this panic has just fatigued me. Whatever the reason, it dawns on me that the whole point of giving up my sleeping-in-at-home weekend is to revel in the bliss that I know is my authentic self—to merge, as in my dream, with the joy that is my true nature. Instead, I've spent the last twenty minutes creating an undeclared war in my head, an epic battle against three female combatants supported by a squadron of swami conspirators. In truth, none of these people means me harm.

I take several slow inhalations. As I do so, I visualize joy, acceptance, and love. This is how one merges with the divine, I remember. It's not about charging in. It's about letting go of the thoughts that restrict its natural flow.

When Carole appears who knows how many minutes later, Janelle gestures for me to go in. I steal a look at my phone: nine minutes remaining. But now, in my calm state, I'm clear on what I want to do. I shake my head and wave her in. She raises her eyebrows, evidently having sensed my earlier panic. I nod.

After Janelle enters the bathroom, I roll out of bed and pull my purple yoga top and stretch pants from my suitcase. By the time she comes out—only three minutes left!—I'm fully dressed. I have time only for a quick run to the bathroom; no shower. But that's okay. Back in the bedroom, Carole and Lucinda are already gone. Janelle is waiting patiently, admiring the altar. I run a quick brush through my hair and tie it with a lavender scrunchie. A dab of lip gloss later, she and I head out the door.

In the hall, I glance at my reflection in an antique wall mirror. Although I'm not wearing makeup and haven't washed my hair, my cheeks are rosy and my eyes are bright and clear.

I make a mental note: Contentment makes for a much better blusher than Clinique.

ॐ

After a half-hour sujal, where my mind is as jumbled as it often is and I experience only a few scattered seconds of actual focus, we prepare for our yoga class—taught by my beloved Miss Gumby, who arrived first thing this morning. I'm relieved to see she'll be teaching, not least because she knows and respects my physical (not to mention mental) limitations.

Once we get going, I'm not surprised to discover I'm the least advanced yogi in the room. My place in the yoga pecking order is further sealed by the fact that the center's full-time residents, including all the swamis, are taking the class. Upside down in the shoulder stand, these yogis are as straight as the Empire State Building; I more closely resemble the pitched roof of a house. In the course of the session, I also discover why *ardha matsyendrasana* is called the *half* spinal twist. I never would have imagined there could be a *full* spinal twist, but Consuela leads us in one. Some swamis spin nearly all the way around.

As we hold the various poses, Consuela tells us to imagine that we are making extra space in our bodies, lengthening not only our muscles and joints but also the areas between them. I do get what she's talking about; as I bend forward and stretch my torso, I suddenly feel taller than my five-foot-five-inch frame.

Sometime in the middle of the two-hour class, I finally stop noticing how strong and flexible everyone else is and begin to focus on myself. I may not have their skills, but I feel good about how much more I can do now than when I started doing yoga. Plus, I'm experiencing more of the subtle benefits of the poses, not least of which is that one of them has opened my sinuses, causing me to catch the faint scent of breakfast wafting from down the hall. I'm so hungry, it takes all my willpower not to jump up and run to the kitchen during the long deep relaxation that ends the class.

Yet when I'm finally able to float to the dining room, my body exhausted but exhilarated, breakfast turns out to be a disaster. Oh, the selection of hot cereals, baked goods, and fresh fruit is certainly enticing. But the silence with which we're expected to eat all this is anything but.

I've always found it deafening when two people sit over a meal in quiet, let alone a whole crowd. At home, I prefer to eat with festive background noises. Typically, if I'm eating alone, I'll turn on the radio or TV, or pick up the phone, calling Brad, Gretta, Anna, or, increasingly, Janelle.

My nerves are rattled before I sit down with the tray of beautiful food I've scored from the buffet line. I settle next to Janelle at one of the dining room's long wooden tables. Janelle is totally focused on her meal, happily digging into the steaming oatmeal (topped with raisins, banana, and cinnamon-sugar), freshly baked slice of bread, and hot herbal tea. But even though I'm famished, I can't take even one bite, caught up as I am in the amplified sounds of clinking spoons and slurping beverages around me.

To get over this discomfort, I try to pretend that a woman across the table whom I recognize from the yoga center—Stephanie, I think her name is, or maybe Samantha . . . no, it's definitely Stephanie—is starting up a juicy conversation with me, chatting about her boyfriend, my ice cream events, the week's hot celebrity news. This helps me feel better for a minute (although I still can't take a bite), but then I panic. *Why am I creating an imaginary dialogue with a woman who's minding her own business? Maybe I'm not just uncomfortable; maybe I'm going crazy?*

After a few more tortured minutes, during which I ponder, and thankfully reject, stealing Janelle's car or just running into the woods to get away, my gaze settles on a woman at the next table. With breathtaking features, perfect brown skin and to-die-for black hair, it's no wonder she caught my attention. But there's something more. She's wearing the same horrified expression that undoubtedly plasters my face, and her food, too, is uneaten. She looks at me and nods. *A fellow sufferer!* I think. I watch as she takes few slow breaths, then closes her eyes. I don't know if it was the breathing or the connection we seem to have made, but something has nudged her past her discomfort. She savors several spoonfuls of oatmeal with obvious pleasure. Then, opening her eyes and grinning, she silently urges me on. *If she can do this, maybe I can, too.*

I focus on the feel of my fingers on the warm, porcelain teacup and the cool metal handle of my spoon. I take a sniff of the oatmeal, inhaling deeply.

Touch and smell now urging me onward, I add sight. Like a baby spying her first banana, I examine its deep yellow color, brown freckles, and oddly shaped tip; I notice the oatmeal, its snowy slopes with moguls and dips.

Finally, I'm ready to eat. I lift my spoon to my lips, and in one swift motion, I experience the merging of color, smell, texture, and flavor. The result is sublime. I'm actually enjoying each meditative mouthful! Before I know it, the bowl is empty.

When I put down my spoon, I look up for the first time since my first bite and discover that Janelle is no longer here. At the next table, though, my compatriot remains. She playfully points to my zucchini muffin, urging me on yet again. I lift the pastry in her direction to make a sort of toast. Then I relish its sugary sweetness until the last crumb is gone.

A few minutes later, after I've guzzled my tea and placed my tray in the kitchen, the woman—whose name tag reads MANDY—links her arm in mine and escorts me to the lecture room down the hall. It's weird not to introduce myself or to thank her, but obviously we can't talk. When we enter the hall, Janelle is already seated on a cushion in the middle of the floor. I plop down next to her. Mandy sits next to me, then grabs my hand and playfully squeezes. Normally, a display of affection like this from a complete stranger would unnerve me, but I allow myself to appreciate her continuing support.

The schedule calls for a swami to discuss the Bhagavad Gita, an ancient Hindu tome. I'd flipped through the Bhagavad Gita a few weeks ago and, quite frankly, hadn't a clue what it was about or why a book concerning the minute details of a war has been praised by people for thousands of years. The swami begins by explaining how the war is a metaphor for the battle in the mind between the expansive, eternal Self and the small-minded self. The book, he says, is a guide for helping the one overcome the other. Oh.

Throughout his talk and the class on breathing practices that follows, I'm able to pay attention and enjoy myself. By lunchtime, I'm feeling pretty pleased with my accomplishments.

As we take our seats in the large, hushed lunchroom room, however, I'm once again rattled by the silence. The techniques that helped this morning prove useless, maybe because I can't see Mandy from where I'm sitting. The spinach salad, grilled tofu, and spelt rolls look divine, but I can't cajole myself to take more than a couple of bites. After a few minutes, I return my nearly full plate to the kitchen and grab an apple from a fruit bowl on my way out the door. I sit on a wicker chair in the lobby and munch alone. *I was doing so good, but I've screwed it up*, I berate myself.

A short while later, I'm able to cut myself some slack. That's because it turns out I'm not the only one who struggles: I discover that even swamis sometimes fall short.

This revelation comes thanks to my period, which makes a surprise appearance when I visit the bathroom after our free-time break, which I spend walking the gorgeous grounds. There's no tampon vending machine, so I approach the young woman at the lobby reception, writing my request on a piece of paper. She points to a small, nearly hidden store out back, explaining that it serves the ashram residents, many of whom are female.

A smiling man in dreadlocks at the cash register waves me into the store. I head toward the personal care items, which I spy on a shelf in the back. Walking down the central aisle, I pass a small table, around which three swamis, including the Cantalope and Jesus swamis who are leading our retreat, are gathered. I nod as I pass them. Then I abruptly stop and pivot. *What's that in their hands? Or rather, what's that in their mugs? It could be yogi tea*, I momentarily consider. *But to my expert eye, it sure looks like . . . yes, it is . . . coffee!* Their sheepish expressions confirm my suspicion.

Consuela has told us more than once that coffee is one of the beverages that are forbidden to swamis: in the ancient Indian health tradition known as ayurveda, it is considered *rajasic*, or overstimulating. But more to the point, I am keenly aware that I was not served a drop this morning. My eyes convey my displeasure.

The swami I don't know jerks his mug away in a halfhearted attempt to hide the evidence. Then he reconsiders, evidently deciding that lying only worsens an already bad situation. I guess swamis know about that DANGER: KEEP AWAY sign, too.

"Yes, we swamis have our addictions," he admits, owning up to the steaming beverage.

"Would you like a cup?" the cantaloupe woman offers, lifting an unused mug in one hand and a coffeepot in the other and brandishing them at me.

She must be kidding: fresh-brewed, sweet-smelling, ass-kicking coffee! Caffeinated black gold! Would I like a cup? *I would love a cup!*

But I shake my head. I rushed to get ready this morning—without taking a shower. Held back my desperate-to-wag tongue for hours. Performed a monkey-mind meditation. Ate two meals in miserable silence. Clearly, I am putting myself through all this for a purpose, and I won't give up that effort now.

I grab the box of tampons from a nearby shelf and rush to pay the man at the register, eager to leave the store before I change my mind.

ॐ

Soon I'm heading for the activity I've dreaded since I first heard about the retreat: the stomach wash. I'd read in one of my books that yogis use dental floss to clear their sinuses, so I shudder to imagine what they do to cleanse their stomachs.

With my unexpected errand, I'm a few minutes late to the session. I rush into the room, my breath heavy from running and from my rising sense of alarm. As the door slams shut behind me, everyone looks up at me. But the funny thing is they don't seem annoyed by my interruption—not even the swami. Unless I'm misinterpreting, they seem to radiate appreciation and love, wrapping me in a cozy blanket of acceptance.

"You are in the room to heal the room. . . . There is no other reason to be here." Those lines from *A Course in Miracles* spring into my head, and feel truer than ever. We *are* here to remind each other that we're all connected and always loved. If only I remembered that more often. . . .

By the time I sit down, the instructor has nearly finished his explanation of the wash. I hear him say that *kunjal kriya,* as the practice is known, was developed centuries ago, when yogis observed sick elephants healing their aching stomachs. The other thing I hear, thank goodness, is that this activity is optional. If others want to treat the inside of their body as if it were a car chassis, let them. I'm happy to just sit and observe.

The swami asks for a single volunteer to pave the way. I'm startled—but not really surprised—when the solitary hand that shoots into the air belongs to Janelle.

Standing in front of the room with the swami, Janelle and he drink large glasses of lukewarm water. "Now, we move around for a few minutes," the swami instructs. "To circulate the toxins before excreting them." Janelle doesn't flinch at the idea, although I notice a few other attendees shifting uncomfortably in their chairs.

Janelle and the swami proceed to leap around the room, two unrehearsed ballerinas dancing to different tunes. I feel a rising laughter desperate to break free. *No, I reprimand myself, the last thing I want to do is giggle at Janelle's expense. Hold it in at all costs!*

I didn't have to worry. My laughter flees a moment later when the swami hands Janelle a large yellow plastic bowl and utters a single directive: "Purge."

Again Janelle doesn't recoil. Sticking her finger down her throat, she gags loudly—as do several others in the room—before she and the swami vomit into their respective bowls.

Now that they've seen this, surely nobody else will volunteer, I'm certain. Yet when I look at Janelle, she is radiant, similar to the glow we always detect around Miss Gumby.

The swami asks Janelle to communicate (without using words) how she feels.

"Lighter and healthier?" he prompts.

She nods.

"Less weighted down? Ready to soar?"

She nods again, more vigorously.

"More connected to your inner being?"

Yes siree, she communicates. And the thing about Janelle is, she does not lie. Sure, she might couch things in a way that doesn't hurt someone's feelings, like that time she told her boss that his weird behavior at a new-business presentation certainly got the prospective client's attention. But she would never say something that was blatantly untrue.

When the instructor asks who else wants to try, I'm the only one who passes. But I'm hardly left out. At the point where they shake the liquid inside, Carole, Mandy, Lucinda, Vinny, and Janelle all gather around my chair, touching my shoulder or patting my back as they leap around. This time I close my eyes when the signal to vomit is given. But when I open them a few seconds later, the tranquillity that previously surrounded Janelle is evident everywhere.

ॐ

The next morning I get first crack at the bathroom—having sensed my anxiety yesterday, the other women signal me in the moment we hear the knock on the door. I'm happy to go first, and to get a chance to shower, but I'm clear that today I'm in a completely different frame of mind. I definitely would not make waiting for my turn the big friggin' deal I did yesterday.

My thoughts race as usual when we sujal, and I'm still not able to keep up with the others during the morning yoga. I struggle a bit during the silent breakfast and lunch, although not so badly as yesterday. During a lecture on the importance of staying in the present, I only partially put the lesson into practice. But since seeing the swamis sneaking their coffee yesterday, combined with the intense appreciation I've felt from so many of the participants here, I'm no longer judging myself for my failings. In fact, I'm feeling pretty proud of the things I *have* accomplished.

Before I know it, it's time for the sharing ceremony that ends the weekend. The swamis instruct us to sit in a circle and prepare to chant as a way to end the silence. I've never liked singing in public, but I adore the idea. Chanting is a practice that combines both earthiness and spirituality, so it will be the ideal bridge back to the world of sound.

The sitar player starts a tune, and the swamis lead the group in several rounds of *"Shanti, shanti, shanti."* Well into the fifth repetition, I realize I'm just mouthing the words. My voice, so blissfully absent these past two days, refuses to return. During the "Hari Krishna" that follows, I manage to eke out a few croaks. Only after the tenth repetition do my vocal cords return full throttle. I sing the final Sanskrit classic, "Om Namah Shivaya"—a greeting to the spirit within us—with gusto, if horribly off key.

After another moment of silence—this one even more striking because now it has followed sound—the Jesus swami asks for volunteers to share their feelings about the weekend. Inexplicably, I begin to cry. Since I've always thought it was weak to weep in public (I know, my mother's voice chiming through), I'm mortified when a staffer walks toward me with a tissue box. But she stops before she reaches me and hands the tissues to Carole. I suddenly notice she and Lucinda are bawling even harder than I am.

Vinny opens the sharing by describing his happiness at watching his wife experience yoga. This lights her up, so she gushes about her own pleasure in glimpsing the inner stillness that her husband has long extolled. Carole discusses her love of the silence—even though I spied her in the back garden this afternoon, whispering a few words to Lucinda. One by one, others reveal the moments they found most profound.

When Mandy speaks, she begins by talking about her challenges. "Yesterday at breakfast, my mind was a total wreck. I don't know why, but it was resisting everything about this retreat, especially the horrible mealtime silence." Then she stuns me by mentioning my name. "It was only by watching Lorna battle, too, that I was able to let go. That one moment—finding someone else who was struggling—changed my experience. So I want to thank you, Lorna, from the bottom of my heart."

The group turns in unison to face me. Once again, I sense their love. I've hardly been the perfect roommate, the perfect yogi, the perfect sujaler, or the perfect silent eater. But the appreciation flowing my way reminds me that I don't need to be. I send that appreciation right back to them.

"Lorna, would you like to share?" the swami gently prods.

My tears stream full force, but this time I'm not ashamed. It's wonderful to allow the emotions I typically hold back to come up for air.

It takes a moment to control my sobs. "I want to thank everyone so much," I finally say. "Even though I'm not a talented yogi and didn't do some of the activities, you all embraced me. I feel a bit like that Sally Field speech years ago: 'You like me!' And I'm really grateful."

The next thing I know, Carole has pounced on me, her hug nearly knocking me to the floor. This display of affection sets everyone tearing up again. Sensing that we're all too choked up to speak, the swami declares the retreat ended. After Carole moves on, I search for Mandy, eager to greet her with words.

She's already making a beeline for me. "I'm so glad I met you. I feel like I've known you for ages," she gushes.

"I'm thrilled to meet you, too," I say, extending my hand. She throws her arms around me, so I do the same.

"I meant what I said, you know. About you being my inspiration. Everything was coming so damn easy for everyone but me. But when I spotted you suffering, suddenly I felt okay."

"It's astounding that you say that, because it was *you* who inspired *me*."

"We're such a great match! I'd love for us to stay in touch. Do you live up here?"

"Naw. I'm from Hoboken."

"Oh, goody! I'm in Brooklyn—not far. Listen, my girlfriends and I sometimes get together for a women's spirituality group. We've got nothing scheduled at the moment, but when we do, I'd love for you to come. I suspect we could both use the encouragement."

I pause, overcome by her desire to include someone she barely knows. Apparently, she takes my silence as concern. "I didn't mean anything bad by that! I just meant—"

"No, I wasn't insulted. So happy, I couldn't speak."

"It's not as serious as maybe it sounds. Mostly it's just a chance for some terrific women to bond over meditation and merlot."

"Sounds heavenly." I jot down my phone number and hand it to her, before moving on to the rest of my good-byes.

A half hour later we're back in our bedroom, packing up our things. Janelle and I exchange numbers and more embraces with Carole and Lucinda.

"We'll be back for another retreat soon. We hope to see you girls here, also," Lucinda says.

Janelle and I answer at once: "Absolutely!"

Chapter 9

The whole next week, everything flows smooth and easy. Details for the Central Park extravaganza are falling into place—and I'm no longer rattled by that stubbornly remaining obstacle: figuring out where we'll store all the ice cream beforehand. I trust that the answer will come in its own time. I'm feeling so good, even the sight of Carletta lights me up.

Brad, who's still in his pre-launch frenzy, sent me a dozen long-stem red roses the night I returned from the retreat, accompanied by a heartfelt note about how much he misses me. I miss him, too, but right now life has me so elated, it doesn't bother me that we're apart.

Love seems to ooze from every person, every project, every square inch of my home and office. It took until Wednesday for me to realize the love is coming from me. The retreat so filled me up that the excess is leaking onto everything.

To ensure I stay in this joyful place, I've taken a suggestion from the swamis and started a gratitude list. I once heard Oprah talk about this on her show, and it struck me as a marvelous idea. As with many good intentions, however, I never got around to putting pen to paper. Until now. Each morning over breakfast— which I happily eat in silence!—I list the things I appreciate:

strangers who embrace me, a boyfriend who cherishes me, friends I adore (my last girls' night notwithstanding), a sister and her family who inspire me, a cozy home, an interesting job, yoga, chocolate, coffee (which has never tasted so delicious!). . . .

I even woke up each morning this week knowing whether my first conscious breath was an inhalation or an exhalation. That is remarkable because I've struggled with this practice since I read about it in a meditation book. Day in and day out as the early light cracked through my bamboo shade, I'd tried to spy my initial breath as intently as a cat eyes a chestnut-sided warbler. But I never had a clue. Now I can declare that Monday and Thursday I inhaled, and Tuesday, Wednesday, and today, I exhaled. These observations are so effortless, I hardly understand why I failed before.

Like every day this week, today has been a joy. Whatever I've wanted or needed has just naturally appeared. So when Doug unexpectedly walks into my cubicle near the end of the day, I know only good will come of it.

He parks himself in the extra chair. "I just got you a raise. Ten percent," he says, getting right to the point.

I leap off my chair in his direction. "Doug, that's fabulous! I didn't think I was up for one till August. Did I remember wrong? Did I—?"

"Calm down before you break your leg—or my leg," he chuckles. I don't bother informing him that this could never happen while I'm feeling so good. "I didn't want to say anything until it was definite. But last month I heard Finance got a few raises through, thanks to the company's better-than-expected profits. I didn't want Marketing to miss a slice of that pie. And the best news is you should get another bump at your annual review."

"Wow!" I restrain myself from giving Doug a big kiss, settling instead for a pat on his shoulder. "Thank you, Doug. I really appreciate you."

"And I appreciate all the things you give our department— especially your creativity." He stands to leave.

"What about Michelle?" I nod my head toward my assistant's cubicle. "Any raise for her?"

"Not till the annual. My talents are vast, but they aren't unlimited. And I'll answer your next question before you ask." He looks over his shoulder as he heads for the exit, then lowers his voice to a whisper. "No raise for Carletta."

ॐ

After work I stop at a small gourmet market to buy ingredients for the lentil soup I plan to make for dinner, part of my effort to eat lighter, healthier foods, as Miss Gumby does. I gather the beans, carrots, tomatoes, and wine vinegar and head to the checkout. Only one register is open, and three shoppers with minimal purchases are already on line. *This shouldn't take long*, I think. But a moment later, the woman at the front of the line brings me up to speed. "Can't you hurry up, already?" she snaps at the cashier.

The gal behind the register is a light-freckled teen in pigtail braids, like Judy Garland off to see the Wizard. With a nervous smile and a deliberate attempt to perfectly center each item under the scanner, it's obvious she hasn't been at this job for long.

The elderly man second in line scowls. "Yeah, hurry up. I don't have all day."

"I'm s-s-sorry," Dorothy nervously replies. "I can't seem to get this frozen orange juice to scan. There's so much ice on the can."

"Just skip the stupid juice, then. I don't want it that badly," the woman gripes.

Dorothy sets the can aside, but ringing up the rest of the order—a brick of premium coffee, a few cans of Wolfgang Puck's soups, a dozen cage-free eggs—proceeds equally slowly. It's a full ten minutes before she gets to the woman ahead of me. When that transaction ends, the rattled customer swiftly snatches up her bags. Too swiftly. One falls to the floor, spilling its cans of aduki beans and boxes of couscous. The cashier is clearly horrified, apologizing dozens of times as she meticulously gathers and rebags the items before the customer races out the door.

Rather than move on to me, she opens the front compartment of her register and begins fiddling with the roll of paper.

"I'm sorry," she squeaks to the long—and growing—line as she pulls out the remainder of what appears to be a substantial roll. "I need to replace this receipt paper before it runs out. It shouldn't take but a minute."

"No problem. I can wait," I say, still feeling calm.

After several minutes of fumbling, she's nowhere near finished. Her lower lip begins to tremble, so she purses it tightly against the top. I feel agitation begin to stir within me, and I wonder if my run of good luck is finally coming to a close. No sooner do I think this than the paper pops out completely from the register, unrolling a long trail around the floor. Dorothy screams in frustration, a sound echoed by others in the line. For some reason, this overreaction makes me realize how foolish we're all being. What does it matter when I get home? In fact, being here now seems to be more important. The Rodney Yee yoga DVD I'd planned to squeeze in before dinner has nothing on this moment. I recall that the yogis have a word for this: *karma yoga,* the "yoga of good deeds."

"It's okay," I soothe. "I'm not in a hurry. Take your time."

I turn to the portly man behind me, waiting to buy a six-pack of beer. "Are you in a rush, sir?" I ask him.

"I am now." He scowls. "This checkout is taking fucking forever."

I glance at Dorothy, who has rewound the paper and pushed it back into the register, but subsequently snagged it in the door. Her lips have vanished completely, and sweat beads so profusely on her forehead, she's soon going to need a mop from aisle ten to dry herself.

"I remember when I cashiered in college," I tell the guy behind me, loud enough to ensure that Dorothy hears, too. "I was so nervous, knowing my customers expected me to be an expert when I felt like anything but. Anyway, I'm in no rush. You're welcome to jump ahead."

"No, it's okay. I guess I can wait," he says, his anger subsiding.

"How about you?" I ask the elderly woman behind the man. "Would you like to move ahead?"

"Well, that's mighty kind of you to offer, seeing how long you've been waiting," she says, hesitating. "No, you were here first. I'll stay where I am."

"If either of you changes your mind, let me know," I say sincerely. "I'm fine with however long it takes."

I turn back to the frustrated cashier. "Is it okay if I help you with that?"

Her face is visibly relieved. "Oh, could you?" she begs.

I remove the roll and tear off the ensnared edge. "I once had an adding machine with a similar setup," I say as I fiddle with the paper and, after a few seconds, hear it snap into its hole. The door closes with ease. "There."

"Thank you so much!" she says. "My boss showed me how to do it earlier. I guess I'm not a very good student."

"No one learns everything after just one lesson. Next time you'll do fine. The main thing is to relax—even enjoy it."

"I don't think I'll ever enjoy replacing receipt paper. Or this job," she confesses.

"This may sound weird, but I'm learning that we can enjoy anything, once we decide we want to."

Dorothy rings up my order in her typical, deliberate pace, but I don't care. When she finishes, I gather my bags and turn to face the group behind me. "Have a wonderful evening!" I say, grinning from one silver earring to the other.

"Thanks. You, too," several of them reply. Before reaching the exit, I turn to look back. I'm thrilled to see many people sporting smiles as wide as mine.

ॐ

After I wake the next morning—exhaling!—I lie in bed and happily recall my calm (and contagious) stop at the market. The funny thing is, when I got home, somehow I still had time to enjoy both my yoga and my supper. Now I'm excited about the day ahead: Janelle and I plan to attend a workshop with a woman who channels spirits.

Weird, I know.

It took me a while to get over that doozy when I first flipped through one of her books at the library. The books are "written" by a spiritual essence channeling through a twenty-five-year-old woman. *Yeah, right*, I thought. But once I started reading, the message felt so perfect and so true that I didn't care if it was delivered by little green men shouting out from Mars.

This spiritual guide teaches that the universe is like a North Pole elf factory, capable of joyfully handing you everything you want, be it a fabulous giant-sundae event, a chic pair of boots, or a mind-set of peace. The way you bring these goodies to you is simple: Think thoughts that are pleasing, and stay confident your reward will arrive.

Janelle honks her Prius just as I finish twisting my hair into my Pebbles 'do. I grab my purse and a water bottle and head out the door. I'm off to what I now refer to as the "mission field" that is the day. I relish opportunities to help others feel as good as I've been feeling.

"You look adorable," Janelle says, eyeing my hand-painted crop pants, jacket, and lilac top.

"Thanks." I check out her cute bolero jacket. "So do you, of course." I lean in and give her a hug, something I'm more comfortable with since the retreat. "I'm so looking forward to this workshop. Amazing that you found out about it in time."

"Talk about a 'coincidence,'" she says, making air quote marks with her fingers to indicate she thinks it is anything but. "I almost never get the newspaper, but something propelled me to track one down yesterday. I had to go to three separate newsstands 'cause the first two were sold out, but I kept hunting. When I opened it, the workshop listing jumped right out at me."

The event is taking place in a midtown Manhattan hotel, normally at least a thirty-minute drive. We've given ourselves an hour to get there because you can never predict city traffic. We arrive in twenty minutes. Every light changes to green just as we approach, and the roads we turn onto mysteriously contain no traffic, even though we can see that nearby streets are gridlocked.

A few minutes later, after we've paid our admission fees, we practically skip into the conference room. Taking advantage of our early entrance, we nab great seats in the second row. An older couple sits down next to us.

Janelle wastes no time starting a conversation. In that way, she's just like Anna. "I'm Janelle, and this is my friend, Lorna. So nice to meet you."

"I'm Helen, and this is Al. We're pleased to meet *you*. Such sweet young women!"

"Have you been to one of her seminars before? I went last year, and it was eye-opening," Janelle says.

"Oh, yes! We've been following her work for a while now," the woman replies, to my surprise. I always expect elderly people to share my mother's narrow beliefs. As if she's reading my mind, Helen squeezes my shoulder. "We seniors are not all fuddy-duddies, you know," she says. I must stop making assumptions.

Helen reaches into her oversized pocketbook and pulls out a bag of chocolate-chip cookies. "I baked them this morning, so they're soft and chewy, the way cookies are supposed to be. In my opinion, of course," she says. "I don't know if it's against the rules to eat in here, but surely a few bites can't hurt anybody."

If only this woman were my mother, I fantasize as I take the bag and retrieve a cookie before passing it to Janelle. I savor every bite. Baked with Helen's love, it is superb.

We chat for a while. Then Helen squeals like an excited child, "Oh, goody! The session's about to start!"

We watch a young woman stroll to the front of the room. The several hundred attendees immediately grow silent. I don't know what I am expecting a channeler to look like, but certainly not like this woman. With her long, sumptuous hair, formfitting V-neck dress, and stylish boots, not to mention her poised, confident saunter, she looks like she's strutting down a fashion runway. The woman is introduced by her mother, apparently also a well-known channeler, who swiftly takes a seat off to the side.

"Hello, so good to see you all." The woman, who goes by the name of Giselle, beams. "I feel the spirit eager to start a conversation with you, so I'll just bring it in." She closes her eyes and makes a few gurgling snorts, the kind you might make underwater. I giggle at the spectacle until Janelle silences me with a firm gaze. The woman opens her eyes, and when she speaks again, her voice is much deeper, as if she's turned into a man.

"Good morning to you all," she says. The hairs on my arms stand at attention. *Can this really be something from another dimension? Is this the energy of our highest source? Has she really tapped into the world of spirit?* I'm intrigued, but not yet convinced of anything. Yesterday, when Janelle called me about the seminar, she said that she'd been to a prior one and felt transformed. I was gung ho after hearing that. But now I can't help feeling that this is strange—and maybe even a scam.

Over the next several hours, this being, whoever or whatever it is, wins me over. The woman brilliantly answers every question from the parade of audience members she calls on, to the point where I'm thrilled I came. Participants ask about money, health, children, even their pets. It seems that every question has a single answer: Focus on what you want. That overflowing bank account, perfect health, desired child, or lovable dog is simply waiting for you to get in sync with it. If you want good health, ponder good health, not the way your achy back keeps you from having it. Desire lots of money? (*Yes, I do*, I answer silently.) Think about the things you'll do when the cash comes. Positive thoughts make you a match to what you want, and once you hold that steady, they must appear. It sounds good to me, and I can't wait to put it into practice!

It's nearly the end of the workshop when the channeler asks for one final question. I haven't planned to ask anything, but a sudden urge propels my hand up. She is looking in the other direction, where hundreds of other hands are raised. But as if her head is pulled by an invisible string, she whips her long mane around and points to me.

"You in the lilac top," she says.

"Are you sure?" I mumble, immediately regretting having volunteered.

"Yes, positive," she replies. "Questioners are selected by the heat they're emitting, and you're practically a furnace. That means you're ready to hear the answer to your question."

I walk to the front and take a seat by the microphone. I don't know what I'm doing here. I hate being the center of attention. Worse, I don't even know what I want to ask.

The words tumble out from my unconscious. "I want to find the perfect life partner," I announce. "There's a guy I'm crazy about, although lately he's been working a lot. But that's not what bothers me; I know that's just till his software launches. He's got a long list of terrific qualities, but sometimes I wonder if he's my soul mate. I'd always thought it would be obvious. But now I keep asking myself, how do you know?"

I pause for what I hope will be another great answer. I am not disappointed. "When you fear you'll never find the man of your dreams, you never will," the woman explains, "because that thought gets translated into your reality. Don't worry whether this particular man is The One or Not The One. Keep focusing on the qualities you want in a mate, and have confidence that as you do so, the best man for you will quickly make himself seen. It might be your current boyfriend, or it could turn out to be someone else. But you won't care, because you'll have him!"

I stumble back to my seat, feeling dazed by the experience but also filled with a sense of calm. As I plop down, Helen leans over. "Honey, how brave of you to ask a question! And what a marvelous answer." I am too stunned to reply.

When the workshop ends, Janelle spins to face me. "I've been to a workshop before and didn't have the courage to raise my hand either time. I'm impressed that you did."

"I didn't plan to," I admit, finally getting my bearings. "It kind of shot up on its own."

"I have to say I'm surprised you asked what you did. I thought you were wild about Brad."

"I *am* wild about him," I answer defensively. "He's smart, funny, considerate, generous, sexy. . . . What more could a girl want?" I pause, deciding to answer my own question. "Well, obviously I have a nagging feeling in there somewhere, of wanting more, or I wouldn't have felt the need to ask."

ॐ

Maybe it's the confusion stirred up by my question. Or it could just be the inevitable passing of time since the bubble created by the retreat. But by early the following week, my skating-through-life aura begins to seriously thin. On Monday, I lose my temper with an Oregon farmer who has the nerve to tell me the five-pound cherry with which I'm hoping to top the giant sundae is out of the question; the largest cherry on record was only a puny three quarters of a pound. "There's got to be some freak fruit somewhere!" I screamed at him. Yesterday, walking back to my office with a Starbucks afternoon pick-me-up, I spilled my latte all over my linen slacks. Today went off track early, when the tailor who's altering a lace-and-cashmere blouse I recently splurged on at Barneys (on sale, but still shockingly pricey) called to say it inexplicably vanished from his shop. After lunch, I took an odd step in the stairwell and broke the heel off my favorite sandals—which means I've spent the entire afternoon walking around my office barefoot. Now I return to my desk to find a bright yellow memo staring at me.

This is the color that management uses for official mail, to inform us they're increasing our healthcare contribution or are axing a personal day from the personnel calendar. I don't have a good feeling as I lift the paper. I quickly realize I was right to be afraid.

To: Marketing department
From: Doug Stevens

Re: Mandatory evening out

Lately I have been dismayed to observe that this department lacks the cohesion it used to have, owing to several new hires and increasing bad blood among some of the longtime employees. To remedy the situation, I am requiring all employees to join us for a night out next Wednesday. The evening will include an early movie, followed by supper. Everything is on the house. No excuses short of death (your own only!) will be accepted.

Ugh. To not only have to spend my workdays with Brendan and Carletta, but to have to deal with them for an evening, also? I won't be able to stand it.

This reversal of my energy is a terrible thing. Because tonight I have plans to visit my mother.

Chapter 10

Last week, I finally accepted her dinner invitation, figuring the aura I'd acquired would protect me from her poisonous assaults. But now that it's fading, I don't know what I'm going to do. I know I can't avoid my mother forever—especially since she doesn't live far—but I had been doing a pretty good job of staying away. The last time I saw her was months ago, at my Uncle Sid's second wedding (to which I stupidly brought Brad; what was I thinking?).

I grab my cell phone and hit FAVORITES.

"Y-ello," a chipper voice sings out after the first ring.

"Hey, Brad, it's me. Can you talk?"

"You know I'd rather chat with you than with the geeky engineers I'm stuck with here."

I giggle at the thought of the guys in his department. Although Brad's got an MBA and business sensibility to go with his computer engineering master's degree, most of his coworkers more closely fit the pocket-protector stereotype.

"I'm having dinner with my mother tonight! How will I survive?"

"Hey, it won't be so bad. Maybe she'll be on good behavior."

"This isn't *your* mom we're talking about; it's mine! It'll be worse than bad! Come, so you can protect me."

"You know I'd love to. First, so maybe I'll see that Wicked Witch side of her you always talk about. She was charming when I met her at your uncle's wedding. And second, to look into your sexy eyes. But my software launches in a month! We're nowhere close to ready."

"I didn't expect you'd be able to come. Anyway, I don't wanna be responsible for anyone else getting hit by one of her flying casserole dishes."

"If you promise to make it out alive, I promise to take you somewhere great as soon as things settle down here. I gotta go to a meeting now, babe. Love you."

I stare at my silent phone. Since that didn't sufficiently mollify me, I dial the one person who I know will understand, even if she is too gracious to admit it.

"Angelica, how are you?" I say when my sister answers on the first ring, happy I remembered to use her preferred name.

"Lorna. So glad you phoned! I've been dying to hear how the yoga retreat went."

"Sorry I didn't call earlier. I don't even have a good excuse. The days just seem to vanish."

"I know what you mean. Anyway, I could've called you." I love how understanding Anna always is, taking the blame for things that are totally my fault.

"The retreat was terrific—the people were incredible. So full of love. But that's not why I'm calling. . . . I'm going to Mom's for dinner tonight."

"That's wonderful! I'm so happy you guys are getting along."

"We are *not* getting along!" I shout. I take a moment to calm myself before continuing. "I was flying after the retreat. My guard was down when I said yes. Now I'm kicking myself for not recycling one of the dozens of excuses I usually use."

"Nothing ever happens by coincidence, you know. You said

yes because you're supposed to be there. Be optimistic that it'll go well."

"You'll change your tune after one of us ends up knocked out on the kitchen floor. The sad thing is, I can't even predict who it will be."

"Look, I know Mom's not easy. But she's not as bad as you make her out to be."

"You just think that because you're her favorite. It's easy to get along with someone who thinks you walk on water. Not only don't I walk on water, but I'm sure she wouldn't even toss a life preserver in my direction if I needed one."

"I am not her favorite!" Anna insists, as she always does when we have this conversation. "I admit she has a stupid habit of criticizing you. But maybe tonight you can make that *her* problem and not yours. Don't take it so personally. So what if she's not conscious enough to see that *we're all* divine creations who walk on water. You're aware enough for both of you."

"How do you do it?" I ask, amazed. "How do you see her as often as you do without wanting to kill her—or yourself?"

"I recognize that her flaws have nothing to do with me. Think how tough she's had it, what with her own mother dying when she was a kid, then Dad walking out when we were so young. It's a powerful spiritual practice to be in the presence of someone who's suffering and not get dragged down. I focus on her glorious, spiritual essence. And I know you can, too."

"Thanks for the vote of confidence. Even if I don't share it."

"You will soon, I promise. Listen, I've gotta run. Gotta pick up Yonatan from the church—he's working on a really exciting project I'll tell you about later. Then I gotta get Radha from school drama rehearsal. Good luck tonight! And remember, the loving energy of the universe is always within you."

"Thanks, Anna—uh, Angelica. Bye."

It's phone calls like this that are the reason I adore Anna.

This hasn't always been the case. When we were younger, I actually hated her guts. Despised her very existence. But that was before I realized it was Mom who set me up to do that, Mom who pitted us against each other like two rats in a single cage, Mom who waited to see which one would emerge victorious: thinner, smarter, kinder, more athletic, the more talented piano player, the more accomplished chef, the better girlfriend, the more caring daughter. Mom always cheered loudest for Anna, so it's no surprise my sister always won.

I used to think Anna was full of herself, that she thought she was God's greatest creation. Only when I began reading these spiritual books did I realize that she's right. Anna *is* God's greatest creation, and that doesn't take a whit away from the fact that so am I. As Deepak Chopra—now that I know who he is—wrote in *The Seven Spiritual Laws of Success*, "The universal mind . . . permeates every fiber of existence. . . . Everything that is alive is an expression of this intelligence."

Since I stopped trying to claw my way past Anna, I've come to appreciate how much I can learn from her—and from her husband Yonatan and her ten-year-old daughter, Radha, who's more spiritually advanced than I might ever be, and certainly than I was as a nail-biting, hopeless, jealous girl her age.

I hobble on my busted heel to my car, where I pray I'll dig up a spare pair of shoes. Fortunately I do find loafers I'd left the other day when I changed into my yoga slippers. I pull them on and start driving. The good news is I am not heading straight to Mom's. I need to stop at the grocery store to pick up the salad Mom agreed to let me bring after I asked (three times) how I could contribute. Maybe I can dawdle around the store for a while, or perhaps the cashier there will need assistance? Alas, I know that I can't delay long. Reality bites me hard: I'm in for a nightmare.

"I don't want to go! I don't want to go! I don't want to

go!" I shout over and over, like a child determined to avoid the inevitable trip to school.

Hoping to boost my mood, I scan for a distraction in the car. I press the window button down, hoping the fresh air will invigorate me. When it doesn't, I seize on the radio. *Why didn't I think of this earlier?* I flip to WNOW.

Serena Robbins's voice emerges from my speakers: "Are you living in the now?" *How does she always know how I'm falling short?* "So often, we spend our time worrying about the future. But this only keeps up from noticing how lovely it is where we are now."

"Yes, that's definitely true in my case," an unfamiliar male voice agrees, and it startles me to realize Serena Robbins wasn't speaking to me, but to a caller on her show. It's not even a live broadcast, but a repeat, an announcer remarks. It's exactly what I need to hear. "Even when I'm in my beautiful garden," the man continues," I don't appreciate it because I'm worried about my business failing or my girlfriend ditching me, or whatever. My fears don't have to be rational. Most of the time they aren't."

I pass the next few minutes consciously appreciating where I am at this moment, which is in my beautiful car, listening to a radio host I adore. *Right now I'm not with my mother.* That thought makes me feel much better.

After my brief stop, where I pick up a premade salad and a bouquet of gorgeous organic flowers, I pull into my mother's driveway. Immediately, I notice a twitch in the front parlor curtains. This is part of Mom's standard drill: Seeing I'm here, she runs into the family room. When I let myself in with my key and walk into the room, she'll be casually sitting, sipping coffee and claiming she hardly remembered I was coming (the gourmet duck or Cornish hens in the oven notwithstanding).

Today, I will not care. I will not rush inside to catch her dashing into the family room, will not answer her, *Oh, I wasn't sure if it was tonight?* with my brusque, *You know it was!* Today, I'm going to be in the room to heal the room, and I suspect that what I am most wanting to heal is that mammoth canyon between my mother and me, the one that has been so filled with poison gas and machine gun fire that I have not ventured into it for a very long time.

I open the front door and head to the family room in the back of the house. Sure enough, Mom is nursing her brew in a bright red mug.

"Hi, Mom. I'm so happy to see you," I sing, words that haven't passed my lips in, well, ever.

"Hello, Lorna. I wasn't sure if it was tonight that you were coming."

I gather my strength. "Well, I hope tonight is good for you because here I am. I brought you flowers." When I picked out these purple pansies and birds of paradise in the store, I knew I wouldn't be able to predict Mom's reaction. In the past, getting flowers from me, even ones as beautiful as these, has elicited everything from graciousness to scorn. Sometimes, after she puts them in water, she'll point out how one bud doesn't look quite up to par—a reference I have always taken to be a veiled shot at me. Today she shrugs nonchalantly at my offering and doesn't reach out to take them.

I cheerfully find a vase in her cabinet, and after I cut the stems and arrange them just so, Mom breaks the silence. "I see you brought salad," she says, eyeing the plastic bag on the counter. "From the store, is it?"

"Yes. I've had this kind before. It's delicious." I don't feel defensive about my contribution. I don't even question my decision last night not to stash a serving bowl in my car in which to empty the bags of greens and tomatoes, as I've done in the past. I knew what my mother meant when she said salad: me standing over my sink carefully shredding dark green, red leaf, and baby lettuces;

slicing orange peppers a quarter inch (exactly!); arranging wedges of tomatoes that had been picked at the height of ripeness; sprinkling in exotic olives and maybe some fresh feta cheese; and topping it all with a carefully measured dressing of cold-pressed extra-virgin olive oil, tangy balsamic vinegar, and freshly cut herbs. In other words, prepared the way she would have done it. But I'm trying to be more authentic about who I am, which at the moment is a woman with no interest in imitating Nigella.

"What about that boy?" Mom asks, shifting from lettuce to lover so abruptly that for a second I wonder if she meant the grocery store produce clerk. "The one you brought to Uncle's wedding. He seemed like a terrific catch for you."

"Yes, Brad and I are still together," I say, unnerved that she's turned to such a personal matter so swiftly.

"Really? Well, he did seem to adore you." I can tell by the puzzled tone that her mind is silently adding, *I can't imagine why*.

I fish a bowl from her cabinet and empty the salad into it. *Stay strong, Lorna, stay strong.* I take a breath so deep, I practically feel the oxygen fill my loafers. I scan my brain for an affirmation— one of the millions I've read by now—to help me through what could be the longest evening of my life, even though Mom will undoubtedly shoo me out by 8 P.M., so she can be in bed in time for her "loveliness sleep."

The New Thought minister Marianne Williamson rushes to my brain: "A good relationship isn't always crystals and rainbows. It's a birth process, often painful, often messy." I read that in *A Return to Love* the other day, and it's perfect. The birth process begins right now.

To buy time while I silently repeat this mantra, I peek into Mom's dining room. Her table setting is breathtaking: gold-rimmed bone china, sparkling crystal glasses, polished silver cutlery, and starched linen napkins. Ever since I was a little girl,

Mom's guiding philosophy has always been, If you're going to do something, do it the right way. By which, of course, she means the way she thinks is right, everyone else's viewpoints be damned. And she's always believed it's right to set a formal table when a guest comes for dinner, even if the guest is her underachieving—and unlovable—daughter.

"Can I help you cook?" I ask when I return my focus to the kitchen, turning the subject away from Brad. I know full well the answer is no. Mom spends days preparing these meals. Besides, she's never wanted my help with any task, the subtext being I would screw it up.

"The correct grammar is, 'May I help you cook?' And yes, you may. If the broccoli pie in the window is cool enough, you could cut it for me. I'm feeling a little tired and would love to sit." It takes all my composure not to yank my mother's cheeks, checking for an impostor. Maybe Anna is right: Maybe Mom and I don't have to be stuck in that same step-on-your-feet tango we've performed forever.

"I'd be honored to." I pick up the knife and get to work. From the corner of my eye, I see Mom get up anyway and walk to the kitchen counter. She picks up my salad and takes it to the fridge, where she adds her own bits of fresh scallions, gourmet Greek olives, and feta cheese.

"So, how're you feeling these days?" I ask, mostly to make small talk. This is when she says everything is fine. Bothering others about her health isn't the "right way," even though later, if I surreptitiously sift through her medicine cabinet, I'll find pills for her high blood pressure, insomnia, and, based on my last foray in her bathroom, type 2 diabetes.

"Actually, the doctor wants me to go in for some tests. Says my liver enzymes aren't so good." Wow. Another blinking neon from the heavens that things can be different. "Nothing to worry about," she adds after spotting the southward plunge of my jaw.

"What's he looking for?" I ask, trying to keep my alarm from cracking into my voice.

"I'm not sure. . . . Really, everything's fine. Anyway, enough about me." She looks intently in my direction, as if to insist the topic is closed. "You know you have dreadful bags under your eyes? I pointed out to Uncle at his wedding that you are prone to 'luggage lids' when you don't sleep enough. Guess you're still having too many late nights out with your girlfriends, huh?"

Her criticism makes me smile. I'd be way too freaked if she didn't at least somewhat resemble the mother I know.

"Truthfully, I haven't gone out much lately. And I don't have any bags, unless you count this adorable number I picked up at Neiman Marcus the other day." I lift the handbag I laid on the counter when I arrived. "Got it for a third of the retail price."

"It is lovely," Mom agrees, taking in the fine stitching and delicate strap and basking in a lesson successfully handed down from mother to daughter: Never pay retail. Mother doesn't pay full price on any item. Even when it's not on sale, she'll wear the saleswoman down by pointing out imagined defects until the woman relents and gives her something off. "It doesn't match your shoes. But I'm sure something in your closet would go nicely."

The phone rings as we head for the table. "Let the machine get it," I say as Mom predictably lunges for the receiver, it not being the right way to pretend you're out when you aren't.

I take my seat, realizing that I'm glad to have time to compose myself. I remind myself of the truth I've read in all those books: The unconditional love I've always futilely tried to get from my mother actually resides inside me. I begin to envision a golden shimmer of love floating up from my feet to my legs, then moving on to my torso, arms, and head. When I exhale, I watch the golden love float out of my body and soften the energy in Mom's otherwise uptight dining room. A wave of contentment overtakes me.

"Don, what is it you want?" I hear my mother say the moment I shift my focus back to the action. My back stiffens at her words. Don? The weasel son of Mom's childhood friend? The guy who can't let a moment pass without wondering what's in it for him? He and I haven't spoken since before Christmas, when he hung up on me, pissed at my refusal to lend him money to buy holiday gifts for, as he put it, "some kids in the neighborhood." I was certain one of those "kids" was a grown man named Don, who was eager to own the new MacBook Pro he saw the photographer using at Uncle Sid's wedding.

I didn't know he and my mother were on speaking terms again. I heard from Anna last month that Mom had physically tossed Don out her front door. I adored playing—and replaying—a mental movie that had her roughly depositing him outside her porch. He'd had the nerve to ask if he could move into her house for a while. Just until he got some check an ex-boss had promised, he told her, or until some (no doubt, super-long-shot) investment money came through.

Mom did take Don in several times over the years, but the first occasion, when he was thirteen and I was nine, is the one that haunts me. Don lived with us for three interminable months, because his mother had been hospitalized with a rare blood condition and his father proved unable to cope with his wretched excuse for a son. Extending herself to help her sick friend is one of the few things I've truly been proud of Mom for. But living with Don fast became a nightmare. He belittled me, lied to all of us, and ran rings around the house rules. Then my things began disappearing: CDs, a gold bracelet, some of my birthday cash. I complained to Mom dozens of times, but she ignored my entreaties, claiming I must have misplaced my stuff, or that I was making waves because I was jealous of her attention to Don.

Thankfully, his thievery finally extended to her. The weekend she demanded he move back home—Anna's missing necklace and Mom's discovery that a pair of skis had been inexplicably charged to her credit card finally jarring her to face reality—was one of the happiest of my childhood. Still, he's managed to slither in and out of our lives ever since.

"No, Don, I can't help you," Mom repeats for the third time, exasperation rising in her voice. "I'm sure it would be good for you to go on a spiritual retreat, especially since you always have plenty of free time. But I cannot—I will not—foot the bill. If you need money, go to work like other young men your age. In any event, I have dinner on the table, so I have to say good-bye."

A spiritual retreat for ol' Don, I think approvingly. That probably would be a great use of Mom's ample bank account, although of course she would never see it that way.

"This soup looks divine," I say as my mother comes to the table and places one of the two bowls she's carrying in front of me. It's a cold melon puree divided perfectly in half, with green honeydew and what I smell to be lime on one side, orange cantaloupe with lemon on the other, and a sprig of mint poised exactly in the middle.

I debate whether to abandon the premeal ritual I've begun doing the past few days. *Things are going along pretty well*, I remind myself, *why rock the boat?* On the other hand, I'm trying to be true to myself, a desire that ultimately wins out. "Mind if I say a short blessing before we begin?" I ask with as much nonchalance as I can muster.

It takes all Mom's effort not to spray out her mouth the spoonful of soup she's just tasted. "Why do I have a feeling your blessing won't be a traditional grace?" she moans. "Isn't it enough that Anna's into such gobbledygook? You have to be, too?"

"It's the same idea as grace, Mom. It's about appreciating how a higher power, in the form of nature, has brought us this food."

I know my mother is mocking me, but I'm trying not to notice. I close my eyes and clasp my hands by my heart, to connect to my loving, internal essence—not to mention to steady my rapid heartbeat, a sign that I am more influenced by her reaction than I hoped to be.

"Annapurne sadapurne shankara prana ballave," I begin to chant. This is the Sanskrit meal prayer Consuela has taught us, along with other traditional Indian blessings. "Beloved Mother Nature, you are here on our table as food. Grant us health and strength, wisdom and dispassion, and help share this with one and all." I pause, then add sincerely, "And thank you to my mother, who lovingly prepared this fabulous meal. I appreciate her generosity and her effort."

When I open my eyes, Mom is wiping away a tear. She quickly removes her hand without saying a word.

Supper is extremely tasty, which is not a surprise. My mother has always been a terrific cook. She took great care that each piece of yellowtail snapper was baked moist and crisp, and that the squash, eggplant, and tomato casserole, not to mention the broccoli and cheese pie, were superbly melded. She insisted that my store-bought salad be served with her homemade dressing rather than with the one that came in the package, and I have to admit it was divine. And she topped off the meal with a dessert of vanilla praline fudge ice cream (not from my company, she made a point to mention) over a strawberry-rhubarb pie that came fresh from the oven.

I suspect there's another reason the meal tasted so good. For the first time in decades, I've eaten in my mother's presence without that telltale knot in my stomach, the one that anxiously anticipates the moment when I'll be compared to her lofty ideal for a daughter and found wanting.

Oh, she is still judging me. Twice she corrected how I keep my fork prongs-side down when stabbing my fish. ("That may be fine in England, but if you haven't realized, Lorna, you're in America," she scolded.) Three times she mentioned those phantom bags under my eyes. And I lost count of how frequently she reminded me that I should snap Brad up right away. *Before he comes to his senses*, I feel her wanting to say. *Like your husband?* I feel myself desperate to reply. My dad skedaddled when I was five. "To jail," she used to speculate. When I was a teen, I laughed to my friends that that would be going from one "corrections" institution to another.

But I've done an admirable job keeping myself out of her gutter. Her aim has always been to puff herself up by belittling me, but now that I'm not defending myself, I feel like I'm getting taller. *You've done it*, I applaud myself. *You've sat through an entire dinner with Mom and stayed centered enough that her shots are bouncing like bullets off Superman.*

"Dinner was wonderful," I say after we've finished our tea and I prepare to leave, knowing she won't let me help clean the kitchen but then will silently fault me for not doing so. "We should do this again soon."

"You know my phone number. Of course, you've always known it, and that hasn't inspired you to use it."

"Well, I definitely will call soon. Maybe next time you'll come to my house?"

"Why would I do that? Mine is so much more comfortable than your little cottage."

I fight to remember Angelica's words that these are Mom's issues, not mine. "Whatever," I answer neutrally.

"My cooking's certainly better," she continues, guns blazing. "God knows I tried to teach you basic kitchen skills. But you never did catch on. No wonder you buy premade salad from the store."

"Your meal *was* lovely," I repeat, aiming to stay on course. "If you prefer to get together here, I'm happy to come again."

"Maybe next time you can bring Gretta. It's wonderful you

girls are still close after all these years. She's such a gem." I nod and smile. Obviously, I have told Mom nothing about the more recent tensions between Gretta and me.

"I imagine I wouldn't say the same for that granola-girl you've apparently been spending time with. You know, the one who went on your little trip. Of course, *you* didn't tell me that. I had to hear it from Angelica. What's her name again?"

"Janelle," I say, my anger rising at Anna for talking about Janelle to Mom, even though I'm sure she meant no harm. I struggle to keep my voice even. "Janelle happens to be one of the nicest people I know. And since you've never met her, I don't think you're in a position to judge."

"Oh, I know the type. Searching for something out there—" She straightens her arm and points away. "—because she's lacking in here—" The hand returns to tap her heart. "—and maybe not much in here, either—" It lands on her forehead. "I just hope you don't get brainwashed from any of her crazy ideas."

Alas, this attack on my dear friend is more than I can bear. The volcanoes of rage I've long felt toward my mother awaken, and start spewing fast. "Don't you insult Janelle!" I scream, unable to hold it in a moment longer.

"Face it, Lorna. Aside from Gretta, you've always picked terrible friends. That mouse Sarah, that bossy Tina—"

The lava flow is unstoppable now, a fury cascading full tilt. "The people I spend time with try to be loving and caring—traits you wouldn't recognize if they smacked you in the head!"

Her own blistering hurricane is stirred up now, the veins on her neck bulging in the thick of the storm. "Look who's talking about loving! You've always been colder than a walk-in freezer. And caring! That's rich, coming from the one who thinks she's better than everyone in the family." Her jaw quivers as the hatred disgorges, yet her eyes radiate satisfaction. She gets such pleasure from attacking me!

What was I thinking, coming for dinner? Nobody can have a normal relationship with you! I grab my purse and take off for the front door, propelled by the desire to get away immediately. I slam the door hard behind me—a tornado added to these converging cataclysms—desperate to reach my car before she finds her way outside. My hands shake as I struggle to dig keys out of my bag. Once I find them, I leap into my car, closing the door at the moment my mother reaches her porch. I sense that insults are still pouring from her frothing mouth, but thankfully, with my windows up, I can't hear her.

I'm blocks away from my mother's house before I realize I'm sobbing, tears so thick, I can barely make out the traffic light ahead. *Why does she still have so much power over me? Why can't I be more like Anna, aloof from Mom's flying arrows? Why does my every encounter with this woman end so badly?*

By the time I pull into my driveway, I'm a little girl, consumed by the rage, humiliation, and unworthiness I've always felt around my mother. "All my spiritual progress down the fucking drain!" I scream as I enter my house and throw my purse on the table. I'm nowhere near as evolved as I hoped. It's like I'm in spiritual kindergarten, while facing my mother requires a damn thesis defense.

I am no more enlightened than when I started my quest, I realize as I dejectedly trudge to my bedroom. *Maybe not even any more than my pea-brained mother is.*

Chapter 11

The next morning on my drive to work, I flip on my radio to WNOW. Since last night, I've been flailing about for something—anything—to put me back on track. Not only did I have a fitful sleep, I don't have a clue if my first breath was in or out—and, really, who the hell cares! And my gratitude list? Pffft. I sat in my kitchen this morning with my pen in hand and couldn't think of one stupid thing to feel appreciative for.

Maybe Serena will be true to her moniker and help me chart a path toward calm.

"Yes, Michael, I agree that seeing the loving soul inside everyone can be difficult, especially when the person is not behaving in a way that makes it easy," Serena Robbins's voice melts over my radio. *She's talking about my mother!*

"Can't someone have so completely obscured their soul that nobody could find it—not even Jesus himself?" a gruff-voiced man asks.

"Well, I don't know that Jesus would have had the trouble that you're having with your father-in-law. Certainly one of Jesus' great gifts was his ability to separate the actor from his or her acts."

"So what the heck am I supposed to do when he sticks his uninvited nose into my business yet again?"

"You could try inviting him. Maybe he's a battering ram because his ego feels bruised at not being included. I'm sure I don't have to tell you that egos try to get what they want in all kinds of warped ways. If you can see your father-in-law as someone just trying his best—as all of us are, really—maybe you'll be able to ignore the meddling. And the great thing is, when you get to that place of accepting and adoring him, his meddling should stop."

Certainly the position Angelica would take, I think as the station breaks for a commercial. But maybe some people are as beyond understanding as a shrieking infant who's already been checked for wetness, hunger, exhaustion, fever, diaper rash, and boredom. Maybe when you have the whacked-out mother I do, a miles-wide berth is the only solution.

I pull into my office parking lot and plod through the busy lobby to the elevators, around which a crowd has gathered. It seems that two of the lifts are broken. When the door to the remaining one opens, the mob crams inside. Two young women and a middle-aged man are pressed up against me. With the mood I'm in, I'm tempted to press back. *Relax, Lorna*, I coax myself. My shoulders are already on the sixth floor, even though we're not yet past the second. I consciously float them down, but it's hard not to feel my impatience rising.

When I finally squeeze myself out in our lobby, I'm hit with a sudden fit of coughing. As is often the case with these attacks, it feels like my lungs might be expelled from my body. I double over, barely able to catch my breath. The barking is loud, like a highway construction zone. After a couple of minutes, the attack subsides. I take a moment to steady myself, then stand up straight. The first person I see is Carletta, hovering by the reception desk, watching me.

"Don't get too excited, Carletta. I'm not dying yet," I say.

"One can always hope." She pauses. "Of course, what would our department do without our superstar Lorna?"

"What's that supposed to mean?" I sneer, happy to engage in battle if that's what she wants. I could use to vent some of my hostility.

"Rumor has it you and Jamal got some sort of stealth raise. The only ones in this department, I gather. Although I find it hard to believe you'd be singled out for such an honor, I have to ask: Is it true?"

I know that Doug wouldn't want me to tell. But maybe an oblique answer will annoy her just as much as a confirmation. "You're asking about a rumor. Unlike you, I don't traffic in them," I say.

"I'm not asking you to talk about other people. It's a question about you: Were you or were you not singled out for extra money?"

"Why would that matter to you?"

"I haven't heard you deny it. If it is true, it's unbelievable."

"I'm not saying it's true. But what's so unbelievable?"

"It amazes me how Doug can't see what a two-face you are—how he buys in to that fake Sweet Lorna persona."

I know I'm supposed to ignore her stupidity, to see past her bruised ego to her higher, more lovable soul. But as I learned yesterday, this is clearly beyond my ability. "We both know which of us is the fake, Carletta," I continue. "And it isn't me."

I storm away before I let loose, and later regret, the other nasty comments gathering in my voice box.

As I approach my cubicle, my phone is ringing. Another woman might think it could be her mother calling, if not exactly to apologize, at least to begin rebuilding our connection. But I know as I lift the receiver that it will pretty much be anyone else. Since my mother believes she is never wrong, no apology is ever required. Hell would not only have to freeze over, the temperature would have to sink low enough to make polar bears quiver, before she would deign a mea culpa.

"Hello," I say, even as I wonder why the heck I picked up the receiver, since there's not one person in the world I want to speak to now.

"Hey. How are you?" Angelica's lilting voice replies. Okay, maybe there is one.

"Mom told you about our dinner, huh?"

"Yeah. She called first thing this morning. Listen, don't sweat it. She'll get over it. I have faith you'll both put it behind you and try again soon."

"Try again?" I stammer. "Are you nuts?"

"Time heals all, my girl, you'll see. Plus, you're making such great progress in your spiritual quest. Soon you'll let her barbs float right to the sky."

"I wish I had the same confidence you have. I think I'm hopeless."

"Far from it. You're amazing!" She pauses, and I wonder if she's reconsidering. "Anyway, Mom's not the reason I'm calling. I've a favor to ask."

"Ask away," I say, thrilled to change the subject.

"Well, a couple of interfaith churches have plans to go to West Virginia on Friday. It's a last-minute thing, to help a Baptist church rebuild. Remember when it was burned by arsonists last year? It was all over the news."

"I remember. It sure sounds right up your alley."

"Yeah. I'm thrilled to do whatever I can to help. But I'll be gone till Wednesday. Radha can't miss so much school, but Yonatan is tied up this weekend. Did I tell you about the retreat he's planning? It's gonna be extraordinary! But he's already behind where he needs to be, so he's gotta work this weekend." She pauses for a breath, but doesn't let me get a word in, which would be an enthusiastic yes for what I suspect—and hope—is coming. "Any chance Radha can stay with you till Sunday night? If you're busy, no worries. I don't have to go."

"I'd love it!" I shout, knowing that spending time with my

ten-year-old niece will be just what I need. A common theme in all my spiritual books is that great benefits come from being around conscious people. I read in *After the Ecstasy, the Laundry*, by the Buddhist teacher Jack Kornfield, about *Sangha*, the Sanskrit word for community, which Kornfield says is "treasured because without it awakening cannot be sustained." I've already seen that wisdom play out in my life, since I always feel good when I'm with Janelle. Spending the weekend with Radha could be just the thing to help me again see my life as a delicious dip in the lake, rather than as the knee-high muddy slog I've made it out to be since yesterday.

"Can I drop her at your place tomorrow after dinner? Say, eight o'clock?" I smile at her grammatical misuse of the word *can*, instead of *may*, although I'm certain Mom has never corrected her.

"That will be perfect."

ॐ

On Friday evening, I'm cleaning my kitchen and scrubbing my pots before Radha arrives. I'm using this opportunity to tackle the Buddhist practice of mindfulness, striving to keep my attention on my effort to eradicate grease stubbornly clinging to the side of my casserole dish. I am not succeeding; each time a car goes down my street, my mind wonders if it's my sister.

The dinner I've just finished was from one of the dozen vegetarian recipes I've collected from yoga and healthy-cooking magazines: shiitaki mushrooms, chopped fresh scallions, crisp pea pods, and little tofu cubes, all stir-fried in olive oil, topped with red wine vinegar and tamari, and ladled over a bit of brown rice. It tasted delicious, if I do say so myself. I even found it fun to cook—something I won't be admitting to my mother.

Eating vegetarian is part of my quest to get back on track, and to be more like my role model, Miss Gumby. In yoga class, she always says that eating flesh (that's how she puts it; it's almost enough to turn you into a vegetarian on the spot!) blocks our full connection with our higher self. Of course, she also says that she sujals for a full hour at sunrise and another hour before bed, but I can take only one Miss Gumby–inspired baby step at a time.

After class one day at the yoga center, I had leafed through some books about transitioning to vegetarianism. Most advocated first giving up red meat, then moving on to chicken and, finally, fish (and even dairy and eggs, if you want to be one of those pure types, which I do not). I figure that even one non-meat meal a week is a step in a positive direction. Of course, I'm nowhere near ready to abandon my beloved burgers and fries.

Radha and her family are strict vegetarians, but she's not set to arrive until after dinner. Not that my fabulous niece would have said anything if I'd whipped out a bloody side of cow in her presence. She wouldn't have eaten it, but like her mother, Radha's got the admirable ability to accept people as they are—a skill that remains as far out of my range as pitching for the New York Yankees. Before I beat myself up further, though, I remind myself that Radha's mother is an interfaith minister, while mine is . . . Well, we know what mine is. It's not surprising that Radha would be so far ahead on the spiritual path that I can barely make her out through the dust.

The phone rings, jarring me back to the moment and making me realize I'd long ago lost my focus on my greasy pot. Oh, well. At least anticipating Radha's visit has put me in a better mood.

"Hellllllooo," I practically sing into the receiver.

"Hellllooo back. Boy you're festive."

"Janelle! So glad it's you. I *am* feeling good. I'm excited about my niece coming over."

"I'm glad for you." She pauses. "Sorry I didn't call you back earlier. I was crazed, trying to finish a project—I just got done."

"No worries. I didn't take it personally—although I think it's the first time in weeks we didn't speak during the day. It felt kinda weird, not getting my Janelle booster dose. But even without it, I managed to stay upbeat."

"So funny you say that. I feel like it's me who gets a booster dose from you! Glad your day was good, seeing how the last few haven't been. By any chance, does this mean you spoke to your mother?"

"Nah. She'll never call—and I can't motivate myself to dial her. I know I'll have to sometime, but not yet. No need to ruin the pleasure of my niece's visit. Speaking of which, I gotta finish getting ready."

"All right. Have a great time with her. Call me tomorrow if you get a chance."

"I will. Love you!"

After I hang up, I dry and put away the last of the cooking utensils, including my favorite: a wooden paddle with a colorful, carved toucan on top, a souvenir from our ice cream promotion in Caribbean resorts a few years back. My boss at the time—who headed the department I now do before she left the company—whipped up the event mostly to get a great trip for the two of us. I certainly didn't complain, although I would never do that sort of thing now that I have her position.

I close the final kitchen drawer just as the doorbell rings. I glance up at my clock: exactly eight. No surprise there. I expect my sister to be on time the way I expect the light to turn on when I flip the switch. A smile crosses my lips when I realize that this time I'm admiring her clockwork precision, not scorning it as I usually do.

The two of them are illuminated by my porch light when I open the door. Clothed in her white minister garb, Anna looks positively angelic—no wonder her teacher gave her that spiritual name. And while Radha is wearing the typical kids' uniform of jeans and a T-shirt, her frizzy hair pulled back in a floral headband, her glow is equally cherubic. It wouldn't startle me if they each sprouted wings and flew inside.

"Thanks so much for watching Radha," my sister says as I usher them into my living room. She settles onto my couch with the grace of a gazelle. Anna was a natural beauty even as a child, but since she's found this inner contentment, she's become even more luminescent. It's as if her spirit guides turned to her and said, *Angelica, let us lighten your load. We'll take some of those heavy bags you've been carrying for such a long time.* I can picture them saying this to her because I've heard them whisper it to me, too. But somehow I haven't yet handed much over. Maybe I've let go of a little backpack or carry-on, but I'm still heaving a big-ass trunk of junk—and I don't mean my backside, which was never all that large and has gotten even smaller from all the yoga, thank you very much.

"Where exactly are you going this weekend?" I ask. "I know you said a church. But remind me where?"

"Remember those terrible arsons in the news last year? Well a Baptist church in West Virginia's been rebuilding—but they're finding it slow going. Several interfaith communities from around here have volunteered to go down to help. I'm sorry Yonatan can't come—he's so much handier than I am. But I started telling you the other day: he got the green light to organize a fantastic retreat. Lots of big-name authors and such. He needs to get the hotel and all the participants nailed down ASAP."

I'm about to ask for more details about this intriguing event when Radha chimes in.

"Why can't I come with you, Mom? You know I'm good with a hammer."

"You're great with tools, as you are with everything," Anna agrees, bathing her daughter in the deep love I always wished someone had rained on me at ten—or at thirty-three. "But we discussed this. I won't be back till Wednesday and you can't miss school. You'll have fun staying with Aunt Lorna."

I blanch momentarily at her use of my name. Ever since I was a kid, I've never liked *Lorna*—it sounds so harsh and ugly, especially compared to those that flow off the tongue, like Anna or, of course, Angelica. Or Radha. Or Janelle. Lor-na. Yuck, yuck, yuck. And when a sugary voice like Anna's says it, it sounds even more discordant.

"I know I'll have a great time here," Radha agrees, an answer that shakes me out of my funk. *I just love that girl!*

"You have time to stay for tea?" I ask Anna. "I've got quite a collection of herbals."

"Thanks. That'd be nice. But if you prefer, we can spend the time before I catch the bus doing a short, guided meditation. If you want to, that is."

Anna knows full well I want to. I adore her guided meditations. Recently, at my request, she made a few MP3 files for me, which I try to listen to at night. But I appreciate that she has asked. For years, Anna would boss me around, so easily falling back into her childhood role as Mom's deputized lieutenant. She'd make proclamations like, "I'll expect you for dinner next weekend," or "I told Uncle we'd swing by his house for brunch." She did this even after she became a minister! Crazily, she'd give the most beautiful sermon at her church about how we are all equal; then she'd swing by my house and not even realize she was making me subservient. We laugh about it now that she's strangled the habit, but for a long time, it was about as funny as finding a shark in the bathtub.

Radha and Anna remove their shoes and silently follow me to my bedroom. My feet are filled with a lightness as I walk. I guess I'm already influenced by their higher vibrations. I lead them to my altar. In addition to the original items—the carved stones, singing bowl, the Kwan Yin—I've added the meditating Jesus and small candles in each of the seven colors of the chakras. A strip of peach silk is draped across the ceiling, as they did in our room at the yoga retreat. I'm thrilled when Anna smiles after spying my setup. Much as I'd like to break my need for my family's approval, it does feel good to get Anna's nod.

I grab three cushions and set them on the floor. After they sit, Anna and Radha pretzel up their legs in the full lotus position. One foot is atop each opposite thigh, with their knees completely relaxed on the floor. I've been working for months to force my legs into this pose, and the best I can do is drag one foot partially up the thigh—a move that is always accompanied by a blast of dynamite beneath my knee. *Oh well, maybe someday*, I think, happily accepting what is. I close my eyes.

"Beloved power of the universe, we revel in our connection with you," Anna begins, and though my eyes are shut, I instinctively raise them to the ceiling, as if I haven't learned by now that God does not sit on a gaudy throne miles above the clouds. "Let us begin by focusing on this energy of the highest spirit, an energy that connects us all. Indeed, we are one with that spirit." She pauses, and I settle contentedly into her words. "Now, let us experience that energy as it courses through our body, one part at a time. Begin with the feet, zeroing in on how this energy animates our toes, and heels and instep. . . . Now feel it in the legs, and the torso, then moving around to our hands and arms, and finally to our head." She pauses again, and I spend the time noticing the happy rumbling inside me. Finally, Anna continues. "Take a moment to visualize this extraordinary body of ours in a wonderful natural setting. Maybe it's a beach, or perhaps a park or a forest. Anywhere you love to be. Imagine yourself there, tuned in to that place in all its detail. Especially observe the life force, the vitality, that abounds there."

Anna stops talking and is, no doubt, already prancing in Yosemite or the Himalayas. Unfortunately, my mind has launched itself on its typical ricochet: *Did I remember to lock the front door after they came in? Is it getting warm in here—maybe I need to lower the thermostat? I probably should have unplugged the phone before we started; if it rings now, it will be really distracting.* I chuckle at this last thought, since I'm quite distracted of my own accord. I wonder if it would disappoint Anna to know I have such trouble settling my mind. *No*, I realize. Anna would say this is common.

I'm finally able to push these intrusions aside and picture myself in my preferred location: Martha's Vineyard, the gorgeous island where Brad and I spent a weekend soon after we started dating. I envision us sitting on the beach, as we did for hours that first evening, watching the waves crash and the sandpipers dance. Brad kept asking to leave the beach so we could ride the scooters we'd rented to check out the local bars. But I wouldn't budge. I was captivated by the incredible beauty of the water. Only after the sun set and the mosquitoes came out in droves did I finally relent. By the following morning, we felt a deep bond to each other, which I was convinced at least partially resulted from our breathtaking surroundings and Brad attributed to the great sex we had when we returned to the hotel. It's no wonder I'm picturing myself back there, relishing water so blue, it's like the sky poured its contents into the sea, and a boyfriend ripe with possibilities— rather than one I have questions about and who, in any case, is too busy to see me or, especially in the last few days (which annoys me to no end), even to call.

After a while Anna breaks the silence. "Now, as we leave that beautiful, magical place, we remember that that beauty and magic always surround us, no matter where we are. And we ask for the continued knowing that, wherever we find ourselves, we remember that we are eternally connected to that magic, which is our higher self, our spirit." She pauses before concluding. "Now, slowly return your focus to the room you're in right now. And let us say, Amen."

"Amen," I echo in the softer, more lyrical voice I've come to expect after one of Anna's visualizations.

I'm still returning my hazy focus back to the room when I realize Anna's already standing, evidently eager not to miss her ride. Radha and I accompany her to the front door, where we exchange our good-bye hugs and kisses.

"Bye, Mom. Love you to infinity," Radha says when her mother finally steps outside.

"Love you to infinity, too." Anna gives Radha another last-minute squeeze in the doorway before she gets in her car and drives away.

I smile at Radha. "I love you to infinity, too, you know. I'm so happy you're here! Why don't we turn our evening into a real pajama party? Let's change, then we can play games, watch a movie, or read together. Whaddya think?"

"Sounds like fun!"

"Wonderful." I drag Radha's suitcase to my home office, which doubles as my guest room. Earlier, I'd put on a clean sheet and an extra blanket. The forecasters predict a chill. I watch as she opens the suitcase and digs through her clothes, pulling out a cute pair of pajamas with a firefighter motif. Once I'm sure she has everything she needs, I head down the hall to my own bedroom.

In the fifteen minutes it takes me to change, wash my face, and brush my teeth and hair, I'm suddenly overtaken by a bone-deep exhaustion. By the time I leave my bathroom, I can barely lift my arms.

"Radha, would you mind terribly if I went to sleep now?" I call from the hall, feeling like I don't even have the energy to walk out of my room. "I don't know what's come over me. I'm suddenly so exhaus—" A big yawn interrupts. "—ted."

"No problem, Aunt Lorna," Radha giggles from the hallway. "I'll just read a book in my room or something." She says this so sweetly that I wish I could find a way to bottle her up and spray myself a little dose of Radha every day.

"You sure? I feel kinda bad about not entertaining you."

"I'm sure. It's totally fine."

"Okay, then. Good night, sweetheart." I drag my limp body to my bed, where I pass out fast.

Apparently, the chill is not limited to the nighttime—at least not to my muscles and bones. Despite two blankets pulled nearly over my head, I'm freezing when I awake in the morning. Did I inhale or exhale? Heck, I'm just happy to breathe. Worse, my throat feels like it's cut in pieces, and when I try to sit up, I discover I'm woozy. *Agh. Ich. How could I have come down with something so quickly? And how will I be able to show Radha a good time?*

"Hi, Aunt Lorna," Radha says, opening my bedroom door and craning her happy head inside upon hearing that I've awakened. She walks in, but when she gets a few feet from my bed, her wide smile disappears. "Are you sick?"

"It's that obvious, huh?" I say, my voice cracking like a budding adolescent's. "I seem to have the flu. I feel awful."

"Don't say that!" Radha commands. "If you say you feel bad, you'll keep that 'awful feeling' energy in place. That's what Mom says. She says I should always tell myself, 'My body is in radiant health,' even if I feel sick. It really does work. Sometimes it takes a while, though, so you should stay in bed. I can be your nurse."

"My body is in radiant health," I croak, my voice so Big Bird–ish, Radha laughs. I'm not sure I believe it, but right now, I'd swallow a quart of horse manure if someone told me it would put the remnants of my head back together. "I'm sorry, Radha. I think I'm gonna need to rest for a while. Will you be okay?"

"Of course. I'm a big kid," Radha insists, although her wrinkled, freckled nose emphasizes her adorable youthfulness. "You don't have to worry about me. You think about feeling better." She skips out of the bedroom and down the hall.

It's one in the afternoon when I emerge from a sleep as deep as the Colca Canyon. Radha's clattering away in my kitchen. I assume she's making herself lunch until I realize that such loud banging could be cooking only if she were pulverizing grain for an army. I slip on a robe and climb out of bed, noting when I'm halfway across the bedroom that I am feeling better. Not quite in radiant health, but closer to it than I was this morning.

I come up short when I see Radha sitting on the kitchen floor near my pantry. Dozens of cans and boxes are scattered all around her.

"Did you have an accident, sweetie?" I ask, nervously scanning the closet to see if shelves are broken.

"Nope," she says, smiling. "Just making myself useful while you were resting. I already cleaned your china closet—boy, you had dusty dishes! Now I'm doing your pantry. You know, you have cans of soup way past their expiration dates." She holds up a dented, dusty can of Manhattan chowder. "A few of your teas are expired, too."

"I didn't know tea expires," I say, picking up a box of green tea from the floor and noting that, indeed, it passed its "best by" date by more than a year. Chalk that up to my coffee addiction, which usually beats out thoughts of tea, even though I've recently bought a slew of herbals. "It's sweet of you to help. And I really appreciate it. But I wish you'd gone out to play."

"I did! You've been sleeping for hours. I jumped rope. Played hopscotch."

"Oh, good," I say.

"I met your neighbor, Ms. Slinkins. What a nice lady! She brought me oatmeal cookies she made, and even went back inside to get soy milk, even though I told her the water I had was fine. We talked a while. She told me about her daughter. Such a sad story!"

My mouth snaps open like a whale spotting prey. I didn't know Ruth had a daughter.

"What'd she say?" I ask, embarrassed to admit my ignorance about the woman's life.

"She said I reminded her of Faith. That we had the same wavy hair and that we both had freckles." Radha pauses, deep in thought. "Aunt Lorna, is it okay that I felt good being compared to a teenager, even though I'm sure Ms. Slinkins was sad to be reminded of her?" Radha suddenly sounds like the child she is, rather than the old soul I've always known her to be.

"Of course it is, honey," I say, still ashamed to admit to Radha that I have no idea what she's talking about. "What else did Ruth, uh, Ms. Slinkins, tell you about her daughter?"

"That she was fourteen when that cancer killed her. That her husband left her after that. Seems like too much sadness for one person to handle!"

My whale mouth returns. I've spoken to Ruth many times— well, more than a few, anyway. Well, maybe *spoken* is too strong a word. She and I occasionally exchanged pleasantries as she worked in her front yard, and of course there were our more recent "talks" about the sprinkler. I knew only that she was divorced. Truth be told, I'd imagined that one morning she'd grabbed her gardening tools and shoveled her husband out the door, perhaps because he turned on the sprinklers too early! I'd pegged her as a selfish biddy. But hearing this story changes everything.

"You look surprised," Radha says, stating the obvious. "You don't think that's a lot of sadness? Or is it that she gave me the soy milk and cookies? Maybe she hasn't been so nice to you?"

"No, sweetie. I haven't been too nice to *her*. I had no idea!"

I recall something Janelle told me about a spiritual workshop she once attended. A woman sitting a row ahead turned to the people behind her and said, "I would love all of you if I knew your stories!" At the time Janelle told me this, I thought, *If that woman was so spiritual, she would love everybody without knowing their stories.* Now I understand that while that may be ideal, knowing what's happened to them does make a difference.

I have a sudden urge to find Ruth and give her a big, apologetic hug for every mean thought I've had about her and, most of all, for not cherishing her enough to learn her story. But I don't. Not only don't I have the courage to do that, the pounding in my head soon returns with a vengeance (so much for being "in radiant health") and keeps me in bed for the rest of the day.

When I wake up Sunday morning, I am completely better. But by then, the impulse to apologize has faded.

ॐ

Radha and I have a wonderful day. We sujal and do yoga in my living room in the morning, and it doesn't faze me when my headstand plops over within fifteen seconds while she holds her pose stock-still for fifteen minutes. After a lunch of soup and salad, which she helps me prepare, we drive to the park and rent bicycles, pointing out the gorgeous flower blossoms we pass. When the sun goes down, we head to a vegetarian restaurant for an early dinner. I'd found the place searching online after I knew Radha would be staying over. The restaurant is run by monks who shower before cooking. They claim it makes the food taste purer. I'm unsure about the notion that well-soaped armpits can influence my taste buds. Then I take a bite. The zest in my "Zen platter"—rice, beans, seaweed, and tons of fresh roasted vegetables—defies any other explanation.

We head back to my house a few minutes before Yonatan's scheduled arrival. Radha quickly packs up her things. "I'm so glad you felt better today, Aunt Lorna. I had a great time."

"I had a great time, too. I'm glad I got into 'radiant health.'" I laugh, and she joins in. I don't want this joyous bond to be broken. "I hope you'll stay over again. You don't have to wait till your mom goes away. Come any weekend."

"I will. I loved our day today!"

When the doorbell rings, we race to the foyer—Radha's

generous words propelling my legs, so I get there before she does. I open the door and am greeted by a bedraggled-looking man.

"Dad!" Radha squeezes him. I'm thrilled to see how close they are, especially since by the time I was ten, my father had been out of my life for years.

"Yonatan, come in." I step back so he has room to enter. "I'd say you're looking well. But I have to be truthful. You look horrible." I'm pleased that I can be honest around my sister's family.

"That bad, huh?" He futilely tries to smooth down his saw grass hair. "I was so busy this weekend, I didn't get a chance to shower. Guess I should have thought to do that before I came."

"No worries. It's fine."

"I suppose Angelica told you about my retreat. It's so much bigger than any I've done, in the caliber of the speakers and the throngs of attendees expected. I guess I'm a bit overwhelmed."

"It sounds like a fabulous event," I say. "When and where is this mysterious retreat—and most important, can I go?"

"I'd love it if you did. It's in the Berkshires. Third weekend in June. I'll have Angelica give you a brochure next time you see her. I'd better have them ready by then."

"Darn. The one weekend I can't make it. My big ice cream event is that Saturday. I guess I'll be there in spirit."

Yonatan smiles. "I'll look for your spirit, then."

"Want to stay awhile?" I ask, aware that I'm not being such a good host, as we're still standing in the foyer. "Want something to eat? I've got nuts, apples, vegetable chips, a few unspoiled boxes of teas—"

"Thanks, but we gotta run. Radha's got school tomorrow, and I've gotta get back to making more calls."

"Another time, then." I realize I've never entertained Yonatan without Anna. Although we've gone out together numerous times, Anna and I usually hog the spotlight. I'd love to get to know Yonatan on his own, since he is a wonderful person. I vow to invite him over soon. "Have you heard from Anna, er, Angelica? How's the build going?"

"It's harder work than she thought. Says her muscles are killing her—even though she's in great shape from all the yoga. But the church people are very grateful. She says their love and appreciation make the exhaustion worthwhile. And they're making tons of progress."

"I'm sure Angelica feels good about volunteering for such a worthy cause."

Radha opens her mouth to respond. I've spent enough time with her today to know what she's about to say, so I head her off. "I know, I know. Your mom tries to feel good no matter what she's doing. But you've gotta admit it's easier when you're doing something altruistic."

"Sure," Radha says. "But Mom would say that's less of a challenge."

"Okay, enough sermonizing for the day," Yonatan interrupts, perhaps because he fears I'll resent being lectured by a ten-year-old—even though I'm thrilled to glean her incredible wisdom. I do detect a hint of pride in his eyes. He looks at me earnestly. "Thank you, Lorna, for taking such good care of Radha. I'm sure she enjoyed herself."

"Thank *you* for letting her stay here," I say. "I'm sure I got more out of it than she did." My mind alights on Ruth, and how Radha has helped me see her through a new set of eyes.

I walk outside with them, then blow big kisses as Yonatan pulls his car away. As I turn to head inside, I glimpse Ruth's shadow in her front bay window. I know exactly what I want to do. I walk over to Ruth's house, noticing the colorful array of daffodils, hyacinths, and tulips surrounding her porch—funny how I've never paid attention to them before, even though I know she works hard on her garden. I breathe in their beauty before ringing the bell. It takes several minutes before Ruth's creaky joints get her to the door.

"Lorna!" she says, clearly stunned to see me. "Is anything wrong? Did my cookies make your niece sick? I thought I should maybe have checked with you before giving anything to her, but she said—"

"Everything's terrific, Ruth. I've just been thinking about what a crappy neighbor I've been, and how I'd be honored by the chance to get to know you better."

"How wonderful! I was just making tea. Would you like to come in?"

I wrap her in a massive hug, which startles us both. "I would love to."

Chapter 12

Still high from Radha's visit, I arrive at work early the next morning, eager for some quiet time to center myself before everyone arrives. I sit at my desk, put my feet flat on the floor, pull my shoulders back, relax my neck, and close my eyes. I consciously ride my breath as it slowly goes in, then out, in, out, in, out. . . .

When a thought pushes into my mind, as it inevitably does, I'm able to watch it in a detached manner without getting pulled in. Just like the books say, it's as if the ideas are a movie on a screen or a cloud passing in the sky. I feel so connected to the timeless energy of my higher self that I have the rare experience of not peeking at my desk clock even once during the fifteen minutes. It's my best sujal ever—a textbook session of joining with my higher self as it witnesses my body, breath, and mind, instead of erroneously thinking these physical aspects are all there is to me.

I'm tentatively emerging from the meditation when I hear lyrical chimes dancing their way toward me. I decide to float on the sound, melting into its sweetness. As I inhale and exhale another round, the sound repeats and I drift on. But rather than becoming fainter the farther I travel, the ringing continues unabated. Eventually, the constant bell yanks me back to the reality of my office. It's the phone.

I'm not going to answer, I think. *I want to end my meditation with a gradual reemergence into this world of form.* I chant softly under my breath. *"Shri ram jay ram jay jay ram."*

"Whadya say?" I hear Brendan's voice ask. I open my eyes and look up to see he's stopped outside my cubicle, eyebrows raised.

"Say? Oh, nothing. I was just humming."

"Oh." He looks dejected. "I thought you were talking to me."

"No. But if you've something you want to discuss, I'm happy to listen." I'm feeling particularly generous right now, even toward Brendan.

"Not me. You were the one mumbling." He walks away.

Focused and peaceful, I turn to my work. I am incredibly productive all morning, generating several program budgets, which usually takes me days to accomplish. I also nail down more details for the sundae event, and still have time to return the calls of five outside companies looking for our co-sponsorships. One proposal, to use the ice cream paintings from our museum event as cell phone wallpaper, has possibilities. All this before eleven thirty!

Still, I have a lot on my agenda for today, so I plan to eat lunch at my office. I break out the sandwich and iced green tea I bought on my way in. The sandwich is avocado salad with sprouts, lettuce, and tomato on pita bread, now that my vegetarian aspirations have gotten a boost from being with Radha. I take a huge bite as my cell phone rings. I glance at the caller ID. It's Brad, who hasn't called or even texted me in five whole days. I let it ring one more time while I chew and swallow.

"Lorna," he says the moment I answer, before I even say hello. "Please forgive me for not calling since your night with your mother. Although I did try you at work earlier this morning. Anyway, how'd it go with your mom?"

I'm not sure if it's because I'm hurt that Brad's been ignoring me or because he mentioned my mother that I react as I do. In any event, I land like a boulder. Thud.

It takes a moment for me to decide how to answer. Then I lace into him. "It was awful, just as I expected it to be. But five days after the fact is a little late to be getting that information from someone you think of as your girlfriend, no?"

"I admit it: I'm a shit. But I have an excuse. Been working twenty-four/seven—not coming up for air. And, sweetie, it's finally paying off, because we're all systems go. You know I'm gonna make it up to you. Although you're certainly within your rights to be pissed. I do find you adorable when you're mad. And when you're not mad, of course. Forgive me?"

As always, I'm sucked in by the magnetism of his charm. It's one of the many things I love about Brad. But I also feel that vague hesitation, the one that caused me to ask that question at the workshop. Anyway, I'm tired of playing second fiddle to his job.

"Why don't you call me after your launch. We're not going to have any time together before then anyway."

"I'm really sorry, Lorna. I miss you terribly. And I understand your frustration. Do know that the blue face you can't see over the phone is me holding my breath till I see you again. I do love you."

"I love you too," I admit.

For the rest of the afternoon, questions about Brad consume my thinking. I'm filled with a tango of competing thoughts: I do adore him, but is he my soul mate? He's fun and sexy, but he puts work ahead of me. And most important, he's everything I've ever wished for in a guy, except for that one, increasingly crucial aspect: spirituality. I'm seeing more and more that my self-discovery is an important part of who I am, but Brad has zero interest.

Despite the rumination, I don't resolve these issues. When

five o'clock comes, I decide to stop worrying about them, and head out to attend a yoga class with Janelle.

ॐ

Wednesday afternoon rolls around faster than I can say *breathe, breathe, breathe.* Okay, maybe this after-work shindig sneaked up on me because I haven't much remembered that crucial bit of wisdom today. Had I been sucking the air in long and slow, keeping my focus on this calming inspiration (literally!), I might not have shoulder blades so tight, they're practically knitted together. I keep telling myself this is only one evening, that I put up with my coworkers all day, so what's the big deal about a few extra hours? But it's because I had to push myself to be gracious to Brendan and Carletta all afternoon, that my brain is screaming. I want to go home to my spiritual books, my yoga, my sujaling, my phone call with Janelle. I don't want dinner and a movie with these clowns.

Plus, it's been a long day. Happily, I've made tremendous headway on my sundae soiree. I've gotten all the necessary city permits, no easy feat in New York. I've sent early teasers to the major media and have heard that most plan to attend. The top network show, *AM Live,* is talking about filming that morning from the park, and their publicity people even asked if one of their hosts could climb the ladder to put on the cherry. We didn't commit, but that would be quite a coup.

After calling just about every farmer in the West and Midwest, I had to concede that the one I spoke with (okay, yelled at) last week was right: No cherry grows big enough to top our whopper. I was in despair over this, but today Michelle spoke with a grower in Linden, California, the self-proclaimed "cherry capital of the world," who offered a brilliant solution. He swears he can glue a huge array of cherries together to look like one giant maraschino. We said yes immediately.

I also got a candy company to donate barrels of chocolate

syrup. And the other day a famous carpenter volunteered to build the bowl we'll need. He's doing it for free, even delaying a kitchen renovation for a big Wall Street tycoon. He told me this will be much more fun. The tycoon's wife took it upon herself to complain to a gossip columnist, so today my event got some unexpected coverage on Page Six. That exposure led to media inquiries from some of the smaller publications and Web sites I hadn't yet reached out to. I'm certainly not complaining about this good fortune. But the upshot is, I'm beat.

The only problem I continue to wrestle with is the logistics of how we'll keep the ice cream frozen that morning. Michelle and I have spoken to dozens of trucking lines, but each tells us the same thing: Their huge freezer trucks are prohibited from driving on the paved pedestrian paths that surround the Great Lawn, and they can't stop traffic by idling on the roads cutting through the park. I've a nagging sense that has plagued me since Day One that there's an obvious solution to the problem, but I can't see it. Doug's starting to get rattled about this crucial detail, and even though I assured him this morning that it's as good as solved, when I'm honest with myself, I admit it's kind of freaking me out, too.

But right now I've got other angst to focus on: this evening. Doug's already selected the film and bought the tickets. I guess he wisely realized that getting consensus from this crazy crowd would be near impossible. The movie he picked is a biopic of a 1940s crooner. Not being into that kind of music, I'd never heard of the guy. Still, that choice is better than some other films currently playing: A horror story about creatures that spring from Boston's underground plumbing. A thriller where a tidal wave crashes over the Capitol. And a drama about a pizza driver who delivers murder with the pepperoni. I've been hoping since first seeing the yellow memo that Doug wouldn't go for these. As part of my spiritual quest, I'm trying to feed my brain positive images, and those films hardly qualify.

It's not the movie that's the problem, though. It's the people. I would never choose to socialize with the vast majority of my colleagues. The more I think about who is going to be there— Carletta and Brendan topping the list—the worse I feel.

After sulking for a while, I decide these thoughts aren't helping me. Maybe I can "reframe" them, as some of the spiritual teachers put it, to be more uplifting. How would those authors see it? I suspect they would view tonight as an opportunity to put into practice all the teachings I'm trying to embrace: to view everyone with loving-kindness and encourage them to do the same with others. I could see this evening as a sort of ministry.

"Could you gag about tonight?" my assistant, Michelle, says as she stands on her chair and sticks her head over the wall separating our cubes, sunny paper in hand. "Doug doesn't pay me enough to take over my social life."

"I know you'd rather be with your boyfriend. But maybe it won't be so bad," I offer.

"What happy juice do you have in that cup?" She points to the coffee sitting on my desk. "Just think, by the end of the evening, we might know every friggin' score Brendan got on every test since the fourth grade!"

"Probably since kindergarten," I commiserate. "But based on the tone of Doug's memo, and the way he's talked about it every day since, he isn't likely to change his mind. Unless you're gonna toss yourself in front of a bus—and if you do, you'd better finish the job, or Doug may do it for you!—we might as well make the best of it. Accept that this is what we're doing tonight. Maybe we can even find a way to enjoy it."

Michelle looks at me cross-eyed. "I don't think I like this new you. I preferred it when you wouldn't go down without a scream to rival Neve Campbell's. This go-with-the-flow stuff makes me wanna vomit." Although I never specifically told Michelle about my spiritual practice, I have discussed my desire to be nicer to others and more accepting of everyone's flaws.

As if a puppeteer pulled her backstage, Michelle's head disappears over the wall. I chuckle under my breath. I can make myself vomit, too. I mean who wouldn't prefer to stay home—or even walk over scorching coals—than go out with these nutters? But it's precisely because I think this that forcing me to socialize with them may be perfect. After all, my evening with Ruth turned out lovely. Although we're dissimilar in many ways—I had nothing to contribute to her long discourse on lilacs and liriope— it warmed both our hearts to bond. And I've developed a level of compassion for her that I didn't know I was capable of feeling.

ॐ

At five o'clock, nearly two dozen of us march behind Doug down the elevator and out the building. As we head toward the theater a few blocks away, I feel a bit like a kid being dragged by her father to a family outing no one wants to attend. Of course, I have no such memory of being taken on such a day—I don't much recall my dad before he went missing. As we wind our way down the street, I'm filled with an odd combination of maybe-this-will-be-valuable scrambled up with a much larger measure of can't-I-please-go-home?

Michelle huddles close to me as we enter the theater lobby. Doug hands the usher the tickets, and we all head down to theater number three. Michelle has practically glued herself to my backside, no doubt because she doesn't want to get stuck sitting next to Brendan. Of course, neither do I—which is why at the last minute, I speed up and step directly behind him. As I take the seat next to Brendan, I know my spiritual cheering squad (aka Anna, Radha, and Janelle) would be proud. I end up on the aisle, so Michelle has to start a new row. Unfortunately (since Michelle is not aiming for her own spiritual trial), Carletta sits at her other side.

I'm hardly confident I can ace this evening. I spend a moment taking a centering breath that turns out to be so deep, it leaves me momentarily light-headed. Once the wooziness clears, I remind myself that sometimes you've gotta earn your angel wings. I envision Brendan pinning mine on me, military-graduation style. This makes me smile.

Brendan must be picking up signals that I'm thinking about him. He abruptly turns in my direction. "Wasn't it wonderful of Doug to bring us all together like this?"

"Yes, fine." I try not to let irony tinge my voice.

"I was thrilled to get Doug's memo. Been wanting to see this movie anyway. I love all the old crooners. I think my voice has that same kind of smoothness. Don't you?"

As his smile widens, I watch Brendan's teeth take over his face. Those pearly whites must be veneers, I think. Maybe he's trying to match the ultra-white shirt peeking out beneath the suit jacket a guy like Brendan never removes. Fortunately, after a few seconds, I stop these wild mustangs before they trample through my brain.

I try to recall what Brendan was saying before his grin exploded all over. "Yes, your voice *is* lovely," I say when the memory returns.

The houselights pick this moment to darken, mercifully ending our conversation.

The movie is tedious, the slow story line exacerbating my lack of interest in the music. Rather than sit and suffer, I decide to use this time to practice nonjudgment. I'm aware that too often my first instinct is to be other people's judge and jury—and a harsh one, at that. It's something I'm committed to changing. Still, I've found that the habit is not easily broken, probably because it's been ingrained in me for so many years.

Recently, I participated in an online workshop about embracing those parts of ourselves we despise. Early in the session, each of us was asked to introduce ourselves on the message board as our most embarrassing trait.

"Hi, I'm terribly judgmental," I typed immediately.

"I'm short-tempered." "I'm full of envy." "I don't feel worthy," others wrote. When several women said, "I'm judgmental, too!" I realized I am not alone. Yet neither owning up to it nor recognizing its ubiquitousness has made it stop. I know that psychologists would say I use these harsh verdicts to cover up my own perceived inadequacies, but I'm eager for them to be gone. I want to see the good in everyone, not home in on their flaws.

Perhaps this practice will be easier if I start with the imagined scenes in the movie, rather than with flesh-and-blood human beings? I quickly find that it isn't. Hard as I try to observe the film without judging, my mind leaps to negative conclusions: What bad casting—that woman looks more like his mother than like his wife. The daughter is so thin, she must be anorexic. That backup singer didn't take sufficient music lessons. Dollar weeds all.

I need a different tack. I settle on a wonderful exercise I learned in that online seminar: appreciating the small things in my immediate surroundings. The theory is that priming the mind on basic items makes it easier to ultimately see the positive in larger, tougher fare. Kind of like preheating an oven before you slide in the soufflé.

I glance around the theater: cheery curtains, comfy seats, crisp clear sound system—thank you all. A bright EXIT sign—I honor your steady light should there ever be a true emergency. The huge, wide screen. The delicious smell of popcorn. A cast that worked hard to make this movie, especially the little guys like the gaffer, makeup assistant, and the people who catered the lunches on the set. I watch my mind take a sharp right turn as I recall a discussion with my cousin years ago. Wade had catered the set of a B movie back when he was getting his party business off the ground. He complained that the actors thought food materialized out of thin air. Feeling completely unappreciated for his efforts, he never agreed to work a movie set again. After a few minutes, I realize I have lost my focus, so I bring it back. Thank you, sun, for providing the gorgeous sunset in this scene in the movie, and you, candles, for the velvety ambience in this one.

Like a Ping-Pong ball, my brain flips again, this time to the candle-lit yoga class that Janelle and I took at our center recently. I'm so happy I know Janelle. Being with her feels warm and soothing. She's so accepting of my flaws. Last week, she spent an hour on the phone trying to convince me I did my best during my horrible dinner with my mother. (I'd told her what happened, but skipped the part about Janelle being the topic that sparked the battle.) Janelle also keeps me calm about my confusion over Brad, reminding me that it's not something I have to decide this instant. I so appreciate that we're friends.

The love in my heart toward Janelle suddenly bursts wide open. That would be wonderful, except this powerful emotion is accompanied by a sudden rush of tears. I start to panic. As much as I admire what I read in Don Miguel Ruiz's masterpiece, *The Four Agreements*, to not take anything personally, I do care—a lot—about not being the butt of tomorrow's office gossip. I can already hear it in my head: *Did you see Lorna bawling her eyes out during the movie?* someone will say. *Yes,* someone else will reply. *And it wasn't even at a part that was sad. She's so ridiculous!*

I refuse to be the blotchy, mascara-faced poster child at tomorrow's water cooler. To prevent Brendan from seeing the tears that are rapidly amassing, I lean over, pretending to remove something from my shoe. I quickly wipe my tears. By the time I pop back up, I'm in control.

"Your foot okay?" Brendan asks, surprising me with his concern.

"Fine now, thanks."

"Do you have a splinter? I've tweezers in my pocket if you need." Offering something without an obvious payback has never been Brendan's style.

"No thanks. I think it was just a pebble. But . . . thanks."

I don't know how the movie ends. I don't care. I spend the

remaining time appreciating my colleagues one by one, visualizing their best qualities, which in some cases I admit are hard to find. It especially takes a while when I get to Brendan, but eventually I focus on how sweet it was for him to care about my "splinter." And Carletta? Well, she certainly is persistent and determined.

After the movie ends and the credits have rolled, the houselights turn on. We stand to leave. Michelle catches my eye, flashing her displeasure to make sure I haven't forgotten. Carletta is prattling on about her pregnant cat, leaving Michelle no choice but to feign interest until we all pour into the lobby.

"So . . . what did everyone think of the film?" Doug asks.

"The ending was so melodramatic. And so unnecessary," replies Carly Harris, one of our new administrative assistants and, if I recall correctly, a recent film school graduate.

"I thought the plot was kinda slow. But the actor who played the bartender was hot," Hallie the receptionist chimes in, her long lashes batting away.

"The music was the best of any film I've seen," the always-sunny Jamal responds.

A similar dialogue is being played out by moviegoers around the lobby. "How was the film?" "Did you like it?" "Was it better than you expected?" I vow not to judge the film anymore—and not only because I didn't pay attention. I'm coming to agree with Eckhart Tolle that this need to lock everything into a mental construct is a sickness in our society, and that our rush to render a verdict on every movie is part of the continuum that leads me to judge other people. Isn't it better to simply enjoy each experience as it unfolds, without jumping in to categorize, label, or condemn?

Doug goes around our group one by one, eliciting feedback, no doubt to validate his choice of movie. When he gets to me, I smile. I feel perfectly contented, but my lack of response unnerves him.

"Lorna, don't you have anything to say?" he asks pointedly.

"I certainly do. Which way to the restaurant? I'm starved."

Chapter 13

Doug's arranged for us to eat at Sybill's, a new Thai place I've been dying to try since a newspaper reviewer raved about the delicious pad thai, calling it a sweet and tangy treat. I haven't had pad thai in years, but I'm eager after that ringing endorsement.

We walk the few blocks to the crowded restaurant, where the owner escorts us to a private back room. Three long tables are set for our dinner, each covered with a shimmering blue tablecloth and exotic china. I'm near the back of the group, so by the time I enter the room, most of the seats have been taken. The remaining ones are at the table with Brendan and Carletta. I take the seat next to Carletta. At least Michelle, Doug, and Jamal are also here.

I raise my eyes to the chandelier—old habits die hard—and silently offer up a little prayer. *Thanks, universe, for giving me this opportunity to practice my generosity and love.* I say this mostly to convince myself that sitting here is not the massive bummer part of me senses it to be.

The waitress walks around, taking orders. Others must have seen the same review because there's a run on the pad thai.

While the waitress makes her way down the table, I look around the room. There are fabulous wood carvings of Asian elephants, stunning golden statues of religious deities, and giant hand-painted paper fans hanging from the ceiling. *It's all magnificent*, I tell myself, *and so, deep down, are the people at this table.* I close my eyes for a moment to let that thought sink in.

When I open my eyes, the waitress is standing next to me, waiting for my order.

"A glass of sparkling water, please. A salad with peanut dressing. And, for my entrée, the vegetable pad thai."

"Good thing the chef's been making extra since that review came out," the waitress replies brightly. "Although I have to admit the guy was right. You all won't be sorry."

We certainly aren't. When the entrées arrive, the pad thai features moist noodles, crunchy vegetables, and a perfect sauce. Chatting with Carletta isn't bad, either. Mostly, she talks about a novel she just finished reading. I discuss a rock band I've discovered on the Internet. At some point, everyone at the table gets caught up in a long riff about the current state of climate change and the environment.

After the waitress clears the table, a lull emerges in the conversation. Suddenly, out of the blue, my hands start shaking. At first, I'm not clear why I should feel nervous. I'm having dinner with coworkers, and it's actually going well. But when I probe a little deeper, the answer washes over me.

For me to call this evening a success, it has to be about more than exchanging pleasantries with Brendan at the movie or with Carletta over pasta. I want to help all of us remove the masks we hide behind every day, to better discover our true connection.

I close my eyes to screw up my nerve. I silently tell myself that it's okay to feel anxious, as long as I don't let it paralyze me.

Now is the time, I coax myself silently. *But really, why do I have to?* another part of me replies. *I had a lovely, if superficial, chat with Carletta. That should be enough.* But my hands haven't stopped trembling; on some level, I know that isn't sufficient. An evening avoiding a faux pas may have been good for the Lorna of old, but the newer me wants so much more.

Just do it, Lorna.

Do it.

Do it!

Still, I hesitate.

DO IT!

An inexplicable calm overtakes me. I take a big breath, face the people at my table, and begin. "We all know we're here because Doug wants us to bond this evening. I'm sure that many of you, and I admit this includes me, are here because he gave us no choice." I nod in Doug's direction. "But since we *are* here, I'm thinking we might as well make the most of it and truly bond."

I continue, more boldly than I'm feeling. "I'd like to propose we go around the table one at a time, each of us sharing something about our lives outside the office. Things people here don't know. Maybe it's something in your personal life. Or from your past that you've never told us." This earns me another incredulous look from Michelle, who sits diagonally across the table. Clearly, I was not in my spiritual mode when I hired her. Right now I wish I had a fellow seeker in my corner.

Everyone seems vaguely stunned, but nobody objects. So I plow on. "Well, it's my idea, so I guess I'll go first." This seems to placate the others. I notice their tense jaws relaxing.

If it's rare for me to open up about my personal life, it's unheard of to do so before a group of sharp-penciled critics such as this one. But I'm inspired by the way learning about Ruth has transformed my feelings for her. That's why it seems like such a perfect thing to do tonight.

What intimacy am I at least moderately okay about sharing? I consider talking about my new bond with Ruth or, even more daring, my relationship with Brad. No one but Michelle knows what's up with him. But what would I say? I'm not sure myself where Brad and I stand. After a moment, I decide to go for broke, to reveal the deepest hole I've always had in my heart.

"Okay . . . well . . . a few weeks ago, I had a huge fight with my mother. A real humdinger. The thing is it was far from our first. . . . The disputes between us go back decades." This admission starts out tentatively, like a bird peering out an open cage. But as the words keep coming, I seem to gain confidence that sharing this burden might finally set me free. "I've always felt she doesn't care about me, and I certainly rank lower than my sister. I keep hoping my mother's opinion won't matter, but it does. She always knows the buttons to press to make me angry—and inadequate."

I fill in the details, and the more I do, the happier I feel. For the next five minutes, I reveal all the ways in which I've always been the "lesser" sister. How all my milestones, from graduating with honors to getting job promotions to buying my house, have been diminished by my mother's inevitable disapproval. How I've spent my whole life trying to get past her perception that I'm not good enough. "I should know better, but I can't help wanting to get her nod," I conclude.

This admission is more honest than I intended. I'm not sure I want to see the reaction. I peek first at Doug. His face radiates compassion. That look is repeated all around. Even Brendan and Carletta seem like they care, even though I just handed them evidence that I'm not lovable to the woman who gave birth to me.

After a moment, of course, Brendan rights himself. "Did you ever wonder if maybe your mother is correct to disapprove?" he asks. "Maybe you're not as good as your sister?"

"I've the same problem, Lorna," Jamal jumps in, overshadowing Brendan. "In my case, it's my father, not Mom. I was valedictorian of my high school class, a top college swimmer, and a pretty good wordsmith. I even won a writing prize from *The New Yorker*. Yet nothing I do impresses that man.

The more I succeed, the more I sense his scorn. Intellectually, I know this is *his* issue. But that doesn't stop it from casting a haze."

Before I fully grasp what I've started, the table is abuzz with true confessions. Hallie shares how she stayed in an abusive relationship before finding the courage to leave the bum last spring. She'd convinced herself that she always provoked her husband, and thought if she figured out how to stop, so would he. Doug's secretary, Olivia, describes the heartbreak of her infertility—yet another miscarriage last month, following a string of unsuccessful IVFs.

Another moment of silence passes, which feels satisfying and perfect rather than awkward and cold. Then Carletta breaks it with a tone so soft, I'm shocked it springs from her usually Amazonian lips. "My mother is ill. Stage Four breast cancer." This leaves everyone speechless. I couldn't talk if I wanted to; my throat has seized up completely. Eventually, she continues. "I'm gonna miss her terribly. Unlike your mother, Lorna, mine's a doll. But my biggest worry is my twin. Brianne's been brain-damaged since birth—they say she got stuck in the birth canal and didn't get enough oxygen. She's so caring and trusting. But she functions like a second-grader. She's lived with Mom her whole life. How's she gonna survive without her?"

Twin sister? Brain-damaged? Stage IV cancer? Instinctively, I put my arm around Carletta. By the time I realize what I've done, it's too unwieldy to remove it. I hold the embrace for several minutes; it actually feels nice.

After a moment of suspended silence, Olivia speaks. "What a heartbreaking story! So much pain for you to be carrying around without ever telling us! I didn't know you had a sister."

"I never talk about her. No one wants to hear. Or maybe I never want to say," Carletta says.

"Isn't it something how we live such compartmentalized

lives," Jamal observes. "Olivia going through IVF and miscarriages and pretending all day long like none of that's happening. Hallie getting restraining orders on the sly. Lorna always ducking her mother's emotional punches, and me my dad's. And Carletta, having a mentally ill twin and a dying mother she can be real about only on nights and weekends. It's insane how we wall off parts of our lives from other people, especially the people we see every day."

"I, for one, feel good some of those walls are coming down," I say, pleased that at least one person appreciates my intention. "Anyone else wanna share?"

Several people turn to look at Doug. He squirms under the glare. I'm sure he didn't envision quite this level of bonding when he conceived of the evening.

"What? Why are you all looking at me? I have nothing to say."

"Well, there is your divorce," Carletta pointedly observes, visibly relieved to move the spotlight off herself and happy to get back to her typical nosiness. "It's been, what, a year now?"

"Yeah, a year," Doug says, his voice less edgy, more resigned. He drops his chin a couple of inches. "One tough year."

"What brought it on?" Carletta bulldozes, no doubt feeling entitled to pry after sharing her own bombshell. Of course, the rest of us are all ears. Rumors ricocheted around the office last year, linking Doug's marriage troubles to hanky-panky during a business trip he took with a finance-department employee just before the split. It didn't help the rumors that the woman, who always wore tight miniskirts and killer heels, left the company soon after the divorce papers started flying.

"Not really your business," he answers bluntly. He pauses. We all keep staring, unsure what to say. Then Doug reconsiders. "Okay. Okay. Since you're all being so honest, I'll bite." He clears his throat and looks directly at me. I'm not sure if it's because he thinks I've always believed the rumors (I didn't), or because I'm the one who sent this evening careening down this unexpected path. "My wife took up with someone else." There's an even longer pause before he adds, "a woman, actually."

"Oh, Doug. We had no idea," I say, feeling suddenly responsible for encouraging him to tear the bandages off this still-bleeding wound.

"It's all right. It kind of feels good to admit the truth. I've been hiding it for so long. But it's nothing I could have prevented. So—" He look at each of us in turn. "—you all can stop repeating those stories about my infidelity. Absolutely nothing happened on that business trip—or on any other."

"Anyone here like dessert?" the waitress asks as she walks toward our table, unaware of what she's interrupting.

"Saved by the cheesecake," Doug says, and we all laugh, happy we had those deep moments of sharing, and now equally glad for the opportunity to lighten the mood.

ॐ

The house phone is ringing as I walk in my front door. My body feels so light, I'm barely touching my bamboo floor. The evening I'd dreaded more than a phone call with my mother turned out to be a smashing success. I'm confident my coworkers feel the same newfound compassion toward one another that I do. Oh, I have no doubt the office backstabbing will start again soon, but maybe behind the barbs and power grabs there will be a little tenderness, at least for a while. My legs do a whoop-de-do jig as I reach for the phone.

"Hello, Lorna. It's Don. It's been a long while since we last spoke," the voice barrels in, even before I have a chance to say hello.

Handout Don. Wanting something, of course.

"Don, I thought I made it clear that you were not to call again."

"Well, um, I wanna smooth things over. There's no reason for us not to get along. Anyway, I hear from Angelica that you're in a more spiritually forgiving mood these days."

Oops. I guess I should be. Especially after this evening.

"I think it's great you're focusing on developing your spiritual side. I'm working on that, too," he continues.

Something inside me shifts. My heart, already full from this blissful night, suddenly overflows with kindness toward Don. I know what I want to do.

"Don, I understand you wanna take a seminar."

Silence. "H-how'd you know?"

"A little birdie told me. Actually, she's a pretty big birdie. Maybe even a dodo." I chuckle, but he doesn't laugh at my little joke. I suspect his mind is trying to wrap itself around how I got the advance warning. "Relax, I don't have E.S.P. I was at my mother's when you called looking to get the tuition money from her."

"Oh," Don says, his voice as meek that of a child who's been forced to turn out pockets filled with stolen candy. "That's not why I called, Lorna," he insists, clearly uncomfortable with being exposed. "I just want to restart the communication between us."

"Don, one day you'll learn that honesty pays. Really, I hope you'll learn it right now, because I'm gonna give you the money you're looking for. It's not even a loan. When you're done with your seminar, pay it forward. Give something to someone else so they can benefit."

"Lorna, thank you so much! I don't . . . I don't know what to say."

"No need to say anything, Don. Just tell me the amount, and I'll mail you a check."

When we hang up, I'm bursting with satisfaction, even though I'm now hundreds of dollars poorer. Once I've changed into loose pajamas and taken off my makeup, I sit at my altar. I set my timer to sujal for thirty minutes. It's longer than I've ever done on my own. But I'm confident that tonight, of all nights, I'll be able to ace it.

Chapter 14

Janelle and I climb the steep steps to the stately front door of the Brooklyn brownstone. She arrives first and presses the buzzer for apartment 3C. It's a glorious day, sunny with a sweet breeze. I look up at the façade of the stone building, impressed by its charm, even if it has seen better days. I've always loved these old townhomes. They make me imagine the generations of New Yorkers who have played, loved, and lingered here.

Someone buzzes us in without asking who's there. Inside, there's no elevator, so we climb the three flights. I'm pleased to see I'm not breathing heavily when we get to the top. I'm in as good shape as Janelle, no doubt thanks to all the yoga we've both been doing.

The door to Mandy's prewar apartment is cracked open, and great peals of laughter greet us as we head inside. Nine women are standing in the kitchen, a clean but ancient room that looks like it's never been renovated. The green appliances, tiny backsplash tiles, and cracked beige linoleum flooring might have made the room dreary, but Mandy's got a festive flair. She's filled the space with colorful dishes, vibrant wall tapestries, a bright throw rug, and an array of silk flowers. The women are a colorful bunch, too—not only because half are black-skinned and the other half are white, but also because they're all cheerily dressed, most in floral or patterned shirts over bright capris or skirts.

I was excited when Mandy called a few days ago to invite Janelle and me to her women's spirituality group. At first, when I saw the unfamiliar phone number and even after she said her name, I couldn't piece it together. But when she called herself "my fellow phobic silent eater," I was thrilled to hear from her. We chatted about the rough patches we've both had trying to keep our consciousness raised since we literally came down from the mountain. I described my horrible dinner with my mother, but also the night out with my colleagues. We both laughed when Mandy said she hasn't eaten in less than a cacophonous ruckus since the retreat. "I happen to prefer noise," she joked. "It hides all my slurps and belches."

Mandy reminded me that she mentioned this women's group at the end of the retreat, letting me know that they'd taken a break but were now getting back together. When she said I could bring Janelle, I quickly said yes.

The moment she notices we've arrived, Mandy rushes over from the counter around which the women are gathered.

"Lorna, Janelle, so glad you made it! Everybody, this is Lorna and Janelle, the women from the yoga retreat I told you about." She goes around the room, pointing one by one to each of her friends. "These are Diana, Soli, Meredith, Jacqueen, Isabella, Teresa, Aliza, and Shareen," she says, introducing the attractive and welcoming women around the room.

"I hope we're not gonna be tested," Janelle teases. "I'm terrible with names."

"I think you'll more easily remember these names once we get into our meeting segment later," Mandy says slyly. "But that's all I'm gonna say about that for now."

For the next hour, we hang out in the kitchen, drinking tea and wine and nibbling all the treats the women have brought, including delicious homemade oatmeal and chocolate-chip cookies, crispy carrots dipped in hummus, assorted fruits, little sandwiches on pita crisps, plus the to-die-for dark-chocolate-covered strawberries that Janelle and I picked up from a gourmet candy shop on our way over. I eat my fill while listening to the women share funny and personal stories, some of which have me laughing until my cheeks are sore. I've never felt so at home with people I barely know, but these women are delightful, and the words flow seamlessly. It certainly is easier to stay connected to my highest, most joyful self in the *sangha* (community) of women like this.

It also helps that I felt superb when I arrived. The last few days at work have gone as I'd hoped—and expected. On the surface, my coworkers seem their same, mean-spirited, selves. The morning after our dinner, Carletta stood in the hall outside my cube. When she saw me crunching numbers, she admonished loudly, in mock horror, "Lorna, how is it that you have not yet finished your financial projections for your summer events?" As if her budgets are always completed when they're supposed to be.

That seemed to inspire Brendan to grandstand before lunch. He stood in the spot where Carletta had bellowed, and, with his voice loud enough for people in Arizona to take note, shouted, "Listen up, people! I've announced that I'm looking for a squash partner for this evening, yet none of you has come forward." He paused, waiting for takers who, not surprisingly, don't materialize. "Well, when one of you realizes playing squash with *moi* is a tremendous offer, I can be found in my office." He stomped all the way back to his cubicle, his footfalls echoing down the long hall.

Michelle, still peeved that I made her sit next to Carletta during the movie, raced through my cube several times to brusquely hand me reports or other documents I'd requested, without staying one minute for our typical chitchat.

But beneath this regular roar was a new harmony I was tuned in to hear. It's as if many of us were suddenly singing the same *om*, even though some were trying hard not to acknowledge it. I noticed that Carletta smiled much more than I'd ever seen her, although each time she spied me, she covered it up by turning away. When I had another one of my coughing fits, she actually came over to see if I was okay. I also sensed Doug walking with a lilt. I chuckled when I caught him yesterday strutting like Gene Kelly singing in the rain. And I overheard Hallie whisper to Olivia the name of an acupuncturist that her girlfriend swears helped her to get pregnant. I'd never seen the two of them share more than negative gossip before.

Then there was this incredible water cooler encounter I witnessed yesterday as I sent a fax nearby—

Brendan: "Carletta, I've been wondering if you might need any help this weekend . . . I mean with your family situation and all."

Carletta swayed, and for a second, I feared she'd fall over from the shock. I worried I might also, but since I was trying not to look like I was listening, I willed my legs to stand firm.

"Why, Brendan, that's very kind. But things are under control. I had a good cathartic cry after I got home that night, and this morning I started making calls to agencies that deal with this sort of thing. Someone from a group home is coming over this weekend to tell us our options for Brianne. But thanks." Woo-hoo!

I myself glided through the past two workdays like there were gel cushions under my feet, ecstatic in the role I played in giving my colleagues a peek behind one another's façades.

After an hour of kitchen chitchat, Mandy invites us into her living room. She's created a circle of colorful chairs and couches by shifting her furniture around. It takes a while to tear us away from our snacking and yapping, but we finally settle into her circle.

"My plan for today is to do a little exploration about our names," Mandy begins. "All day, every day we walk around hearing ourselves called these names. I think it will be great to see if our names can point us to a trait or a goal we can aim toward. For someone with a name like Hope, that would be obvious. But with a little digging, I think the rest of us can find similar inspiration."

Our names? We're going to explore our names? Double ugh. What lofty goal could the name Lorna possibly inspire? Being forlorn? Being a thorn? Maybe a Lorelei—one of those mythical German sirens who lured river boatmen to their ruin. I can't imagine the name Lorna having any kind of positive meaning, seeing how it's always felt to me to be ugly and plain.

Oblivious of my silent objections, Mandy prances around the room, distributing foreign-language dictionaries, baby-name books, and pages from various Web sites that she's printed out.

"Okay, let's get started," she announces after each of us has at least one resource on her lap and some of the more enthusiastic women are teetering under the weight of several. "Remember, there are no rules here. Just look up your name in different places, and see if anything jumps out at you."

Less than a minute later, Aliza, whose voraciousness about this project has been evident since she yanked the first dictionary out of Mandy's hand, leaps out of her chair. She announces with a flourish that, according to the Hebrew dictionary, her name means "joyous one."

"That's a marvelous example of what I'm talking about," Mandy says. "Now take it one step further: Can you use that knowledge to uplift yourself? When you hear your name being called, Aliza, can you remind yourself to *be* the joyous one?"

"This is a great exercise," Shareen says. "Aliza *is* joyful most of the time. But when she gets off track—as all of us do—maybe hearing someone say her name can help her get back on it."

"Exactly!" Mandy enthuses.

We pass the next half hour flipping through the materials Mandy has collected. Every so often, someone shares her discovery: It seems *Mandy* comes from a Latin root, "worthy of love." *Janelle* springs from the Hebrew phrase, "God is gracious." *Shareen* is French for "darling one." Teresa's not thrilled to learn that she's a "harvester," but the other girls quickly remind her that harvest also means the rewards of one's labor, and that she shares a name with one of the most esteemed laborers in modern history, Mother Teresa. Quite an icon to live up to.

"Lorna, we haven't heard anything from you," Mandy says, after we've been at this awhile and all the other women have spoken.

"I've always hated my name. And now I know the reason," I say glumly. I turn to the Latin dictionary that's been sitting open on my lap since we began. "Lorna: 'solitude.' 'Alone,'" I read sullenly. "I guess it's my destiny to end up that way, isn't it?"

"The word *alone* doesn't have to be bad," Janelle says, always looking for that sliver of silver, no matter how black the sky. "Alone can mean forging your own path, not limping along with the masses. You know, like Robert Frost said—taking the road less traveled by."

"That's right. You can interpret it to mean anything that works for you. Anything that helps you reach for your highest self," Shareen adds. *That's easy for the "darling one" to say*, I think.

What hurts worse than the fact that it may indeed be my destiny to end up alone is that a few minutes ago, I looked up my sister's name. Not Angelica, the spiritual name she was given when she became a minister—that's easy to decipher. Anna, the name my mother, the same woman who selected Lorna for me, bestowed on her. It was like a kick in the teeth to see that Mom gave her favorite daughter a name derived from the Hebrew word for "gracious." *She's gracious; I'm lonely. That sums it up,* I brood.

"Hey, this exercise is intended to inspire you, not bum you out," Mandy says, reading my dour expression. She walks toward me. "Like Shareen says, the idea is to make your name mean something positive to you. To me, solitude is a wonderful thing. When I'm by myself at the ocean or in my backyard, I'm most likely to get inspired, to connect with my higher essence."

"Or if you can't see any good in it," Diana jumps in, "and you truly do hate your name, maybe think about changing it? There can be great power in consciously taking one of the million names out there and making it your own. I chose Diana a few years back. The Roman goddess of the moon!"

"If I remember correctly, she was also a symbol of virginity—something I know you don't aspire to," Nancy interjects, giving her friend a playful tap. Everyone laughs.

I laugh, too. But I'm intrigued by what Diana said. Why can't I take another name? Diana did. Heck, my own sister did, even though her given name was already inspirational. No law says I have to stick with the name my mother pinned on me at birth.

Mandy gives us a few more minutes to finish our research and consider all that we've discovered before she plans to lead her closing meditation. I take the opportunity to pick up another baby-name book and look up *Radha,* a name I've always known must have special meaning, but which Anna has never explained. Radha is Sanskrit for "light," the book says. It's not surprising that Anna preferred to let Radha's brightness shine through on its own, without needing to announce its meaning. But seeing how Radha's name is another apt description only depresses me further.

Following the meditation—during which my monkey mind is in full swing—and a round of friendly can't-wait-to-see-you-agains that lasts a half hour, I drive Janelle home in silence. I had hoped this gathering would lift my spirits beyond the lofty heights they've been recently, to propel me further on a positive trajectory. But while I adored seeing Mandy and meeting her delightful friends, I can't shake my disappointment over the discovery about my name.

"You know, you *can* change it if you hate it that much," Janelle says, finally breaking the long, cold chill. "I know a woman who was inspired by the Native Americans she met on a trip to South America. She came back here and became Aponi, which apparently is Blackfoot for 'butterfly.' And this was an Orthodox Jewish girl from Queens!"

I laugh at a mental image of this woman announcing to her religious parents that they should stop calling her Hadassa or Sarah. Truthfully, their reaction couldn't have been worse than my mother's when she learned Anna was becoming Angelica, as if a mother should be able to label you forever. But as with everything having to do with Anna, Mom got over it pretty easily, even if, like me, she doesn't call her Angelica as often as my sister would like.

"Even if I did want to change it, I have no idea what I'd change it to," I say, feeling further dejected. "It's not like I've had this secret yearning to be called something else all my life." I make the left turn into Janelle's street.

"Why not put it on the back burner and see if anything comes to you?" she says, gathering her things in preparation to leave the car. "Maybe at the grocery store or the office, you'll hear someone say a name that gives you goose bumps, and you'll know it's meant for you. We never know what the future holds."

"So true," I reply, brightening as we embrace. "We never do."

Chapter 15

Before exiting my car, Janelle asks if I want to come in and hang at her place, but I decline. I don't think I'll be such fun company right now. As I drive to my house, I ponder the possibility of changing my name. It's not something I've ever considered, so the concept feels strange—but also liberating. I don't know that I'd have the guts to do it, but I like mulling the idea. Still, I'm mostly looking forward to washing off my doldrums with a hot bubble bath and an evening of yoga.

When I turn onto my own street, though, there's a car in my driveway. As I get closer, I see that it's a gleaming Bimmer. Brad.

I've been avoiding calling him, or more accurately, returning one of the sixteen messages he's left on my cell phone the past few days. In increasingly desperate tones, he let me know that his launch was red hot, that he's the office star he'd hoped to be, and that he's "as eager as an *American Idol* contender before his final sing"—the exact words on his voice mail this afternoon, knowing as he does that I adore that show—to have me back in his arms. But I've been mad that he shut me out of his life in the run-up to his launch. And, more important, I'm not sure what I want to say.

Seeing his car excites me. I suddenly have no idea why I've been avoiding him.

I pull into the driveway, ecstatic to find him slouching on the Adirondack chair on my front porch. As I leave my car, he grins that wide, sexy smile that lights up his eyes.

"I hope it's okay I've come unannounced," he says tentatively. I realize he's not sure how I'll react to seeing him. "I've been waiting more than an hour, hoping you'd show. I really want to be with you."

"I love that you're here! I'm sorry I haven't returned your calls." I rush into his arms. After several minutes, I let go. "I've been mad that you've been too busy for me. But now that you're here, I'm glad you persisted."

"You mean, you don't think fifteen phone calls is going overboard?" He smiles. "Especially when you didn't return a single one?"

"Sixteen, actually. Maybe I like being pursued." I open my front door and usher him inside.

"I thought we could go out for something," he says. "To celebrate. Plus, I'm famished. It's nearly dinnertime."

"It's only dinnertime if you're living in a Florida retirement community," I laugh, as it's barely four thirty.

"We could start with cocktails. There's a romantic little Northern Italian place I've been dying to take you to. It has wonderful atmosphere."

"Sounds lovely. I'll need about a half hour to shower and change."

"Could that shower be for two, or are you set on taking it solo?"

Solo. Alone. Lorna. My elation at seeing him crashes down. Fortunately, I catch it midfall. I'm not going to let a feeding "pain-body" ruin any part of another evening with Brad. "A shower for two would be wonderful. But may I suggest the Roman tub instead?" I yank him down my foyer and lead him to my master bathroom.

Two satisfying hours later, we're finally ready to go for dinner. "At least you don't have to worry about meeting early bird retirees anymore," Brad jokes as he tucks his shirt into his slim-waisted pants, adjusts his belt, and combs his thick blond hair. "I hereby announce that anytime we're going for dinner, I volunteer to help kill time so we're not too early."

The restaurant he takes me to is indeed romantic, with candle sconces on the walls and lace curtains on the windows. We skip the bar, since by now we're both starving. Throughout the delicious spicy bean soup, vegetarian antipasto for two—which Brad orders to please me; ordinarily, he's a hard-core carnivore— and my to-die-for eggplant rollatini, Brad delights me with an endless parade of stories. Most involve the last-minute blunders and near misses that almost sank his launch, which were funny only because they didn't.

"Enough about me. I've been hogging the spotlight," he says as the waiter brings us two homemade napoleons, each with a thick, decadent layer of chocolate swirled on top. I can hardly wait for the man to put them down so I can dig in.

"I'm not complaining. Your escapades are entertaining," I say between mesmerizing mouthfuls. "You're a wonderful storyteller."

"You're sweet. But now I'm ready to hear what's been up with you."

"Not much to say." I hold up a fist and raise my index finger. "My niece Radha stayed over for a weekend, which, even though I developed a twenty-four-hour bug, was fantastic. She's an incredible girl." I add my middle finger. "I went over to my neighbor Ruth's to get to know her better, since I realized my assumption that she's a bitch sprang from not really knowing her. Now that I do, I'm clear that she's not." Ring finger. "Doug made us all go out to that movie-and-dinner thing. As you know, I was as eager for that as for a rectal exam, what with Carletta and Brendan there, but it turned out great. Under my prodding, we all opened up about what's going on for us, and it's made us all closer." Pinkie. "Went to a women's spirituality gathering today—"

He cuts me off. "Whoa. Back up and tell me about that work thing again? Whaddya mean 'opened up about what's going on'?"

"It was me who started it. Part of my spiritual mission. I wanted us to get past the bullshit and see what each of us is really living. So at the dinner, I shared the problems I'm having with my mother, how she always belittles me. . . . That inspired others to talk about real things in their lives. You wouldn't believe what came out. Carletta's got a sick mother *and* a brain-damaged twin sister! I've gotta tell you, that's made me much more compassionate toward her."

"But she's after your job! And she'd stomp over your still-warm corpse to get it!"

"Probably. But I don't have to let that affect how *I* feel. I can view her negatively or positively, and since that night, it's been much more of the latter."

"You're amazing," Brad says, taking my hands in his and looking me in the eyes. "I don't think I could overlook the fact that someone I worked with was praying I'd have a heart attack, regardless of the tragedies she's suffered."

"I'm not saying I do it all the time. I'm saying that's what I'm aiming for. I'm trying to see people the way my higher self views them. I believe that in some deep way we're all connected. So why have enemies? I mean, when you get right down to it, my thinking badly about Carletta hurts me a lot more than it hurts her."

"I think that says something terrific about you," Brad says, kissing my extended fingers. When he's gotten to them all, he continues. "There's a guy in my office, Daniel. I've told you about him. He's set himself up as my rival. You can imagine, he's not happy with the kudos I've been getting since the launch. Frankly,

I can't stand the sight of him. Knowing about his personal life—which truthfully I don't give a damn about—wouldn't change that."

"I bet it would. Why don't you ask him what's going on in his life? Maybe there's something that's causing him to behave the way he does."

"No way! Maybe it's not in my nature to care as much as you do about the good bits that may—and I only say *may*—lurk behind someone's evil exterior."

After a few minutes of stilted silence, Brad moves his delicate kisses up my arm, which pretty much ends the discussion.

During the drive home, I consider trying to persuade Brad to get to know that Daniel better, but I decide it's a lost cause. Instead, I share details about the get-together at Mandy's house, how we set about to explore the meaning of our names.

"But your name's as beautiful as you are!" Brad insists after I share the definition I uncovered. "Plus, many great women have had that name. There's, um, Lorna Luft . . . and that sexy Hispanic actress Lorna Paz—not that she has anything on you, of course. . . ."

"But what if my name does turn out to be my destiny?" I say, glossing over his compliment. "What if I'm gonna end up alone? Like my mother!"

"Start answering my calls instead of ignoring them, and you won't. I'll see to it myself."

"I'm serious, Brad. Think about it. If people had called me 'darling one' or 'worthy of love' all my life, don't you think that would be so much more uplifting than that they call me 'alone'?"

"They're not calling you 'alone.' They're calling you Lorna. But I guess if you want to look at it that way, be grateful your mom didn't name you Moon Unit."

"Or Chastity," I laugh, thinking of a few more weird celebrity kid names.

Naturally, this is the moment we pull into my driveway. Brad asks to come in. "To save you from the thought of having to live up to a name like Chastity!" he jokes.

I'm happy to invite him. I'm enjoying his company and wouldn't mind exploring those sexy lips a few more times. We end up having a delicious lovemaking session well into the night. We sleep soundly, snuggled in each other's arms. When we awake the next morning, it's nearly ten o'clock. At least this time he isn't thinking about running back to the office!

I pad into the kitchen to make coffee, pour orange juice, and toast and butter some whole wheat bread. I carry the tray back to bed. After we've eaten, we talk some more, about his launch's success and my anxiety over my impending ice cream sundae event. Brad has no suggestions that I haven't explored about storing the ice cream. Soon we go another round with each other for dessert.

"Hey, I've a great idea!" I say a while later, once we've both showered and dressed. "Let's do yoga together."

"Yoga? Not for me. I'm not flexible like you are."

"It's not like that. In yoga, you stretch only as much as you feel comfortable. Anyway, it's not so much about twisting your body, the way people think. Yoga is really about stretching your mind. And helping you connect with your inner self. I always feel incredibly peaceful. I think you should try it."

"Nah. Yoga's your thing. Anyway, I need to get going. I've got a ton of personal errands I've put off for way too long. I'll leave soon, so I won't keep you from your cute little yoga session."

Cute? Little? I'm taken aback by this belittling comment. "Some of the poses are quite strenuous and challenging, you know."

"All the more reason for me not to join you," Brad says. "I'd just cramp your style."

A short while later, Brad's heading out the door. I give him a long kiss, but I realize I'm happy to see him go. I bound to

171

my bedroom, roll out my yoga mat, and light my incense and a candle.

I decide to begin with some balancing poses, starting with the Tree. As soon as my right leg leaves the ground, though, it's as if a twenty-mile-an-hour gust blows through. I'm quickly knocked off-kilter. The same wobble strikes when I try another balancing pose, the King Dancer, one that's usually my best. After I've grasped my ankle and begun tilting forward, other hand extending out, I lean over so far I have to quickly drop my leg to keep from falling.

This is a great metaphor for my relationship with Brad, I realize. We have terrific fun when we're together. But I worry that if I stick with him, I'll lose the upliftment I've been working so hard to achieve.

Chapter 16

The following Thursday, after some wonderful workdays and numerous sweet phone calls (and delivered flowers!) from Brad, which again confuses me about my intentions, I leave my office to accompany Janelle to her doctor's appointment. She's been begging me to go with her for ages—not because she's worried that anything's wrong, but because she's been dying for me to meet her practitioner. The first time she gushed, "You absolutely must meet this doctor," I was sure she was trying to set me up with him. When I finally confessed this to her, she laughed. The guy is gay. Turns out Janelle is just hot for the energy-healing method this Dr. Fallyn swears by, and like all new converts, she's trying to reel me in. Twice I made up excuses why I couldn't go. This week I finally relented.

I'm not sure why I feel such resistance. After all, part of my spiritual beliefs includes being open to all kinds of possibilities about the universe. And I'm certainly clear that there's a force beyond that which we can see, hear, and feel. As Janelle keeps saying, the idea that there's invisible energy in the world is not even that out there: we all believe in electricity. I know that the body is made from the energy of the universe, so why couldn't it be harnessed to help you heal? But I grew up with my mom's very narrow approach to health, which I'm having trouble shaking. Still, I know that my own family physician, an M.D. with Harvard training and an overreliance on a prescription pad, can't possibly have a lock on healing.

The funny thing is Dr. Fallyn has his own Harvard training, a Ph.D. in biochemistry, along with his naturopathic physician degree. It's just that he doesn't seem to be using one bit of what he learned at the Ivy League. On his Web site, which I scanned last night, he claims he can treat most diseases with his machine. The Web site featured a picture of the device; it looks like a crystal ball. No matter your complaint, this doctor's treatment seems to be the same: several sessions in front of the machine as it "beams out targeted energy waves at a frequency designed to fix what ails you." Naturally, these are waves a client can't see. All I could think as I scrolled through the site was, at $100 a pop, this guy's got a great business!

Janelle has seen Dr. Fallyn three times. A friend from the yoga center told Janelle the machine cured her insomnia, and Janelle was eager to see if it could do the same for the dust and mold allergies that swell her eyelids. Although her symptoms haven't completely disappeared since she started, even my cynical brain has to admit she seems vastly improved. I'm not entirely convinced her recovery isn't attributable to less contact with dust and mold, positive thinking, or even those horse-pill megavitamins the girl somehow swallows daily. Janelle is certain that Dr. Fallyn is the sole reason for her turnaround, but I'm of the mind-set that it's equally plausible the man is a total quack.

Displaying her usual impeccable timing, Janelle swings her Prius around the corner just as I step out from my office lobby.

"Hey, how was your day?" she asks as I climb in her car (we decided to leave mine in my office parking lot, to be picked up later), even though I gave her the complete rundown when we chatted on the phone not one hour earlier.

"Great, as you well know."

"I'm so glad you agreed to come. I know you have doubts, but I think he's on to something big. Maybe he can help you with that chronic cough."

"I hope that's not why you've brought me. My cough's mostly fine. Anyway, I've been hacking since the first grade. I think I'd miss it if it disappeared."

"Don't worry. I brought you because I want you to see this. Opening your mind's a good thing. If you never wanna have your cough treated, that's okay by me."

"Really, my cough strikes only every couple of weeks. It's no big deal. You should have heard me as a kid. I used to bark every hour!"

"Sounds awful. But I bet it's something Dr. Fallyn can fix."

"I'm sure he'd be happy to try—at a hundred dollars per. I can't believe you think his Frankenstein machine is worth that kinda money. Think of the great clothes a gal could get for that!"

"Honestly, I'm surprised you're so dubious, considering that I'm Exhibit A. My allergies are so much better. And I know you believe the same as I do: Everything in the world is energy. Solid things merely move at slower speeds. So why wouldn't changing the energy in your body have a huge effect on your health?"

"You underestimate the extent to which I absorbed my mother's faith in FDA-approved pills and potions," I chuckle. "But I agreed to come. So clearly I'm a wee bit open-minded."

A few minutes later, we pull into the doctor's parking lot and head inside. While Janelle signs in, I notice two model-gorgeous women, one with cropped short blond hair, the other a brunette whose mane is long and curly, in the waiting room. I head over to an empty chair near them to get their perspective.

"Are you patients of Dr. Fallyn?" I jump in, surprising myself with my assertiveness.

"Yes—," the brunette starts to say.

But the other interrupts her. "Who wants to know?"

"I'm sorry if that was too personal," I say sweetly. "Let me start again. My name's Lorna, and that's my friend Janelle." I indicate the reception area, where Janelle is quietly chatting with the nurse and filling out papers. "If you're worried about privacy, you don't need to discuss your condition. Janelle's here for an appointment, and I'm curious—okay, I admit, skeptical—about his treatment methods."

"I'm sorry if I was rude," the blond woman says, extending her hand with a complete attitude reversal. "I'm Tabitha. This is Ashanti. Yes, we're patients. I thought you might be with the medical board."

"I don't understand," I say. Janelle finishes with her forms and slips into the chair beside me.

"Well, Dr. Fallyn practices in a way that threatens traditional physicians, so he comes under a lot of fire. Several doctors have filed complaints to get his license taken away. I thought maybe you were part of their investigation. My girlfriends Soli and Jacqueen, who are patients, told me someone was snooping around the last time they came here."

"Soli and Jacqueen—the ones who know Mandy Adams?" I'm sure they must be the same women I met in Mandy's spirituality group, not only because the names are unusual but also because they seem likely to travel in these alternative medicine circles.

"Yes—and we know Mandy, too! What a small world," Tabitha says.

"God forbid you ruffle the feathers of some physicians," Ashanti continues, ignoring our game of people geography and getting back to the topic at hand. "So many of them have tried to run midwives, chiropractors, homeopaths, and, in this case, naturopaths, off the map. They want to keep every healer from doing anything creative."

"I see we're of like minds," Janelle says, leaning forward to introduce herself and officially join the conversation.

"Do you think this treatment really has helped you?" I ask the women pointedly.

They look at each other and laugh.

"Oh, you could say that," Ashanti says. "Tabitha's one of Dr. Fallyn's big success stories."

"My regular doctors practically left me for dead," Tabitha says dramatically, pausing for further effect before continuing. "Two years ago, I was diagnosed with a brain tumor. The oncologist told me outright I'd be lucky to last the summer. Nothing like nipping all hope in the bud."

"Naturally, we found a different oncologist right away," Ashanti says. "Someone who wasn't ready to call the funeral home yet. I'm Tabitha's best friend—we've modeled together since high school. I got online and started doing research."

"As you can imagine, I was in shock about the whole thing. Kind of paralyzed," Tabitha adds. I lean forward, eager to hear more.

"I found her a doctor who agreed to shrink the tumor with radiation. He thought there was a chance that if it got smaller, it could maybe be surgically removed, although he wasn't making any promises. Something about it being complex, and close to her speech center."

"I had eight weeks of radiation," Tabitha jumps in again, and my head flips from one woman to the other. "X-rays showed the tumor getting smaller. But radiation is so freaky. They're pointing this machine right at your head! I was nervous about the harm the radiation might be doing to the rest of me. I kept recalling the joke about the doctor who says he knew the treatment helped his patient because the autopsy showed the tumor had gotten smaller."

"Tabitha and I got to talking," Ashanti says, and my gaze swings again to her. "I mean, what is radiation if not energy? Why couldn't her tumor shrink with energy that wasn't so toxic? Soli, who's my neighbor, told me about Dr. Fallyn. It sounded weird, I admit, but Soli swore the treatments had shrunk her uterine fibroids, like down to nothing." *Leave it to the girl with the "sunny" name to be so optimistic*, I think.

"Dr. Fallyn encouraged me to stay with the radiation, and even do the surgery if my oncologist thought it was safe," Tabitha continues. "He wanted his treatment to be complementary. But I decided to stop the radiation cold for a month to see what happened. My oncologist was pissed, but I figured that was his problem. I came here every day for four weeks. At first my eyebrows were raised as high as yours are." She points to mine, and I realize they're practically in my hairline, so astounded am I by this information. "But I had to give it a try." I try to consciously relax my face, but my eyebrows quickly pop up again. "By the second week, I could sense that something was working. Hard to explain exactly what I was feeling. After a month, I went to my oncologist for another X-ray. He stood there stunned. Couldn't find but a tiny trace of the tumor! I tried to tell him about Dr. Fallyn, but he just laughed. Swore that the radiation he'd given me before must have worked wonders."

"No operation. Nothing. Tabitha's been in perfect health for a year and a half! Comes here now for weekly tune-ups. I come myself when I've a cold or headache. My story isn't so dramatic, but I'm a satisfied customer, too."

Janelle is smiling wider than a beauty pageant contestant. She knows this tale will go far toward convincing me that Dr. Fallyn is not selling the energy version of snake oil. Plus, there's the added bonus that they know the women we've recently met; it makes it seem more like karma.

"That's incredible," I say, trying to put the *wow* I'm feeling into words. "But are you sure his machine treatments *are* what cured you? Maybe it *was* the radiation? Or . . . something else?"

"Truthfully, I do think the machine is only part of the story,"

Tabitha says. "Dr. Fallyn believed in my body's ability to heal itself. That's not something I got from any of the dozens of other doctors I saw during my care. When you think about how you get over the flu or a cut in your skin, or how a woman grows and births a baby . . . the body's such a wondrous machine. Why shouldn't it have that same ability to dismantle runaway cells clumped up in my brain? With Dr. Fallyn, I started having faith that my immune system could cart that icky stuff away. I think the energy treatments just sped up the process."

"You guys should go on a talk show, or something! The world needs to hear this," Janelle says.

"I think that would only make more trouble for Dr. Fallyn," Ashanti sighs. "Jacqueen said it was an MS patient's neurologist who complained the loudest, even though the woman is supposedly walking for the first time in years!"

"I hate to break up this little kaffeeklatsch," a voice says, and the four of us turn in unison to see a thin, middle-aged man in black pants and a bright red shirt, his straight black hair down to his shoulders, standing by the door.

"Dr. Fallyn! Hello!" Tabitha, Ashanti, and Janelle reply together.

"Hello to all of you! Janelle, whenever you're ready, come on in. And of course, your friend is welcome to join you."

ॐ

As we walk through the office, I feel like I've taken a wrong turn into a day spa. Silk screens line the walls, creating the same relaxing effect as the silk in the bedroom at the yoga retreat and over my home altar. An indoor waterfall and several small fountains fill the air with the bubbling sound of running water. Rather than antiseptic alcohol, green tea incense scents the air.

We pass a hallway lined with diplomas—everything from a master's at Northwestern University to the Ph.D. from Harvard to fellowships at the National Institutes of Health. A Jewish mother's dream, I think with a chuckle, certain any Jewish mother I know would wonder how such a promising, mainstream career swung so drastically off course. On the adjoining wall are diplomas in equally large frames, under spot lighting that gives them more prominence: his Naturopathic degree, a School of Light diploma for hands-on healing, and certification for mastering this gizmo in which Dr. Fallyn now puts most of his faith.

He leads us into a treatment room, and I immediately notice it has no exam table lined with crinkly paper, no bright overhead light, no blood pressure cuff. A cozy floral couch fills the main wall; behind it is a poster of beautiful men and women, while across the room hangs one of a white-powdered beach. What appears to be a crystal ball is tucked into the corner, on a small table next to a wooden stool.

"Why don't you both take a seat on the couch and I'll set Janelle up," Dr. Fallyn says as he pulls the little table to him and begins pressing tiny buttons barely visible on the orb.

My cough picks this moment to erupt, and lasts a solid minute. When I was with Brad the first time it unleashed, he called it my "Luciano Pavarotti." Right now it sounds more like a dying old man.

"Wow, that's some cough," Dr. Fallyn says when it finally subsides.

"It sounds worse to others than to me. I've had it so many years, I hardly notice. Of course, when I was a kid, I hated it—so embarrassing. Plus my mother insisted I take this horrible medicine. Swore 'one more dose' would cure me. I'm surprised it didn't kill me instead."

"You might want to let me treat it sometime. If you've had it for decades, I'd venture there's some stuck emotional energy keeping it in place. I've seen enough success stories to know this machine can knock that out pretty easily."

I don't answer. Tabitha's tale was inspiring, but in my mind, the jury is still far from settled. Fortunately, Dr. Fallyn doesn't press it.

Dr. Fallyn positions the table directly in front of Janelle. Then he presses flat, round magnets onto Janelle's arms, chest, and forehead. Janelle sits peacefully, oblivious of the weirdness of the situation.

"I'm going to run the diagnostic program first," Dr. Fallyn says. Janelle nods and settles back into the couch, familiar with the drill. For the next five minutes I watch as swirls of light dance around the contraption. Finally, a list of seeming unrelated words appear in the ball: VITAMIN B_{12}. VITAMIN E. MOLD. DUST. KIDNEYS. STRESS. . . . Dr. Fallyn leans forward, raptly studying the list as if it were the code for the atomic bomb.

"Interesting," he says after a time. "The same allergy stuff as before, of course, but this time some vitamin deficiencies are also being flagged. That could be contributing to your strong reaction to the everyday dust that doesn't bother other people."

"Should I take more vitamin supplements?" Janelle asks. "I already take a daily multi, plus some antioxidants and calcium."

"Does she ever," I chime in. "Monster pills."

"No need to take anything else. This machine will energize your body so you'll more efficiently metabolize the vitamins you do take."

"A crystal ball can't cure a vitamin deficiency," I pronounce, unable to disguise my incredulity any longer.

"In this country, with all the food we eat, most of us get all the vitamins we need without supplements. But the body doesn't always use them properly, since stress, toxins, preservatives, and whatnot interfere," Dr. Fallyn politely explains. "More pills are rarely the answer. This machine helps eliminate the interference, so your magnificent system can work as it was designed to."

"I'm sure you didn't learn that at Harvard," I say.

"That's for sure," Dr. Fallyn laughs. "I've had plenty of

training since. Don't get me wrong; I learned great things about how the cells work in conventional school. And I certainly would take full advantage of Western medicine if I were in a car accident or my appendix burst. But I know now that healing involves much more than chemicals and cutting, especially for the chronic illnesses so many people have. I haven't abandoned anything I've learned. I use it all."

For the next forty-five minutes, the computer "treats" Janelle for her allergy and vitamin deficiencies. Dr. Fallyn leaves the room for a time, periodically peeking in to check on the progress. To my untrained eye, "treatment" seems the same as the diagnosis: color and light dance around the circle.

Finally, in huge letters, the word HARMONIZED appears.

Alerted by the whistling sounds that accompany this apparently major accomplishment, Dr. Fallyn enters. "Before I take the magnets off, let's run an overall check to make sure nothing else needs to be done," he says.

As he presses a few more buttons, I stifle a snort. I sense that my original impulse was right on target. Now that Janelle's allergy treatment is complete, a few mouse clicks will be all the doctor needs to uncover some other problem requiring additional appointments.

My mind leaps to the ultimate skeptic: my mother. Heaven forbid she should discover us here! If she went nuts about my saying a Hindu grace, seeing Janelle with magnets on her body, with me sitting next to her, would blast her into a straitjacket. And she'd try to put me into one alongside her.

"What's happening?" Dr. Fallyn asks suddenly. "Janelle, your energy just went wacky."

"I didn't do anything," Janelle says. "What do you mean, wacky?"

"What about you?" Dr. Fallyn turns to me. "Did you dramatically change your thoughts? This machine is sensitive enough to pick up a big shift in anybody in the room, not just the person plugged in."

"Well, I did start thinking about my mother, about how she would mock my sitting here if she knew."

"And it made your energy go weak. Interesting."

"What do you mean 'go weak'? You could see something?"

"The sensor dipped quicker than I've ever seen. You must be strongly attached to your mother's opinions."

"Is she ever," Janelle pipes in. "Lorna might have her own doubts about this treatment, but I'm sure her mother would freak. And Lorna cares a lot about her mother's approval."

"What does my mother have to do with this? How could you see that in a stupid crystal ball?" I say, suddenly defensive.

"Your energy drop was so dramatic, I bet we'll be able to detect it even without the machine. Stand up," Dr. Fallyn instructs.

I get to my feet, sure that if Janelle weren't here, I'd use them to run right out the door.

"Put out your right arm."

I raise my arm to shoulder height, and Dr. Fallyn tells me to ponder something positive. I look at a poster on the wall behind the couch: dozens of people from around the world are lined up by skin color, the blackest African on one side, Asians and Native Americans in the middle, and a pale Swede on the other end. It's a wonderful example of how all of humanity falls along a continuing spectrum.

Dr. Fallyn pushes down on my arm. It doesn't budge.

"Now, think about your mother."

When Dr. Fallyn presses again, it drops all the way.

"That's not fair! You pushed harder the second time," I protest.

"No, he didn't," Janelle says. "I watched closely. If anything, he used more force before."

"I'm happy to try it again so you see that I didn't do anything different," Dr. Fallyn says.

"He definitely didn't," Janelle says. "Give it another shot, Lorna. Think about your mom."

I recall my mom's hurtful comments about Janelle the night of our dinner, about how she always tries to destroy everything that's important to me. I try to keep my elbow locked as I think this, but it's no use. My arm collapses under what I see is Dr. Fallyn's slight touch.

"Unbelievable," I say. "What causes that?"

"Applied kinesiology. Also called muscle testing. In the seventies, a doctor named John Diamond understood that negative emotions zap our strength and positive ones enhance it, and he popularized that quick test. It never fails. I've seen a football player push down on a ballerina's arm, and if she's thinking positive thoughts, he won't get it to weaken."

"Can we try again, with me pressing on you?" I ask, still feeling unmoored by all this.

"Sure. So you don't think I'm cheating, I'll write what I'm going to think on this paper here. Then you try your hardest to push my arm down."

He scribbles something on a notepad, turns it facedown, and sticks out his arm.

He doesn't stand a chance, I think, with my muscular biceps from all the yoga poses I've been doing. Still, I begin by pressing moderately; I'm surprised when his arm quickly succumbs. He turns the notepad over. "September 11, 2001," he reads.

"One more time!" I demand.

"Okay. I'll write something else. But you won't know what to expect. It could be another negative comment." More scribbling, and then he thrusts out his arm again.

I push, careful to use the same amount of strength as before. His arm stays firm. I press harder, but it doesn't dislodge. Finally, I use everything I've got, but it's resistant.

I turn the paper over: *Energy healing can cure a lifelong cough.*

"All right. I'm impressed," I admit as Janelle and I gather our things. "I'll definitely consider making an appointment."

Chapter 17

After the session, Janelle and I drive to a nearby bookstore. My mind is spinning, and I want to research more about this kinesiology stuff. I ask the clerk about John Diamond. She says they don't carry his books, but she points me to a more modern adherent, David Hawkins. His book, *Power vs. Force*, is a spiritual classic I somehow missed in my quest to gobble the whole New Age library. Janelle stands near me as I pull the book off the shelf and flip through it. I'm immediately intrigued.

"Hawkins believes you can quantify the energy level of people, emotions, and ideas with muscle testing," I summarize to her. "Says he's tested thousands of people while they've thought about different concepts, individuals, religions, even humanity itself. The tester asks if the item's level is higher than one hundred, then two hundred, and so on, until an exact number score is given."

"Sort of like a spiritual *Price Is Right*!" Janelle jokes.

"Exactly! Hawkins says spiritual things—people meditating, inspired books, honesty—consistently register at very high numbers."

"Wouldn't the energy of the person being tested have an effect? Or the energy of the tester?"

I scan the page further. "Nope. Says in his studies people were tested, and I quote, 'on top of mountains and at the seashore . . . in moments of joy and of sorrow,' and that none of it mattered." I can barely control my enthusiasm. I keep flipping pages. "Wow, listen to this. Humanity as a whole calibrates only at two hundred seven. Albert Einstein and Freud were each four hundred ninety-nine."

"Such a big difference."

"Two hundred fifty's apparently the threshold where human satisfaction comes into play. So by his reckoning, most of the world's in the dumps."

"That's depressing," Janelle says. "But I guess it makes sense when you consider the billions of people who live in fear—of poverty, dictators, and, of course, their image of God."

Janelle reaches over my head and grabs her own copy off the shelf. Even though she's leafing through it, I'm so pumped, I continue reading aloud. "He says asking people to think about the ancient spiritual giants—Jesus, Krishna, Buddha—registers at close to a thousand, the highest level on his scale! Oh, and here's more good news: A single person at that enlightened level counterbalances the lower energies of millions of others."

"That reminds me of something I once read in a Kabbalah book," Janelle says, looking up from the page she'd been silently perusing. "That there are thirty-six 'righteous' people, called *Lamed Vavniks*, always on earth. Without them, the world would stop existing. The interesting thing is, you never know who those thirty-six people are, because even *they* don't know. It could be you! Or me!"

"I'm pretty sure it's not me," I chuckle.

"The idea is that anyone could be key to the world's survival, including people who don't seem righteous to anyone else."

"Are you saying my mother could be a *Lamed Vavnik*?" I ask in the most incredulous voice I can muster.

"You never know," Janelle replies with a wink.

"I'm certain I know." We both laugh.

An hour later, we've each read Hawkins' entire book.

"Let's grab a drink at a café and digest all this—along with some food," Janelle suggests.

"Great idea. Especially the food part. I'm starving."

ॐ

We walk up to the counter of a nearby coffee shop, behind which stands a heavy teenage girl, arms with lines of tattoos spilling from her too-tight tank top. Although I'm no fan of this body art, I admire the delicate blue and gold butterfly landing on her shoulder and tell her so. When she opens her mouth to reply, I expect the voice of a trucker, but she is surprisingly melodic— reminding me once again to stop prejudging. I order a tomato soup, veggie sandwich, an oatmeal raisin cookie, and a decaf mocha light. Janelle orders the same soup and sandwich and chamomile tea.

"My brain's exploding from these ideas," I say as we sit down and dig in. The food tastes especially delicious, both because I'm famished and because I'm feeling so high. "The idea that a thought or emotion can be quantified is mind-blowing—and simply by pressing on someone's arm!"

"I know. Incredible, isn't it?"

We eat our food and sip our drinks while continuing our discussion.

Janelle puts down her cup of tea suddenly and looks right at me. "Hey, this is reminding me of an energy exercise I learned from a guy I dated ages ago. Haven't thought about this in years . . . . It's fun. Wait here. I'll show you."

She walks over to the tattooed barista and orders a bottle of water with two glasses—not paper cups, she insists. The woman has to scramble, but finally turns up real glassware. Janelle returns to the table, pours half the water into each, and sets one before me.

"Keep your palms down and fingers flat, and swirl your hands in a circle a few inches over the cup," she instructs. "Be sure they're going in the same direction."

"Like this?" I demonstrate, waving my hands over the rim—a magician about to pull out a rabbit—and feeling ridiculous not for the first time today.

I'm not the only person who thinks this is odd. A geeky twentysomething at the next table is staring. "May I ask what you girls are doing?" he interrupts after watching for more than a minute, his tone implying we may be missing a few crucial screws.

I'm feeling awkward enough, but I restrain myself from telling him to please go back to his cappuccino. Naturally, Janelle responds from a more loving perspective.

"It's a test. We're proving everything's made of energy. We're moving the energy in the water even though we're not touching it. It looks to anyone watching like the liquid's staying still, but if we do it right, the taste will be affected."

"Is *that* what we're doing?" I ask. "I thought we were exhausting our arms before another round of kinesiology!"

"If you want to change the taste of a cup of water, why not just pour salt in? Or sugar?" the guy jokes. "Save your arms a ton of trouble."

Janelle again ignores the bait. "This way's more interesting—and more fun. Want to taste the water when we're done?"

"You betcha! This should be good for a laugh. Not to mention a distraction from this boring differential equations book. Exam next week." He points to an open textbook on his table that to me might as well be in Russian, with all the math-speak on the page. Then he thinks better of his rudeness. "Sorry to be snide. I'm really a nice person. Name's Ed. Pleased to meet you." He starts to extend his hand but retreats when he realizes ours are surfing above our glasses.

"Can we stop yet?" I plead to Janelle a few minutes later. "My arms are exhausted." *So much for my yoga buffness!*

"Another minute should do it."

The next sixty seconds are some of the longest in my life. My biceps are screaming. Finally Janelle nods. "Okay, that should be enough."

"Thank heaven!"

I plop my arms down while Janelle retrieves a third glass from the woman behind the counter, who, now that she knows where they are, quickly obliges. When she returns, Janelle pours some of her water into the extra cup and passes it to our waiting critic. Janelle and I raise our glasses to make a toast.

"To uncovering the mysteries of the universe," Janelle says.

"To the intriguing world of energy," I say.

Ed lifts his. "To quenching my thirst."

I take a sip. The water tastes like someone added a dash of soap. Or sawdust.

"Yuck," Ed replies after his own gulp. "You girls are up to something. You put something in the water before I noticed you doing this parlor trick."

"We did put something in the water," Janelle says, as much to me as to Ed. "Air. Moving our hands caused the molecules in the water to swirl, creating an invisible vacuum in the middle. Nature abhors a vacuum, as you learned in school, so air jumped in. That's what causes the water to taste funky. Yet another example of how we can't see all the energy in this world," she beams at me.

"That's fascinating!" I say, setting my glass down. "I wish I'd had a science teacher like you when I was in school. Would have made learning more fun."

"I was never taught that in my school, either," Ed says, still uncertain whether we're for real. He pauses. "Wait a minute! Something's coming back that I learned years ago. Hold your arm out," he demands to me.

"Applied kinesiology? We already did that today," I say.

"Nope. Karate chops. From the sixth grade. Come on. Stand up and hold out your arm."

In the spirit of cooperation, I do as I'm told. My arm stretches like before. Instead of telling me to think of something good or bad, Ed pushes down unexpectedly. Spent as my arm is from the water trick, I'm surprised it stays straight.

"Nothing happened," I say.

"Keep watching," he answers.

Like a character in a martial arts movie, Ed chops at the air above and below the arm. It takes all my effort to keep from laughing. I don't want to give him the leverage he is obviously seeking. I take a deep breath and focus on staying strong.

Once he stops chopping, Ed pushes again. My arm slumps like a deflated balloon. Incredibly, I don't have enough strength to lift it back up. It remains limply hanging by my side.

"It's the same idea as your water game," he says triumphantly. "I disturbed the energy around your arm, and that weakened the muscles. My buddies at Walker Elementary would be pleased to know I remembered that. We used to do it to each other in the boys' bathroom—when we were supposed to be in class, of course. It does remind me that invisible energy can be tampered with, but I'm still not convinced you didn't monkey with the water."

"You get to believe whatever you want," Janelle says. "And so do we. And I have to say, what I believe gets more intriguing every day."

ॐ

A half hour later, we're back in Janelle's car.

"Mind if I flip on the radio to WNOW? I'd love to hear Serena Robbins," I ask.

"Go right ahead. I'm starting to get hooked on her myself, thanks to you. The dial's already set to the station."

"Goooooood evening to you!" Serena Robbins sings out after I press the power button. "So wonderful for you to be here, sharing this moment in our lives together."

"How'd you know Serena Robbins would be on now?" Janelle asks. "Doesn't her show usually air in the morning?"

"Just a hunch—or, rather, a sensing of energy." I smirk. "I know she sometimes fills in for other hosts, and I had a feeling she'd be on."

"You're becoming an energy-sensing machine!" Janelle chuckles.

"Let's go right to the calls, since I love speaking to each and every one of you," the lilting voice on the radio continues. "Hello, Paul from Centerville."

"Thanks so much for taking my call. I don't have a problem like many of your other callers. I just wanted to say thank you for your inspiration. It seems that no matter what I'm working on in my spiritual growth, you seem to say something that hits it right on. I'd call it a coincidence, but I know there are no coincidences. We all have the power to call what we want into our lives exactly when we want it. It's mostly a question of whether we're aware enough to know that."

"Beautifully said, Paul! When you focus on what you want and open yourself to it, good things must flow your way. It's the law of the universe," Serena replies.

As Paul elaborates on all the ways his life is grand, I realize things are going pretty darn good for me, too. I'm happy with my spiritual progress, now that I've finally accepted that it isn't a linear process and will always zig one way before zagging another. It hit me the other day that I don't need to be whipping my horse to get to the finish line; I just need to relax and enjoy the beautiful ride—because there never is a finish line. Now that I know the universal life energy is flowing through me, I'm confident the answers to my every dilemma—from dealing with my coworkers to figuring out what to do about Brad, not to mention getting along with my mother—will appear.

Janelle pulls into my office parking lot near my car. We say good-bye with double cheek kisses—something I've never done with my other girlfriends but somehow feels natural with Janelle. I drive home in a state of elation. When I walk into my house a while later, I'm not surprised to discover I missed a call from Brad. His voice mail offers to take me to a fancy mountain retreat next weekend. Or, if I prefer, to Miami's South Beach.

I love being with Brad. And I know he's a terrific guy. But there's something crucial missing in our relationship. What exactly do I want to do about him?

Not a second after I ask this, the answer hits me.

I walk out the door and head for Ruth's house. Although it's dark outside, I hear her in her backyard, as I often do in the evening. I find Ruth kneeling over a Laura Ashley–esque army of pink, white, and yellow tulips, illuminated by a dazzling row of solar-powered garden lights.

"Lorna!" she says, no doubt surprised to see me in her yard, since I've never ventured here before.

"Wow, this garden is beautiful," I say, surveying the dozens of species blooming all around.

"Gardening keeps me sane. It helped me get through my difficult time with Faith, and now it gives my day purpose. There's nothing better for connecting to my higher essence than digging my fingers into freshly turned soil."

"Ruth, I had no idea you were so spiritual," I say.

"Not religious. But spiritual? Yes. I believe we're all linked to a higher power. And to me, no prayer reminds me of that more than a day in the dirt."

"Ruth, you do keep surprising me! Do you meditate, too?"

"You mean sit crossed-legged, singing *om*?"

"Uh, something like that, yes."

"Never tried it. But I believe I meditate every day while

gardening in this paradise." She waves her arms to encompass her magnificent flowers, shrubs, and trees.

"I've no doubt you do. But if you ever want to try the crossed-legged variety, lemme know. I've been meditating daily for months now—and I love it."

"I might take you up on that sometime." She pauses, suddenly realizing I may have come over for more than small talk. "Did you need something in particular, Lorna? Eggs? Sugar? Your sprinklers turned on earlier?" She smiles.

"Actually, I need a favor. Won't take but a minute."

"I wouldn't care how long it takes. I've no place to go."

"This may sound strange. I've been learning about energy and something called kinesiology. I'm hoping you'll give me a hand—well, an arm—to help me test something. All you have to do is push down on my arm when I tell you to."

"Sure thing. Gimme a minute to go inside and wash up. I wouldn't wanna touch that beautiful outfit of yours with these fingers." She holds up hands that are as black as coal.

As she heads inside, I begin to formulate the sentences I want to test. After trying a few versions, I decide the best approach is to be direct. Finally, Ruth emerges, hands as clean as a gardener's fingers can be. She's changed her clothes, too, from the frumpy sweats she usually wears to a formfitting metallic top over stylish jeans. I nod approvingly.

"I'm ready," she sings. "This sounds like fun. What do I do?"

I explain how I'm going to think a thought, hold out my arm, and have her push on my limb. "Press with medium force. Don't be scared you're gonna hurt me, because you won't," I say.

I close my eyes and take a few slow deep breaths to collect my thoughts. Then I whisper so she doesn't hear, "Brad and I make a wonderful couple and should stay together." I shoot my hand out while silently repeating these words twice more.

Ruth lays her hand tentatively on my arm. I hear her take a

breath; then she presses. My arm goes south faster than a bird in winter.

"Maybe I pushed too hard," Ruth exclaims. She can tell by the alarm on my face that this is more than a game to me.

"No. That was perfect. Gimme a minute to think something else and then do that again."

"The same amount of force? Or maybe a little less?" she asks uneasily.

"The same, or as close to it as you can get."

Eyes closed, I breathe deeply again. "I should leave Brad, confident in the knowledge that a guy who's better for me is waiting around the corner," I murmur inaudibly, repeating this again before extending my arm. Ruth presses. My arm doesn't waver.

"One more time, just to make sure?" I ask without opening my eyes.

"Whenever you're ready."

"It's time for Brad and me to go our separate ways," I mumble. She pushes. Again, it stays.

"Are you all right?" Ruth asks after several silent minutes, during which I stand stock-still. I drop my arm.

"I'm fine. I just need to go home and process all this. Thanks so much for helping."

"I'd be lying if I said I had any idea what this was all about. But if there's anything else I can do, or anything you want to talk about, please let me know," she says, kindly but not intrusively.

"I will. Thanks so much." I envelop her in a hug, which doesn't feel awkward at all, before walking back to my house.

Emotionally out of sorts, I decide to do some yoga to help calm me down before trying to make sense of what this means. I lay out my mat in my bedroom and prepare to do the Sun Salutation. I used to hate this twelve-step pose; it was murder on my wrists, left me breathless, and seemed to take forever to finish one round—and you're supposed to do several! But when I told this to Miss Gumby a while back, she suggested a visualization for each of the positions. It's been my favorite ever since. I step to the front of my mat and begin.

Position one: Palms together at my chest. I connect with the loving energy inside my heart.

Position two: Stretching my arms out, up, and back. I envision the warmth of the sun and indeed the entire universe dancing on my face.

Position three: Folding forward toward the ground. I expand my appreciation to all of Mother Earth.

Position four: Left leg back, left knee on the floor, back arched, arms stretching up. I remember that even when I feel low, I'm always connected to my higher self.

Position five: Both legs back, arms straight in a plank. I get in touch with the inner strength that never leaves me.

Position six: Lowering knees, chest, and chin to the ground. I remember to be humble around other people, since they, too, are extensions of the universal energy.

Position seven: Pelvis to the floor, chest rises up in a cobra pose. I extend my sense of oneness to all the animals in the world.

Position eight: I make the upside-down *V* that is Downward Dog. I can't remember what Miss Gumby said about this one, so I just give the universe a quick, friendly wave of my butt.

Position nine: Left leg forward, right knee on the floor, back arched, arms stretching up. I start to rise up to my full potential.

Position ten: Folding forward as in position three. I remember to pause to gather my inner resources before taking action.

Position eleven: Stretching up and back. I open to the full universal energy once more.

Position twelve: Palms together at my chest. I realize this higher power always resides inside me.

After three rounds, my mind feels completely at peace. I walk over to my nightstand and pick up the photo of Brad and me. I gaze at the picture for several minutes, admiring his gorgeous face and sexy body. I remember the first time I saw Brad. He was across the room at a party hosted by Gretta's colleague. Those liquid blue eyes instantly struck fire in my heart. My breath catches even now as I recall the moment he headed my way. Our first date— and every date since—was tremendous fun. And of course, he is the most generous, sensual lover I've ever had. Still. . .

Brad's not on the same spiritual path as I am. Heck, he's not on any path at all. In his book *Conversations with God,* Neale Donald Walsch wrote that the first question to ask yourself about a relationship is, Where am I going? Only then can you ask the second question, Who is going with me? While journeying with Brad would be wonderful on many levels, ultimately we're not heading in the same direction.

I know Brad will make a great partner for someone. Yet I feel a lightness in my heart as I accept the fact that that someone won't be me. Maybe I will end up "alone." But I have a sneaking suspicion that my perfect guy is waiting just around the bend.

Chapter 18

Early on Saturday morning, I'm roused out of a soupy sleep. It takes me a few minutes to realize that what I'm hearing is the phone. In my dream, the timer on my oven is beeping and beeping, while the turkey I'm cooking for a thirty-person dinner party is burning to a crisp—the smoke belching into every room. The scary part is that I'm oblivious of the fiery fowl, because I'm turned completely inward. Sitting cross-legged on the floor by my bedroom altar, I'm in a deep sujal.

When I shake myself into full wakefulness, I'm totally unnerved. Could such a thing happen? Could I become so intensely entwined with my ethereal side that I lose my grip on my material surroundings?

I snatch one of the books off my nightstand, pulling it from the middle of the stack. This causes the whole pile to tumble down onto the floor. I'm so desperate for the answer, I don't care about the mess. I'm also not bothered to let my voice mail answer the phone. *Brad, I suspect.* Even though I'm at peace with Thursday night's decision to end our relationship, I'm not ready to confront him with the news.

The book in my hand is a treatise on meditation, *Coming to Our Senses*, by the Zen teacher Jon Kabat-Zinn. I flip around, snatching bits and snippets, until I find a passage that soothes my jangled nerves. Meditation, he writes, "is really an inward gesture that inclines the heart and mind (seen as one seamless whole) toward a full-spectrum awareness of the present moment just as it is, accepting whatever is happening simply because it's already happening."

Whew! At least if my house caught fire while I was sujaling, I'd be aware enough to grab for the fire extinguisher—and presumably the meditation would help me stay calm. I chide myself for worrying. After all these months of landing my (continually shrinking!) butt on my cushion, how could I not know the true goal of meditation? Awareness and acceptance of the present moment, here I come!

I brush my teeth and change into the comfy gray yoga pants and green tank top I bought the other day at the store in Om Sweet Om. The front of the shirt features an adorable illustration of a kitten doing the Cat stretch. I roll out my yoga mat, eager to begin a long hatha session.

First up is a pose I'm coming to love: headstand. When I initially saw a woman in my yoga center turn upside down, I swiftly concluded this pose would be beyond my ability forever. Until recently, I did fall over whenever I tried. But Janelle kept encouraging me, pointing out some of the heavier, less limber women in our class who are nonetheless able to get their feet skyward. I began repeating some positive affirmations: "I am as balanced in headstand as the Cat in the Hat, with his stack of teacups on his inflatable ball." I didn't just tell myself this; I tried to feel it emotionally. A few days ago, it felt so real, I knew I'd be able to accomplish it.

I understand now that having the thought resonate is crucial to getting what you want. You can't just fake it till you make it, great as that expression sounds. If I had continued believing I was the Queen of Klutz, my words wouldn't have had one iota of creative power. But I realize that my view of myself as having two left feet results from thoughts burned into my brain long ago by my mom, ideas I no longer choose to live by. Once I began believing in my ability to master this pose, I kicked up into a bowling-ball-can't-knock-me-over headstand and remained, unmoving, for ten solid minutes.

Now, as my legs soar toward my bedroom ceiling, I don't even pause midway for a balance check. I hold this pose for nearly fifteen minutes, savoring the delicious perspective of my room from this vantage, not to mention the energizing rush of blood to my head. When I finally come down, I rest in child's pose to let my brain adjust. The first day, I popped up too quickly and thought I might be swirling toward Oz.

Since it's Saturday and I don't have plans until this afternoon, I have time to do an extensive yoga practice. For the next hour, I work through numerous poses—with increasingly impeccable form, I happily observe. I end the physical session with a soothing deep relaxation, tensing and releasing all my muscles in progression, then savoring the repose.

Totally rested, I move on to thirty glorious minutes of sujaling. I recently upped my daily morning session to this quota, and an amount of time that once would have felt like a jail sentence speeds by in a flash.

Having discovered that my best sujals begin with a focus on my physical body, I put my attention on the feeling of my butt on my cushion, the straightness of my spine, the pressure of three fingers on each hand connecting in a *mudra* position on my lap. While I'm sitting with this concentration on the here and now, an inner peace overtakes me. Actually, I know that that peace is always there, that it doesn't fly in on a magic carpet during my meditations. But typically I'm too frenzied to notice. During my thirty minutes this morning, the peace settles easily. Of course, thoughts periodically flit into my mind, but when I don't give them my attention, they dissolve. By the time my alarm dings, I am filled with contentment.

Maybe this would be a good time to call my mother, whom I've been avoiding since the screaming match that passed for our family dinner. Last night, as I was thinking about how I need to speak to Brad, it struck me that I also need to dial my mother. Holding on to my anger isn't helpful to either one of us—even if my feelings are justified.

I rise from my mediation cushion, overflowing with a sense of calm, and lift the phone. I don't even need to take my signature deep breath before she answers. But when she says hello, I realize I haven't figured out what I plan to say.

"Mom. Hi. It's Lorna." *A good start.*

She pauses, her mind undoubtedly darting through a series of alternative answers she might choose from. Since I have no strategy save to make amends, I plow on.

"Mom, I want to put our relationship back on the right footing," I say sweetly.

"Well, it's big of you to realize you did wrong." *A size you will never grow to,* I think, before snapping that nasty vulture back into its cage. I don't recall admitting I did wrong, but whatever.

"I was wondering . . . do you wanna come over for dinner next weekend?"

There's a long pause. Maybe she's checking her calendar or, more likely, spying on a neighbor. Finally, she speaks. "I don't think so. It's pretty evident our last dinner doesn't warrant repeating."

She hasn't changed a bit in my absence—which I knew already because Anna's been filling me in on their discussions. But since I'm aspiring to mimic the way Anna, uh, Angelica, lets Mom slide right off her, I don't take no for an answer. "How about afternoon tea at a restaurant, then? My treat."

"I've been reading in the paper that things aren't so great in your business," she says, a complete non sequitur until I realize she's commenting on my ability to pay for her mug of English breakfast. "Something about a drought and high prices for cow feed. Of course, with all the obesity out there, a little less ice cream could be a good thing. . . ."

I let her ramble until she runs out of steam. "My company's great, Mom. My salary is, too. In fact, I got a raise. I'll call during the week and we'll firm up the time and place."

"Fine, fine. I'll be happy for the change of scenery, seeing how I've been sitting in my house by myself for ages."

"That's not true. Anna and Radha come over often."

"Well, once or twice, maybe," she says, embarrassed that I know more than she thought. "Mostly I'm here without company."

Another time I might have said, *That's how you've set it up, Mom: running everybody out of your life.* Happily, I don't need to go there. "I'm looking forward to seeing you."

"Fine." She hangs up quickly.

"Love you, too, Mom," I say into the dead phone, playing out how I've always dreamed our conversations might end, but for once not really caring that it doesn't.

A moment later, I hear ringing again. Could it possibly be my mother, reconsidering her role in our unhappy tango? I doubt it, but I'm intrigued enough to grab the receiver. I'm met with a dial tone. How can there be a dial tone when the ringing is so clear? I hear it again and realize my brain jumped the gun. No one is on the phone; it's the doorbell.

I peek surreptitiously through my bedroom curtains, praying that it isn't Brad. I'm not ready to tell him of my decision.

Thankfully, it's Janelle. I head for the front door, and open it, smiling. "Hey! So glad you're here. Was I expecting you?" Today is the one Saturday a month Janelle and I never get together. I have a long-standing, monthly shopping date with Gretta.

"I was hoping you were. Tried calling a while ago, but you didn't answer. I left a message."

"Oops. I remember hearing it ring when I was getting up. I started doing yoga and forgot to check. What's up?"

"Mostly I had an errand to run nearby, so I thought I'd swing over. Am I interrupting anything? Anyone?" She smiles, looking around.

"No one's here but me. I guess that's the way it's gonna be for a while."

I discuss again my decision to end things with Brad, which I've told her over the phone, and also describe my talk this morning with my mother.

"Good for you about your mother!" she says enthusiastically. "You've no idea how much negative energy you've been carting around that you'll release by making amends." She enfolds me in a supportive hug. I notice she didn't mention Brad—another reason I adore her. I've always sensed that Janelle wasn't wild about Brad for me, likely because of his lack of spiritual curiosity. But she never said one word against him.

When she releases me, I ask, "Are you here just for a hi and a hug—which is fine—or is something going on? Or did you find out any more about that amazing energy stuff? I didn't hear your message."

"Those teachings *are* brilliant! But that's not why I'm here. Now that you ask . . . I've been thinking about that ten-day silent retreat this summer. I figured you might need an in-person arm-twist to sign up with me."

"You're mad!" I shriek. "There's not a chance I could keep from talking ten days. My tongue would be wagging like a dog's in a sweltering summer."

"How do you know? You didn't think you'd make it through the one weekend. But you not only kept your mouth shut, you went without coffee. Despite the fact that it was offered to you on the black market." She grins, recalling the story I told her about the swamis during the ride home from the retreat.

"Not a black market exactly," I smile. "They did have milk and sugar."

"You're changing the subject. But I'm not gonna let you get away with it. Think about how deep we can go in ten days of silence."

"You and I have trouble going five minutes without yapping about what's on our minds," I say, recalling our many phone check-ins. "Plus, these days—what with my mother, Brad, and my sundae event—my brain's on terminal overload. There's no way I'd be able to shut it down."

"Your event's in June; the retreat's not till July. I think it'd be the perfect way to decompress. Anyway, you know they understand if you can't keep silent the whole time. Remember what Lucinda said? They expect people to cheat—and that was only a weekend."

"Okay, okay. I promise I'll give it some thought. But that's all I'm promising."

"Think how much easier it'll be to connect to your spirit after those ten days—and what an influence you'd have on others. Remember what Hawkins wrote: A single person at a high vibrational level counterbalances the lower energies of millions." She turns to the front door, pleased with the case she's made. "Meditate on it long and hard before coming to a decision. Of course, if you decide 'yes' right away, there's no need to meditate on it at all!" We laugh and embrace again before she makes her exit.

"See you at yoga class Monday?" I call out as she opens her car door.

"Wouldn't miss it! Wear your fabulous purple outfit. It's a knockout on you."

That's what I love about Janelle, I think as I watch her Prius shrink smaller and smaller until it disappears. *She speaks to both my highest spiritual self and my highest feminine self—and she's smart enough to know they're intertwined.*

🕉

The phone is ringing again. This time I know it is the phone because I'm standing by the open and empty door. *Time to bite the bullet with Brad.* I take a long, slow breath (two phone rings' worth, to the point where I'm wondering whether my real intention is centering myself or getting him to abandon hope and hang up).

Finally, I head to the living room and pick up the receiver. "Hello?"

"Thank goodness you're home. I thought maybe you weren't." It's a man's voice, but not Brad's.

"Yonatan?" My brother-in-law has never phoned me before. He leaves the social planning to Anna.

"Yeah. Listen. Angelica's been hurt."

"What do you mean, 'hurt'?" I feel the blood drain so fast from my legs, I grab hold of the wall.

"Car accident. We're at Northwest Medical." A really long pause. "It's bad."

"I'll be right over," I say. My trembling hand starts returning the phone to the cradle when I realize he might need to say more. I yank it back to my ear. "Are *you* okay? Do you need anything before I get there?"

"Prayers. Lots of prayers." The line goes dead.

I'm dressed in sweaty yoga clothes, but I'm not about to take time to change, even though my mother's voice silently scolds me for going out dressed improperly. If calm, cool Yonatan says it's bad, it must be awful.

The hospital is a forty-five-minute drive away. My arms are shaking so badly, I'm not sure I can helm the steering wheel.

Maybe I should call Janelle to drive me, since she can't have gotten far? But I don't know how long I'll need to stay at the hospital, and besides, I might need my car. I dry the tears I've just realized are gushing down my cheeks, slip on some loafers and stumble into the driver's seat.

The trip seems endless. For some reason, my car has trouble picking up WNOW without a ton of static, so I suffer through a lite FM station offering an endless parade of what Brad jokingly calls the golden moldies. Only when I finally pull into the hospital parking lot does it occur to me that I could have turned the radio off. I would have much preferred silence.

I fly into the lobby and ask at the desk for Angelica's room. A cute guy working there (some part of my normal brain seems to working, or I wouldn't have noticed his looks) directs me to the fifth floor, intensive care. Those two words send my panic thermostat rising higher.

Yonatan's standing outside her room when I blast around the corner. I pull up short.

"We can't go in right now. The doctor's putting in a breathing tube," he says in a voice so low, I have to strain to make out the words. I initially think he's saying *breeding tube*, as if Anna's here for some sort of experimental reproductive procedure.

"Can't she breathe on her own?" I respond in horror once I grasp his words.

"The doctors were hoping. They say once they put in the tube, it can be hard to get her to breathe without it. But now they say they have no choice."

"What . . . what happened?" I ask timidly, not sure I want the answer.

"We don't know everything yet. The police are investigating. Apparently there was a witness. He didn't see the crash, but says a minute before the accident, the other driver was juggling her cell and what seemed like a satellite radio remote. She might have been distracted at the intersection Angelica was going through."

"Did she hit the back of Angelica's car?" I ask. "That couldn't have done too much damage."

"No. Angelica was going straight. The woman was turning, and slammed into Angelica's door. She's in this hospital, too. Not hurt as seriously, from what the cops say. But it's bad enough that they haven't questioned her yet."

I struggle to recall that peaceful place I'd encountered during my morning sujal, which feels like centuries ago. It's beyond elusive. "What are Angelica's injuries exactly?"

He answers as if the mute button has been pressed on a phone, so I have to lean in to hear. "A lot of internal bleeding— ruptured spleen, colon, lung, I think. The biggest question is her brain. There's bleeding there, too. The doctors worry how much damage is already done, and how much more there could be if she has a stroke."

"Is that possible?" My anxiety leaps even higher.

"With her injuries, they tell me it's likely."

My legs wobble again and I decide to let myself go to the floor. My hands break my fall on the cold linoleum. I look at my palms: they're plastered with dust. *Don't they ever clean? Shouldn't a hospital, filled with sick people, be spotless?* I realize these thoughts aren't productive, so I bring my attention back to Yonatan. He looks as panicked as a drowning puppy. I reach out and touch his leg; he leans over and holds my shoulder. The contact feels good, as if by hanging on to each other, we can keep ourselves afloat.

"Where's Radha?" I ask after a time, amazed I haven't thought about her until now. I'm coming to see that a traumatized mind is like a randomly pelting ice storm rather than an even blanket of snow.

"Home with our neighbor. She was sleeping when I got the call, so I had Susan come to the house. I wanted to assess things first, so I could know what to tell her. Your mother's going to pick up Radha when she comes over."

My mother. The news drops like a guillotine. I'm glad I called her this morning to make amends. But I'm not eager to see her now, when we'll both be so emotionally fragile.

"When, um, do you think my mother will arrive?" My tone aims for nonchalance, even though I'm sure Anna has kept Yonatan abreast of my mother maelstrom.

"Within the hour. She needed time to shower and do her hair. I don't have to tell you—"

"No. You don't have to tell me anything that has to do with my mother."

"Listen. Your mother has about a thousand unresolved issues, but you don't have to let any of that affect you."

"Look at you! Consoling me—at a moment like this!"

"I think we need to console each other. That's why I called you first. I was being selfish. I figured it would help me, having another spiritual person here."

"Between me and my mom, that's no trophy. But I know what you mean." I pause, trying to pull myself together. "Well, if you're wanting my higher self, I should probably make a better effort to give it to you. Should we spend a few minutes meditating?"

"Wonderful! We can send Angelica our healing energies, too."

I'm not totally convinced it will help her, but I'm willing to try it. What I know for sure is that sujaling will make me feel better. "Think we can go to her room?"

Yonatan walks over to the nurse at the center station. He comes back and reports that the doctor is finished but that ICU visitors can go in two at a time, on the hour, and stay for only fifteen minutes. I glance at my watch; three minutes before noon. Close enough.

I'm a few paces ahead of Yonatan when we get to the closed door. I try to take a deep breath before pushing it open, but rather than tunneling down to my abdomen, the air catches high in my chest. My meager effort at calming myself doesn't help once I get inside. It's like a war zone: bleeping monitors, tubes attached to Anna's face and chest, her body battered and bandaged. My weak knees return with a vengeance, giving out so fast, I crash to the floor again. Before Yonatan says a word, I signal that I'm okay. I'm disgusted to notice the floor is filthy here, too.

Yonatan plants himself on the linoleum beside me, pretzels his legs, and closes his eyes. He begins to chant softly, *"Om Namah Shivaya."* I straighten my spine, cross my own legs, and join in. The repeated melody feels like a feather caressing my nerves, and the lyrics—which I remind myself is a call to connect with spirit—soothes me. When we finish chanting, fresher oxygen seems to have filled the room. We sit in silence for several minutes. I figure it can't hurt to visualize a golden healing light surrounding my sister.

Our stillness is shattered by the banging of the door. A nurse, or rather, a five-foot, 200-pound thunderbolt, blasts into the room. The juxtaposition between her harried entrance and our peaceful presence is apparent even to her. She stops in her tracks, but after a pause resumes her frenzy.

"Visiting time's over. This patient needs her rest," she barks as she bustles over to Anna to adjust some tubes.

She was resting nicely until you barged in, I feel like saying, bristling even at her phrase *this patient*, as if Anna were the bed rather than the living woman in it. But I don't think it's wise to make enemies of the staff. Yonatan evidently agrees.

We stand to leave, but instead of heading to the door, he walks over to the nurse. Her back is to him as she brusquely changes a bandage on Anna's arm. Right at this moment, I feel like slugging this compassionless technocrat, so it's particularly eye-opening to watch Yonatan in action. He places a loving hand on the nurse's left shoulder, a gesture that leads to her involuntary sigh. Since she doesn't shoo it off, he gently adds his other hand to her right side.

"Bless you for all you do with such love and caring," Yonatan says, his voice as melodic as if he were still chanting. "I'm so pleased my wife is in your capable hands. If there's anything you yourself need during this time, please let us know. We're happy to serve you."

The nurse lights up like daybreak. "Don't you worry. I'll do my best for her. I've got thirty years' experience, and I'm gonna use every one of them in your wife's behalf."

"Thank you so much. I'm Yonatan Simke. That's my wife, Angelica, in the bed. And this is her sister, Lorna Crawford."

"Helen Stiver. Nice to meet you, although I'm sorry it's under such tragic circumstances," she says, warmth overtaking her as she thrusts out her arm for a firm handshake. "I'll do everything humanly possible to help Angelica pull through."

As we leave the room, I feel a new sense of confidence that she will.

Chapter 19

The two of us head for the waiting room down the hall. When I push open the swinging door, I'm assaulted by the sight of the orange flea market–quality couch and love seat that take up much of the otherwise Spartan room. A wan, fake tree hides in the corner. Almost instinctively, I look down at the floor. It's so sparkling clean, I could do a locust pose without a mat.

"I don't get it," I say, appalled. "Where the healthy people are, the floors are spotless, but the sick people get layers of dust?"

"I'd venture to guess this room was scrubbed by some family member with lots of time on his hands," Yonatan answers nonjudgmentally. "Cleaning can be cathartic."

"You think? I'd much rather mope than mop."

"That's what makes the world go round." He shrugs.

I flop onto the love seat, which squeaks as loudly as a whoopee cushion. Yonatan and I laugh at the noise, relieved to have a break in the tension. We've still got smiles on our faces when the door swings open and my mother barges into the room, followed a few paces behind by Radha.

"What could possibly be cause for levity at a time like this," Mom snarls, stopping so short that Radha nearly crashes into her.

"Hello, Mom," I say, the smile automatically wiped from my

face by her mere presence. "No matter how dire times are, some things are funny, and you just gotta laugh."

"I don't think your sister being near death is the least bit humorous!" For dramatic effect, she marches past me, arms swinging. She plops down on the couch—and is greeted by the same whoopee cushion sound. Yonatan and I muffle our giggles.

"How are you, Radha?" I bound toward the person I'm genuinely happy to see. She's still perched near the door, perhaps trying to create both physical and emotional distance from my mother. I scoop her in a full embrace.

"I'm okay, I guess. Any more news? Grandma said the last she heard, they were putting tubes down Mom's throat."

"That's right," Yonatan answers. "To help her breathe. But now that she's got the tube, she's breathing fine. It's serious, but Mom's a fighter. And she's got lots of help—from the people in the hospital and, of course, from her guardian angels."

"I keep repeating, 'She's recovering, she's recovering,'" Radha says softly. "I hope Mom's saying that to herself, too."

"You know she is," Yonatan replies.

ॐ

For the next few hours, we're silent zombies on the pumpkin couches, Mom's presence sucking all life from the already depressing room. Radha and I sit hip to hip on the love seat, Yonatan and Mom on opposite ends of the couch. I can't help thinking we look like mannequins in a department store, except I'm wearing sweaty yoga pants with expensive loafers. Mom's perfectly coiffed hair and Armani cream blazer make her window-ready, but her charm is negated by those red-lipsticked sneers she keeps sending my way, even as she simultaneously fingers her rosaries.

Every hour on the hour, Yonatan and one of us trek into Anna's room for our allotted visit, returning each time to report that nothing has changed. I try to comfort myself with the knowledge that no shift is better than a downhill dash. The second time I accompany Yonatan, Helen's in the room, adjusting Anna's tubes and bandages. Maybe it's my imagination, but I'd swear she's handling Anna with a lighter touch. Helen gently grazes my hand—I'm not sure if by accident—when I step close to whisper loving sentiments into Anna's ear. At exactly fifteen after, however, Helen shows she's still Nurse Ratched at heart: "Visiting time over," she barks, and shoos us out the door.

Back in waiting room hell, Radha's seat is vacant. When I ask Mom where she went, she doesn't know, and doesn't seem to care. She mumbles something about maybe Radha being in the bathroom or getting a drink. "Didn't she say, when she left?" I demand, my issues about my mother's lack of concern for children in her care rising like a coiled snake. But Yonatan walks over and puts his hands on my shoulders in the same tender way he won over Helen, and his peaceful palms pacify me, too. Radha returns a short while later, cup of water in hand, and, relieved, we take up our familiar places.

Until now, I've done a spectacular job keeping my mind tuned to willing Anna's recovery. But as darkness begins to descend outside, a parallel blackness settles in me. *What horror on wheels dared do this to my sister? How could a driver pay attention to her phone and stupid radio and not to the woman she might have killed with her hurling weapon of steel!* I hate this excuse for a woman. I can't even say I hate her action, separating the doer from the deed. I deeply loathe her every cell. *Why isn't she the one badly hurt? Why can't it be her with the miles of tubes crammed down her gullet?*

During the next hour, I work myself into such a state of anger, I'm ready to rip the head off the next person who walks into the room. Just as I think this, the door swings open. I will myself not to do anything stupid. I expect the visitor to be a doctor with some hopeful (I pray!) news, or another waiting family dealing with their own personal purgatory. Shockingly, it's Handout Don.

I've seen Don sporadically over the years since my mother temporarily took him into our home. In the times I'd seen him in adulthood, he always looked like the scruffy misfit I knew he was. But now, standing by the door, he looks stunning. He's dressed like a model for a men's suit ad: crisp blue pinstripe; monochrome burgundy shirt and tie; and drop-dead chain-stitched, ankle-high dress shoes. His typically ruffled black hair is combed into neat waves, and he holds a black leather briefcase.

"Don! What the hell are you doing here? I mean, how the heck do you even know?" I stammer, trying to prevent the fuse in my firecracker rage from lighting.

"I'm so sorry I wasn't able to come earlier," he says. "As you can imagine, I wanted to the minute I heard from your mother. But I had to work—I know, it's the weekend—but I had a big meeting today I couldn't miss."

"Mom called *you*? I thought she didn't want anything to do with you!"

"It was the old me she didn't want anything to do with. The new me is so much better to be around: Honest. Caring. Genuine. Hardworking."

"Exaggerating," I snort. "Let's take that last one for starters. You haven't worked hard a day in your life!"

"Actually, Lorna, I got a great job right after I took that spiritual retreat. While there, I realized I could change the direction of my life anytime I wanted, so I have. I'm training to be the new public affairs manager for an advocacy group to protect New Jersey's rivers."

"If you weren't dressed the part, I'd add *delusional* to your list of traits. But I have to admit, you look fabulous."

"It's you I have to thank, Lorna. From the bottom of my heart. Your donation is what made the retreat possible."

I hadn't even remembered I sent Don that check. As I recall, I was flying after that night of bonding with my colleagues and wanted to do something to blast me to even greater heights. Hearing his words, my heart swells, and my anger at the world softens a bit.

"Who knew, our little Lorna's a makeover maven in disguise?" my mom chimes in, but I'm feeling so contented, she doesn't get the rise she's obviously after.

Don walks over to Radha and gives her a loving hug. This same klutzy Don who, when he would go into Mom's kitchen for a glass of milk, made such a racket, you'd have thought a cow was somehow involved. Yet his stride now is almost regal. After embracing Radha, he pats Yonatan on the back. Then he reaches Mom and kisses her cheek, professing great pleasure over her appearance. She glows from the attention. Finally he glides over to me, stopping so close, I can smell his minty breath.

"Lorna," he says more quietly, perhaps so my mother doesn't hear. "I've been wanting sooo much to tell you how you've helped change my life. I started to call several times, but I feared the phone wouldn't do my gratitude justice. Yet now a face-to-face thanks doesn't seem adequate, either."

"Really, Don. There's no need to thank me," I reply, equally quietly. "I'm glad you're finally getting yourself together."

He blushes. "How's Anna doing?" He asks this louder, to reengage others in the room. "The nurse at the desk said she's unconscious."

No one else replies, so I dive in. "Right now it's all wait and . . . Well, in truth, there's not much to see. We can't go in but once an hour."

"I want to wait with all of you, if you'll let me. I know I've had a funny way of showing it sometimes, but your family's always meant the world to me."

I halfheartedly wave him to the open spot on the couch

between Yonatan and Mom. I return to my seat next to Radha. Don and I hit the cushions simultaneously. The big whooshing sound filling the air brings a smile to everyone. Except, of course, to my mother.

ॐ

At some point during the long night, I must have fallen asleep. My first clue is the daylight streaking into the waiting room. Not surprisingly, the windows have no curtains. The second is that I'm the only one in the room. Third: my neck is killing me. I blink several times, trying to regain my bearings.

An aching dullness in my gut reminds me where I am. I wonder whether everyone is gone from the room because they were summoned to Anna's bedside to deliver a hasty good-bye. But before that terror has a chance to overwhelm me, I force the opposite idea through my brain: Maybe Anna's remarkably recovered, and they're in her room celebrating.

I'm eager to go down the hall to confirm that hopeful scenario, but first I need to work the stiffness out of my body. I rotate into a sitting spinal twist, crossing my right leg over my left to generate resistance, then spinning my torso and head around to the right. This feels delicious. I hold the pose for several minutes, breathing into each vertebrae as I continue stretching and twirling. I'm coiled like a corkscrew when the door suddenly swings open.

"Oh, I'm sorry. I didn't realize anyone was in here," a woman says, readying to retreat.

"It's okay. There's plenty of room here." I unwind myself and shift over in the love seat to take up less space, even though the couch is wide open. The woman, about my age, has luscious dark red hair, which, while a little tangled, cascades gorgeously over her lime silk blouse. She walks over to the couch and sits so gently, no sound emerges.

"I'm Lorna," I say.

"Dolores."

"Nice to meet you." I wind around to stretch in the other direction, and our conversation comes to a temporary halt. Finally, the worst kinks out of my neck, I swing back to face front and, fearing an awkward silence, speak again.

"Who're you here visiting?" I ask because I can't think of what else to say.

"My mum. I've been staying in her room to be with her, but the doctors asked me to leave while they examine her this morning. Anyway, I had to get out for a breath of air."

"You won't find much air in this waiting room." I laugh, dropping my right ear to my shoulder and relishing the stretch on the side of my neck. "It clearly wasn't designed with people in mind."

"You mean, you don't love this orange sofa?" She points to a particularly crackly spot. "I was thinking of asking where they got it so I could buy one for *my* house!"

"Is your house around here?" I ask, mostly to be friendly, as I drop my left ear.

"Not too far. Hoboken."

"Wow," I straighten up. "That's where I live! I have a house off Elm. Don't you love it there?"

"I do! I love the people, the energy, the history. The funny thing is, my grandpa used to live in Hoboken. Now he's in California, but every time he comes East, he marvels at how Hoboken's been transformed. Says it used to be a real pit. A pit with potential, I guess."

For reasons I can't discern, I'm starting to warm to this Dolores. I abandon my yoga to concentrate more intently on her. "Have you been to the new Spanish café on Washington Street? The tapas are fantastic—and the décor charming."

"You mean it's nicer than this place?" She sweeps her arms to indicate the room, then gets more serious. "Well I haven't been there. But you're the third person who's told me about it, so I will definitely check it out."

"There's a new bookstore on that corner, too. Also divine."

"Wow, a bookstore opening rather than closing. That's worth noting in this day and age."

"You like to read?"

"Love to! All kinds of books: women's novels, memoirs, mysteries, self-help. You might say my taste is eclectic."

"Well, you'll love this store. The staff's incredibly smart. Last time they pointed me to several gems I hadn't heard of. And *their* couches are incredibly cozy."

"Sounds dreamy. I love curling up on a sofa with a great book."

"You definitely won't wanna curl up on this sofa," I say, absentmindedly rubbing my neck. "This furniture's not only tacky, it's uncomfortable. Though maybe it'll be better now that my mother's left the room."

"You don't get along with your mum, huh? I'm always sorry to hear people say that. I adore mine, which is why it's so upsetting she's here."

"I certainly got the booby prize in the mother lottery," I confess, pausing after I say this because it strikes me I've overshared. "I'm sorry if I'm being too personal about myself. I haven't known you five minutes, but I admit I feel a connection between us. Still, I shouldn't be talking ill of mothers when yours is sick."

"It's fine, really. More than fine. It's great to have someone besides that Nazi nurse to talk to. And I feel that connection, too. I was going to ask if you wanted to go to that Spanish café or bookstore with me sometime, but I stopped myself because we hardly know each other."

"I'd love to do that!" I say, touched by her openness.

"I'm not offended when you bash your mother. It's a shame, but I know not everyone has one as great as mine. But I bet you have other relatives you adore. Your dad, maybe?" She smiles again, a slightly crooked arc that for some unknown reason endears her to me further.

"I hardly knew my dad. But I've a sister I treasure. Her husband and daughter are marvelous, too."

"I always wanted a sister. I'm an only child."

"Mine's terrific. She's the reason I'm here. She was in a car accident yesterday; hit by some woman not paying attention to the wheel. Plowed right into her. My sister's barely hanging on. It makes me just wanna strangle that bitch driver."

Dolores's smile wanes. "Your sister's name?"

"Anna Simke. She goes by Angelica, though, which is perfect since she really is an angel. She's the only person I've ever known who gets along with everyone—even my mom. Well, her husband does, too. He's another angel."

"I think I need to leave now," Dolores says, brusquely standing and rushing to the door, gorgeous green-and-gray slingbacks tapping out her speedy exit.

"I don't understand. Did I say something to offend you?"

Dolores answers over her shoulder in her final step to the door. "In case you were wondering, the bitch's name is Ada. And I'm her daughter."

Once the door closes, it takes a minute for this interaction to sink in. I feel terrible that I disparaged Dolores's mother, but the ire I feel toward that menace on wheels remains as biting as ever. The angel on one shoulder tells me I should run after Dolores to apologize, but the devil, who holds great sway right now, wins out. I wait till I'm sure Dolores is out of range; then I stagger down the hall to the nurses' station for an update on Anna's condition. A genial-looking woman behind the desk tells me that Anna's situation remains unchanged, and that my relatives went to the cafeteria a short while earlier.

I head back toward the waiting room, hoping for the chance

to fortify myself in the quiet before my mother returns, when outside the door, I practically crash into Gretta and my neighbor, Ruth. Gretta is dressed in a blue-and-yellow-striped cotton dress and jeweled flip-flops, her hair constrained by a bright blue headband. Ruth looks different somehow, and it takes me a minute to realize she's wearing an outfit straight out of *Vogue*: She's layered a tank under a bright cotton sweater, with a short skirt and leggings. Even her usual grandma shoes have been replaced with two-inch-heeled baggy boots. Her formerly severe bun hangs in a looser knot, pieces floating attractively around her face.

"Gretta! Ruth! What are you doing here? You guys don't even know each other! And how did you know I was here?"

"You didn't show up for our lunch and shopping date yesterday," Gretta says. "At first I thought maybe you blew me off to hang out with your yoga girlfriend, but when you didn't answer my calls to your house or cell into the night, I got worried. Swung by your house first thing this morning."

I completely forgot I was supposed to meet Gretta for our standing monthly shopping spree. I'd also left my cell phone on the kitchen counter when I raced out of my house yesterday.

"I still don't understand. . . . How would you know I'm here? And how did you and Ruth get together?" I wonder whether this puzzle would be less confusing if I weren't so worried about Anna.

"The world is a marble!" Ruth says, pausing after that pronouncement as if it explained everything. Finally, she continues. "A few minutes before I saw Gretta pull up to your house, I had phoned a good friend. She's a nurse. She told me she'd met a lovely man and woman yesterday who showed their appreciation for her hard work, something she rarely gets. Imagine how startled I was when she mentioned your name."

"You mean that short, plump woman?" I ask, not grasping until the words are out how unflattering they sound.

"The same." Ruth doesn't seem offended. "I told Helen to take extra care of your sister, and she said she'd already promised you she'd go the extra mile. I don't know how you did that! Helen's got a heart of gold, but her exterior's tougher to crack than a bank vault. Took me a year before I saw that kind of softness from her."

I suddenly realize how Ruth knows Helen: from when her daughter battled the leukemia, which we've had several long conversations about since our first evening of bonding. As if reading my mind, Ruth continues. "Yes, this is the hospital where Faith was treated. And where she died." The look on Gretta's face reflects her surprise. Ruth turns to her and continues. "My daughter Faith was diagnosed at eleven and lived till fourteen. With all her treatments, we got to know this hospital—and Helen—quite well."

"Tell me more about Faith," I say, feeling a desire for a deeper connection with Ruth right now.

"In every day of her short life, she showed what a gem she was. Never complained, even through the roughest treatments. Never asked, 'Why me? Why not somebody else?' Toward the end, when she was so sick, she could barely lift her head off the pillow, she talked about how blessed she was to be able to see the flowers in her room, hear the singing birds outside, and be with wonderful doctors and nurses. No one cried harder than Helen when she passed on."

"How long ago was that?" Gretta asks, barely getting the words out.

"Three years." She pauses for several seconds, trying to swallow a lump in her throat. But after a moment, she continues. "I'm clear she's in a great place now. I don't believe people are finished when they die. Faith went on to another dimension. Maybe she's even planning to come back as another wonderful human being."

"I don't know what I believe, but if it gives you comfort to have those thoughts, I'm all for them," Gretta says, to my great surprise. Normally, anything to do with spirit sends Gretta flying away faster than the Concorde. "Ruth's been telling me how much you've influenced her," Gretta adds, turning to face me, and I see her eyes glisten. "How after you went to visit her that first night, she started caring about herself again."

"I get no credit for that," I say. "It was Radha who got to know Ruth, who helped me see the light in a neighbor I'd, frankly, ignored."

"Maybe that's true. But Ruth says it was after *you* visited that she saw it was time to move on with her life."

"I can't explain it, Lorna, since we didn't talk about much that evening," Ruth says to me. "And I know I bored you, prattling on about my flowers."

"Not at all!" I protest. But the need to be honest overtakes me. "Okay, maybe a little. But I *would* like to learn more about flowers. Your garden is gorgeous."

"To me it didn't matter what we talked about, just that you'd come over. I saw that it was time to put joy back in my life. That it wasn't dissing Faith's memory if I did that. In fact, she'd be the person who'd most want me to."

"Well, I must say you look terrific. I thought I saw something different in you the other night, but I was too wrapped up in my boyfriend question to pay close attention. You've transformed."

"Thank you. But Gretta and I didn't come to talk about me. How's your sister? How are *you*?"

I take them to see Anna—Helen lets us sneak into the room even though it's the bottom of the hour. Seeing Anna's still-battered condition, the three of us dissolve into a mass of embraces and tears.

Ruth and Gretta want to stay the afternoon, but I tell them there's no need, that there's hardly any room in the waiting area. It's not that I'm not thrilled to see them. But I want to sit in silence for the rest of the day, to try to calm my still-festering anger toward Ada. After a few more minutes of bonding, I walk them out to Gretta's car.

The fresh air feels like life itself, so after they drive away, I linger outside. When I finally head back towards the waiting room, Yonatan ambushes me in the hall.

"Please feel free to say no, but I've been thinking Angelica would love to have the healing things on her altar: her crystals, angel statues, and what she calls the 'wisdoms of the world'—her mini Bible, Torah, and Qur'an. Might you be up at some point to going to our house to get them? If you don't want to, I hope you'll be honest enough to say no."

"Of course I'll get them," I reply brightly. "I think those would do her, and me, some good. In fact, I'll go now."

"You're a treasure, Lorna. I hope you know how much I appreciate you."

Blushing, I give Yonatan a hug, and he gives me his house keys. A few minutes later, I walk toward the elevator that leads to the parking lot from which I just came. Heading down the hall, I pass several open doors I hadn't noticed while chatting with Ruth and Gretta. In one room, two young children are climbing all over their father in bed. I don't know what he's here for, but I hope it isn't a broken limb! In another, a group of middle-aged women are singing "Happy Birthday" to an elderly man. His daughters, I think, silently adding my good wishes.

After I press the elevator button, I glance into the closest room. The door is open wide enough for me to see a woman sitting on a chair at the foot of the bed. Although I can't see her head or much of her torso, I'd know those sling-back shoes anywhere. Dolores. Which means, of course, that the woman in that bed is the idiot who slammed into Anna. I try to look away, waiting eons for what I'm sure is a spitefully sluggish elevator. I press the button a dozen times. Still, my eyes keep drawing back to that room. How ironic that in other circumstances, Dolores and I might have turned out to be friends.

Thankfully, Dolores doesn't see me. I feel the rage rising up again, my hatred for her mother boiling my insides. When the empty elevator finally arrives, I leap inside. Only when the doors close do I realize my hands are shaking, my head is throbbing, and I can barely catch my breath.

"Bitch!" I pound my fist on the elevator wall. "Bitch! Bitch! Bitch!" But rather than reducing my rage, the outburst only fuels my fury.

Chapter 20

The trip to Anna's house passes in a fog so deep, it's like Seattle in a steam room. I'm not sure how I even got here. Crumpled on Anna's favorite living room chair, I have no memory of my key turning over the engine, of driving out of the hospital garage, of the familiar landmarks I must have passed—the county park, the oversized Whole Foods, the restored old train depot where I make that left turn. I don't recall leaving the car, walking past their garden Buddha statue near the bougainvilleas, opening the front door, or plopping into this chair.

I knew at the hospital that I was barely holding it together, but now I'm surprised to see how unhinged I truly am. It scares me to realize that I drove here completely unaware of the road. But apparently I made it without hitting anyone—which is a heck of a lot more than I can say about the beast who tunneled into Anna.

I finally get enough energy to pull myself off the chair and aim my body for the master bathroom. My head is pounding, so I hope to find Tylenol or, better yet, something stronger. I fantasize about turning up a Valium, even though I'm certain I will find nothing of the kind in any medicine chest belonging to Yonatan and Anna. Once I enter the rose-colored bathroom, I notice a pair of Yonatan's dirty socks tossed around the floor, which reminds me of Brad's similarly strewn-about undergarments in his home.

The medicine chest is completely bare. *Do they never take any painkillers? Not even for a pounding headache?*

Once I leave the bathroom, I see that the door to the bedroom closet is open and Yonatan's clothes are crumpled underfoot. Even items that *are* hung up are done so haphazardly, wrinkling the shoulders of dress shirts and running crazy zigzag pleats down trouser legs. How does this not make Anna nuts, especially since the dresses, slacks, and blouses on her side are hung to perfection? For the next half hour, I'm oddly driven to organize his clothes, my annoyance at his slovenly style rising with every snap and fold. I know it's ridiculous to get worked up over this nonsense (I don't even live with the guy!), but I can't help myself. Once the clothes are organized, I move on to lining up his wayward shoes. He's got all these unused shoe trees stashed in back, so I stuff them into his wingtips and loafers. When I'm finished, I stand and look at my handiwork. I'm completely unsatisfied. Not even a morsel of relief.

Empty-hearted, I drag my spent self to the kitchen to rummage through the cabinets, hoping somehow a bottle of Dewar's or Absolut will magically appear between the organic beans and spelt flour. I dream of downing a whole fifth and passing out on the floor. No such luck. There's not even a damn bottle of wine. *Why can't these people come by their mentally altered state with a little assistance every once in a while?* I know that Miss Gumby also believes alcohol interferes with efforts to sustain elevated consciousness. Referring to the Hindu God of Righteousness, she laughs that she prefers "Ram over rum." But right now, I could use a booze-infused shortcut.

The thought of Miss Gumby inspires me to head back to the living room and slink to the floor. I get ready to press into Downward Dog. Maybe getting my butt into the air will shake me out of this funk. I don't enjoy doing this pose, because it takes too much effort to keep my back aligned. Still, every yoga book describes Downward Dog as the perfect asana for relieving stress and energizing the body, two things I frantically need right now.

The moment I put my weight on my hands and feet, however, I tumble down. Maybe that pose was too ambitious. Staying close to the Mexican tile I'm already lying on, I straighten my torso and legs and fold my hands beneath my shoulders. A cobra can't be too tough, can it? It's distressing to realize that just one day ago, during my long yoga practice, I'd have considered such a question absurd.

Pressing on my palms, I stretch my neck and lift my head. Oxygen flows into my back and shoulders, releasing the tight muscles. I hold this posture for several minutes. Then, under the mistaken theory that if a little feels good, a lot will be better, I straighten my elbows and raise my chest and abdomen off the floor. On a regular day, I could hold this pose forever. But I collapse quickly, banging my cheek so hard a welt starts rising. Stinging tears flow. I feel completely overwhelmed.

I force myself back to the kitchen, where I wrap ice in a towel and press it against my face. I trudge over to the living room, to a leather club chair that I normally find so comfortable. Today I resent how it wants to swallow me whole. I actually kick its leg in anger.

At some point during my stupor, I decide I should boost my energy by eating, even though I'm not the slightest bit hungry. I drag myself to the kitchen again, and rummaging through the pantry, I find a box of honey O cereal—the organic kind, of course. There's soy milk in the refrigerator, but the thought of chewing something sodden nauseates me. I decide to eat it dry. I lug the box to the kitchen table, plop myself onto the carved wood chair, and dip my hand in.

After a time, I notice the box is empty. That's impossible, since it was nearly full when I sat down. I look on the floor to see where the cereal has fallen. Bending over, I feel a roiling in my stomach that lets me know where the O's have gone. I can't believe I ate all that—and mindlessly, too. I vaguely recall that mindful eating was something I'd once mastered. Hah! *How did the O's taste? Sweet? Crunchy?* Who the hell knows.

A while later, I'm back in the swallowing chair, again uncertain when I got here. I wonder if grief can make you senile. I know for certain, it can make you mad. I'm furious at Yonatan's messiness, and even at this stupid chair. Of course, that's nothing to what I feel about that Ada—a witch who should have flown her broomstick rather than driven a car. How dare she get inside a two-ton weapon of steel and not keep watch where she is going! The bile in my throat rises with every thought until it threatens to choke me. Would that I could use it to strangle Ada!

"You horrible, miserable, person!" I scream, hoping Ada hears my words across the miles. "Why do you continue to live?"

I must have repeated this crazy raving over and over, because when I finally get a grip on myself, my larynx is exhausted. Worse, somehow I'm standing atop the coffee table, veins popping out on my neck. I climb down and skulk back into the chair.

I'm desperate to gain control over my suffering. Surely, after hundreds of hours of the now seemingly useless reading I've done, there must be some spiritual truth I can latch on to. Is there no brilliant wisdom that can calm my mind and make this moment okay?

I can't recall a single word.

All I can think of is how I wish I could change what happened. If only I could turn back time, return Anna to that moment when she hit the gas pedal, but this time entice her to pause one teeny second. Or, what if I had called Anna yesterday morning, delaying her trip with a tale of my decision to break up with Brad or the progress of my ice cream sundae event. We could've giggled over the firefighters I've arranged to squirt chocolate syrup from their hoses, or the famous TV news people who are jockeying to be the one who puts the giant cherry decoration on top. She wouldn't have been at that intersection at that fateful moment, and we'd both be laughing today.

"Why did it have to turn out this way? I'd do anything to have things be different!" I'm shouting again.

"You can get things to be different," a strange, powerful voice inside me answers. "But the only way to get there is to accept things as they are right now."

Normally, a voice from the blue would terrify me. But I know this voice. Or, at least, I have a passing familiarity. It's the calm, inner me that I've glimpsed during a good meditation or one of the powerful deep relaxations that end Miss Gumby's yoga class.

I also recognize the wisdom behind the voice. That sentiment hails from the spiritual teacher Eckhart Tolle, whose books I've read dozens of times and whose insights helped me quell my pain-body during that almost-ruined night out with Brad. Tolle's words remind me that it's always my choice how I view and react to any event.

I shuffle to the bookshelf across Anna's living room and pick up a copy of Tolle's *The Power of Now*. "Surrender to the grief," I read aloud from a random page I've opened to. "Embrace it. Then see how the miracle of surrender transmutes deep suffering into deep peace."

Surrender to the grief? Even if I wanted to, how could I do that? The lucid answer comes immediately: Start with the body. Focus on what my body is experiencing right now.

At another time or place, I would judge these thoughts ridiculous. But maybe it's because I'm in a house where masters live, their loving molecules suffusing the air, that I'm convinced this is a good idea. I sit in my chair, close my eyes, and steel myself to peek inside.

The first thing I notice is that my abdomen is hosting a veritable parade. There's a gymnast doing flip-flops, a gyroscope swirling in circles, an elevator on a local route up and down. All this action frightens me, though I resolve to maintain my focus. After a time, I realize that underneath those frenzied sensations there's a lizard in my gut, thrashing about.

I watch the lizard run in circles, until it hits me: The lizard is fear. I'm terrified Anna might not pull through. How can I live without my Anna, the rock I've always counted on, my surrogate mother, and more recently, my steady spiritual guide? Other fears about my life—wanting to break up with Brad but not to end up alone, balancing my friendships with Gretta and Janelle, protecting my job from Carletta—come bubbling up, too. Rather than trap the lizard in a cage, I spend the next half hour letting it run free. I don't try to distract myself with happy thoughts. I make it okay to feel the fear.

Eventually, my focus moves to my chest. My heart's still beating—a good sign. But there's a murkiness below my breastbone, a thick sludge. I take a deep breath, preparing to wade in. I enter cautiously, and immediately sense sadness all around. Sadness not only for current events, but also for the past, for all the times I let my mother's poison affect me. Sadness that she drove away my dad. Sadness that my own life hasn't always gone the way I've wanted. Sadness that I can't solidly stay connected to my highest source.

I don't pretend that things are okay. I allow myself to wallow in the sorrow. I rub my sad feelings into my skin, pour them over my head, squish them between my toes. In the process, something buried beneath the muck becomes uncovered. It's the pure, raw grief in my heart, completely exposed. I let it be.

Some minutes later, I shift to my throat. A snake is tightening my airway. I know that I have long run away from this snake: anger. Anger at that horrid Ada, of course. But in truth, I'm pissed at a long parade: Gretta and my other girlfriends, Carletta, Brendan, Brad, my mother, my dad. Even myself, for the missteps I've made over the years. I don't try to strangle the snake, and for the first time, I don't worry he will strangle me. I watch and allow.

I observe these emotions for minutes—or is it hours? I am inside time, which means it doesn't pass quickly or slowly, or seemingly at all. Yet I don't feel impatient.

Eventually, a strange calm washes over me. I've fully embraced my fear, sadness, and anger, and this permission has diminished them. Taking their place is a gracious acceptance. It's not that I'm happy about Anna's condition or any of the other mountains challenging my life. But I no longer feel ill equipped to scale them. I understand in a powerful way that where I am is fine, because from here I can get anywhere I want to go. The embankment may still be steep, but if I take one mindful step at a time, I'm certain that my higher self will remove some of my heavy baggage, enabling me to reach the top.

I open my eyes and, remarkably, spy a copy of Jon Kabat-Zinn's *Coming to Our Senses* on the bookshelf. I get up and retrieve it. When I return to my chair, which, oddly, feels comfortable now, I flip to the same passage that reminded me yesterday of the purpose of meditation. Now I realize it's also meant to remind me of the purpose of life: "It is really an inward gesture that inclines the heart and mind (seen as one seamless whole) toward a full-spectrum awareness of the present moment just as it is, accepting whatever is happening simply because it is already happening."

I truly understand. I need to stop flailing, to let the currents gently carry me down the river, to allow the universe to move me through what is ultimately a glorious life. The ability to embrace everything exactly as it is is the true objective of the yoga and sujaling I've been doing. The goal is not momentary inner peace in the corner of my bedroom. It's the lingering calm that sustains every moment, regardless of what transpires.

I put down the book, close my eyes, and melt into the most profound and peaceful silence I've ever encountered.

Chapter 21

After sitting for an amount of time that completely eludes my linear brain, I feel as refreshed as if I'd been on an around-the-world vacation. I can't wait to get back to the hospital. I'm in the perfect space to comfort Yonatan, Radha, my mother, and even Dolores and her mom.

Remembering that I came here to retrieve the objects from Anna's altar, I head for her meditation room—a whole, glorious room, not simply the corner of a bedroom! Seven healing crystals stretch across the altar, one for each color of the chakras, the energy centers that run through the body. The green one catches my eye. After a minute of staring, I understand: this is the chakra of the heart, the area I'm most connected to right now. I gather them up, along with Anna's four angel statues and the three holy books, placing everything into a canvas bag I find on a corner table. Then I head out the door.

I hop into my Volkswagen, determined this time to concentrate on the road. No more foot-on-the-gas-pedal, brain-in-the-clouds excursions, lest I end up in the bed next to Anna's. As I start the car, I'm conscious of a heightened sensation of my fingers making contact with the steering wheel, and my foot resting lightly on the brake pedal.

A few minutes into my drive, a fast-moving Chevy cuts me off. I'm pleased to see I harbor no ill will toward the driver—a young, lanky guy with long, stringy hair. Maybe he's got to get home quickly because his mother or girlfriend needs him. Or perhaps he's just come from a terrible trauma; I wonder how fast I drove on my way to Anna's house from the hospital.

I consider whether I can generate that same compassion toward my mother. The answer may finally be yes. At that channeled seminar Janelle and I attended, the spirit extolled the benefits of setting clear intentions for each upcoming situation. "When I get to the hospital, I will feel appreciation for my mother," I say loudly and proudly.

I pull into the hospital parking garage. Although it's packed and other cars are circling, I easily find a spot when a Jaguar pulls out right in front of me. At first I feel guilty that other drivers have been waiting longer, but then I realize that the spot opened for me because of my loving mind-set, a mind-set that is available to everyone.

I want to center myself before going up to the ICU, so I sit on a couch in the lobby and perform a few rounds of the alternate-nostril breathing that served me so well in the bathroom of LeHot. When I finish, I feel fully prepared to learn what's up with Anna, and to see my mom. I gather up the canvas bag and my purse and head down the hall.

Overflowing with energy, I decide to bound up the stairs to the fifth floor instead of waiting for the elevator. At the top, the stairway opens to an unfamiliar hallway. It takes a minute for me to get my bearings, but eventually I navigate the maze of passages and find my way to the waiting room. I'm around the corner from the closed room door when I hear my mother's voice booming from inside. A few steps later, the voice becomes clear enough that I can make out her hurtful words.

"Why did it have to be my Anna? My beloved Anna! The

daughter I love more than life itself!" she wails.

"Take a deep breath, Mrs. C. You're understandably upset about her condition. But Anna will be okay. You'll see. She's going to recover. Soon you'll be back to having two healthy daughters," Don's soothing voice responds.

"I can't bear the thought of life without my Anna! I've always treasured my Anna most of all!" She's sobbing through her words, but I hear them fine.

"I'm sure you love Lorna as much as Anna," Don says, and I grin at his valiant, if futile, effort to defend me.

"Don't talk about what you don't understand! Anna is my pride and joy. Lorna is . . . well . . . she isn't." Her voice trails off.

In the past, these words would have sliced through me like a fiery chain saw. Now, while they seem to have rendered my legs immobile, my heart and mind feel strikingly calm.

A warm hand lands on my shoulder. I spin around to face Yonatan, who must have come down the hall the other way, after his visiting time with Anna. From the look of compassion on his face, it's obvious he also overheard.

"Lorna, I'm so sorry," he says, sympathy swimming through his creamy dark eyes. "There's been no improvement in Angelica's condition. Your mother's out of her mind with worry. . . ."

The door to the waiting room swings open, and Don's head pops out. "I thought I heard talking," he says nervously. "How— how long have you been standing here?"

"Long enough," I reply, and without waiting for another word, I push past him and head inside.

Don and Yonatan don't follow me in, perhaps sensing my need to work through this alone. I take several slow, deep breaths, even though I already feel remarkably peaceful. My mother is sitting alone in the room, her Armani blazer a wrinkled mess, her hair more tousled than I've ever seen it. Her face sports a scowl. It's her effort to hide the embarrassment she feels at knowing I might have heard her ugly words.

I look into her eyes, and for the first time, I do not see my tormentor. Instead, I see a scared, lonely woman who was emotionally abandoned by her own mother and, later, by her spouse. She may not know it, and she'd certainly never admit it to me, but this wounded woman belittles me to keep me in the trenches alongside her.

Remarkably, I feel none of the pain, anger, and desperation that always accompany visits with my mother. I feel only the desire to accept this woman, warts and all—even if she is covered in a million of them. I've wanted her to be different for so many years that it never dawned on me until right now that I could choose to embrace her if she never changes at all.

A fantasy plays out in my head, similar to that children's parable I read by Neale Donald Walsch, *The Little Soul and the Sun*. Mother and I are dancing together in the spirit world, before either of us is born.

"I'll be the mean mother, you the yearning daughter who struggles to get past my seemingly hardened heart to see my true inner essence," I suggest.

"Nah, we did that last time, and the time before. Let's do it the other way this time."

We shake hands to seal the deal, and off she goes to her poverty-laden birth and sterile existence where she would come to feel inadequate, the better to later play out her role with me.

Maybe that scenario is fantasy, but who really knows what goes on before we're born? Anyway, if it helps me see my mother through tender eyes, if it can mend two horribly broken hearts, isn't that story as good as any other?

I recall how in *Tuesdays with Morrie*, the dying old man tells Mitch Albom we must "love each other or die." A part of my mother and of me has been dead for decades; this is the moment I choose love—and life.

My euphoria must be leaking out of me and heading her way, because my mother seems to be blooming. Her cheeks radiate aliveness. Or maybe she's still chagrined, and I'm just seeing through a rosier gaze.

"I love you, Mom," I say, feeling joyful as I vocalize these odd words. "I'm sorry for everything that's gone on between us. I'm going to make things different." I enfold her in an embrace, which, not surprisingly, she doesn't return—but doesn't repel, either.

"You know the problems were always your doing," she says stiffly. Then she reconsiders, her voice breaking. "I'm sorry it's been this way, too. I would like for us to be better."

"Well, we can. All we have to do is resolve to think different thoughts about each other. Actually, I've already resolved that, so I'm certain we will."

"I'm not as certain. But I'm willing to try," she murmurs, a stunning comment.

Yonatan picks this moment to pop his head into the room. "Angelica's opened her eyes. She's going to be okay!" he shouts.

"That's wonderful!" I answer. "And Mom and I are also."

ॐ

The next week is a blur of waiting. After that first moment when Angelica responded to the doctors and they knew she had no lasting brain damage, she's taken constant steps toward recovery.

For the first few days, Yonatan, Radha, Mom, and I practically live in the waiting room. Janelle, whom I finally had the presence of mind to call after my sister turned the corner, comes by daily during her lunch break, bringing fresh sandwiches and salads for all of us, plus affirmations for Angelica's continued progress that she's beautifully hand-lettered and decorated in watercolor. Each evening, Ruth and Gretta stop by together. The first day, they brought two large baskets full of blankets, sheets, and pillows from their houses. "Leave the floral sheets here when you go home," Ruth instructed. "You can cover up that horrid orange couch so nobody has to look at it again." Each day since, they've come bearing delicious dinners, everything from avocado sushi rolls to platters of grilled tofu to vegetable kebabs. Ruth's a fabulous cook, and she says she's enjoying cooking vegetarian, which she knows I'm trying to follow. She carefully ensures there's enough of her food so all the nurses can nibble, too.

Between visitors, Yonatan, Radha, and I often chant and sujal in Angelica's room. On the third morning after her breakthrough, Angelica feels well enough to join in from her recumbent position. Yonatan has arranged the healing crystals near the window, so when the sun shines, colorful beams of light dance around the walls. Radha is convinced these helped Angelica return to us. Don (yes, Don!) joins in our sujal when he arrives in the early evenings, having gone back to his new job the day after Angelica regained consciousness.

Several times over the course of those days, my mother utters more of her nasty comments about me, but I never consider rising to the bait. Even though she hasn't changed—not counting her visible relief over Angelica's steady recovery, seen in her reemerged erect posture, and fresh clothes and refreshed hair from a quick trip home—she looks completely different to me now.

Thankfully—that's how I truly feel—Dolores's mother had surgery to set the broken bones in her hip and leg, and she's recovering beautifully. Janelle told me yesterday that she looked up *Ada* in a name book and it means "rich gift," which, of course, is perfect. Nurse Helen, who's been a total doll, told us this morning that Ada will be leaving tomorrow. My sister will likely need another week before she's transferred to a rehab center.

On the seventh day after the crash, the police report comes

back, shocking us all. (Although she is quite lucid now, Angelica has no recollection of the moments before the accident.) It seems that an office building near the intersection was set up with security cameras, and the police finally studied the film. It clearly shows that it was Angelica who ran the red light just before Ada made her legal turn. All my initial hatred toward her, and Ada was the innocent victim! My sister's a terrific driver, so I can't quite work out how this could have happened. Maybe she sneezed as she approached the intersection and didn't see the light turn. Or maybe she blacked out for a second from some undiagnosed illness—which could explain her lack of memory leading up to the crash. Or maybe . . . a blast of irony snorts through my nostrils as I realize I hadn't dreamed up any of these scenarios for Ada when I thought the fault was hers.

On Sunday, I decide I can finally leave the hospital and return to work the following day. After all, my big event is fast approaching, and I have a lot of work still to do. Happily, I no longer wonder how I'm going to get all that unmelted ice cream into Central Park. I've had plenty of time to ponder this during my time here at the hospital, and I've latched on to a masterful plan.

As I'm saying good-bye to everyone in the waiting room, Don comes over and presses a book into my hand. "I bought this the other day," he says. "I want you to have it. Consider it my thank-you gift for what you did for me, paying for my retreat and all."

"No gift required, Don. Seeing what a changed man you are is present enough."

"It would make me happy to share this. Ironically, I bought it the day before Anna's accident, prompted by nothing in particular. The book leaped out at me from the bookstore shelf. I assume you agree that there are no coincidences, that we call everything to ourselves, whether we know it or not. Now I realize I bought it for you."

I examine the spine of the book. *Broken Open: How Difficult Times Can Help Us Grow*, by Elizabeth Lesser. I flip open to a page: ". . . the Odyssey, the Grail quest, the great initiation. . . . All of these names describe the process of surrendering to a time of great difficulty, allowing the pain to break us open, and then being reborn—stronger, wiser, and kinder."

I give Don a hug. "I'll be back tomorrow after work," I say. "Will you be here?"

"Absolutely."

ॐ

After saying good-bye to Angelica, I take the elevator down to the hospital lobby. As I walk toward the front door, I hear a familiar voice.

"Are you certain he's on the third floor? I'm pretty sure yesterday he was on seven," a woman asks sweetly.

I glance around but don't see anyone I know.

"Yes, it's spelled *B-y-r-o-n*. As in the poet, which he certainly is in his own quiet way," the lilting voice continues.

I trace it to a middle-aged woman standing near the reception desk, talking to an elderly man sitting behind the computer. Her curly auburn hair frames her face in ringlets, and combined with her prominent cheekbones, she's adorable, in a mature sort of way. Yet I've never seen her before.

"Oh, I see. He's been moved to three to start physical therapy," she replies after hearing the man answer. "Thank you so much for your help, and have a blessed day."

Like an apple falling from Newton's tree, it hits me where I know that voice from: the radio. It's Serena Robbins!

"Excuse me," I blabber, racing to catch her before she reaches the elevator. "You're Serena Robbins, aren't you? The radio host?"

"Yes, that's me. I'm sorry if I was speaking so loud I disturbed you. I've been trying to find my father for the last half hour. He isn't in the room he's been in all week."

"Wow! I can't believe you're Serena Robbins!" I know I'm gushing like Gretta, but I can't help myself. "I'm such a big fan—I listen to your show all the time. May I touch your hand or something?"

"If you're a big fan who listens all the time, may I touch *your* hand?"

"Come on! You must have so many listeners."

"Not as many as you think. Let's just say people on the leading spiritual edge are a distinct minority."

"Sorry to hear that. And sorry your father's ill." I pause, trying to figure out what to say next. "I guess what I want to tell you is, thank you. You've helped me become a better person—which has come in so handy here, with my sister being in a freak car accident and all."

"Oh, sweetheart. How awful for you and your family," she says, enfolding me in an embrace. "What's your sister's name? I'll send a healing to her, along with my dad, on my show later. We'll get all our listeners to join in."

"Wow, that would be great. Angelica would love that. Anna's her real name, but Angelica's the spiritual name she prefers. She's much better now, although it was touch and go for a while. I was an emotional wreck, but somehow I found my center and started accepting what life is throwing at me. It was profound how much that transformed everything."

"That's terrific. And if I may say so, you have a glorious glow about you, no doubt from how you used this experience to reconnect with your highest self."

"An actual glow? Can you see it?"

"Since you're the type of person who listens to my show, I'll go out on a limb here. I can see auras, the colored energy that surrounds everyone. Yours is a magnificent green—the color of a healer."

"A healer?" I laugh. "Hardly. I do special events marketing for ice cream."

"Ice cream is very healing. I've eaten a ton of it since my dad's been here, and it's helped a lot!" She giggles. "But that's not what I mean. You don't have to be a doctor or nurse to be a healer. I've never mended a busted bone, and I consider myself one. I bet you uplift people all the time."

"Well . . . I'm working on it."

"Listen, I've gotta go see my dad. Call in to my show sometime, and I'll definitely take your call on-air. Sounds like you could share a lot with my audience."

Chapter 22

As the doctor predicted, Anna recovered fully. I've gotten back to my regular life. Except nothing is the same.

On a Saturday several weeks after Anna's accident, I spend much of my day tending to my garden. I've done that so much lately, flowers are thriving everywhere. Ruth's taught me her secrets: not only how to enliven my yard, but also how meditative it can be to till earth and pull weeds. I adore hanging out here nearly every evening after work, and for hours on weekends. By late afternoon, I'm a mess, my hair and hands streaked with sweat and dirt.

I take a long, hot shower, rubbing my skin with energizing salt scrubs followed by a jasmine-scented sugar wash. I inhale deeply, breathing in not just the jasmine but also gratitude and awe. That's something that comes easily now.

Feeling fantastic in my own skin, I toss on comfortable shorts and a T-shirt and sit on my sujaling cushion in lotus position—each foot fully up on the opposite thigh! For the next forty-five minutes, I experience a sublime meditation, watching my mind tack back and forth without ever getting pulled in. I've come to realize I'll never banish those intrusive thoughts, but that's not the point. I need only to stay detached from the to-do list or the replaying conversation or whatever mental mumblings inevitably kick up their heels.

This time, during my sujal, I actually tune in to the faint hum I hear as I breathe the energy of the universe deep into my body and back out again. *Ohhhhmmmm*, it says. *Ohhhhmmm. Ohhhhmmm.* When my timer dings, I have to drag myself out of the *om*—which the yoga masters believe is the primordial sound underpinning all of life. Part of me wants to sit here for hours, relishing this energy, but the other part knows I'll carry it with me through the rest of my evening. Om. Yum!

I had to do my evening sujal early because tonight I've got a date with the girls. Since Angelica's release from the hospital, I've faithfully sujaled twice each day without fail—and I can surely say it hasn't failed me. No matter how I'm feeling beforehand, I'm always centered and calm by the time I'm finished.

In my kitchen, I throw together a salad of organic baby lettuce, grape tomatoes, and freshly cut cucumbers, then top it with canned black beans, artichoke hearts from a jar, and bottled vinaigrette dressing, my newfound effort to merge healthy with speedy. Even though I don't have much time, I make it my business to sit mindfully at the table and savor every bite. Food tastes so much better now that I'm really paying attention. This heightened focus on the taste, touch, and smell has made it pleasurable for me to eat at least occasionally in silence. Plus, I'm drawn to eating much less junk.

My cell phone rings, and I grab it from the counter. Once I see who it is, I heartily answer.

"Hey, Brad. How are you?" Even though I broke up with Brad the day I went back to work, we've remained friends. I think back to the Big Talk, when I swung by his house after hours, before heading to the hospital, and told him of my decision the moment we sat down on his living room sofa.

"I know you're mad that I ignored you before my launch, but I can't do more than apologize, and I've already done that a hundred times," he begged, trying to get me to reconsider.

"It isn't that," I said, gently taking his hand in mine.

"Well, you can't be mad that I didn't come to the hospital. You never called! I left you a hundred messages, wondering where you'd gone."

"Of course I'm not mad about that. I'm not mad about anything. I've just been thinking a lot about what I'm wanting."

"And how can what you're wanting not include me?" he implored. "We're great together. And you know I adore you!"

This wasn't going the way I intended. So I stared into his eyes and mustered all the love and sincerity I felt in my heart, and the right words flowed. "Brad, it's because I adore you that I want you to move on. You're a fabulous guy, and you deserve a girl who wants to get serious with you. With my yearning to connect to spirit, and your equally valid lack of interest, we're just not going in the same direction for that girl to be me."

He was sad, of course, and tried every which way to change my mind, but eventually he understood that I was firm. In the end, he wants to stay friends, a prospect that thrills me.

I turn my attention back to the fact that Brad is now on the line. "Sorry, I was daydreaming. I was just thinking how terrific you are," I say.

"As are you. I was wondering if there's an update on your sister's progress." I fill him in on how ecstatic her doctors have been that she's nearly returned to normal. Brad catches me up on how he's faring with his promotion. Thanks to his stellar launch, they've made him president of the whole division.

After we hang up, I skip to my bedroom to change into my going-out clothes—the black-and-white, lace-and-cashmere blouse my tailor recently found after it inexplicably went missing, black leather pants, wedges, and of course, my Pebbles hair—and head out the door.

Ruth's already waiting by my car. She's wearing a flattering coat dress over decorative leggings and red leather flats. "Am I dressed all right?" she asks hesitantly. "I haven't gone to a bar in ages; I had no idea what to wear. I saw a dress like this in a magazine, so I thought it might be good . . . but now I'm thinking it's maybe more for daytime?"

"You look great," I say, and mean it. Ruth has shed lots of weight and started sporting these magazine-inspired outfits, and she's developed her own Miss Gumbyish radiance.

"Are you sure your friends won't think I'm too old for them?" Ruth asks, unsettled. "I'm practically old enough to be their mother."

"They'll love you! Gretta already does, and she's the fussiest. She told me five times this week to make sure you were coming."

"Yes, Gretta is lovely. And of course, you know you are."

I give Ruth a squeeze, and we hop into my car. "Mind if I turn on the radio?" I ask.

"Sure, go ahead . . . but you're not into that rap stuff, are you?"

I chuckle. "I thought we'd both enjoy my favorite talk station." I flip on the radio, where my dial's already set to WNOW.

"Goooooood evening to you! So wonderful for you to be here, sharing this moment of our lives together. This is Serena Robbins, host of *Onward and Upward*. I'm going to jump right into my calls tonight, since I've got a special caller on the line. Regular listeners will probably remember Liz from Cleveland. She's called us in the past, trying to overcome her feelings of lovelessness and lack of acceptance."

"I've heard that Liz woman several times!" I exclaim. "Poor girl. She's so caught up in what other people think of her, which I sense isn't much."

"Hello, Serena and everyone," Liz's voice rings forcefully over my speakers. "You all know I've called often. . . ." She pauses, and I suspect she's once again listening to the sound of her voice over her household radio. You'd think she'd be over that by now.

"Uh, sorry. . . . Well, I used to think I was such a loser. I couldn't get people at my office to like me, and I even had questions about my so-called friends."

"Yes, and as I recall, you took it so personally," Serena Robbins chimes in, her voice reassuring as always. "I suggested that you were too invested in how other people saw you. It's like a loop. When they view you negatively and you notice they're seeing you that way, you attract more of it. The only way to change that is to break the cycle, starting with how you see yourself."

"Yes, I get that now. It's why I'm calling," Liz continues. "Last week I decided to try something different. When someone at work said something nasty about me, I said something good about me. Under my breath—but still. . . . Someone said I was a moron. I told myself, 'I'm smart.' Someone said I don't know how to talk to people. I said, 'I'm a perfect conversationalist.' This went on for days. And then the most incredible thing happened! They started seeing me like I was seeing me! A woman in my department came to me for advice on a project, which no one ever did before. A coworker invited me to lunch. My life is completely upside down from how it used to be!"

"Liz, that's wonderful. You've put the Law of Attraction into action. This law says you get what you put out. By lifting your own energy, you've allowed a higher energy to come back to you. I'm thrilled how it's working out. And what a great lesson for everyone listening out there."

"That's incredible," I say to Ruth as I turn down the volume so we can talk. "You should've heard her the first time she called. It was January, I think. Such a lost soul. And now she's found. Or, rather, she's found herself."

"Sounds like me! A lost soul in winter, a budding flower in spring. And it's all thanks to you."

"No, it's not. It's thanks to *you*. You're the one who changed yourself."

"Yeah. I felt defeated before, like my life was over. Now I realize that was just a chapter, not the whole story. I finally got that Faith—more than anyone—would've wanted me to move on. She would've loved the day spa I've been to, the gym I joined, the shops I've visited. I love them, too! And it all happened because you reached out to me that first night. It was such a surprise to learn that somebody cared. You are a true healer."

"You're the second person who's called me that!" I say, thinking of my talk with Serena Robbins. "The host of this radio show—who I told you I met at the hospital—she said that, too."

"In my book, anyone who brings out the light in other people is a healer. Faith was one. And so are you."

"I'll tell you a secret: Serena Robbins said I should call in on her show, so she could talk about my being a healer on the air."

"Oh, you definitely should! I'll call in after you to tell everyone how you've helped me change."

I feel a blush rise from my neck through my face, until even my forehead is crimson.

ॐ

Later that evening at Scoffo's, we're sitting at our usual spot, with an extra table tacked on the end to fit all the new women. There's not only Ruth, but also three other pals I've invited: Janelle, Mandy, and Dolores. Dolores and I have become tight friends despite our rocky beginning. It sure didn't help that I called her mom a bitch, especially since it turned out that Angelica caused the crash. But a few days after my epiphany, I got her number from the nurses and phoned to apologize. The old me would have been too embarrassed to admit I'd been so stupid, but I knew I'd done wrong and wanted to atone. Thankfully, Dolores was gracious. She said she understood that I was stressed out about my sister. I confessed that it was more: that I always needed to target my negative energy toward someone (Carletta, my mother . . .), and that day her mother was the lucky recipient. I confided that I'd been working on my spiritual self and hoped those days were behind me; that her mother sounded like a wonderful woman whom I'd love to meet sometime; and that, in those few minutes in the waiting room before I knew her identity, we seemed to have a fabulous connection.

That link has become more solid since. Dolores and I have gone out several times, chatting over dinner or coffee about life, fashion (our mutual passion), God (she's a devout Lutheran, which I respect, and I'm not, which she respects), and mothers. I've learned a few things about the mom department from Dolores. It was she who advised me to support my mother by accompanying her to her favorite places. Mom's main love is church (unless you count discretely spying on the neighbors from her living room window, which I wasn't game for). So last week I went with her to Father Jimmy's Mass. I can't say the service much moved me, but I loved feeling the elevated energy of the people in neighboring pews. And watching Mom beam over my presence (although of course she never said thanks) was as heart-opening as any homily.

When I first thought about inviting Mandy, Dolores, and Janelle to our standing girlfriend gabfest, I was nervous, knowing that Gretta can be jealous of my other friendships. Plus, I wasn't sure the new girls would fit in. Then I decided to just do it and have faith that everyone would mix together fine. Even if they didn't—if, say, Mallory ended up dissing Dolores, or Gretta revealed her jealousy of Janelle—I knew I could take it in stride. So far, though, everybody's getting along brilliantly.

"Janelle, how long did it take you to get good at yoga? I've been thinking of trying it—ever since I read a study showing it helps you lose weight," says Sarah, who once again came to our gathering late, after changing her outfit umpteen times.

"Really? Then I'd love to learn how to do it, too," Mallory singsongs.

"Despite its reputation, yoga's easy to learn," Janelle answers. "It takes a while to master the challenging poses, but the easy ones are just as powerful."

"Can *you* do the hard ones, Lorna?" Gretta asks, intrigued rather than contemptuous of my yoga practice, as she has been.

"Not like Janelle," I reply. "I'm finally getting to where I can do some of the medium poses. I'm contented with that."

"Can you stand on your head?" Tina asks me.

"Finally, yes!" I say. "After a million unintentional backflips, including one where I knocked over my living room bookcase on top of me, I finally found the magic balancing point. Of course, right after that, my yoga teacher gave us this huge lecture about how the most important part of yoga isn't standing on your head; it's being able to stand solidly on your feet. Doing a headstand is great fun, but I have to agree."

My old girlfriends look puzzled, and I don't belabor the point. "Headstand's nothing for Janelle," I continue. "She can take the pose even farther, lifting her head off the ground and balancing on her forearms! It's called the scorpion—no doubt because it stings most people who try it. It certainly would bite me." We all laugh.

The conversation segues into everyone discussing the most contorted position she can do. Gretta describes her wide-legged straddle, a holdover from her gymnastics days. Sarah says she can bend backwards so far, her hands touch the floor. Mandy claims that, while standing, she can reach over her head and grab her stretched-up free leg. I brag about my newly developed lotus pose. Dolores, with double-jointed fingers, can pile them one on top of the other. She demonstrates this to applause. Ruth's body isn't quite so flexible, she admits, but she delights us with the stretch of her tongue, which reaches her nose. We all try this, but it seems Ruth has a gene the rest of us lack. We're quite a sight, with all our tongues wagging, but no one besides Ruth even comes close to her nostrils.

At some point, the discussion comes around to Brad. They've all heard that I broke up with him, but I haven't seen most of my girlfriends since. They pepper me with questions.

"Was he heartbroken?" Mallory sighs.

"He wasn't thrilled," I answer, "but he understood."

"He did like you a lot," Gretta says. "And I think at least for a time, the feeling was mutual."

"I definitely adored Brad! Still do. We're just heading in different directions, so it didn't make sense to keep the relationship going."

"Can I ask you something, Lorna?" Sarah asks shyly.

"Shoot."

"Would you mind terribly if I gave Brad a call? I've always thought he was quite the catch."

The other girls' eyes widen, knowing that Sarah has crossed an electrified line in girlfriendom, and they're waiting to see whether she gets her deserved shock.

"You know, Sarah. I think you and Brad would make a great couple. You have my blessing."

"She does?" Gretta asks, incredulously. "If I'd known he was up for auction, I would've placed a bid!"

"Wow. It seems this Brad's a popular guy," Dolores says. "Maybe I should line up, too."

I laugh. "Uh, Dolores. You're engaged."

"A minor inconvenience!" she chuckles.

"Well, Lorna, you must really be over Brad if you're willing to let these man-eaters have a piece of him," Tina says. "Not you, Dolores," she adds, smiling across the table. "I don't know you well enough to say."

"I believe in appreciating what was, then moving on to what

will be," I say. "My next great relationship is right around the corner. Actually, it may be closer than that. There's someone I'm sort of interested in."

"Who? Tell! Tell!" they all shout in unison.

"I'm not saying yet. I don't want to jinx it. We've mostly spoken on the phone; he's only come over twice. I'll let you know if it becomes something more."

"Do you know who it is?" Gretta asks Janelle.

"No! This is the first I'm hearing."

Relief washes over Gretta's face: She hadn't lost her place as my supreme confidante.

"I may know who it is," Ruth says slyly. "I've seen a young man come to your house a couple of times." I squirm, realizing my secret is about to be exposed. "Don't worry, I'm not gonna say. I make it a point to respect people's wishes. When you're ready, you'll share."

"Thanks, Ruth," I say, my affection for her deepening further. "Let's move on to another topic, shall we?"

"How 'bout we play 'What's up with that person'?" Tina says.

"I'll need another drink before playing that," Sarah says, gulping the dregs of her second apple martini. Janelle and I have been sipping Perrier, while Mandy and Ruth each nurse small glasses of wine. Dolores, as much a drinker as the other girls, finishes up her second cosmo.

"Crystal, can we have another round?" Gretta shouts to the harried waitress who's served us for years.

"Be right out with them, girls," she replies, as she rushes a tray of highballs to another table.

I thought I'd feel awkward not drinking alcohol tonight, since we always go through several rounds of drinks and shots during our outings. But since I'm in such an accepting mode, not judging the girls for heavily imbibing, I feel that they're not judging me for not doing so.

"So what's this game?" Janelle asks.

"It's really fun," Mallory trills. "We pick a person at another table or the bar, and make up a story about their life and what brought them here."

"Right," Tina jumps in. "So, for example, that heavy woman at the bar. The one wearing the muumuu. If it was my turn, I'd say something like—" She pauses, apparently thinking. "—I'd say she's let herself go these past few years because her husband walked out on her. He started cheating with his secretary, and later married a dancer at a strip club. He was unhappy with his wife because—" She ponders again. "—her daughter died and the woman just fell apart, unable to function. She gained tons of weight, and now comes to the bar every day to drown her sorrows."

A choking sensation rises in my throat. Tina knows nothing about Ruth's history, yet except for the secretary and stripper details, she's nailed her past. I glance at Ruth's contorting face, desperately trying to hold back the tears.

"I've got a twist on this game I think could make it even more fun," Janelle says, somehow picking up vibes that a flood is about to break from Ruth's welling eyes, even though she doesn't know Ruth's tale and she doesn't have a good view of her from where she's sitting.

I know Tina didn't mean anything, and I don't want to make her feel guilty. But I worry that if I don't support Ruth, I won't be honoring our budding friendship. I waver for a moment before realizing that struggle is always a sign that I'm not tapped into my highest self. I close my eyes and focus on my heart. Within seconds, I'm clear what to do.

I leap up and walk past Dolores to get to Ruth, who's sitting between Gretta and Mandy. Angling next to Mandy, I gently place my hand on Ruth's shoulder. She grabs it and tightly squeezes. Gretta, who's gotten friendly with Ruth since

Angelica's accident and does know her past, begins stroking Ruth's other arm.

"What's going on?" Mallory says, reflecting the confusion of the others at the table. I give Ruth a chance to settle herself. When she's back in control, I look around at the staring gazes.

"Tina didn't know this, but Ruth lost her daughter several years ago, and her husband left her after."

"Ruth! I'm . . . I'm so sorry! I had no idea," a mortified Tina stammers. "Of course that story wasn't about you!"

Ruth gains her composure enough to speak. "No, it *was* about me. That's what's so upsetting. Deep in my heart, I knew my daughter was okay, that her spirit lives on, that she went to a better place. Yet I didn't let myself move forward. I held it together when Faith was dying by distracting myself in the details of her care, but once she passed, I gave in completely to my grief. I don't blame my husband for leaving. I was stuck. I felt like I didn't deserve my life, because Faith had been denied hers. Only recently, thanks to Lorna and her niece, have I been able to let that go."

Mallory jumps down Tina's throat. "You're such a dumb-ass, Tina! Saying those terrible things about Ruth!"

"I didn't say them about Ruth!" Tina fumes. "You think I woulda made up that story if I'd known about Ruth's daughter? There are a zillion stories I could've invented about that woman. And don't call me a dumb-ass again, you jerk!"

"You're the jerk! Why would Ruth ever want to come back and hang with us after this?"

"Whoa, slow down!" I say, returning to my seat. "Everybody's losing her peace here. Can we all take a minute to get back to the place we were at a few minutes ago? You know: appreciating each other. I know—let's try this: Everyone hold hands and close your eyes."

"No way. This is gonna be stupid!" Tina says.

"Just give it a try," I insist.

"Lorna, I think you're getting a little too 'out there' for us again," Sarah says, turning to Tina, who rolls her eyes in agreement.

"Maybe so," I say, holding my ground. "But I think you might like this."

"What're you gonna have us do?" Mallory whines.

"Nothing too weird. It's not like I'm asking you to wash the insides of your stomachs." I smirk at Janelle.

"I think Lorna just wants us to get back to a calm place. Her exercise can't hurt, can it?" Janelle says to the women.

"Exactly!" I say.

"Sounds good. I'm in," Dolores says, trying to shepherd the others.

Her excitement fails to influence them, probably because they barely know her. With a neutral countenance, I look around the table at each one of my pals. If they don't want to do this, I won't press them.

Finally, when I make eye contact with Gretta, she breaks the silence. "Okay. I'm in. Just make it quick."

I give her a big thank-you grin. Following Gretta's lead, the others nod their reluctant acquiescence.

After everyone holds hands, I paraphrase a guided meditation I recently discovered on YouTube. I instruct them to close their eyes, place their feet flat on the floor (or as flat as they go in the three-inch heels most of them are wearing), bring their shoulders back and down, and center their heads. "Now begin to envision a swirl of golden energy starting at your feet," I coo, "slowly working its way up your legs and torso, stopping when it gets to your heart. This energy is love. Feel it feeding your heart, and in turn getting fed by it. Enjoy the sensation of opening to its boundlessness." I give the girls a few minutes to experience this. Then I guide them to send that energy down their right arm and out their hand to the girlfriend sitting next to them, simultaneously soaking in the loving energy coming from the hand of the woman on their left. I focus on my adoration flowing out to Dolores. The love flows into me from Sarah, but really from all the wonderful women I'm blessed to know.

Five minutes later, I'm no longer sitting in a loud bar. Instead, I peacefully float on a fragrant, timeless sea. I peek open my eyes. From their relaxed and joyous expressions, I sense the other women are floating out there with me.

Eventually, I instruct them to open their eyes. For more than a minute, none of them does. They don't want to climb out of the water.

"I liked that," Sarah says when she finally looks around. "I'm not sure why, but it made me feel good."

"I'm not sure what that was, either. But I have to say I feel closer to all you guys," Dolores says.

"That *was* pretty neat," Tina agrees, sounding surprised. "I was so pissed at Mallory, and now I'm not anymore."

"Thanks, Lorna. There's nothing like reconnecting with your core to make even big conflicts seem meaningless," Janelle says.

"Yes, thank you, Lorna," Ruth says, looking more contented than I've ever seen her. "As that Serena Robbins woman told you, you *are* a powerful healer."

Everyone (except Janelle, who constantly hears me gush about the radio host) asks who Serena Robbins is and why she'd say I was a healer. Mandy jumps in with a (mercifully!) short sermon for healing as a lifestyle, not a profession, and how we all do it when we're at our best. I don't know that any of them buys it, but they're impressed that I met a radio personality—even one they've never heard of—and prod me to take her up on her offer to be on the show.

Janelle picks up where we left off before Tina's huge blunder. "I'd like to propose we try again with the 'What's up with that person?' game—only adding a bit of a twist."

"Oh, I don't think we should go there," Sarah says, alarmed.

"I agree we shouldn't go *there*. But this goes someplace else. I promise it'll be fun—and kind," Janelle replies.

"How's it work?" Dolores asks.

"Same as the other game, only we pick people who look troubled and say positive things about them. Even though they don't hear what we say, I believe seeing the best in them lifts their energy—and I know it elevates ours."

"I love that idea!" I say. "Who knows? We might even turn someone's life around."

"Sounds supremely hokey," Tina says. "But since the game we usually play didn't work out, to put it mildly, we might as well try something different."

"I'll go first." I scan the room for someone who looks unhappy. I'm excited about the possibilities. I once heard Wayne Dyer say on a PBS special, "When you change the way you look at things, the things you look at change." It's certainly becoming true in my experience.

As I look around, most people seem to be having a great time. *There must be someone,* I'm certain. Finally, I spy a woman sitting at a corner table. The guy she's with has his back toward us, but I can see her face, and it's miserable. Although probably in her early twenties, she has a wan appearance and deep frown lines that give the impression of a long and difficult life. She's got a large tattoo running up her forearm, which initially provokes a negative reaction in me, but then I recall the sweet woman who served us at the coffee shop and the spiritual men who dragged their wives to the weekend yoga retreat.

In past games, I might have tagged this woman as a lost soul, someone who married at seventeen because she was pregnant for the third time and couldn't afford another abortion. I might have invented that she'd stayed with the abusive man sitting across from her (his neck is the size of my thigh, with tattoos all over it, so he would have been simple to pigeonhole) because she's too weak to stand up and be counted. Now I see her in a completely different light.

"That woman over there," I say, surreptitiously pointing until everyone's stolen a peek. "She got pregnant at eighteen and decided to get married rather than abort the baby. Her partner was nervous because he was so young and didn't have an income, but he stayed in school and became, uh, an EMT. They came here tonight to celebrate their fifth wedding anniversary. They're a happy couple. Still, life's been rough because their daughter was born with a major defect and, um . . . has spent her life in a wheelchair. But tonight her husband brought her here to surprise her with great news: Their doctor learned of an experimental treatment that may help her walk, one that's worked miracles on other kids."

"Ooooh. I like that! It makes me feel good! This is more fun than I expected." Mallory says.

"I'll go next," Sarah jumps in, just as eager. "I'll take those two women over there." She points to a couple of midlifers to her right. When I look at this depressed pair—even a festive Dolce & Gabbana floral scarf on the blonde can't mask their gloom—I fear Sarah will say that one is confessing she's had a torrid, if ill-conceived, affair that's led to an impending divorce, and the other knows exactly from whence she speaks. But bless her heart, Sarah wanders far from there.

"The blond woman's been unhappy in her job as a stock trader for a decade, but she could never figure out what else to do. Yesterday at work was the final straw, when her portfolio plunged and her horrible boss made things more wretched than ever. She's venting now. What she doesn't know is that her friend here is about to tell her she's starting a new business, and she's inviting the woman to be her partner. They're gonna buy crafts from tribal women around the world and sell them on the Internet. Not only will they get rich, but they'll also help thousands of indigenous women make a better life for themselves and their kids."

"Uh, you're predicting the future. That's a no-no with this game," Tina scolds. "Although I do admit I love happy endings."

"In my version, predicting the future is fine—so long as it all ends well," Janelle says.

"Everyone's future is always fine, because we're eternal beings," Mandy says, a sentiment with which I agree, but that causes Tina and Mallory to simultaneously wrinkle their noses.

"Okay, my turn," Ruth says, scanning the crowded room. "Oh, this is gonna be good! I'll take *him*," she says, gesturing toward someone at the bar. My cough picks that moment to crank up its machine gun fire. I close my eyes and will it to stop. *My body is in radiant health,* I say to myself. This seems to slow the cough for a moment, but just when I hope it's finished, the gunning resumes. I catch sight of Janelle. She gives me the Look, the one that says if I'd only go to her Dr. Fallyn and his healing machine, my cough would vanish. She doesn't know I've already decided to try it.

Ruth is midthought when my cough subsides and I get back to the game. "Some might think it's weird for a priest to go to a bar, and maybe to an outsider, he looks kinda lonely sitting by himself, but this priest is having fun. He knows that opportunities to connect to the Divine happen everywhere, not only in a church." I spin around to where Ruth previously pointed, certain she must be referring to Father Jimmy.

"Excuse me," I say, after I see I'm right. "I know that Father!"

"Oh yeah, I remember you talking to him once," Tina says, intrigued.

I smile at her. "Don't get any ideas. He's an old friend, and a nice guy. My mom's taken me to his Mass."

"Tonight one of his sometime parishioners is gonna be thrilled she saw him here, because he's gonna help her feel good about herself." Ruth finishes up her narrative, winking at me before I rise and scurry away.

"Hi, Father Jimmy!" I say as I get to the bar.

"Lorna! So good to see you here again. And I must say, it was great to see you at Mass, too."

"Yeah, I went with my mother."

"It's wonderful that you and she are getting on so good lately. Terrible that it took your sister's accident to bring you closer, but I've always believed tragedy has its hidden glories. I guess your mom's nearly losing one daughter made her finally appreciate the other."

"Not exactly. Let's just say it made me realize there's no point hanging on to an unattainable dream. She's what I've got, and she's not gonna become a different kind of mother. I'm finally accepting that that's enough."

"How marvelous! That mind-set will serve you in all of life. And it's clear it already is. You're looking wonderful. When I saw you in church, I wanted to tell you, you have a peace about you. Of course, I'd like to believe my inspirational service played a part in that."

"You know, Father Jimmy, it has. I'm coming to believe there's no need to run from anything. Every place I go is an opportunity to lift up someone—which is the best way for me to also elevate myself. Even church—though I never thought I'd hear myself say that."

"I would hope especially church. But I'm not gonna give you my church sermon now."

"Thanks for refraining." I give Jimmy a friendly pat before I head back to my girlfriends. "See you one Sunday soon!"

When I return, Ruth asks, "So you know that priest? Glad I said only good things about him."

"I'm working on saying only good things about everyone, whether I know them or not," I reply.

"Uh-oh, Lorna the Lecturer's returned." Gretta scolds.

"No lecture. I'm zipping it." I pull an imaginary tab across my lips.

"I think this game's been terrific," Janelle says. "Look at us: We're all so happy. And look at the people we've talked about. It could be my imagination, but they seem better, too."

I look around and see that Janelle is right. The young couple is holding hands, the woman joyfully gazing into the guy's eyes. The older women, standing in preparation to leave, embrace in a monster hug. I don't know if they'll be starting a business—or saving the world—but they're definitely pumped. Father Jimmy looks radiant, too.

Tina figures out the split of the bill, and we all throw money on the table.

"I've really enjoyed hanging out with you girls and appreciate your letting me into your circle," Janelle says, a remark quickly seconded by Ruth, Mandy, and Dolores. "I don't know if any of you are into this, but Lorna and I are planning to go on a ten-day yoga retreat this summer, and we'd love to have any or all of you join us."

"I never said I was definitely going!" I protest. "Last we left it, I said maybe."

"Can I say maybe, too?" Gretta says, causing me to nearly spit out the final sip of Perrier I'd just taken.

"Gretta, it's ten days of silence—no gabbing, gossiping, nothing—not to mention hours of meditation, yoga. . . . Somehow I don't think it's for you."

"Well, Ruth here's been telling me a lot about the meditation you've been teaching her. Sounds like something I could use. Immersing myself in a ten-day retreat could be a great way to learn it—like going to Paris to study French," she says.

"I might be interested, too," Ruth says.

"Well, if it's good for all of you, I'd like more info," Mallory declares.

"Me, too," Dolores chimes in.

"You guys never cease to amaze me. I love you all," I say.

At that moment, a song starts playing over the sound system. Louis Armstrong croons about those blue skies and loving friends, and how it's such a wonderful world.

It certainly is, Louie, I think, as we all get up and head toward the door. *It certainly is.*

Chapter 23

The morning sky over Central Park is a perfect sapphire blue. The weather forecast for this June day, which I'd known in my gut would come through for me, calls for highs in the mid-seventies, a delightful temperature that will keep both the crowds and the ice cream from wilting. Most important, there's not a rain cloud in town. The gray canopy that normally hangs like a permanent awning over Manhattan scooted out yesterday and hasn't made an appearance since.

Surprisingly, I'm not nervous about our attempt to set the ice cream sundae record. During special events in the past that weren't half so large or unpredictable, I was always so panicked that my stomach regularly visited my toes. I'd pop a dozen Rolaids while mentally rewinding again and again all the glitches that could occur. But here at the park at eight in the morning, after a great night's sleep (and a first breath that was definitely an inhalation), I'm confident everything will be terrific.

Since the day when I came to know that my power comes from accepting whatever comes at me exactly as it is, I've opened a valve of well-being into the universe. How ironic that, now that I'm ready to embrace everything, even failure, success is the only thing flowing.

"You feeling optimistic?" Michelle asks, pausing from her jaunt around the Great Lawn while taking care of the million last-minute details.

"Absolutely! It's gonna be terrific! All the newspapers ran huge articles again this morning, so we're guaranteed a massive turnout. And the national TV people—including both news and talk shows—confirmed they're showing up. The weather's perfect, the ice cream crisis is solved. What more could I wish for?"

"I always knew you were clever, but solving the cold storage problem was even better than your usual. Gotta go. The TV guys need help figuring out the best locations to set up their cameras." She darts away.

The event's not scheduled to start until eleven. Between the well-organized Michelle, our hired production crew, and the employees pitching in from numerous departments at Favored-Flavors, there's not much I need to take care of, short of staying present and remembering it will all go as flawlessly as I've envisioned.

I look around, pleased with the progress so far. A team of about three dozen workers is hammering away, constructing a stage in the center of the huge expanse of grass in the jewel of Central Park that is the Great Lawn. Dozens of other men and women with walkie-talkies—employees of a company that specializes in the logistics of these big events—comb the grass for trash, sharp objects, dog poop, dead pigeons, and anything else that might distract from the fun. Near the stage, about fifty college kids from Columbia and NYU, based on their hoodies, are rolling up their sleeping bags. I heard they camped out last night so they could be closest to the action. A few early representatives from the police, firefighters, and mayor's offices are chatting under a tree near the lawn's edge. Many more will be showing up later. City officials are supporting this effort big-time, figuring it's great publicity for New York.

I look across the lawn and spot Brendan and Carletta strolling toward me. I can see Brendan's whitened grin from halfway across the field. For an instant, I chuckle that it could prove useful should we have an unexpected solar eclipse. But a compassionate thought quickly follows: Maybe he's overcompensating for having ugly, gray teeth as a child.

"Hello, Lorna," Brendan says, chin held high as usual. "Well, you certainly couldn't have picked a more magnificent day for your event here. The sky will make a perfect backdrop for your crazy ice cream concoction."

I feel not a whiff of need to push back. *It's a shame to be trapped by an ego that always has to be on top,* I muse sympathetically. *It has to exhaust him.*

"You've gotta be thrilled with how everything's been going. So glitch free!" Carletta says, giving my forearm a friendly tap.

"Totally. It's gonna be great." I return a warm pat to her shoulder. "I can't thank you enough for all your help, especially putting in those late-nighters this week so we could get everything done."

"It's been my pleasure. And thank *you* for getting Doug to pay for someone to watch my sister those nights. What a load off my mind not to have to worry how she's doing now that my mom's way too sick to manage her."

A conversation like this would have been unimaginable a few months back. But my relationship with Carletta has transformed. We'd been nicer to each other for a while, since she opened up about her disabled twin sister and dying mom. You can't know someone's in pain and not reach out to them, so I did. But still, clear she'd snatch my job from me in a nanosecond, I kept my emotional distance.

After my revelation at Angelica's house, however, I let all that go. I stopped worrying about whether she might someday get my position and began to appreciate the joy the job brings me. I'm no longer desperately clinging to it. When the time is ripe to move on to another slot, I'm glad Carletta will be a ready replacement. Our bond intensified this past week when she offered to help Michelle and me in our mad scramble to get everything finished. It was the least I could do to arrange for her sister's care while she assisted us, knowing she's been going to her mom's house every evening to take care of Brianne.

During one of our late-evening talks, while we were compiling the press kit for the media, I mentioned to Carletta that I was planning to take that ten-day silent retreat. I don't know what made me say it, because as the words tumbled from my mouth, I fully expected her to burst into hysterics about the absurdity of such a "vacation." Incredibly, she asked for more details. It seems yet another person may be joining Janelle and me. Whoever said the universe works in mysterious ways surely knew my friends and colleagues!

"Did you speak to Angelica today? Think she'll be able to come?" Carletta asks, as Brendan, clearly uncomfortable with our newfound coziness, scoots away. I've been keeping Carletta—and several other new friends from the office, including Doug's secretary, Olivia—informed of Angelica's recovery, which doctors say has been remarkably swift. With Angelica's positive attitude, I'm not surprised.

"Yeah, she's coming with my mom. Her husband's putting on a major retreat in the Berkshires this weekend. I thought for sure Angelica would have gone up yesterday, but she said my event's just as important. She's coming here and then catching a ride up to the mountains after."

"That's so great. I know it means a lot for you to have her here."

"To have my mother here, too!" I say. Another comment I never would have uttered before. "This event's important to me. I wanna share it with my whole family."

"I'm gonna help Michelle with the TV people. If you need me for anything else, just holler." Carletta smiles sweetly before walking away.

I notice that the hammering has stopped. I look to the front of the lawn. The workers have finished constructing a five-foot-high stage around a giant weighing scale. Behind it, they're setting up the colorful tent we'll be using to prepare our entertainment, and next to that, they'll build a low platform for the musicians. In the center of the main stage, on top of the scale, carpenters are attaching the enormous bowl to its special pedestal—an eight-foot-tall, carved piece of pristine mahogany, which glistens in the sunlight. The bowl and pedestal are gorgeous, as I knew they would be. They've even gotten their own publicity on design Web sites.

Nearby, metal barrels of chocolate syrup are lined up alongside a wide slatted box. The container was flown in last night, filled with sewn-together cherries that, once the sundae is complete, will ceremoniously be placed on top. Shivers go up my spine— kundalini energy, I've been told by Janelle—when I think about who I finally decided would crown the sundae, and how thrilled I am that she said yes. The people in my office thought I was nuts turning down two national morning show hosts—each of whom begged to do it—but I didn't care. Even my boss and the president of my company thought I'd lost a few brain cells, but they agreed that since the event was my idea, it was ultimately my call. With all the morning and "magazine" shows coming anyway, my choice doesn't seem to have hurt our publicity.

I flop down under a tree to touch up the welcome speech I'm going to give, check in on my walkie-talkie that the mayor's top assistant's arrived, watch people begin to stream into the park, and answer the occasional logistical question from staffers working the event. I look at my shoes—ugly numbers I bought last week because they're so comfortable. In the past, I wouldn't have been caught anywhere, let alone at a big event, in less than gorgeous footwear. But lately I've come to see that I can adore and appreciate everything, no matter how they look, and I'm already grateful for the fact that my feet, which I'll be standing on for hours, feel so pampered.

Before I know it, it's nearly eleven. I shake my mind out of preparation mode and look around the Great Lawn, examining the tens of thousands of people who have gathered. Like the city itself, they're a tapestry of ethnicities and ages: parents pushing strollers, school-age kids, single young professionals, cabbies and messenger boys in uniform, and numerous midlife and elderly couples. Most stand next to ice coolers of all shapes and sizes. I smile. My plan is going perfectly.

On my cue, the big band set up on the platform near the stage brings the morning to life, jazz trumpets and saxophones blaring. Realizing the event is starting, the crowd erupts in wild applause. After a few minutes, several dozen male dancers, dressed like old-fashioned ice cream soda jerks—in crisp white clothes and paper hats—file out of the tent. The band switches to early rock 'n' roll, and the men begin a medley of old dances, starting with the twist. The crowd bops along. This continues for fifteen minutes.

When the music suddenly crescendoes, a small truck drives through the path we've left among the crowd, stopping on the side of the center stage. It's painted to look like the traditional ice cream truck that still circles many neighborhoods. This one is a bit larger; in fact, it's the biggest freezer truck the city would allow us to drive on the lawn. Actually, they balked even at a truck of this size, but when we told them we wanted Mayor Jones to make his entrance by emerging from the cab, they made this one-time exception. The fact that we could pack many gallons of ice cream in the freezer compartment was the payoff for us. Of course, we couldn't cram even a fraction of the ice cream we need to break the record, but it will get things started.

The crowd hushes as the truck's cab door opens—and out comes the mayor, a tall, elegant black man, also dressed in the soda jerk garb. He's accompanied by our celebrity honoree, Veronica Swanson. I didn't think she'd return my call when I dialed her agent out of the blue, but she actually remembered our LeHot encounter. When she called me back, she told me—her words— that she'd thought that night that I'd had "a fabulous energy." *If you thought my energy was great then,* I wanted to tell her, *you should see me now that I finally understand what it means to be "enlightened."* But I just thanked her profusely for agreeing to participate.

The two of them make their way up the platform steps, and I walk several paces behind. Hunter Stanton, the silver-haired president of our company, is already standing on the stage. Hunter thanks the mayor and Veronica for coming, and each gets whistles and cheers when they say a few words. The thunderous applause grows even wilder when Hunter says it's time for the main attraction. "It's wonderful to go to a local ice cream parlor to have a nice sundae." He strains his voice to be heard over the shrieking crowd. "But how often do you get to make—and eat—a record-setting bonanza?" Veronica steps up to the mic to add the line I drummed up last evening: "It may be Saturday, but I think . . . it's sundae-time!"

At the mention of these words, the back of the truck opens, revealing a monstrous blob of vanilla chocolate swirl. Several men hook a sterilized conveyer belt between the truck and the huge bowl, and a dozen more start shoveling the ice cream onto the moving belt with specially designed golden shovels. Each time some ice cream makes it up the conveyer and plops over the edge into the bowl, the crowd roars. Finally, the truck is empty. This is my cue. I climb the platform steps and head to the microphone.

"Hello, everyone!" I pause for more screeching. It's amazing what people will scream at when they're having fun. "Are we gonna set a new world record?" More pausing for more roaring.

"Many of you know Favored-Flavors specifically chose the fabulous city of New York to break the world's largest sundae record —a record that has stood for two decades. You also know we can't do this without you, the residents of this wonderful city. That's because we couldn't bring all the ice cream we need into Central Park on our own. So we've asked you, the people who are the heart and soul of this great city, to join forces with your neighbors and fellow apartment and co-op dwellers to bring ice cream here in coolers. I want to thank the supermarkets in the city for accepting our coupons so you could get the ice cream for free, and also for stocking the dry ice you needed to keep it from melting." Even though I have a mic, I realize I'm shouting. I pause to give my voice a brief rest. With this restless crowd, I don't dare stop for long.

"It's my hope that we not only break this sundae record— which I'm confident we will—but that linking up with your neighbors will have the side benefit of building new connections among you. We hope these friendships continue long after the record is broken and the ice cream is eaten."

The crowd screams again, so I take this moment to grab a quick sip from the water bottle Michelle stored earlier by the microphone. "As you can see, we've got the base of the sundae already started," I continue. "During the next hour or so, we need everyone to slowly and orderly come forward and place their ice cream on top of what's already here. We're going to start on the left side of the platform, and in a methodical fashion, work our way to the right. Please wait for a guide to accompany your section, then walk carefully. If we lose ice cream in a mad dash to the bowl, we might endanger our world record. Okay, everyone, let the games begin!" I step off the stage, satisfied with my talk, to watch the electrified action.

The tent flaps open to reveal a hundred women dressed in the female version of 1950s ice cream fun—full-skirted pink dresses, white bibs, paper hats, bobby socks, and saddle shoes, all holding trays with attached (fake) ice cream soda glasses with two long straws—who disperse around the field. As the band plays a eclectic array of ice cream hits, everything from *Sesame Street*'s "Ernie's Ice Cream Cone" to Van Halen's racier "Ice Cream Man," the women escort groups to carry their coolers to the platform. There their ice cream containers are checked to ensure they are still factory sealed before being opened by our staff and their contents—a rainbow of colors and flavors, although a disproportionate amount of vanilla, I notice—dumped onto the conveyer belt, which lifts it to the bowl. Some of the coolers are large and packed full, requiring four or five people staggering together to carry them forward. Others coolers are petite, but nonetheless often carried by two or even three neighbors grinning and giggling over to the stage. I'm impressed by how orderly this process is, even though it takes nearly two hours before everyone gets a turn. It's after one o'clock when the escorts approach the final group.

I return to the stage, ready to energize the crowd once more. "Thank you all so much for your invaluable ice cream contributions," I say, to growing applause. "But of course, no sundae is complete without terrific toppings. To help us get delicious chocolate syrup on this ice cream tower, I present to you: the Fire Department of the City of New York!"

The crowd comes alive again as twenty members of New York's Bravest, as the department is affectionately known, dressed in full blaze-battling regalia, pick up the golden hoses that we've connected to the metal barrels. They look similar to firefighting hoses, but, like the shovels and conveyer belt, these are sterile versions we had manufactured for this event. As the hoses turn on, the band plays "The Candy Man." Fire department members direct the hoses over the ice cream. Out comes a choreographed spray of chocolate, raining down in a dance to the music.

When they finish, I look up and admire the sweets twinkling

in the gigantic bowl—it's listing a bit to the left, but thankfully is in no danger of falling over. A hush falls over the crowd as we wait for the official certifiers we hired from a national accounting firm to confer with Carletta, who's been assisting them.

Carletta smiles and heads my way. "You did it!" she whispers, hugging me while handing over a card with the official number.

"We all did it," I tell her as I turn to the microphone.

"Thank you, New York!" I scream, my heart exploding with excitement. "You came together with your friends and neighbors to build this ice cream masterpiece. And I've just been told the official certifiers have weighed in our sundae at seventy-seven thousand, two hundred forty-three pounds! We have all set the world ice cream sundae record!"

The crowd erupts like New Year's Eve. I wait for several minutes until their enthusiasm travels the inevitable path from raucous to restrained. All the while, I focus on how perfectly this event—not to mention my life—is going.

While the sundae dazzles in its chocolate patina, Michelle and some hired assistants carry over a ladder and set it next to the big bowl. It's time for the sundae's crowning achievement.

"And now, the grand finale: the cherry on top," I bellow into the mic. "You may not know the person we've selected to do the honors, but I urge all of you to find her station on the radio and listen to the beautiful message she has to share with us all." Right on cue, Serena Robbins comes out of the tent, lifts the cherry decoration out of its box, comes on stage, and begins to climb.

"Ladies and gentleman," I continue. "Topping our sundae is Serena Robbins, host of the show *Onward and Upward*, on the radio station WNOW. Let's all give her a big hand as she indeed goes onward and upward to complete your masterpiece."

Serena Robbins stops near the top of the ladder and delicately places the fruit on the sundae, trying to center it. The ice cream isn't quite even, so it slips a bit to the side. *Even this sundae wants to be unique, to make its own mark on this world,* I laugh to myself. Like a beret tipped on a Frenchman's head, it looks charming. That farmer was right—from afar, you can't tell it isn't one huge maraschino. After the sundae is topped, the band strikes up Queen's "We Are the Champions," and the audience explodes for a final time. Photographers from newspapers around the world begin snapping pictures—their flaring flashbulbs making it look like I've arranged for strobe lights, an effect I hadn't even planned.

To end the event, we've hired helicopters to fly overhead and drop thousands of sealed packages, each filled with a paper cup, napkin, and plastic spoon. Right on schedule, here they are! Their drops are planned for the edges of the Great Lawn, so as not to clobber people on the head. Everyone—including the toddlers and the elderly—gleefully runs to pick up the utensils, leaving a sea of temporarily abandoned coolers where they had stood. A huge, winding line quickly forms as people rush to get a taste of our historic dessert.

I walk over to Serena Robbins, who's descended the ladder, which is quickly carted away by a hired helper. The crew has also already detached the bowl from the pedestal and brought it down to the stage, so our assistants can help people dig in to the creation. I watch Serena eye the first people licking their spoons. Her auburn ringlets dance around her face, which is beaming.

"Thanks so much for making me a part of this day," she says, crushing me into a gigantic embrace. "I'm sure you had your pick of the litter. I'm still shocked that you chose me."

"And I'm shocked that you don't see how much you've helped change my life," I say, returning her squeeze. "I want everyone to know who you are!"

After a minute, we both finally let go. "I don't deserve too much credit," she says. "You were looking for the transformation. What's that expression? When the student is ready, the teacher appears."

"Well, thank you for being one of my teachers."

Michelle runs up to us, huffing and puffing. "Several TV reporters want to interview Ms. Robbins. I hope you don't mind if I steal her away." Not waiting for my answer, or to catch her breath, she steers Serena toward the waiting cameras.

"Excuse me, miss." I turn to see a group of people gathered behind me, with a fortysomething man in front, speaking to me.

"Yes?" I assume they're wondering if they can have seconds, or where to throw their empty bowls. (*Yes*, and *in the bags being held by all the dancers,* I prepare to tell them.)

"All of us want to thank you so much for this. We live in an apartment building on East Seventy-fourth Street," the man says, his arm gesturing to the dozen people around him. "Many of us have lived there for years, yet we were all strangers. When I saw the newspaper article about your event, I put notes in everyone's mailboxes. I got a great response; people volunteering their coolers, and their muscles, to schlep all those gallons over. It's been fun being a part of this record-breaking effort. But the best part is how we've gotten to know one another. I don't know what role you exactly played in organizing this event, but we want you to know that we appreciate your getting us to meet."

"Wow! Thanks so much for telling me. That was one of my motives for doing it this way. I was hoping it would bring people together."

"It certainly has!" the group replies in unison.

"Our building, too," says a twentysomething woman in jeans and a cute lace blouse standing with another group to my left. "We're from West Eighty-ninth Street. We also want to thank you for the great friends we've made in the past few days—from right next door!"

I'm buzzing from all this gratitude when I spy my mother, Angelica, and Radha under a tree by the edge of the tent. Angelica's still walking with a cane, and is avoiding the crush of this crowd.

I again thank the people surrounding me, and head over to visit with my family.

"I'm so happy to see you," I say, embracing first my mother, then Radha, then, more gingerly, the still fragile Angelica.

"We wouldn't miss it for the world," Angelica says. "Looks like everything's going perfectly, huh?"

"Just as I envisioned. And I did spend a lot of time visualizing it, which I think contributed to its turning out so great."

"I'm so happy for you, Aunt Lorna," Radha says.

"So am I, dear," my mom adds. "You've really put your all into this and certainly deserve to have it go your way."

I'm momentarily stunned by my mother's kind words. But then I realize that her improved relationship with me is just one more of the delights that have occurred since I tapped into that stream of positive energy.

"Lorna! Lorna!" I hear Gretta calling, and look up to see a group of women rushing toward me: Gretta, Ruth, Janelle, Dolores, all my drinking buddies, Mandy, and even Carole and Lucinda from the yoga retreat, who got in touch a few days ago, after reading publicity for the big event. "We've been looking all over for you! We're dying to tell you how much we loved this day!"

"It's been sooo fun!" Mallory says. "We brought over ten gallons ourselves, so we were a key part in making history here." One by one, I kiss them all. My heart is so full from all the love I'm feeling that I'm surprised no one's noticed it's expanded out of my chest and is surrounding not only me but the entire park.

Ruth sidles up to me. "Is your new man going to make an appearance?" she asks, loudly enough to perk up all ears, including my mother's.

"Yes, he's here somewhere, although in this crowd, I have no idea where. Things are great between us."

"Oh, goody. I was hoping it'd go well. He seems so excited

whenever he comes to your house." Ruth puts her arm around my waist and gives me a squeeze.

"You've been spying!"

"Just a little neighborly peek."

I lean in and whisper, more quietly so only she can hear, "There's something else I've been wanting to tell you, Ruth. I've shared how I've always hated my name, and even more so since I discovered it means 'alone.' But what you don't know is that I've given serious thought to changing it to Faith, to honor your daughter and the qualities she stood for. But after today, I've decided I'm gonna keep my name. It doesn't mean I'll have to be lonely. I can make it mean I'm blazing a unique path, one that helps others connect to their highest selves. Not to mention to their neighbors!"

"That's a great decision," Ruth says. "Just like you once thought you had to leave your ice cream job to do something meaningful, and look at the wonderful relationships you've nurtured today. I've no doubt you can keep your name and embody every quality you desire."

"So where's this new man?" my mom interrupts, impatient with my private discussion. "I'd love to see who has an interest in you." So the old mom hasn't completely disappeared. There's something to be said for the comfort of the familiar.

"Is it someone I know?" Gretta asks.

"Actually, it is," I say as I glance around the field and finally spot him heading this way. The sight makes my heart expand further, something I didn't think was possible. His gait is strong and steady. Thick black hair billows in the breeze as he approaches, forming a sort of halo around his beautiful face. At least to me it looks like a halo, since everything about him seems divine.

"Don?" a stupefied Gretta says as she spies him running toward us. "You're dating Handout Don?"

"I don't believe it," my mom says. "You've always hated him."

"I knew from the beginning that's who you'd been seeing," Ruth says triumphantly. "That first time he came to your house, he seemed concerned about impressing you. He stood outside combing his hair and trying to get up his nerve before knocking."

"Yup, I'm dating Handout Don. Only he's changed so much, I think of him now as Hand-up Don. He's lifting me up plenty."

"What was the turning point?" Janelle asks, intrigued.

"Something changed in how I saw him at the hospital. Well, even the fact that he was there spoke volumes. Then he came to my house, under the pretext of telling me how he 'paid forward' the money I'd given him for his retreat. That night we really hit it off. He's changed, of course, but the biggest shift was that I wasn't seeing the way he'd been. I was open to seeing him as he is now. We talked for hours, about yoga, great spiritual thinkers, life after death—we have so much in common."

I turn toward Don as he comes close enough to hear me. "Hi, sweetie. So happy you could make it!"

"Make it? I wouldn't miss this for the world." He gives me a deep, genuine kiss. The girls applaud.

For a second, I'm embarrassed, but I decide to plant my own kiss right back. I'm crazy about this guy, and the people in my life might as well know it.

"I told you I'd be here, though I had to scramble all morning to prepare for my meeting tomorrow. I got here just as the festivities started—what a spectacular event! I'm sure you're thrilled with how it went."

"How it's going, you mean. It's not over yet." I survey the sundae, about half its once-stupendous size, the serpentine sampling line still wrapped around much of the lawn.

"I never would have envisioned you with Don," Angelica says as she hobbles to me. "But since he makes you happy, I'm thrilled for you both." She clasps both Don and me. Her legs have gotten strong enough that she stays steady.

"You should get to know him as he is now," I say to my sister, loud enough for everyone to hear. "After years of floundering, he's truly discovered who he is and what's important—something people go through their whole lives not understanding. He's such a joy to be around."

Gretta, who's heard me vent about Don since middle school, remains wide-eyed. "It's gonna take me a while to get used to this," she admits, an honesty I appreciate. "Maybe if I contemplate it during our ten days of silence, by the time I speak again, I'll have adjusted!" We all chuckle.

"Who's having ten days of silence?" my mother asks, horrified.

Hands go up around the group. I'm touched. A few months ago, I had trouble hanging out with some of these women, because I feared they didn't share what was significant to me. Now in a few weeks we're going to embark on a thrilling new chapter of this journey together.

"I don't know about you, but I'm in the mood for ice cream!" Dolores says, picking up a handful of cup-and-spoon combinations from the ground.

"I can't imagine why you're craving ice cream, but I am too!" Mallory laughs.

"Can we cut the line, since we have an 'in'?" Tina asks.

"Sorry," I say. "It won't look good if I sneak you past people who've been waiting. Besides, if you get in line, you'll be able to chat with people around you—maybe make a new friend. I know firsthand that there are some incredible souls here."

The girls go off to sample the ice cream. Mom, Radha, and Angelica also say good-bye, since Mom has to get my sister and niece to the hired car that's taking them to Yonatan's retreat.

I turn to Don. "I'm gonna have to stay here for hours, making sure all this is eventually cleaned up. Why don't you go home and meet me around eight at my place for a celebratory dinner. Of takeout food, of course. I'm too exhausted to cook."

"You sure you don't need my help here?" he asks sweetly.

"Nah. I've got plenty of assistance. Plus, you have that meeting with the environmental coalition. I'm sure you could use the time preparing. I'll see you later."

"We're definitely gonna celebrate later. And not only about your sensational sundae event." He kisses me big again and turns to walk out of the park. As I watch his sinewy body stroll down the path, I recall another passage from the spiritual master Eckhart Tolle. Relationships "are not here to make you happy," he wrote, they are "here to make you conscious."

I can't help but think that, when you're as connected to the energy of the universe as I am, maybe they can do both.

About the author

Award-winning writer Meryl Davids Landau has seen her work published in such esteemed magazines as *O, the Oprah magazine, Reader's Digest, Glamour, More, U.S. News & World Report, Self, Redbook*, and *Whole Living*. This is her first novel. Meryl lives with her husband and two teenage children in South Florida. Although she tries to meditate, do yoga, and connect with spirit on a regular basis, like Lorna Crawford throughout much of this novel, she sometimes falls short.

Acknowledgments

The idea for this novel struck me some years ago, when I was in the kitchen making breakfast. The TV was on in the nearby family room, the host of a morning show interviewing a bestselling author. The sound carried faintly, and I couldn't discern who the writer was. But I stopped in my tracks (mid-scrambling my egg) when the author described how she came up with the idea for her books: "I asked myself, 'Where are the novels for women like me?'" Although all my writing to that point had been nonfiction, I was immediately inspired to start my own novel, one for spiritually seeking women like my girlfriends and me. I still don't know the identity of that author, but I feel deep appreciation to her for getting me started.

I also applaud and adore the women in my fiction-writing critique group: Leslie Pepper, Lynn Wasnak, and especially the indefatigable Sophia Dembling. Readers of earlier drafts who also provided feedback include my dear friend Leslie Lott (whose optimism and inspiration never faltered), Ruth Hathorn, Sandi King, Lori Landau, Suzy Anand Garfinkle, and Michele Anderson. Thanks, too, to my wonderful copyeditor, Eliani Torres, and to Fern Reiss, Stacey Joiner, and attorney Sallie Randolph for their invaluable assistance.

I also owe a debt of gratitude to all the members of the American Society of Journalists and Authors, where I got tremendous advice—not to mention the encouragement to keep going when the process seemed to take forever. (It didn't take long for me to discover that crafting a novel is a lot more intricate than writing a magazine article!)

Of course, a spiritually based novel like this one would not have been possible without all those who participated in my own personal evolution. Special thanks go to the numerous, rotating members of our longstanding Tuesday night study group, as well as to those in other study groups I have been part of; teachers of the many spiritual workshops I have attended; the talented energy healers who have worked with me these past few years; and the spiritual leaders and members of Temple Adath Or and the Center for Spiritual Living in South Florida and Integral Yoga Institute in New York. I am also indebted to the spiritual masters I have cited in this novel—all of whom set me on this glorious path!

Finally, I wish to thank my family: my darling husband Gary, who gave me the time and space to write, and my kids Richard and Kelsey. And to my parents, for their lifelong love and encouragement.

I hope the novel inspires you to reach for your own wonderful dreams, and to acknowledge all the beautiful souls who have and will continue to help you reach them.

Reading Group Questions

(Additional reading group material can be found at
www.DownwardDogUpwardFog.com)

Questions about Downward Dog, Upward Fog

1. Discuss the agitation Lorna feels at the novel's beginning, and why she can't shake it.

2. Lorna's girlfriends—old and new—can each be seen as representing various aspects of Lorna, as well. Describe each girlfriend and the qualities of Lorna you see in her.

3. Lorna pigeonholes people she meets based on their appearance, even though she claims to know better. Discuss this and other traits of Lorna's that are less than admirable but that she has trouble changing until her spiritual transformation.

4. Did you think early on that Lorna was exaggerating about her mother's flaws? Do you think that Lorna's expectations of her mother's behavior contributed to their failed relationship?

5. Lorna's relationships at work also present challenges for her. Yet she feels it's particularly important to bring her budding spirituality into the office. Why do you think that is, and how does it work out for her?

6. Brad is obviously a wonderful guy and, as Lorna says, a fabulous catch with whom she is clearly smitten. Discuss the pros and cons of their relationship.

7. As Lorna begins to transform, it seems like she might have to leave all her old friends behind. Why do you think she needs to push away her girlfriends for a while? Why is she able to bring them back into her life? Why is this harder to do with Brad?

8. Once Lorna faces her real-life crisis, she realizes that to mentally survive she must stop dabbling in her spiritual pursuits and seriously embrace their principles. How is she able to do this? Were you surprised it transforms her as much as it did?

9. Do you think Lorna will be able to sustain the gains she has made in her spiritual growth? What do you hope for her going forward?

Questions about your own spiritual development

1. Meryl Davids Landau admits that this book was written so spiritually seeking women can have a women's novel with a protagonist whose life they can relate to. In what ways do Lorna's spiritual pursuits mirror yours?

2. Describe your own attempts over time to connect with your higher self. Have you found it as hard to sustain this as Lorna does throughout much of the novel? How can you expand your soul connection going forward?

3. Do you practice yoga and meditation? What holds you back from doing more? Consider "sujaling" for five minutes this evening before going to bed, and trying the sun salutation with the visualizations that Lorna finds so effective.

4. Is there a person in your own life like Carletta or Lorna's mother whom you find it difficult to love unconditionally? What can you do to move in that direction? (Hint: waiting for that person to change is not an option.)

5. Do you feel that you wear a "mask" at work or in other situations that cover who you really are? Discuss ways this can be beneficial, and ways in which it hides your true and beautiful light.

6. Lorna learns that "healing" others can happen in any job or situation. How can you uplift the people who surround you in all the various parts of your day?

7. Have you ever had a transformative spiritual epiphany the way Lorna does? If so, how did it come about, and how did it change you? Do you think it requires a crisis in your life to achieve this?

8. What do you think about the Law of Attraction? Do you believe that positive expectations cause things you want to flow your way? Test this law by expecting three specific good things to happen (small items, where you don't have psychological resistance, like seeing a yellow rose) and observing if they materialize.

9. Although the novel ends with Lorna anticipating that everything will go well for her forever, most of us find it hard to stay permanently connected to our higher selves. When this disconnection happens to you, what can you think or do to get that connection back as quickly as possible?